DRIFTERS VOLUME 1

To find a comics shop in your area, call the Comic Shop Locator Service toll-free at 1-888-266-4226.

publisher
MIKE RICHARDSON

editor
CHRIS WARNER

book design
KAT LARSON

Dark Horse Manga
A division of Dark Horse Comics, Inc.
10956 SE Main Street
Milwaukie, OR 97222

DarkHorse.com

First edition: August 2011
ISBN 978-1-59582-769-2

1 2 3 4 5 6 7 8 9 10

Printed at Transcontinental Gagné,
Louiseville, QC, Canada

GANTZ

HIROYA OKU Works.

The last thing Kei and Masaru remember was being struck dead by a subway train while saving the life of a drunken bum. What a waste! And yet somehow they're still alive. Or semi-alive? Maybe reanimated . . . by some kind of mysterious orb! And this orb called "Gantz" intends to make them play games of death, hunting all kinds of odd aliens, along with a bunch of other ordinary citizens who've recently met a tragic semi-end. The missions they embark upon are often dangerous. Many die—and die again. This dark and action-packed manga deals with the moral conflicts of violence, teenage sexual confusion and angst, and our fascination with death.

Dark Horse is proud to deliver one of the most requested manga ever to be released. Hang on to your gear and keep playing the game, whatever you do; Gantz is unrelenting!

VOLUME ONE
ISBN 978-1-59307-949-9

VOLUME TWO
ISBN 978-1-59582-188-1

VOLUME THREE
ISBN 978-1-59582-232-1

VOLUME FOUR
ISBN 978-1-59582-250-5

VOLUME FIVE
ISBN 978-1-59582-301-4

VOLUME SIX
ISBN 978-1-59582-320-5

VOLUME SEVEN
ISBN 978-1-59582-373-1

VOLUME EIGHT
ISBN 978-1-59582-383-0

VOLUME NINE
ISBN 978-1-59582-452-3

VOLUME TEN
ISBN 978-1-59582-320-5

VOLUME ELEVEN
ISBN 978-1-59582-373-1

VOLUME TWELVE
ISBN 978-1-59582-526-1

VOLUME THIRTEEN
ISBN 978-1-59582-587-2

VOLUME FOURTEEN
ISBN 978-1-59582-598-8

VOLUME FIFTEEN
ISBN 978-1-59582-662-6

VOLUME SIXTEEN
ISBN 978-1-59582-663-3

VOLUME SEVENTEEN
ISBN 978-1-59582-664-0

VOLUME EIGHTEEN
ISBN 978-1-59582-776-0

VOLUME NINETEEN
ISBN 978-1-59582-813-2

VOLUME TWENTY
ISBN 978-1-59582-846-0

$12.99 EACH

AVAILABLE AT YOUR LOCAL COMICS SHOP OR BOOKSTORE
TO FIND A COMICS SHOP IN YOUR AREA, CALL 1-888-266-4226

For more information or to order direct:
·On the web: darkhorse.com ·E-mail: mailorder@darkhorse.com ·Phone: 1-800-862-0052 Mon.–Fri. 9 A.M. to 5 P.M Pacific Time.

DARK HORSE MANGA

DarkHorse.com

DRIFTERS

1

story and art by
KOHTA HIRANO

translation
MATTHEW JOHNSON

lettering and retouch
STUDIO CUTIE

DARK HORSE MANGA™

CONTENTS

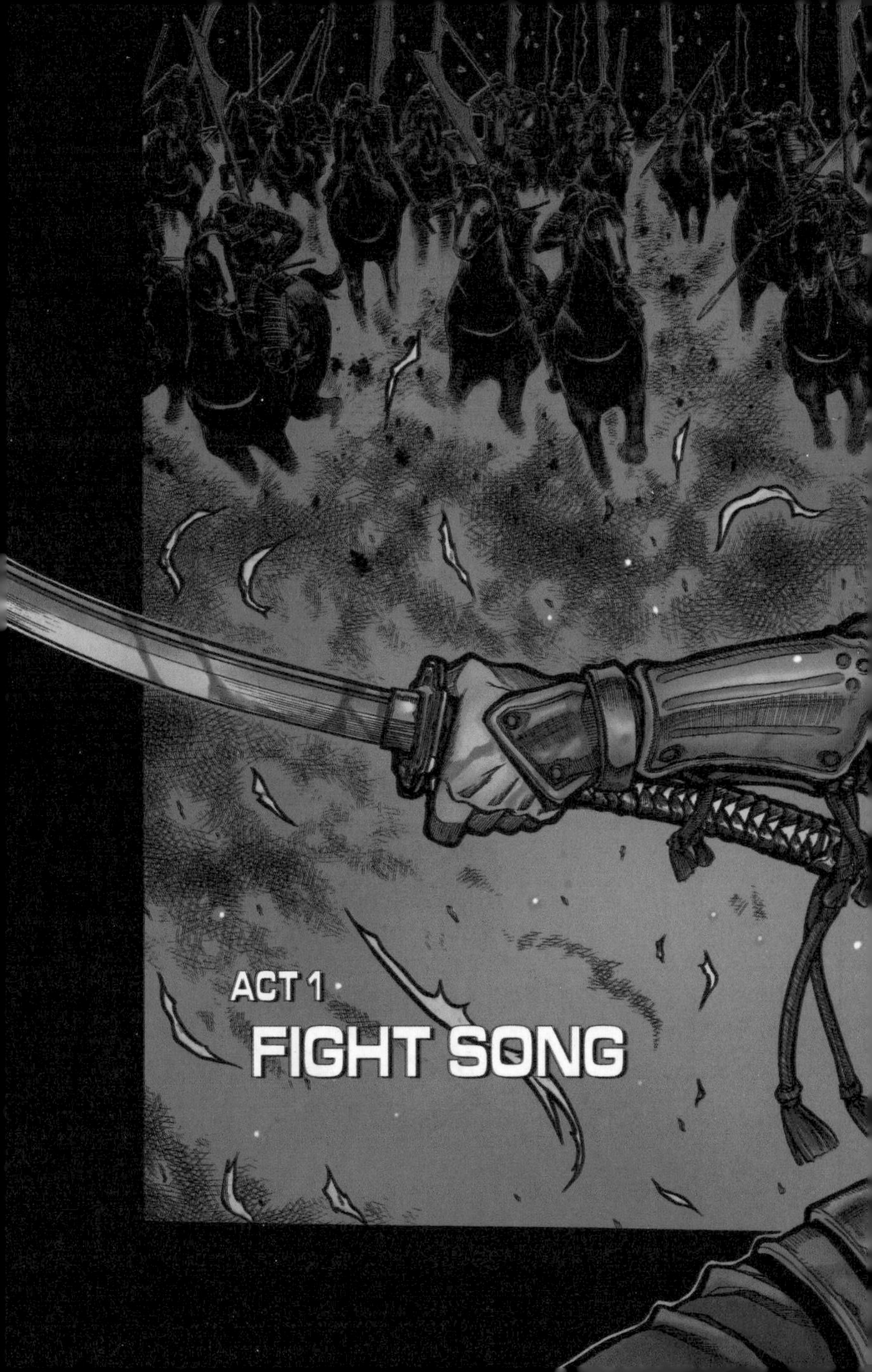
ACT 1
FIGHT SONG

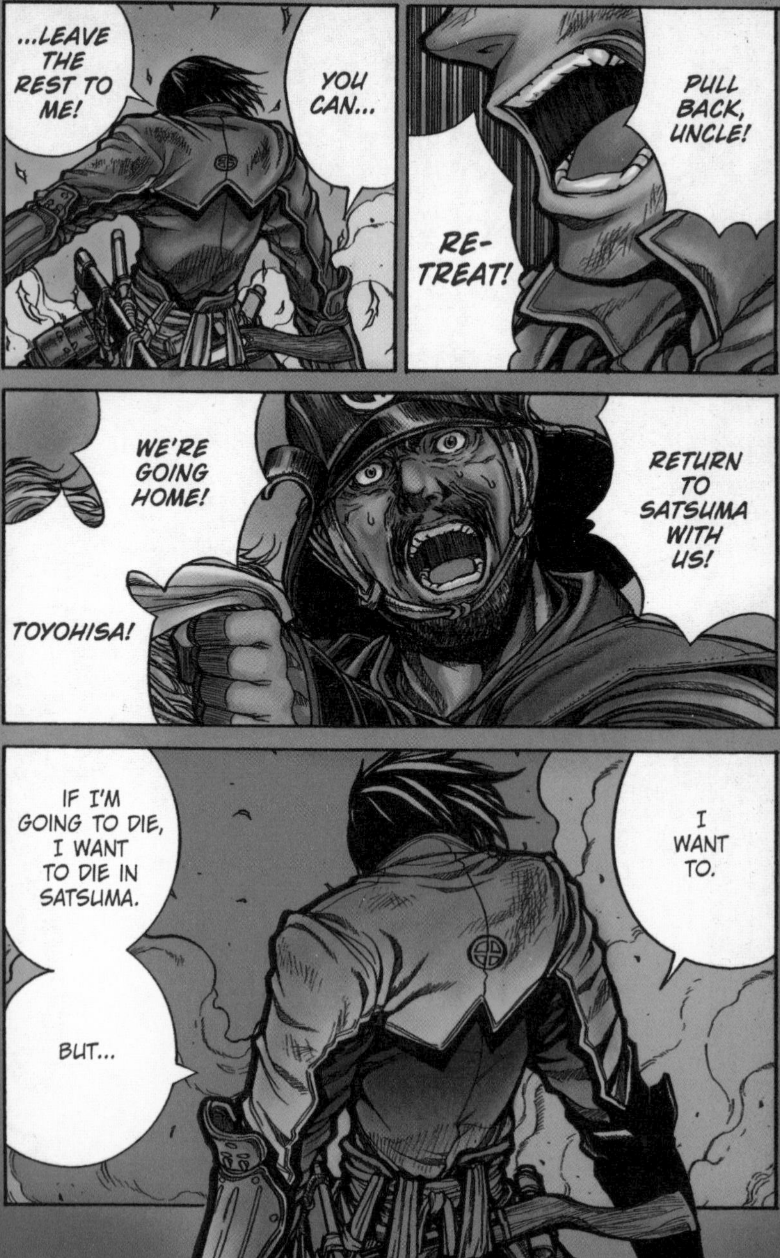
PULL BACK, UNCLE!
RE-TREAT!
YOU CAN...
...LEAVE THE REST TO ME!
RETURN TO SATSUMA WITH US!
WE'RE GOING HOME!
TOYOHISA!
I WANT TO.
IF I'M GOING TO DIE, I WANT TO DIE IN SATSUMA.
BUT...

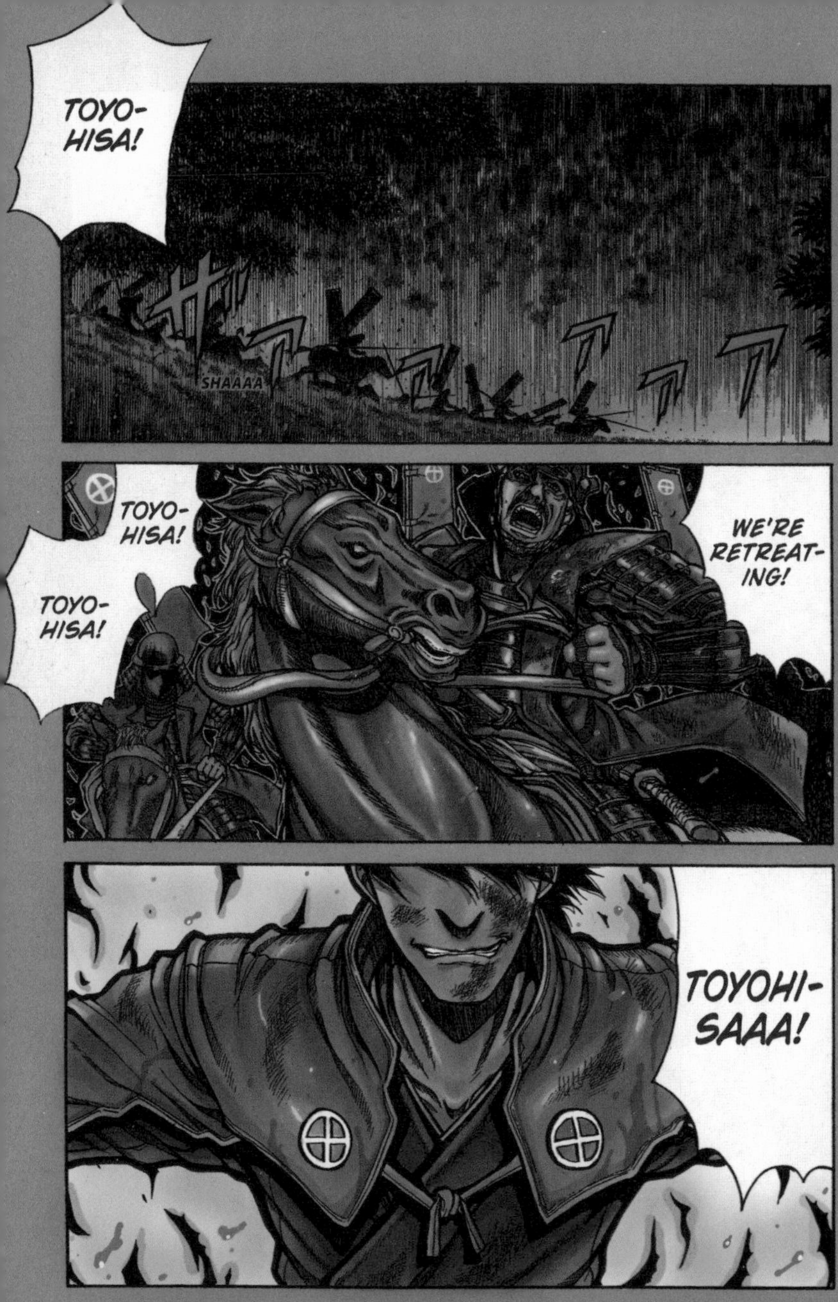
TOYO-HISA!
SHAAAA
WE'RE RETREAT-ING!
TOYO-HISA!
TOYO-HISA!
TOYOHI-SAAAA!

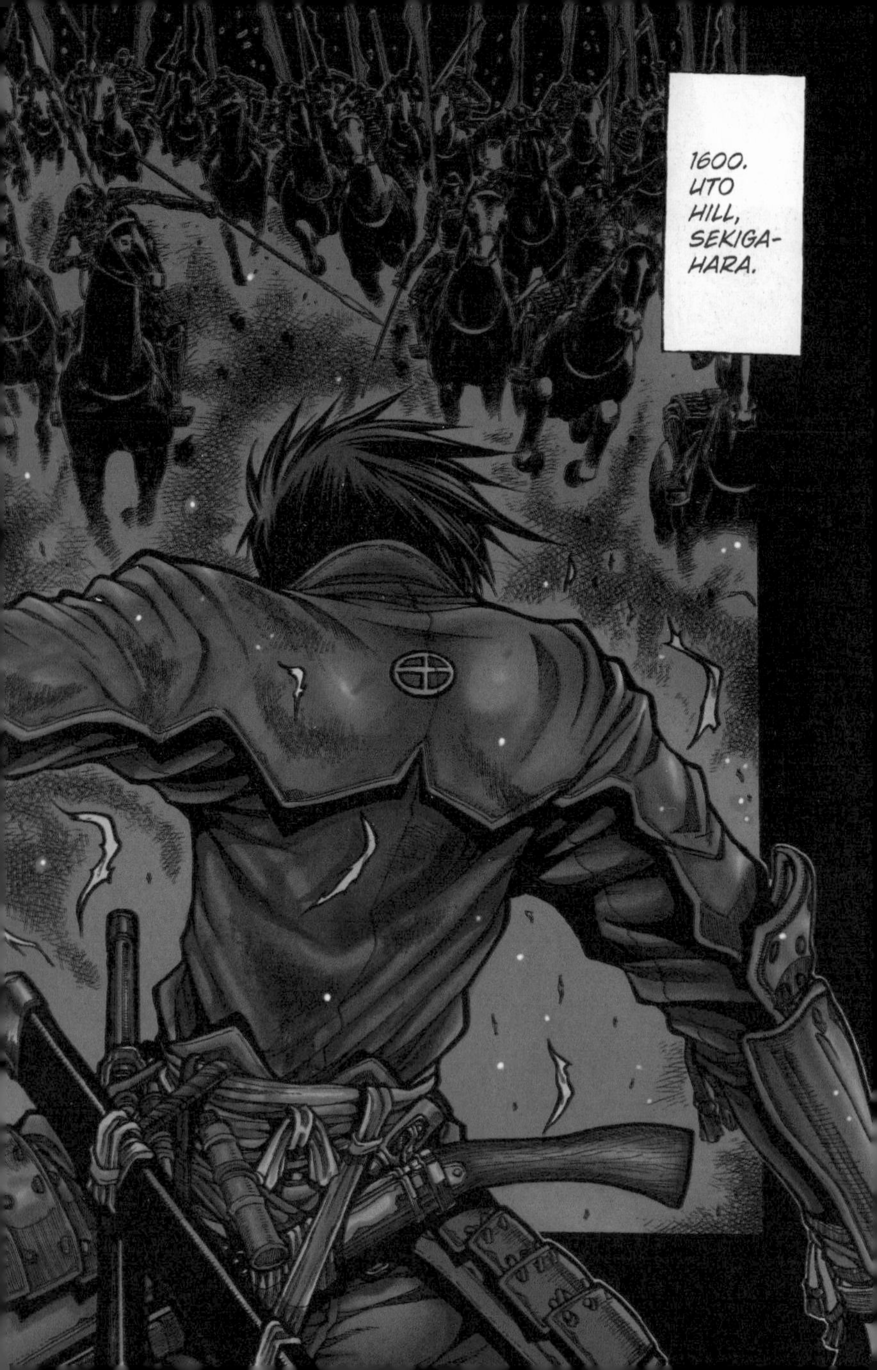
1600. UTO HILL, SEKIGAHARA.

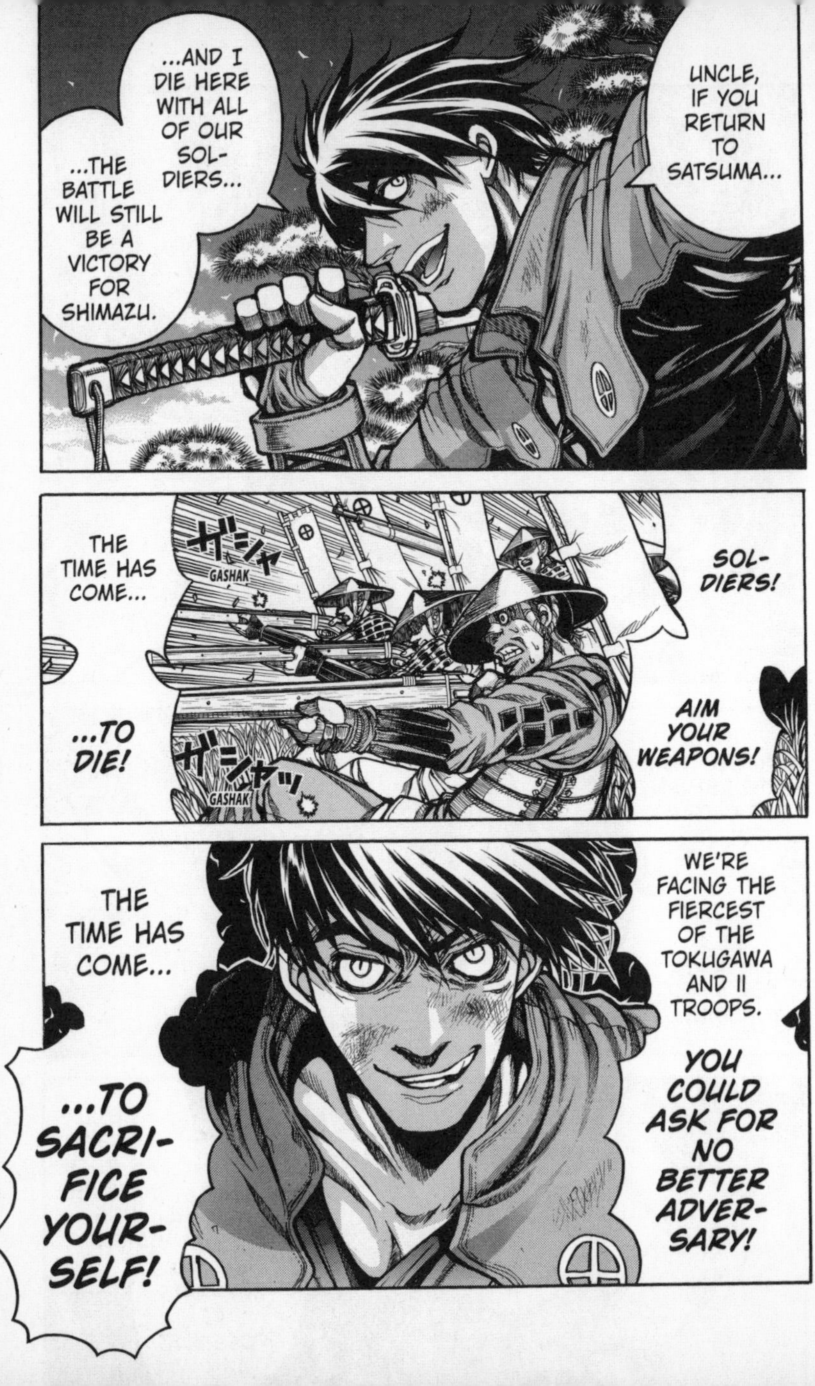
UNCLE, IF YOU RETURN TO SATSUMA...
...AND I DIE HERE WITH ALL OF OUR SOLDIERS...
...THE BATTLE WILL STILL BE A VICTORY FOR SHIMAZU.
SOLDIERS!
THE TIME HAS COME...
GASHAK
AIM YOUR WEAPONS!
...TO DIE!
GASHAK
WE'RE FACING THE FIERCEST OF THE TOKUGAWA AND II TROOPS.
THE TIME HAS COME...
YOU COULD ASK FOR NO BETTER ADVERSARY!
...TO SACRIFICE YOURSELF!

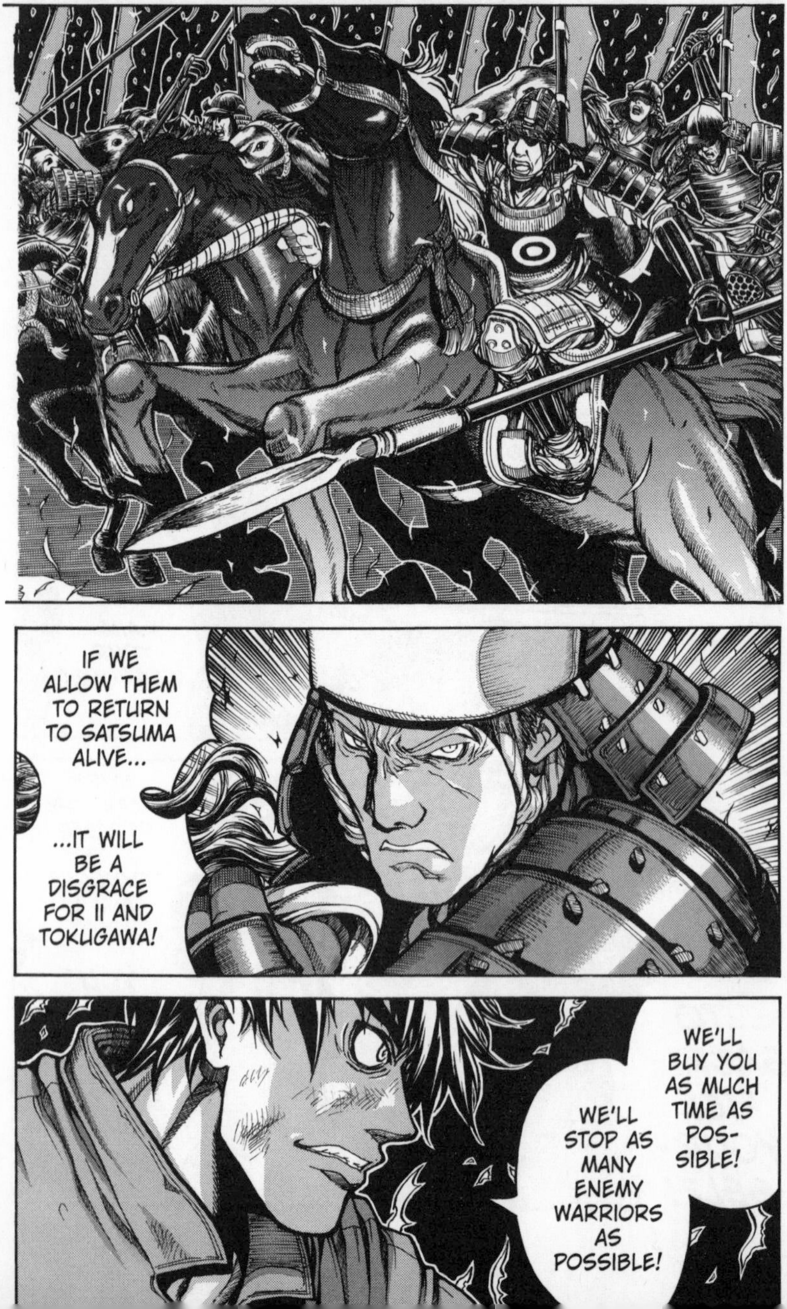
IF WE ALLOW THEM TO RETURN TO SATSUMA ALIVE...
...IT WILL BE A DISGRACE FOR II AND TOKUGAWA!
WE'LL BUY YOU AS MUCH TIME AS POS-SIBLE!
WE'LL STOP AS MANY ENEMY WARRIORS AS POSSIBLE!

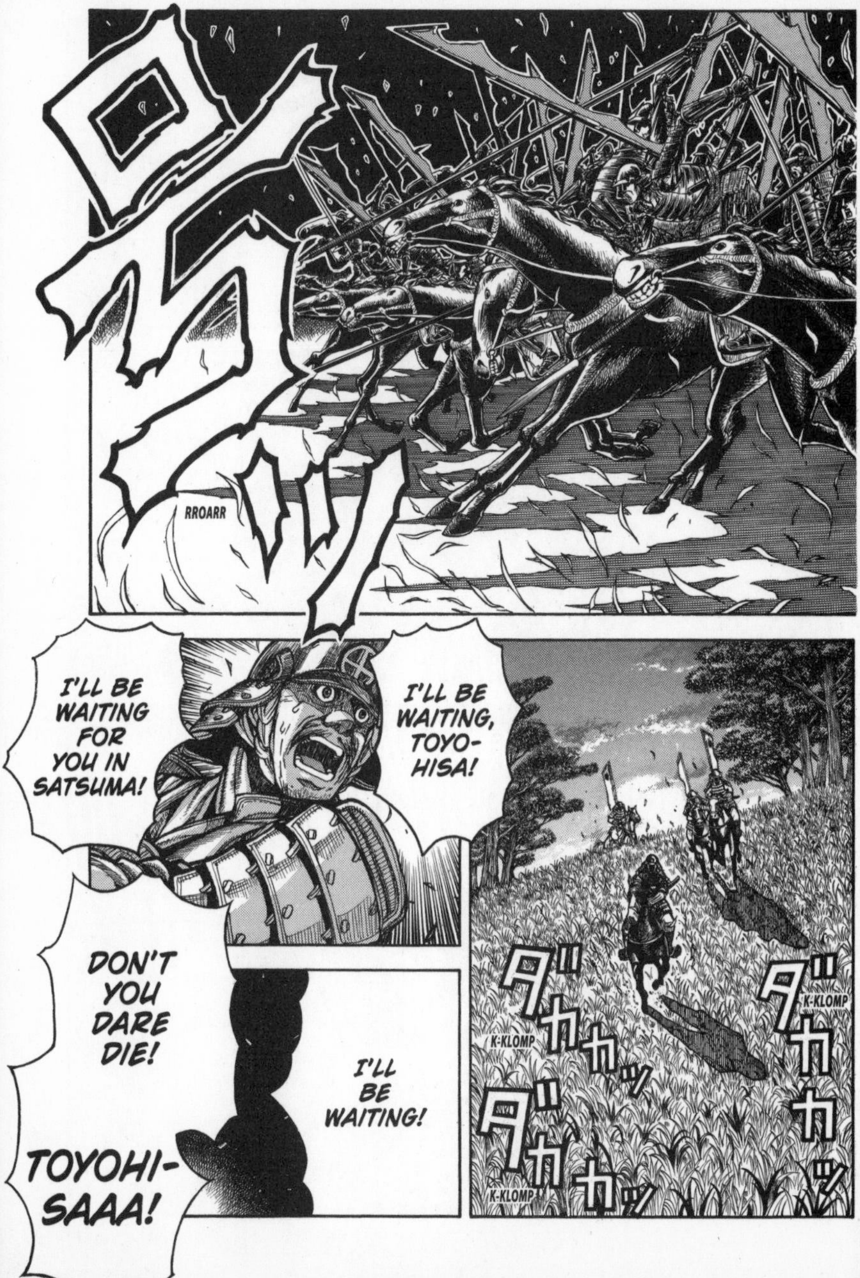
RROARR
K-KLOMP
K-KLOMP
K-KLOMP
I'LL BE WAITING, TOYO-HISA!
I'LL BE WAITING FOR YOU IN SATSUMA!
I'LL BE WAITING!
DON'T YOU DARE DIE!
TOYOHI-SAAA!

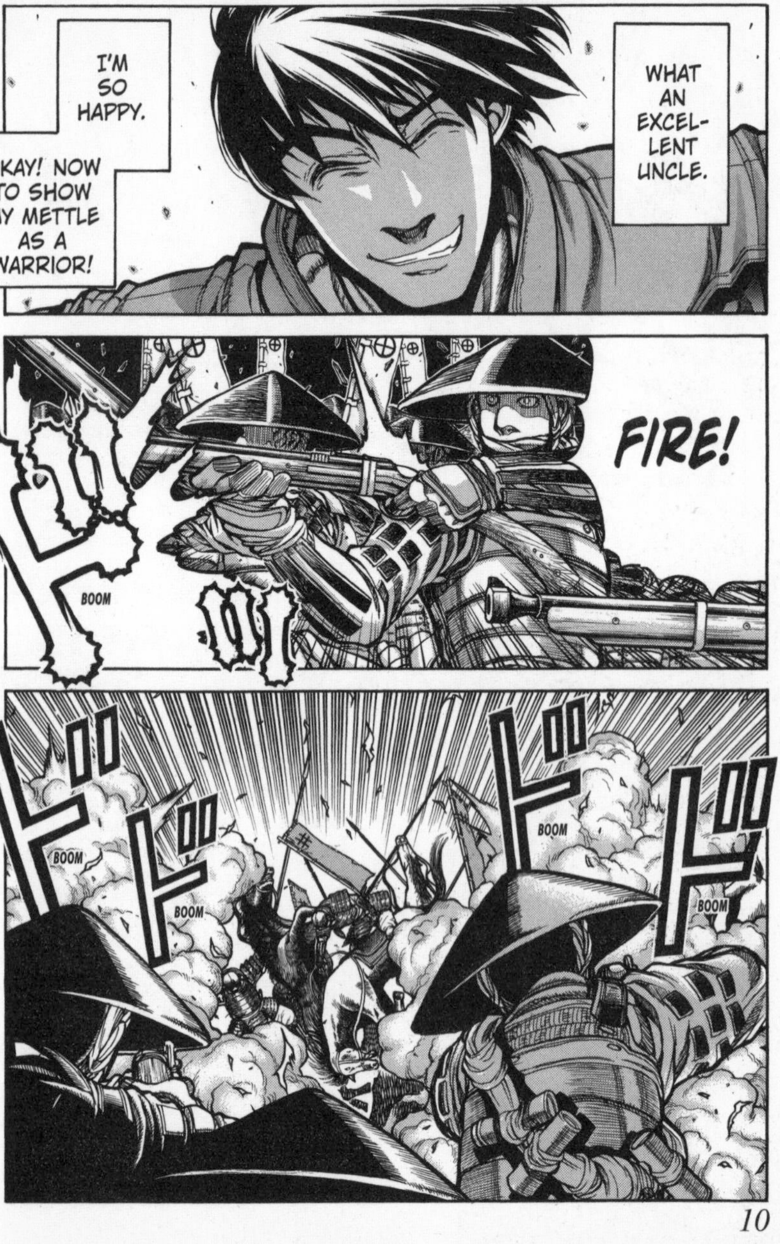
WHAT AN EXCEL-LENT UNCLE.
I'M SO HAPPY.
OKAY! NOW TO SHOW MY METTLE AS A WARRIOR!
FIRE!
BOOM
BOOM
BOOM
BOOM
BOOM
BOOM

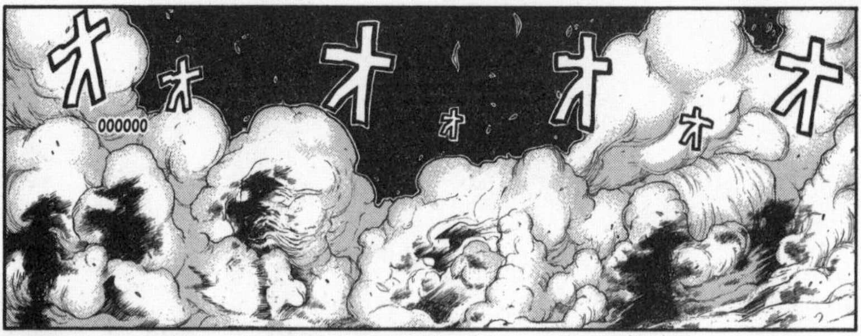
OOOOOO
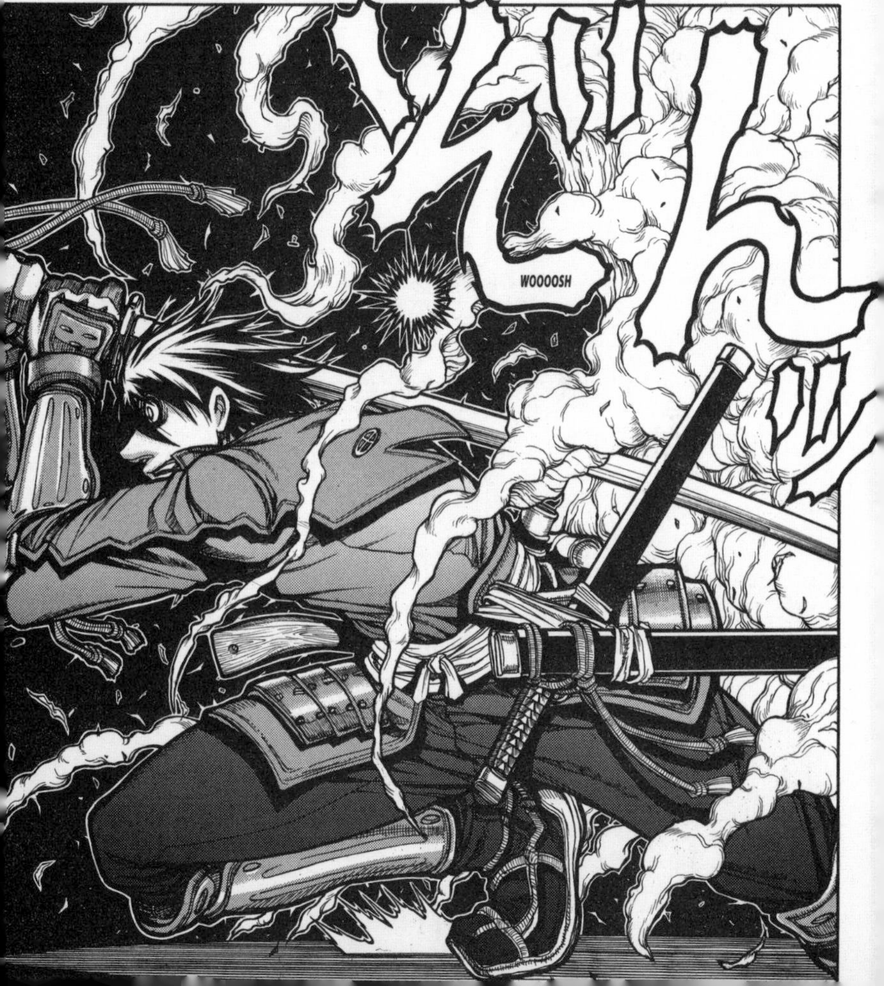
WOOOOSH

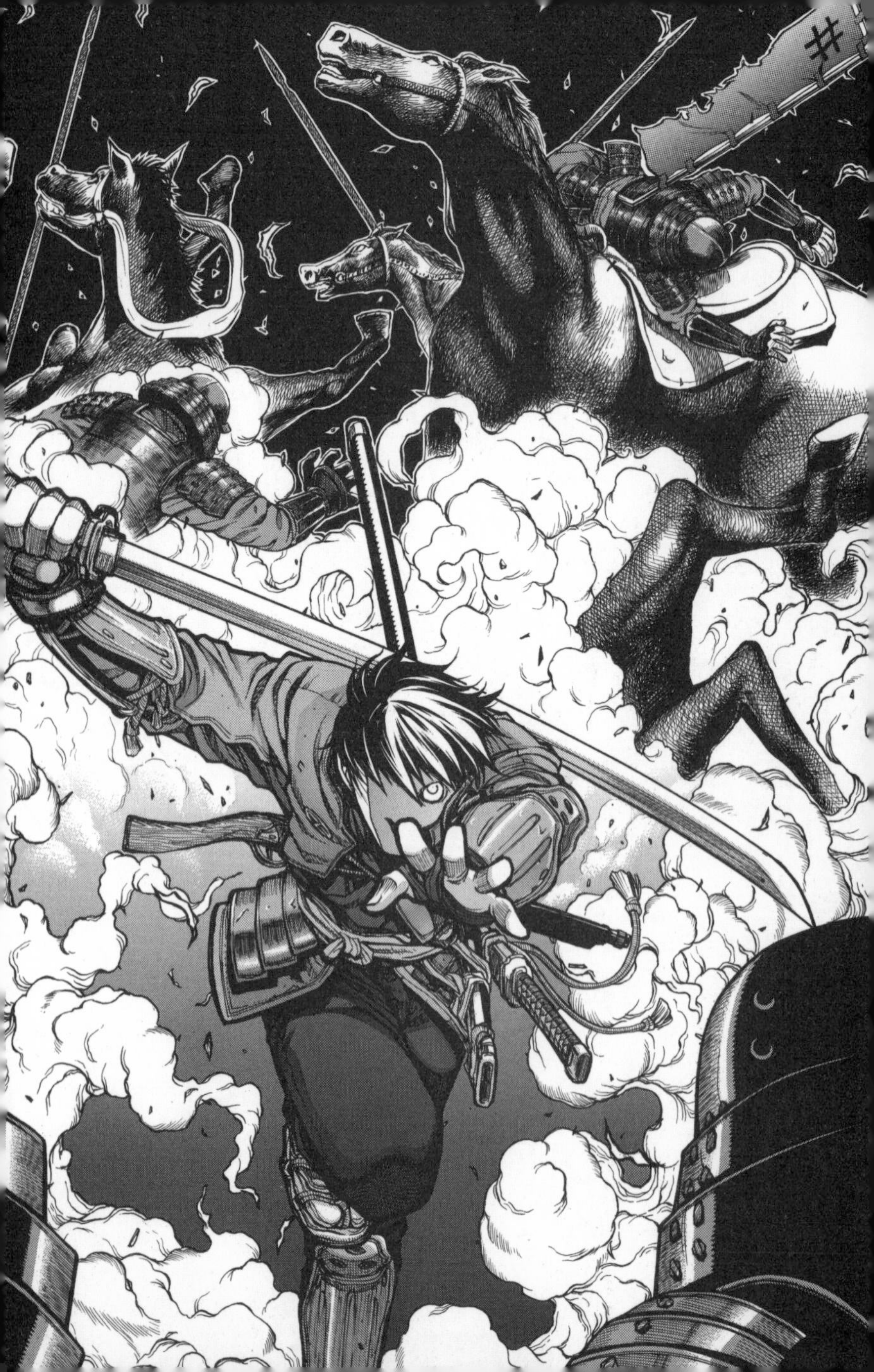

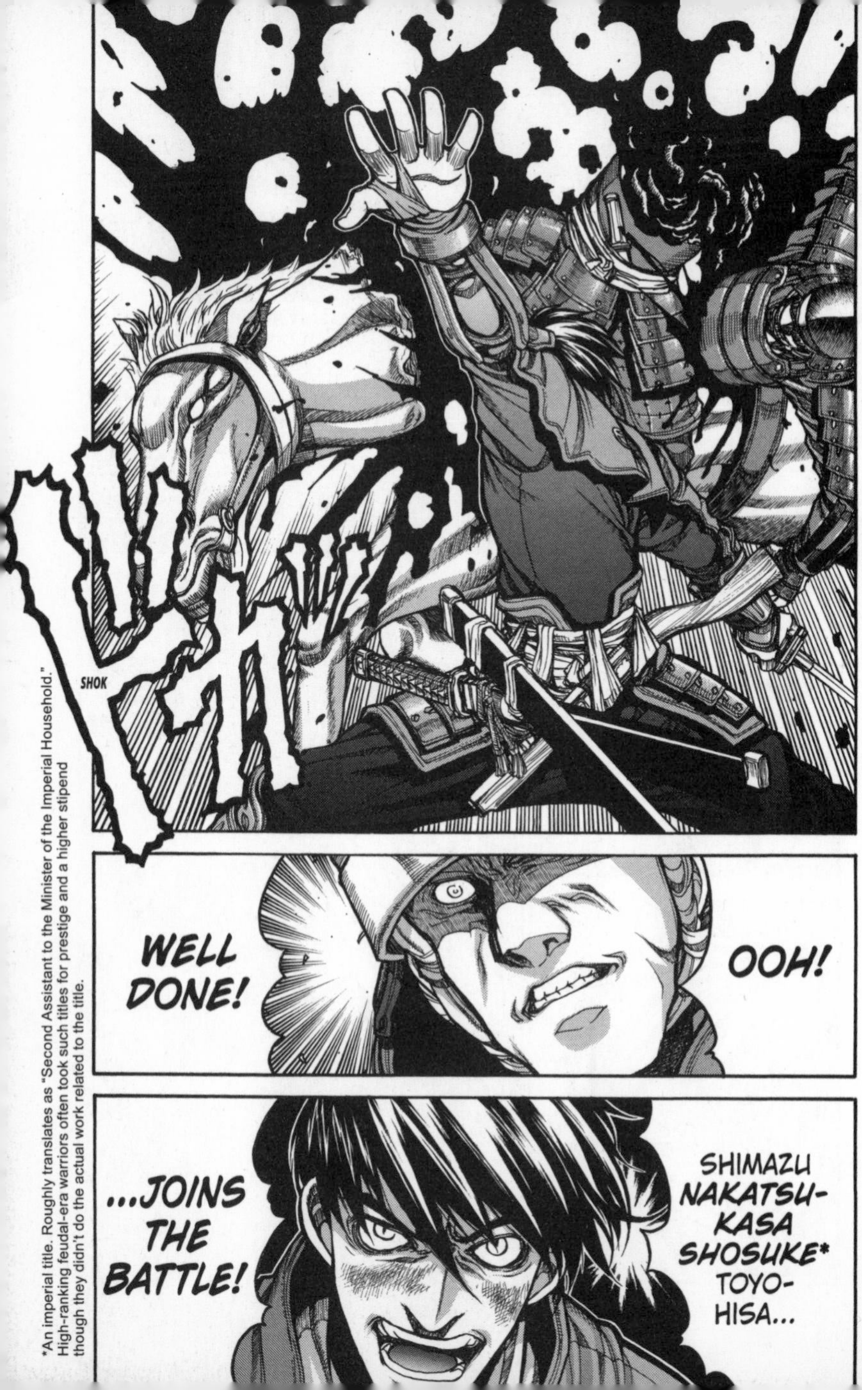
SHOK
OOH!
WELL DONE!
SHIMAZU NAKATSU-KASA SHOSUKE* TOYO-HISA...
...JOINS THE BATTLE!

*An imperial title. Roughly translates as "Second Assistant to the Minister of the Imperial Household." High-ranking feudal-era warriors often took such titles for prestige and a higher stipend though they didn't do the actual work related to the title.

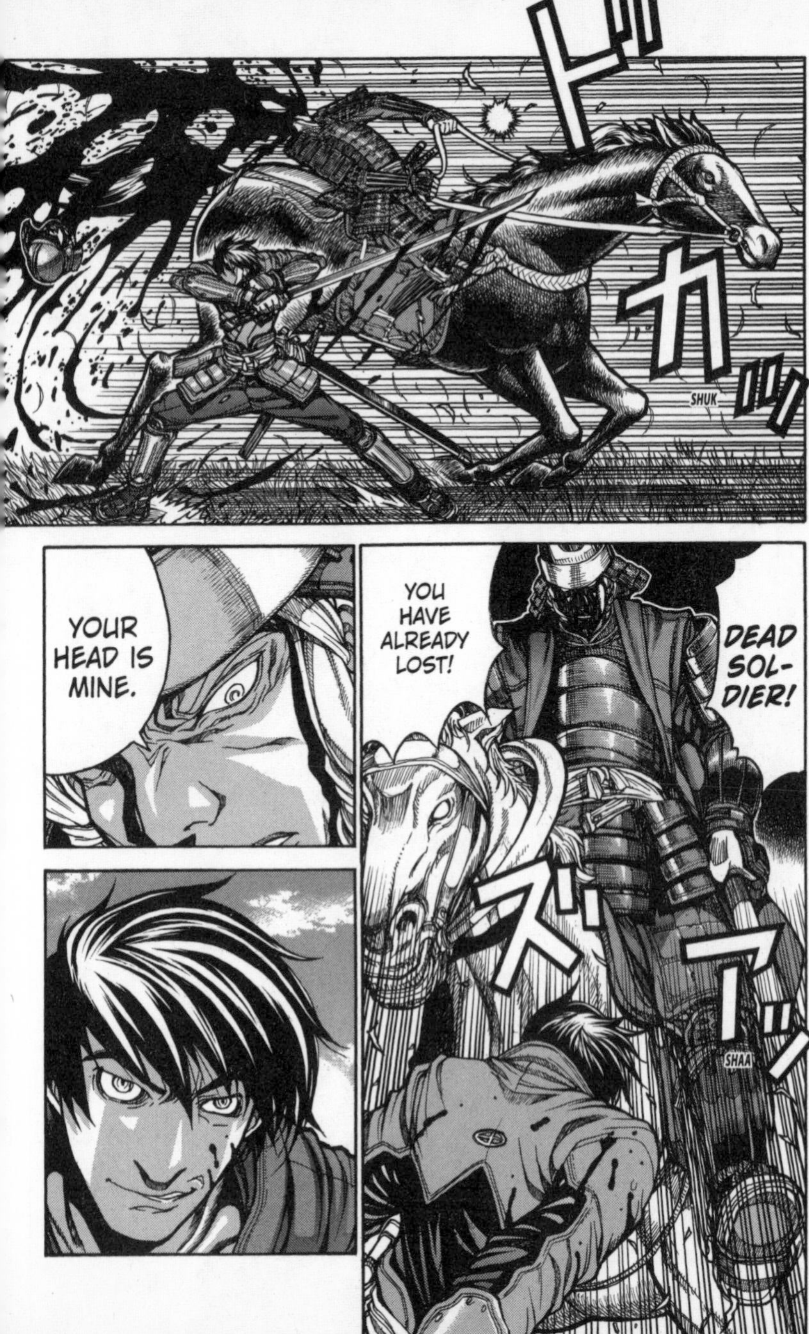
ドカッ
SHUK
DEAD SOL-DIER!
YOU HAVE ALREADY LOST!
ズァッ
SHAA
YOUR HEAD IS MINE.

WHAT NONSENSE YOU SPOUT.

THE ONE SAYING FAREWELL TO HIS HEAD...

...WILL BE YOU!

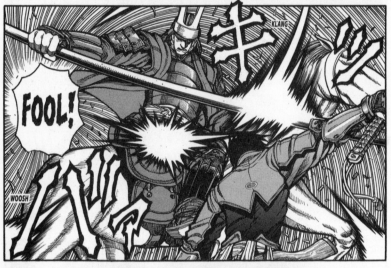

FOOL!

KLANG

WOOSH

OUR LORD!

PRO-TECT HIM!

LORD NAO-MASA!

ZA

ZA

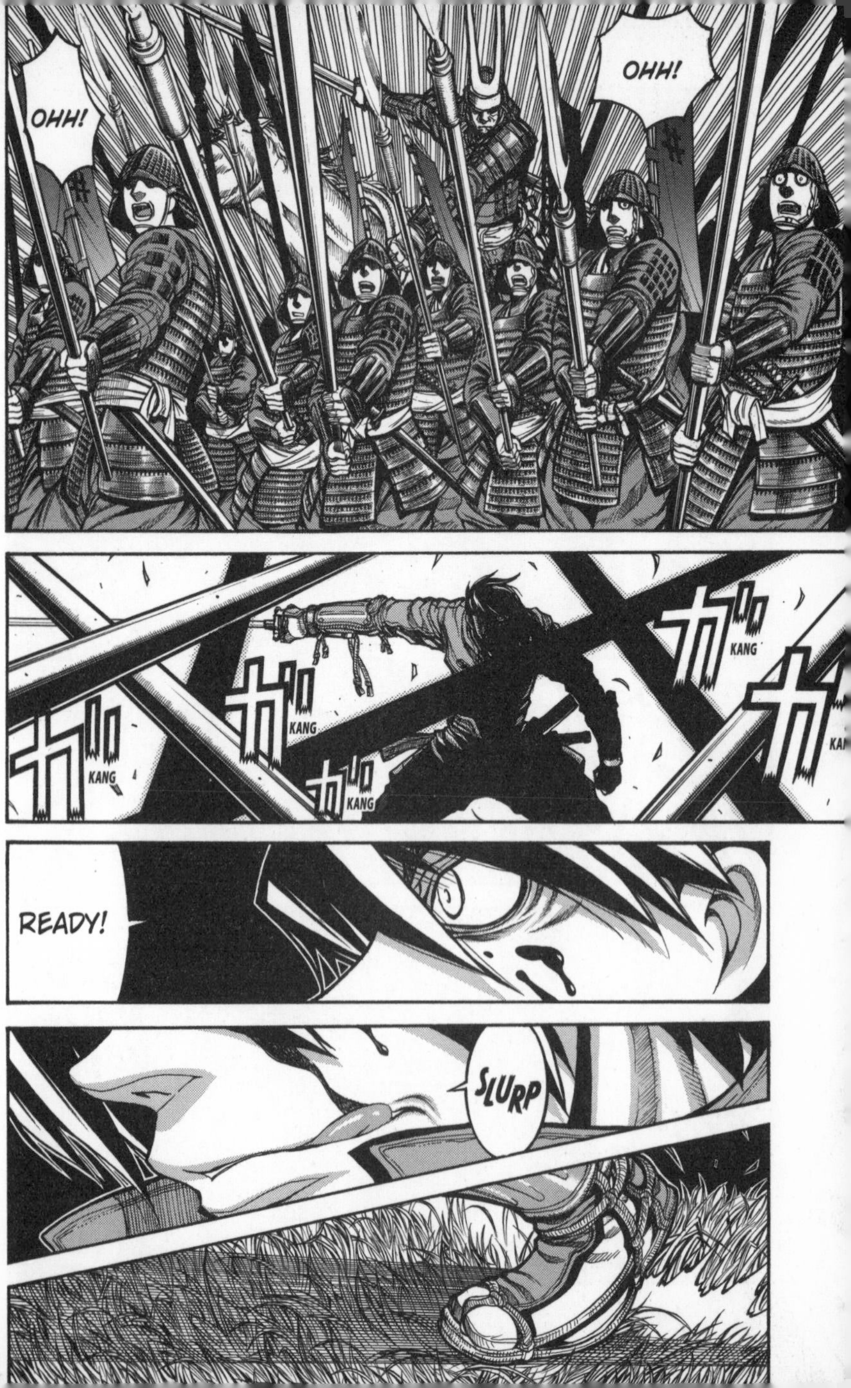
OHH!
OHH!
KANG
KANG
KANG
KANG
READY!
SLURP

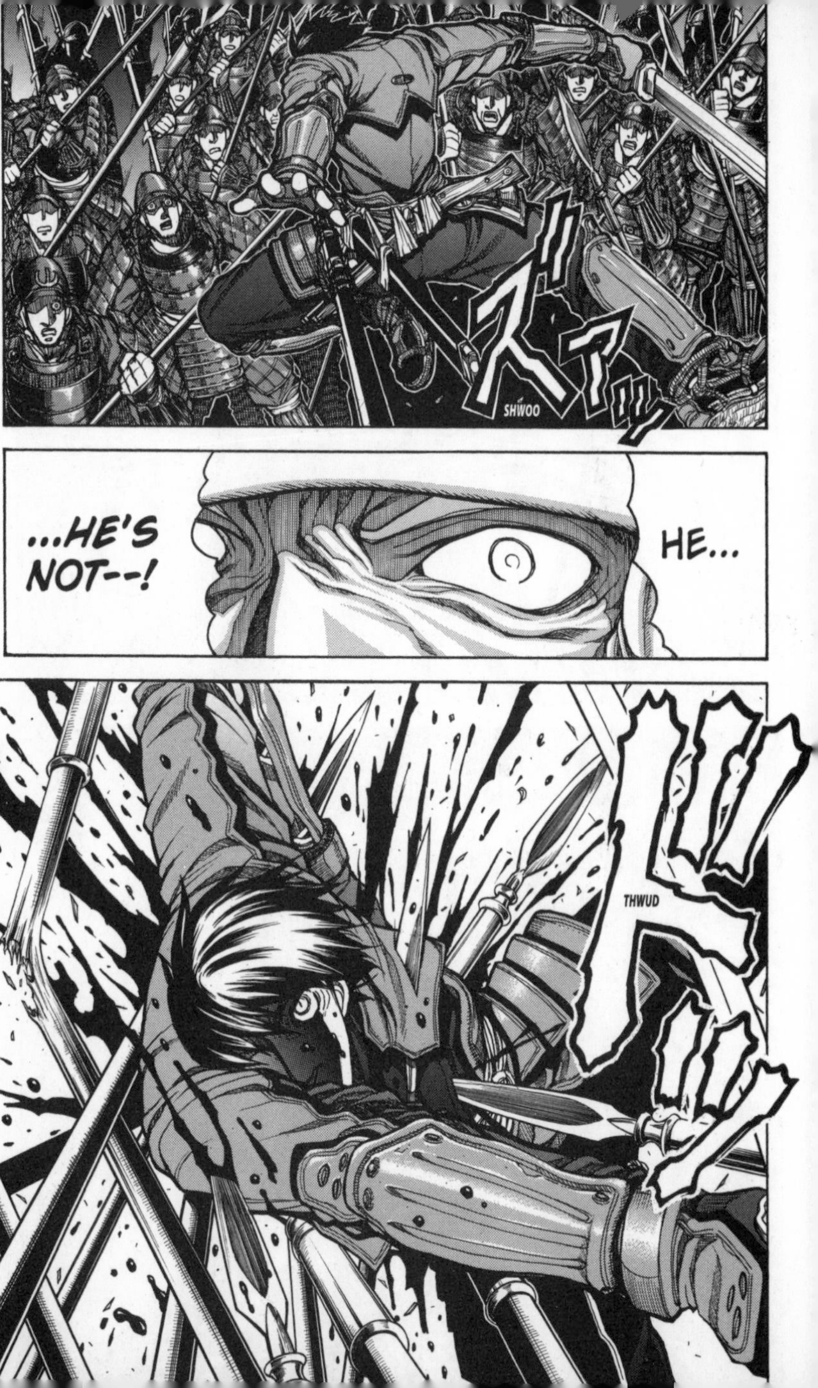
SHWOO
HE...
...HE'S NOT--!
THWUD

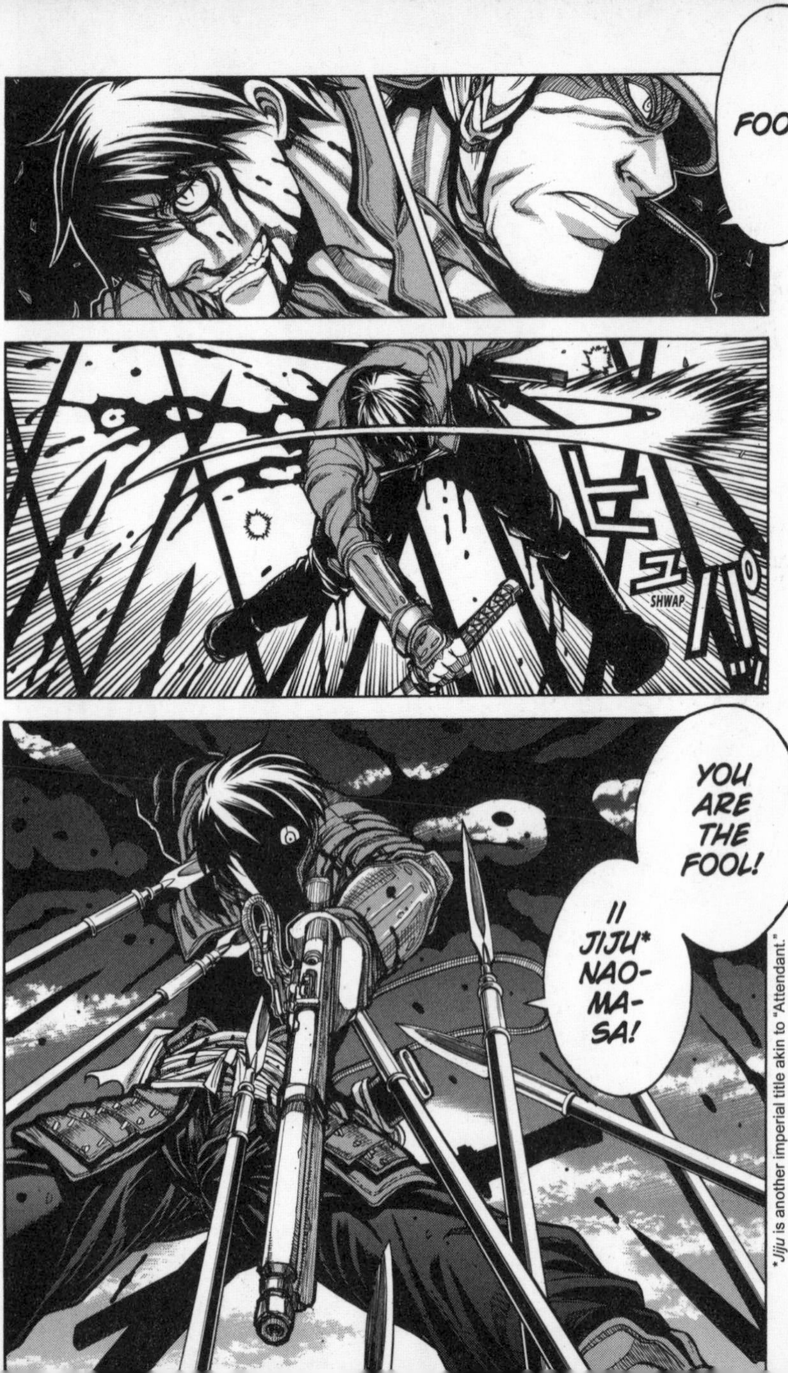
FOOL!
SHWAP
YOU ARE THE FOOL!
II JIJU* NAO-MA-SA!

*Jiju is another imperial title akin to "Attendant."

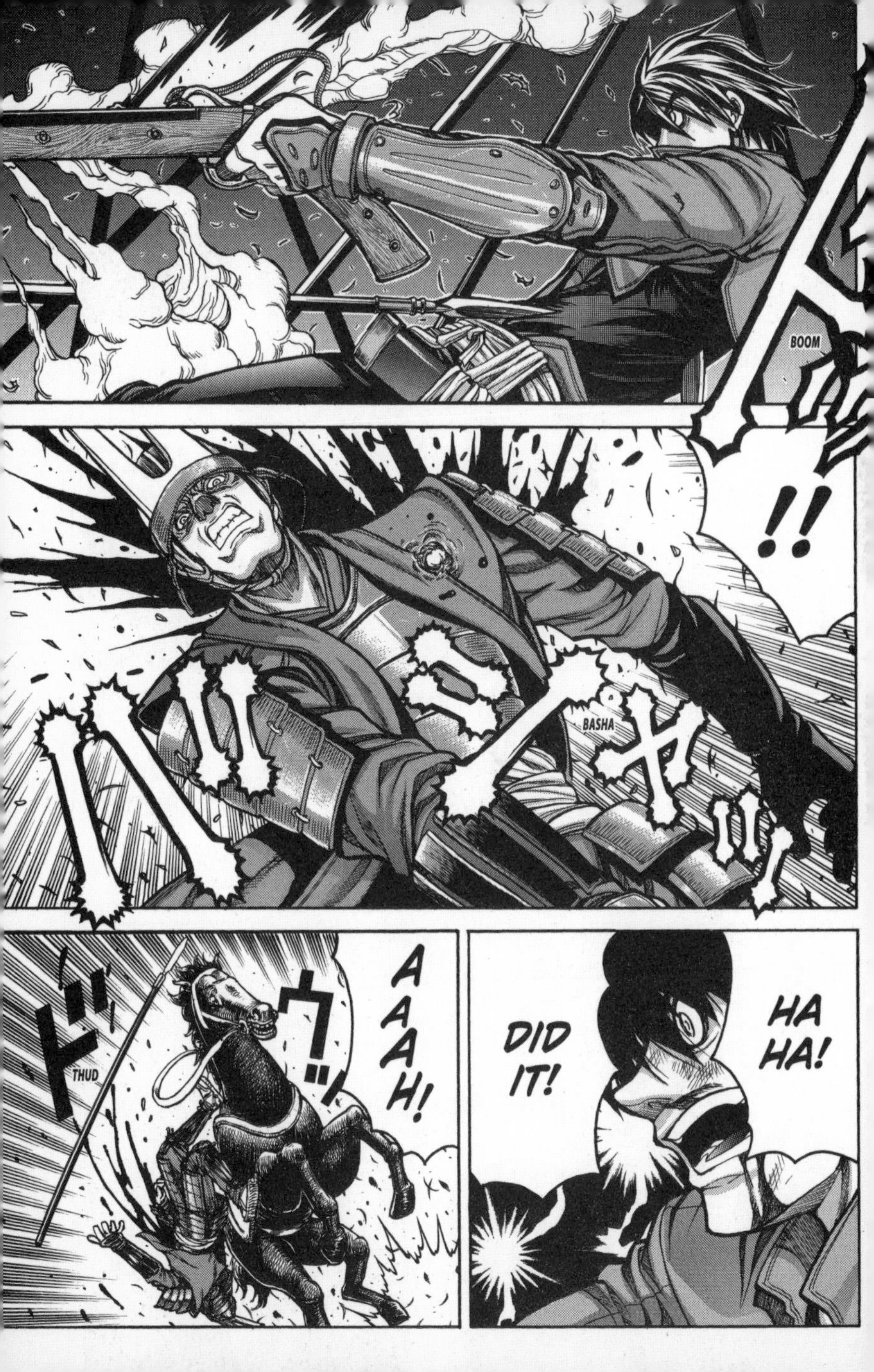
BOOM
!!
BASHA
HA HA!
DID IT!
AAAH!
THUD

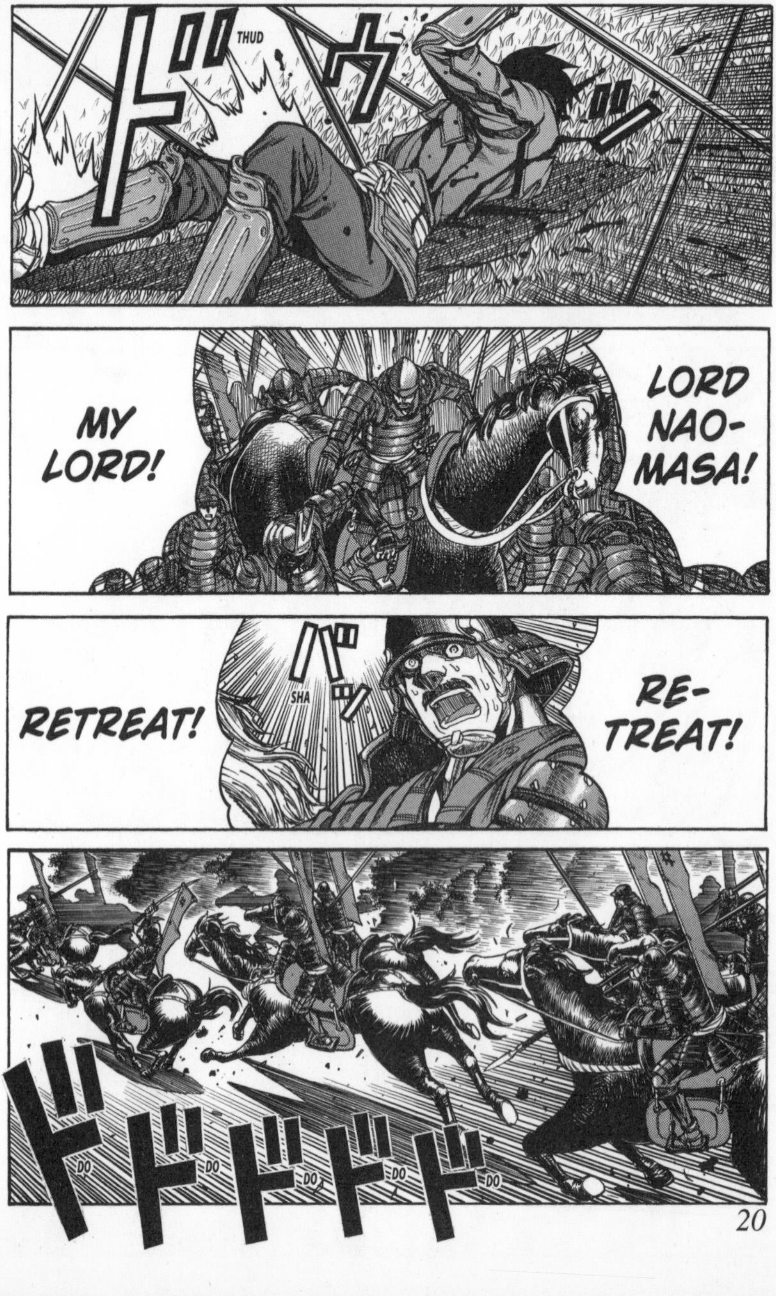
THUD
LORD NAO-MASA!
MY LORD!
RE-TREAT!
SHA
RETREAT!
DO
DO
DO
DO

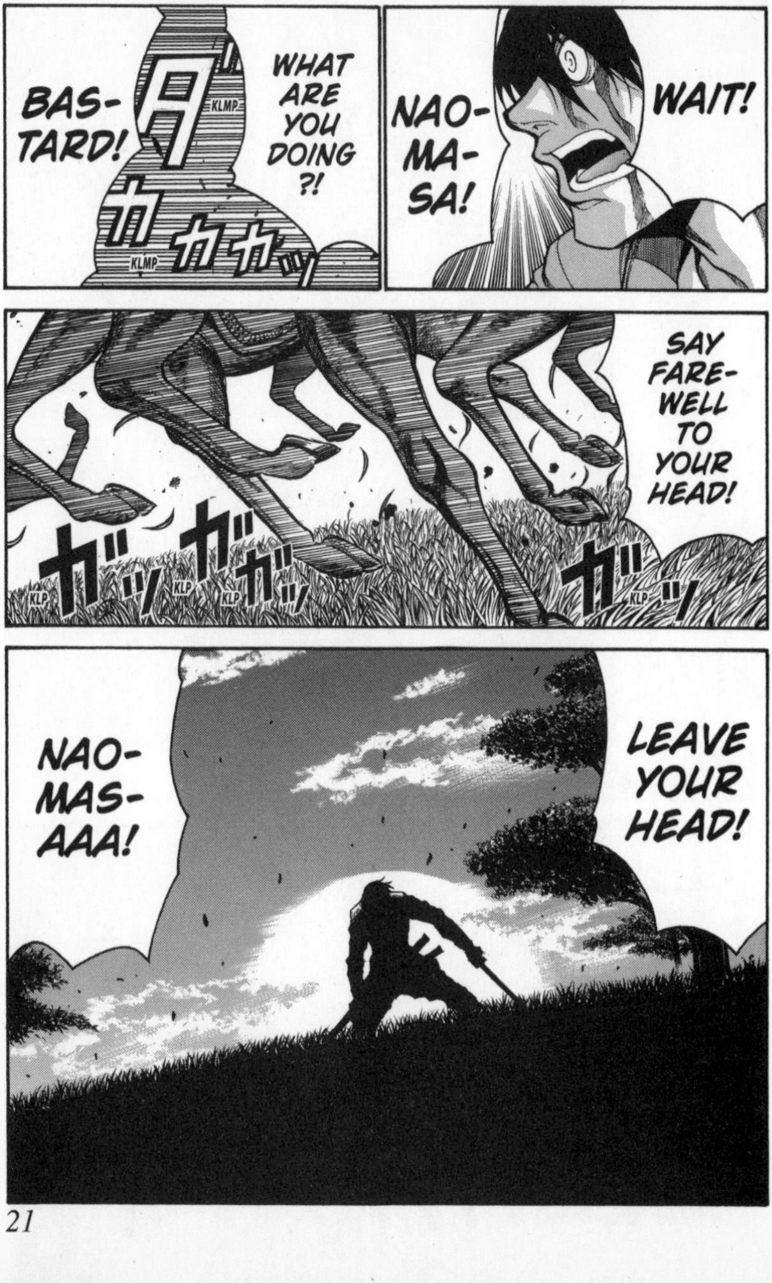
WAIT!
NAO-MA-SA!
WHAT ARE YOU DOING ?!
BAS-TARD!
KLMP
KLMP
SAY FARE-WELL TO YOUR HEAD!
KLP
KLP
KLP
KLP
LEAVE YOUR HEAD!
NAO-MAS-AAA!

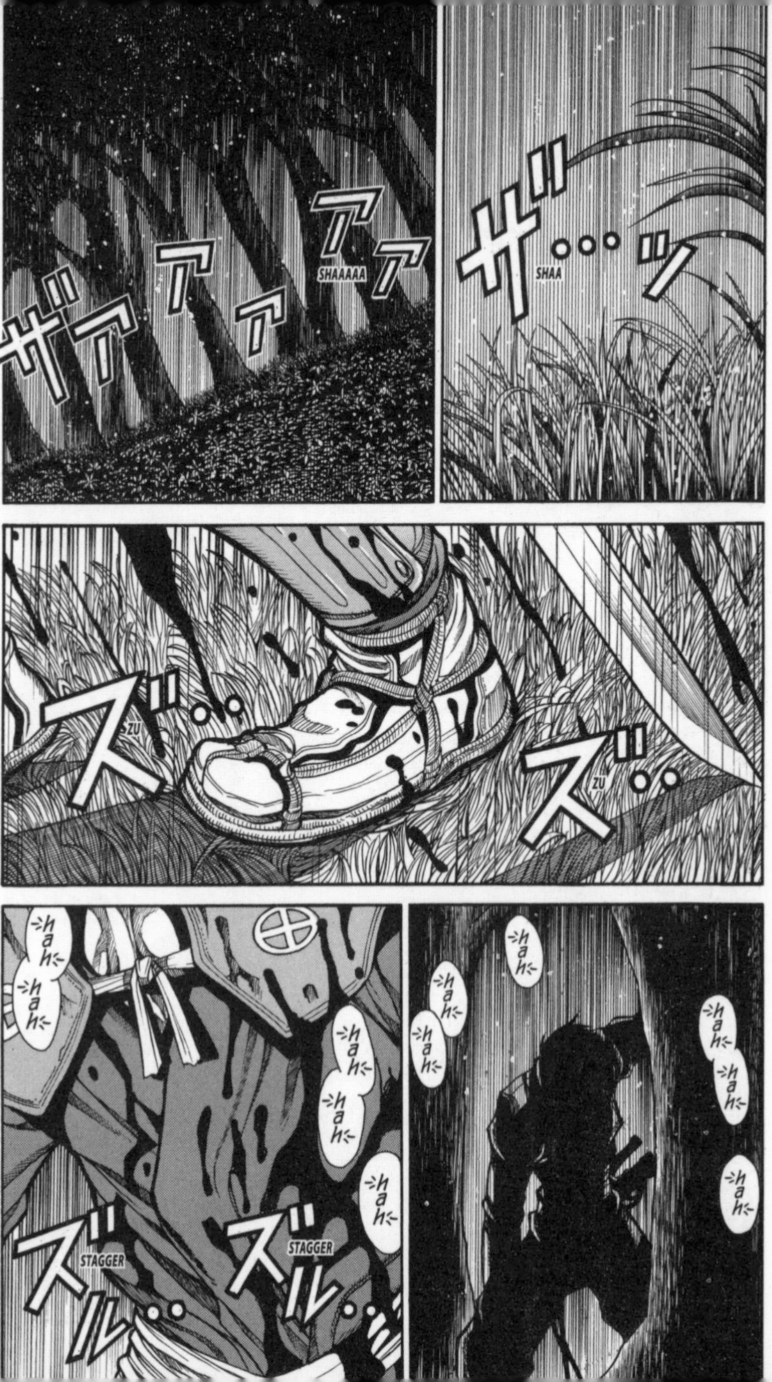
ザ…ッ
SHAA
ザアアアア
SHAAAAA
ズ‥
ZU
ズ‥
ZU
hah
hah
hah
hah
hah
hah
hah
hah
hah
hah
hah
ズル‥
STAGGER
ズル‥
STAGGER

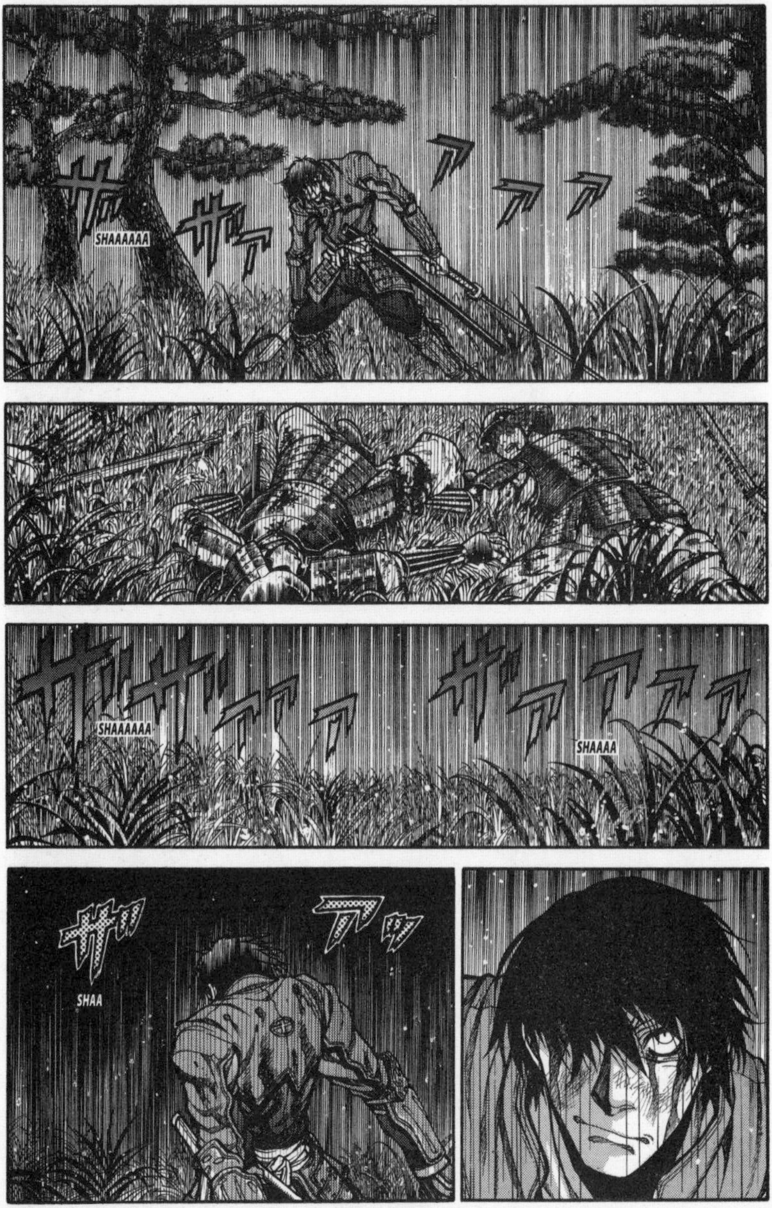
SHAAAAAA
SHAAA
SHAAAAAA
SHAA

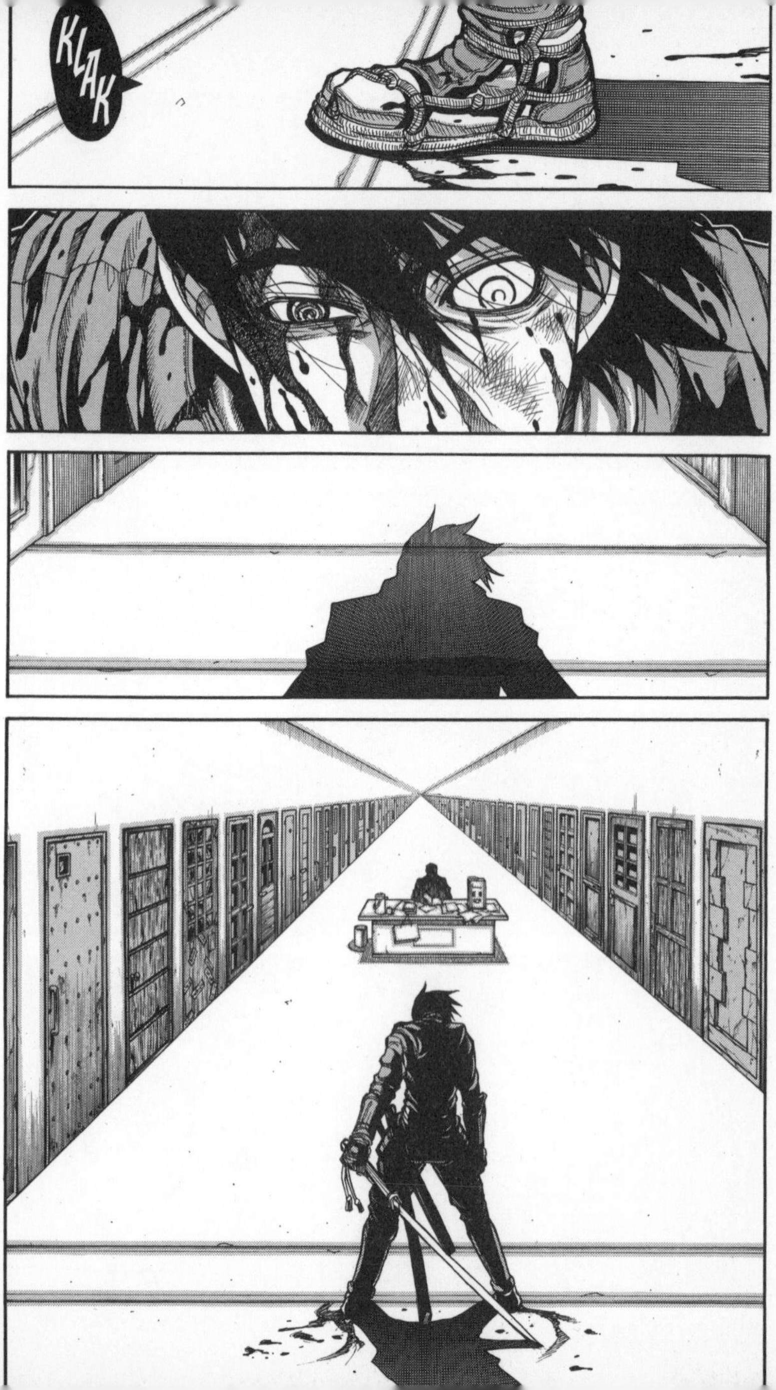
KLAK

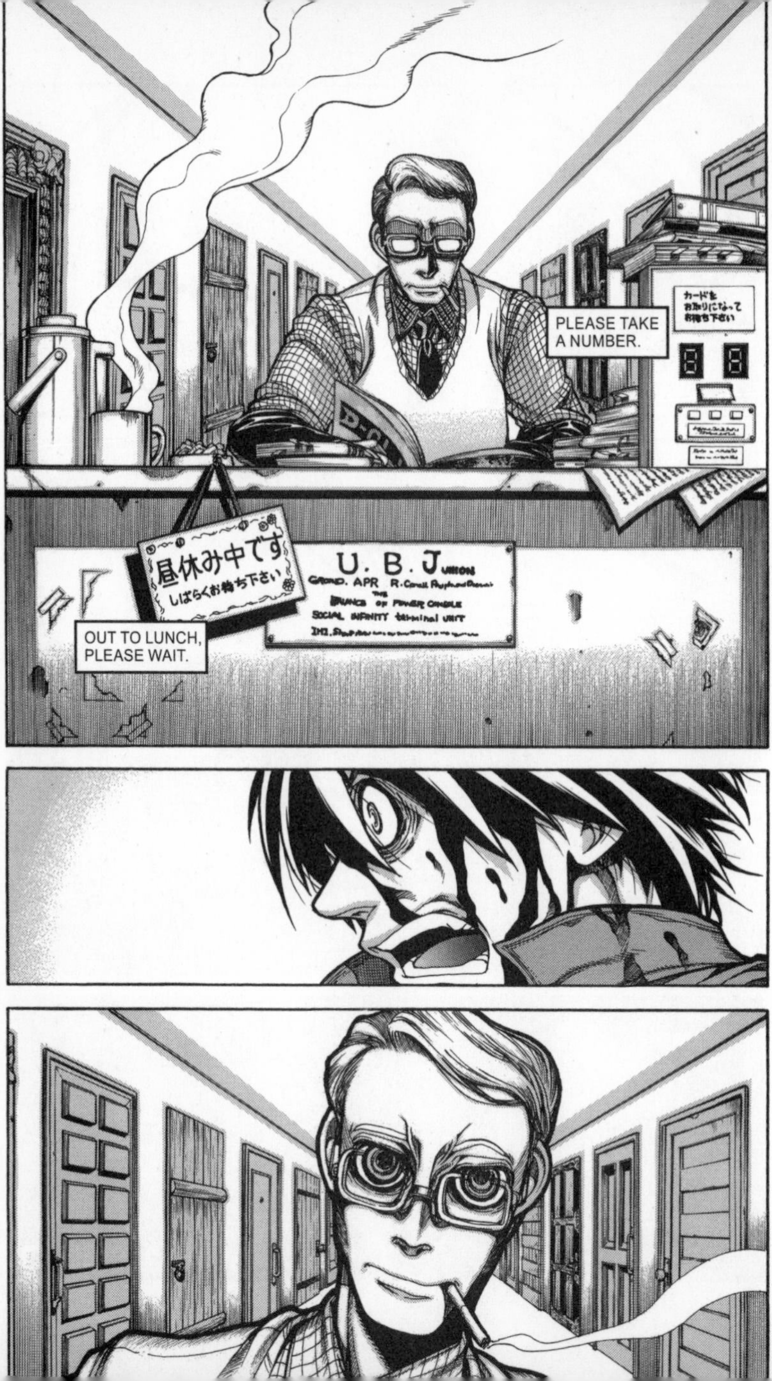
カードをお取りになってお待ち下さい
PLEASE TAKE A NUMBER.
昼休み中です
しばらくお待ち下さい
U. B. J
OUT TO LUNCH, PLEASE WAIT.

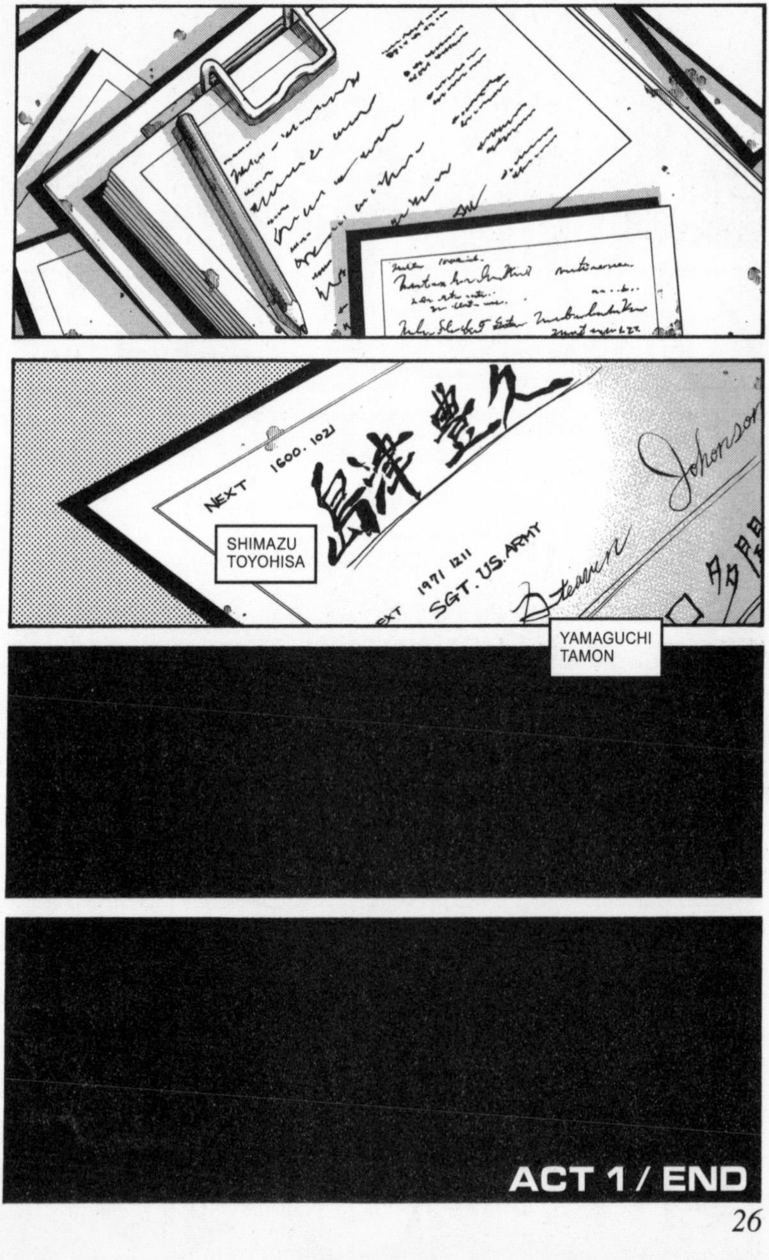
NEXT 1600. 1021
島津豊久
SHIMAZU TOYOHISA
1971 1211
SGT. US.ARMY
YAMAGUCHI TAMON
ACT 1 / END

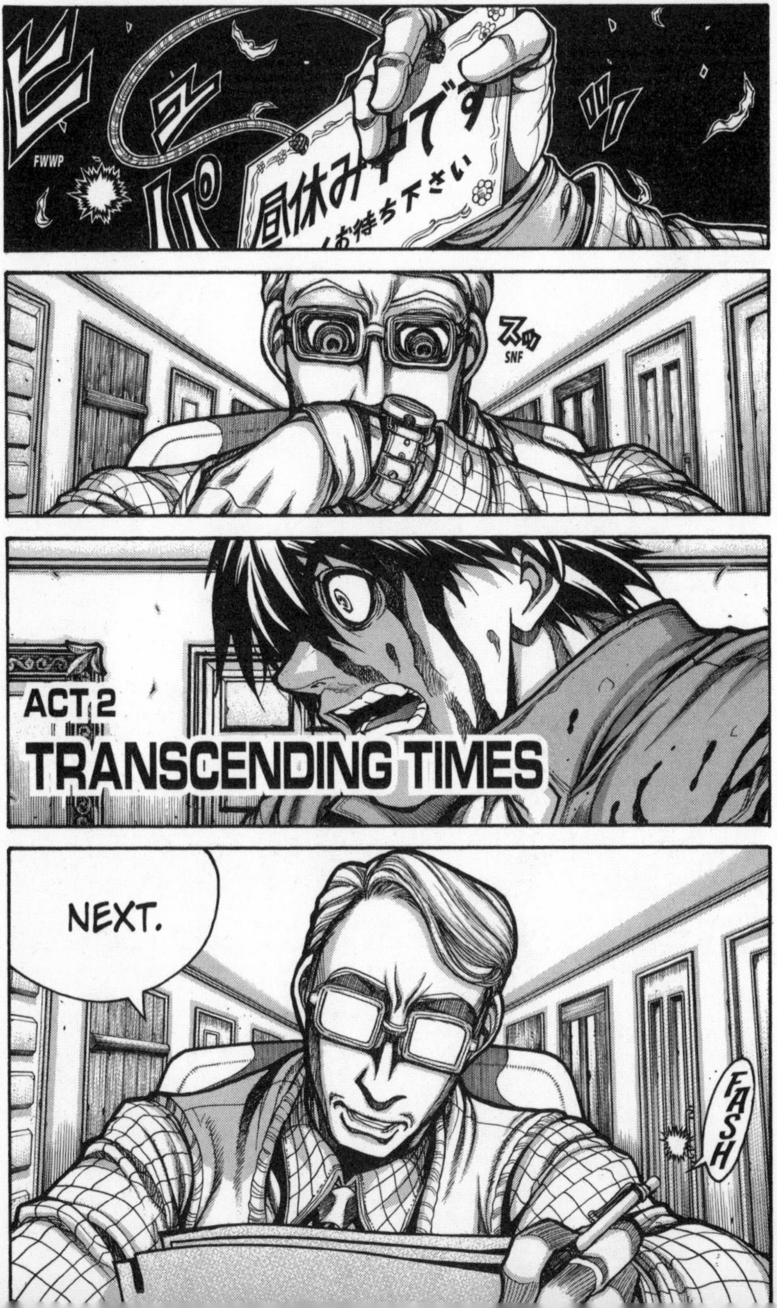
FWWP
お待ち下さい
SNF
ACT 2
TRANSCENDING TIMES
NEXT.
FASH

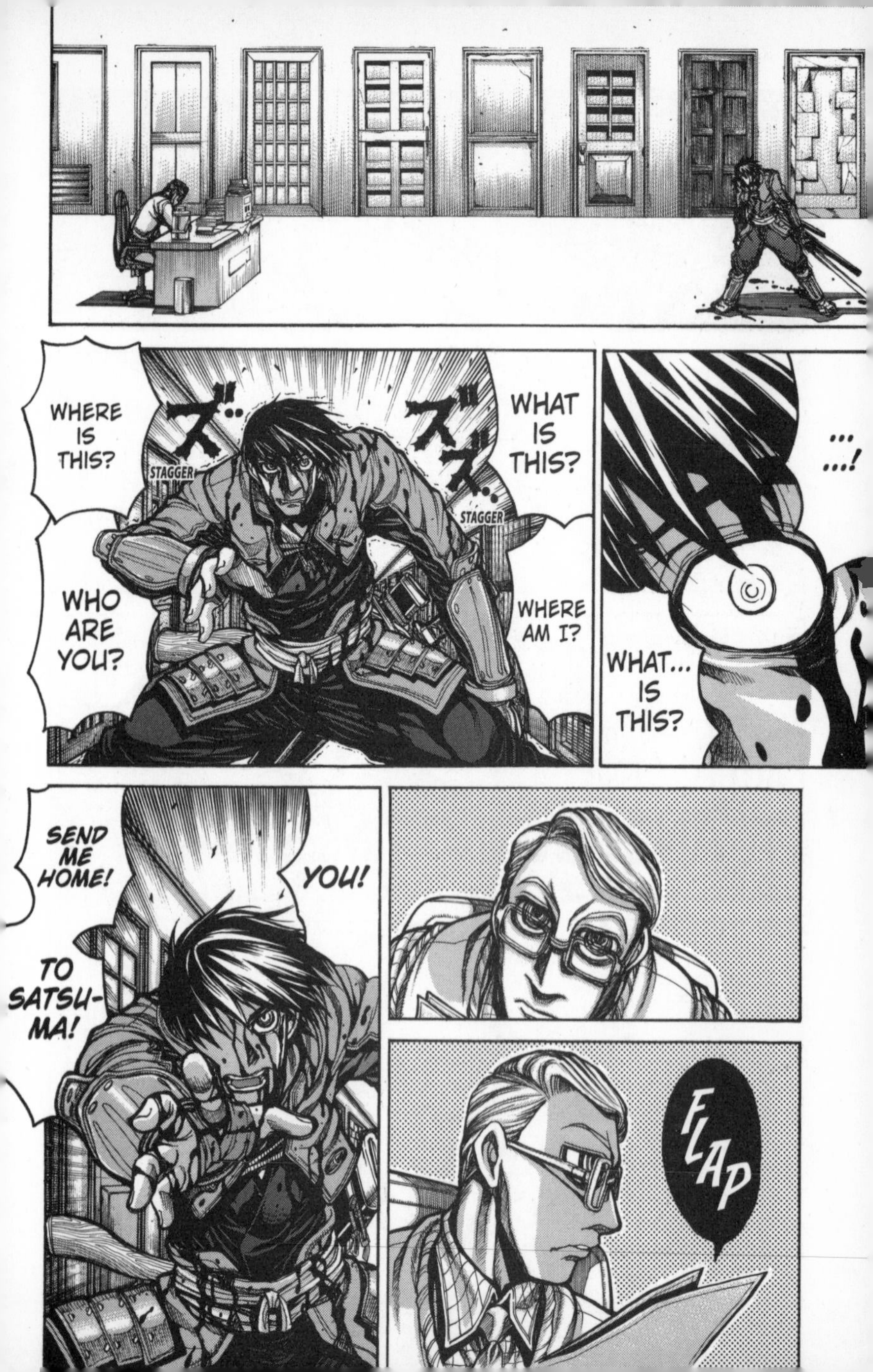
...
...!
WHAT... IS THIS?
WHAT IS THIS?
STAGGER
WHERE AM I?
WHERE IS THIS?
STAGGER
WHO ARE YOU?
FLAP
YOU!
SEND ME HOME!
TO SATSU-MA!

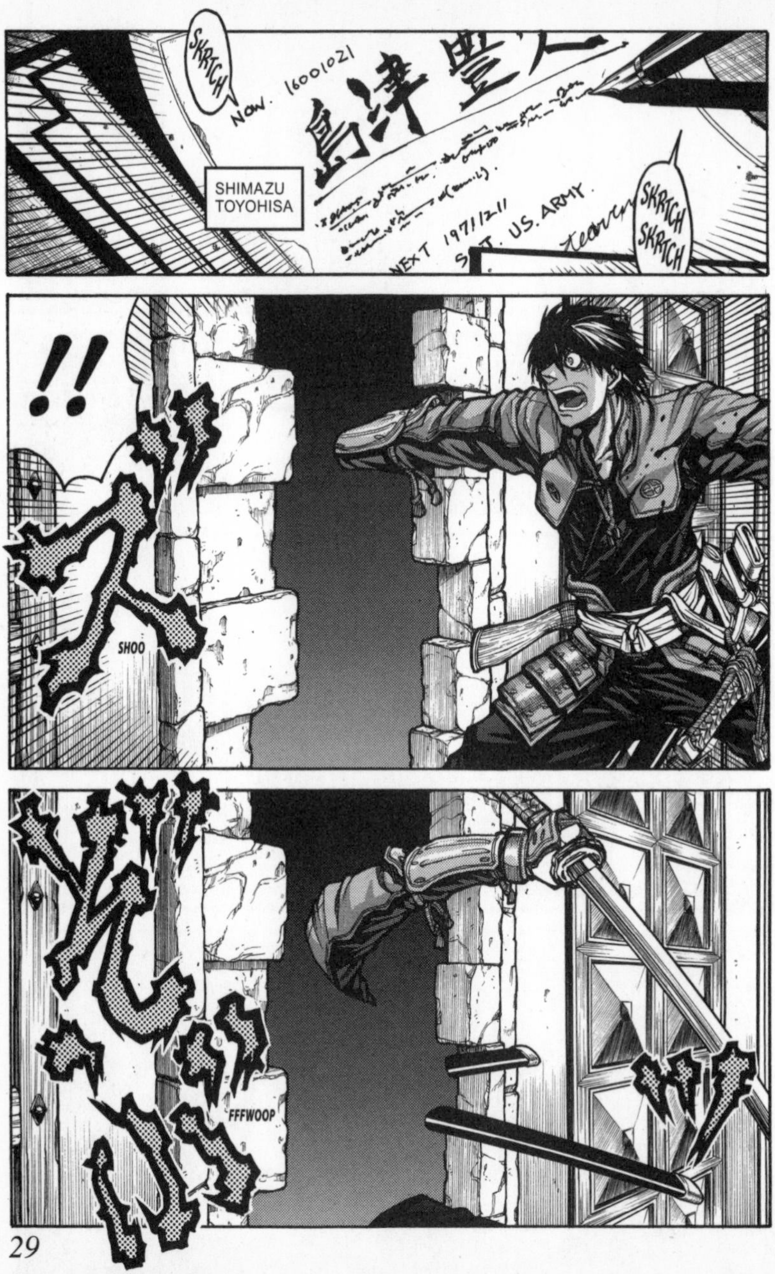
SKRICH SKRICH
島津 豊久
NOW. 1600/021
SKRICH
SHIMAZU TOYOHISA
NEXT 1971/2/11
SGT. U.S. ARMY
!!
SHOO
FFFWOOP

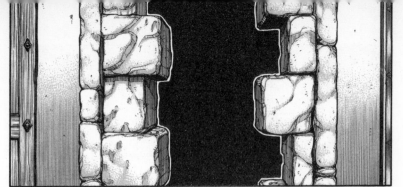

NEXT.

WHAT...

...THE
...ELL?

HUH?

ズ
ズ
ZRCH

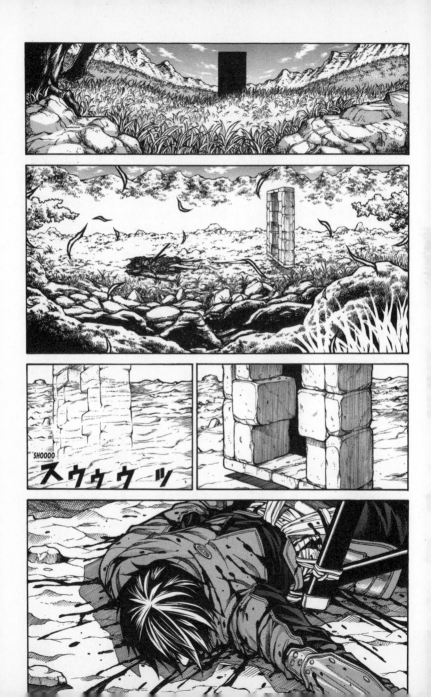

SHOOOO
スウゥゥッ

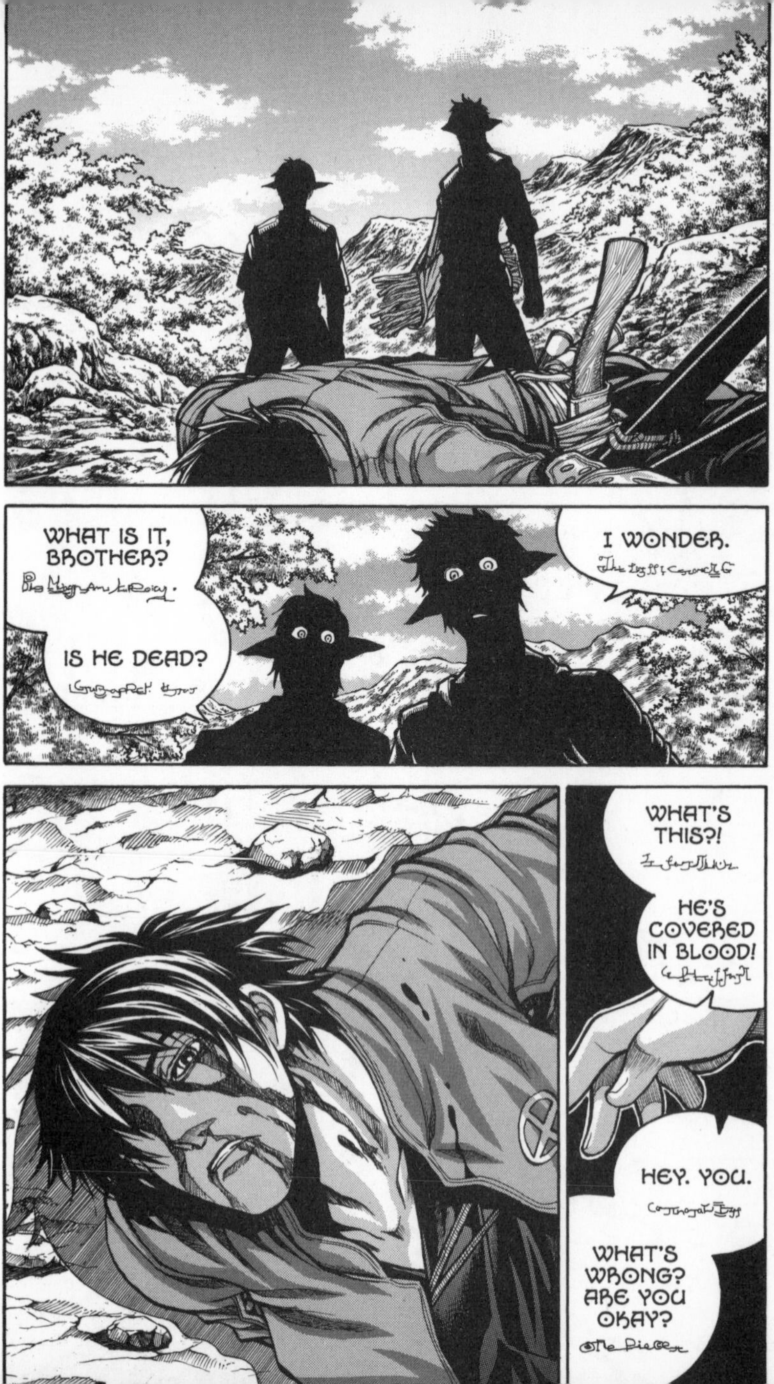
I WONDER.
WHAT IS IT, BROTHER?
IS HE DEAD?
WHAT'S THIS?!
HE'S COVERED IN BLOOD!
HEY. YOU.
WHAT'S WRONG? ARE YOU OKAY?

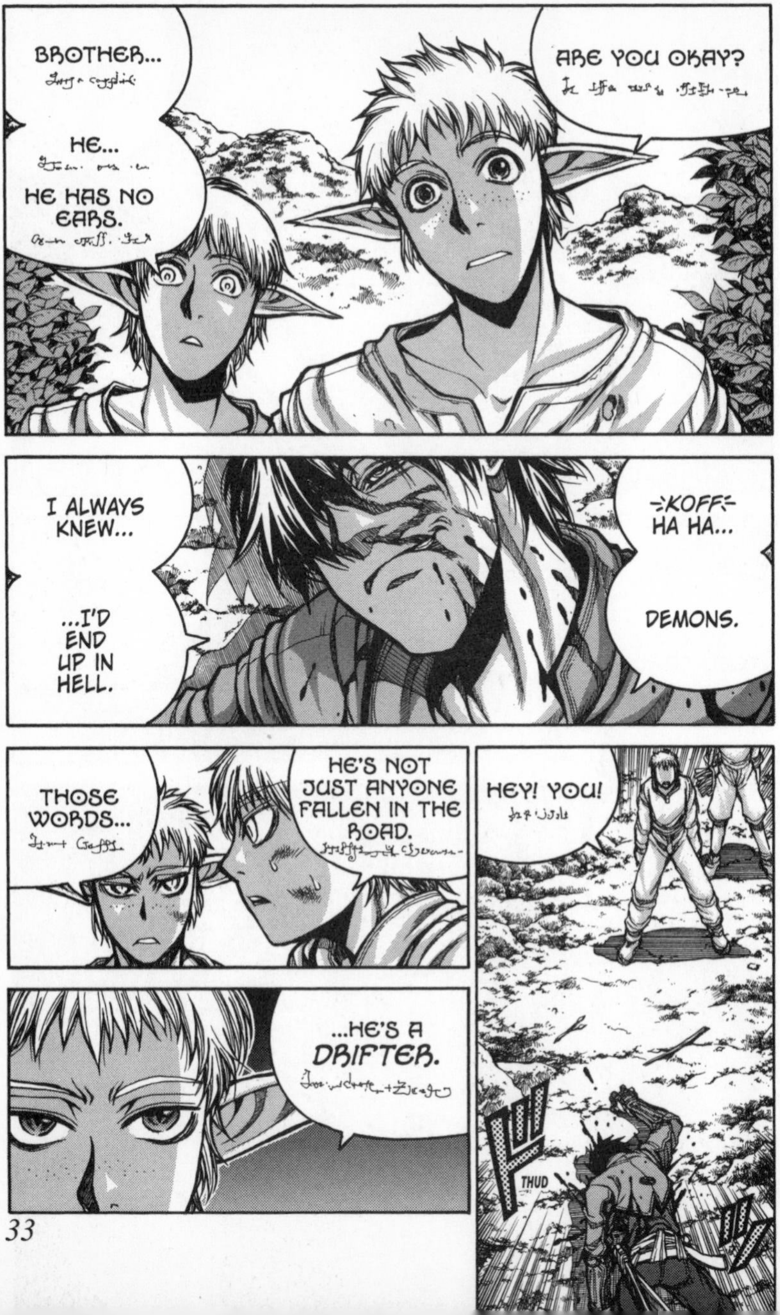
ARE YOU OKAY?
BROTHER...
HE...
HE HAS NO EARS.
-KOFF-
HA HA...
DEMONS.
I ALWAYS KNEW...
...I'D END UP IN HELL.
HEY! YOU!
THUD
HE'S NOT JUST ANYONE FALLEN IN THE ROAD.
THOSE WORDS...
...HE'S A DRIFTER.

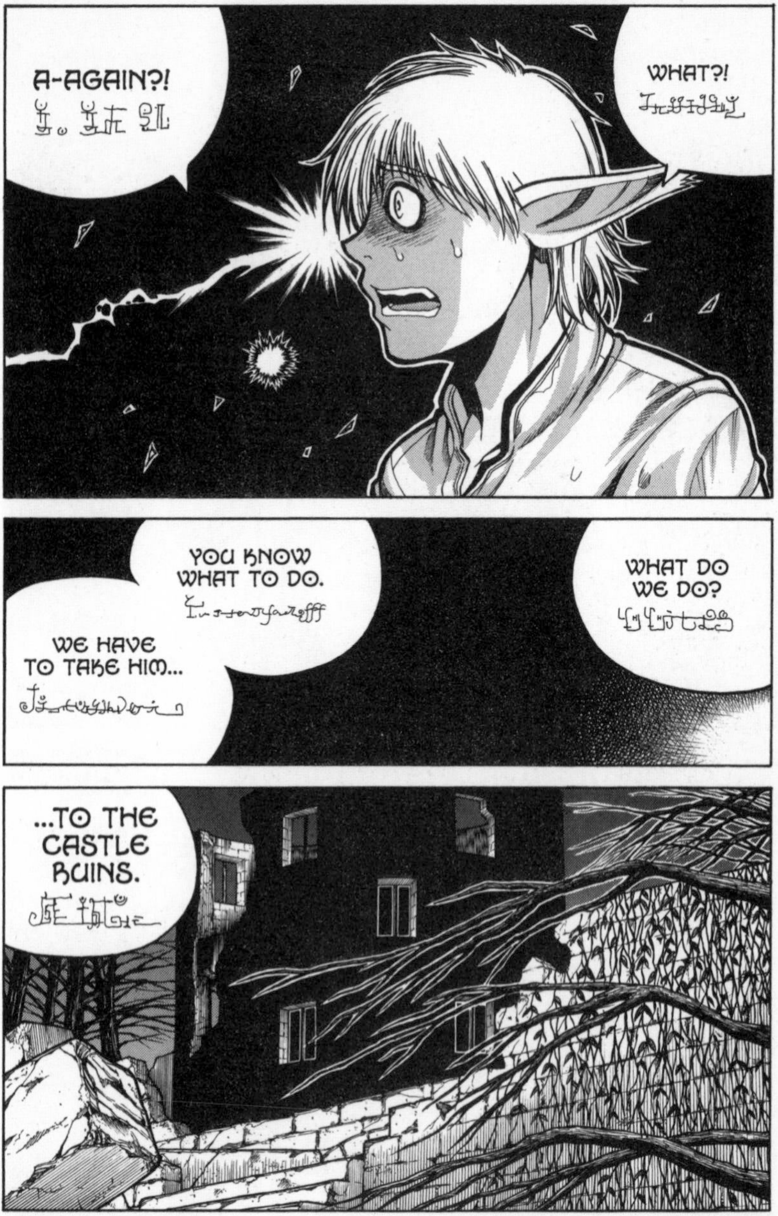
WHAT?!
A-AGAIN?!
WHAT DO WE DO?
YOU KNOW WHAT TO DO.
WE HAVE TO TAKE HIM...
...TO THE CASTLE RUINS.

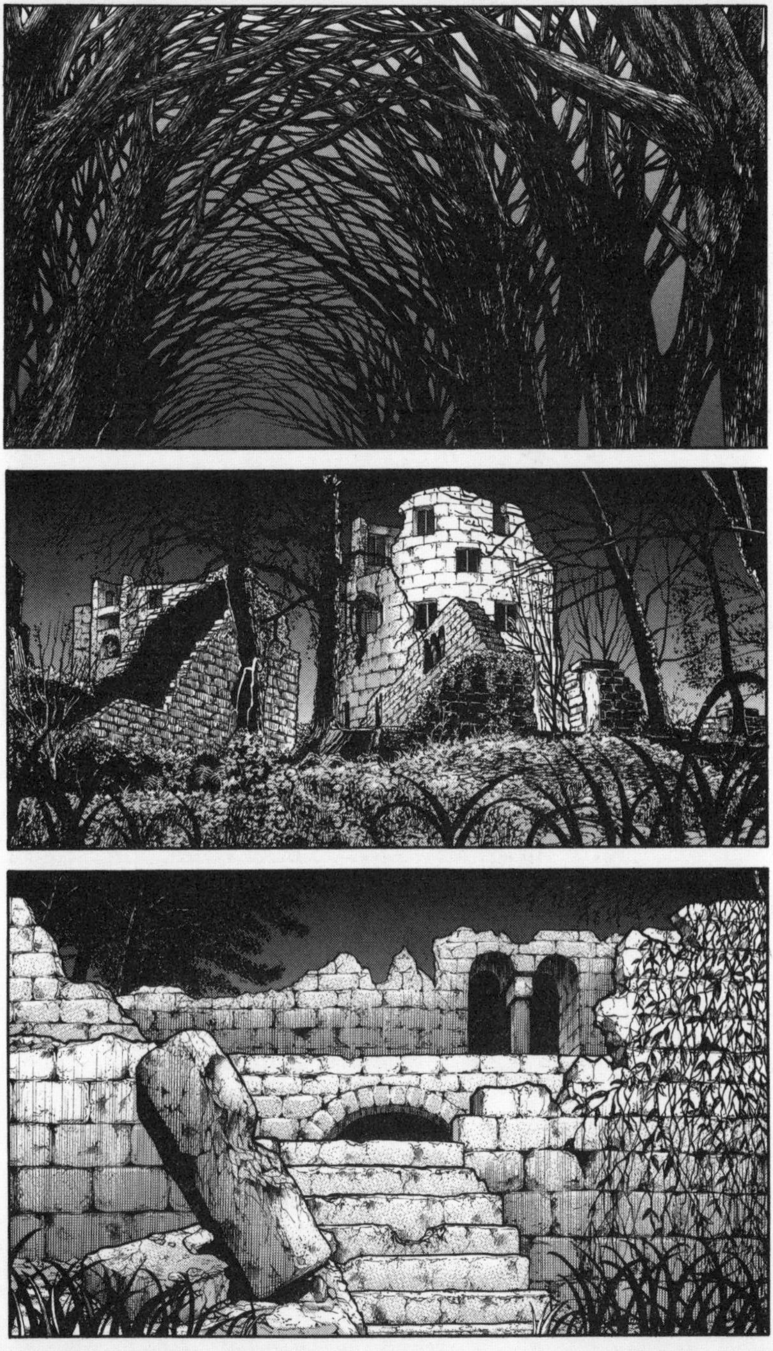

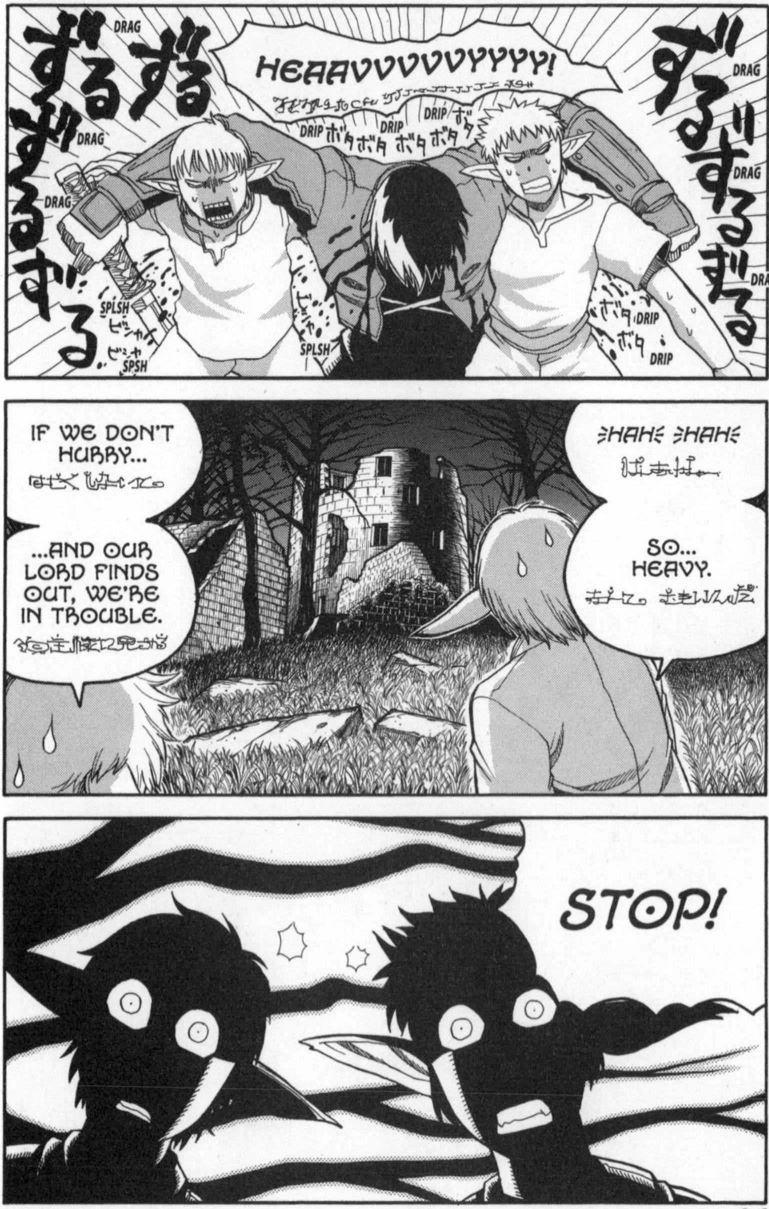
ずるずるずるずる
DRAG
DRAG
DRAG
HEAAVVVVVYYYY!
DRIP
ずる
DRIP ボタボタ
DRIP ボタボタ
DRIP ボタ
DRIP ボタ
DRIP
SPLSH ビシャ
ずるずるずるずるずる
DRAG
DRAG
DRAG
SPLSH ビシャ
SPSH ビシャ
HAH HAH
SO... HEAVY.
IF WE DON'T HURRY...
...AND OUR LORD FINDS OUT, WE'RE IN TROUBLE.
STOP!

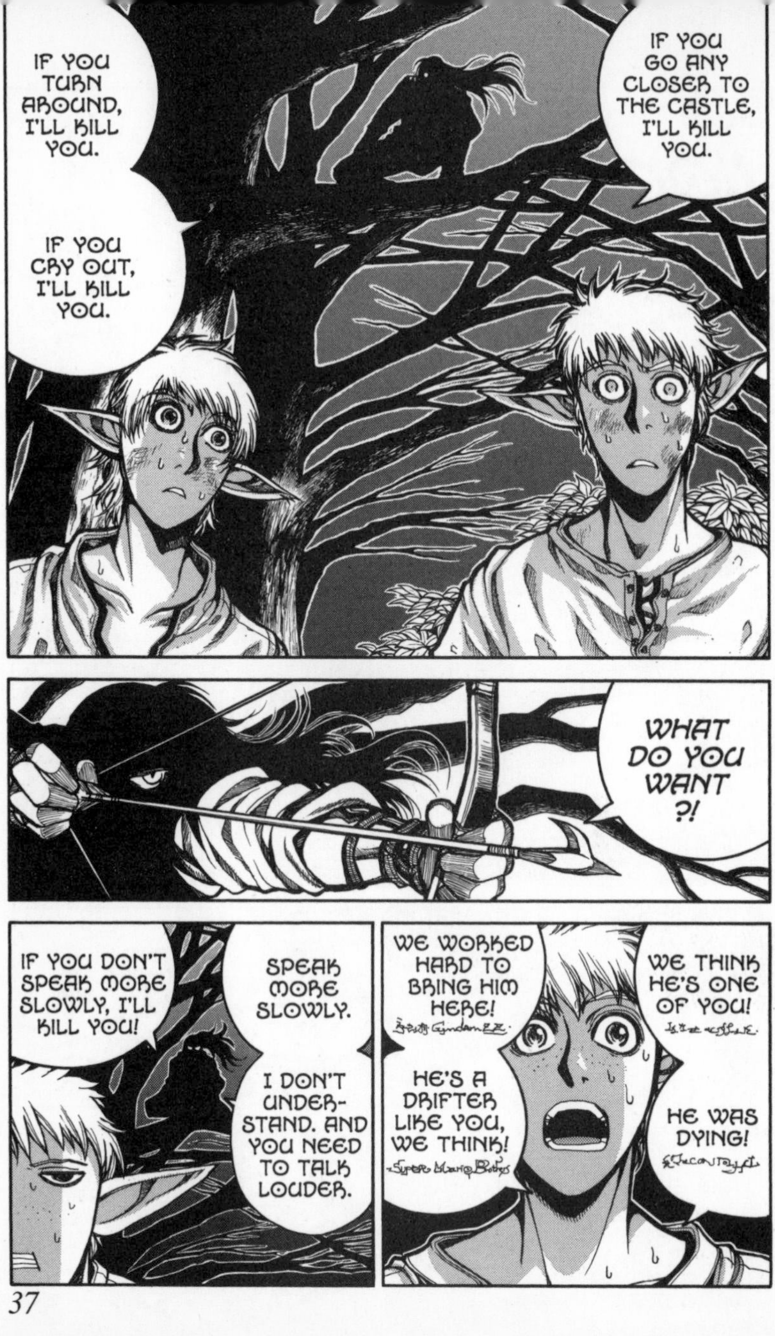
IF YOU GO ANY CLOSER TO THE CASTLE, I'LL KILL YOU.
IF YOU TURN AROUND, I'LL KILL YOU.
IF YOU CRY OUT, I'LL KILL YOU.
WHAT DO YOU WANT ?!
WE THINK HE'S ONE OF YOU!
WE WORKED HARD TO BRING HIM HERE!
HE WAS DYING!
HE'S A DRIFTER LIKE YOU, WE THINK!
SPEAK MORE SLOWLY.
I DON'T UNDERSTAND. AND YOU NEED TO TALK LOUDER.
IF YOU DON'T SPEAK MORE SLOWLY, I'LL KILL YOU!

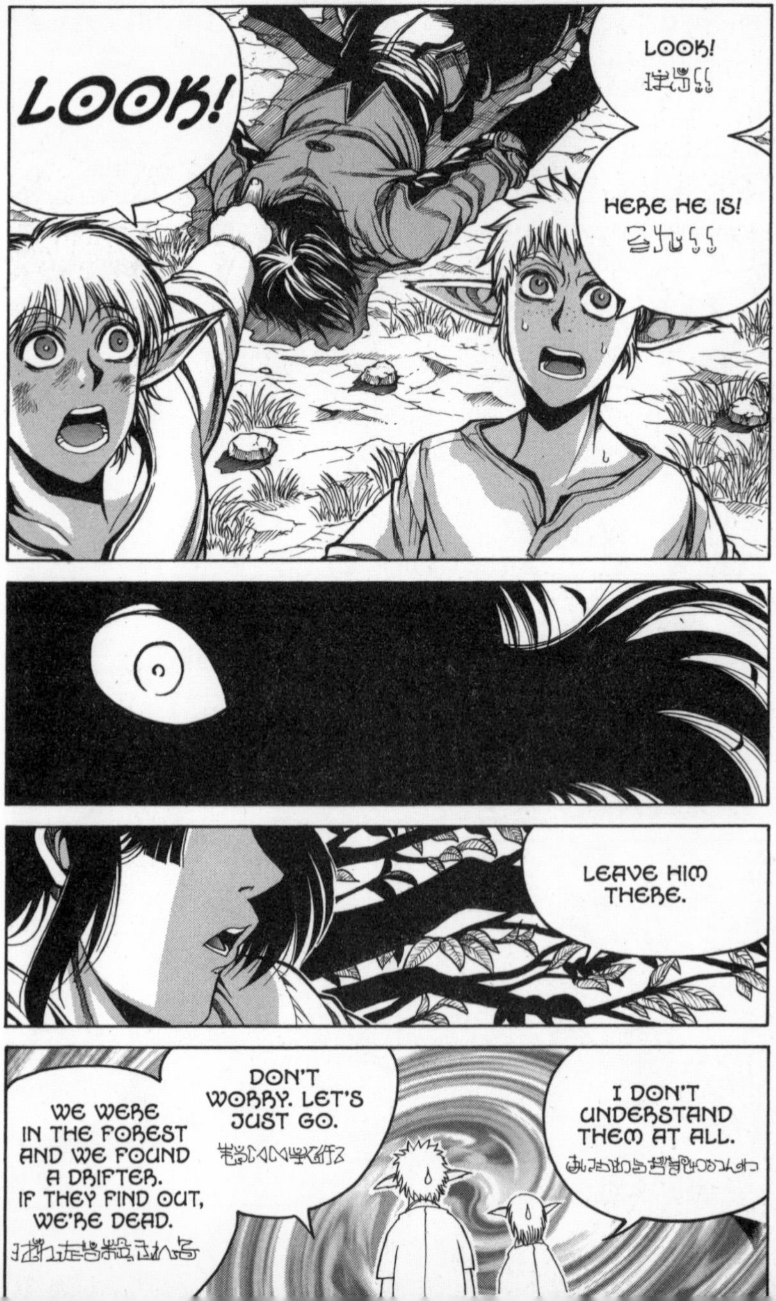
LOOK!
HERE HE IS!
LOOK!
LEAVE HIM THERE.
I DON'T UNDERSTAND THEM AT ALL.
DON'T WORRY. LET'S JUST GO.
WE WERE IN THE FOREST AND WE FOUND A DRIFTER. IF THEY FIND OUT, WE'RE DEAD.

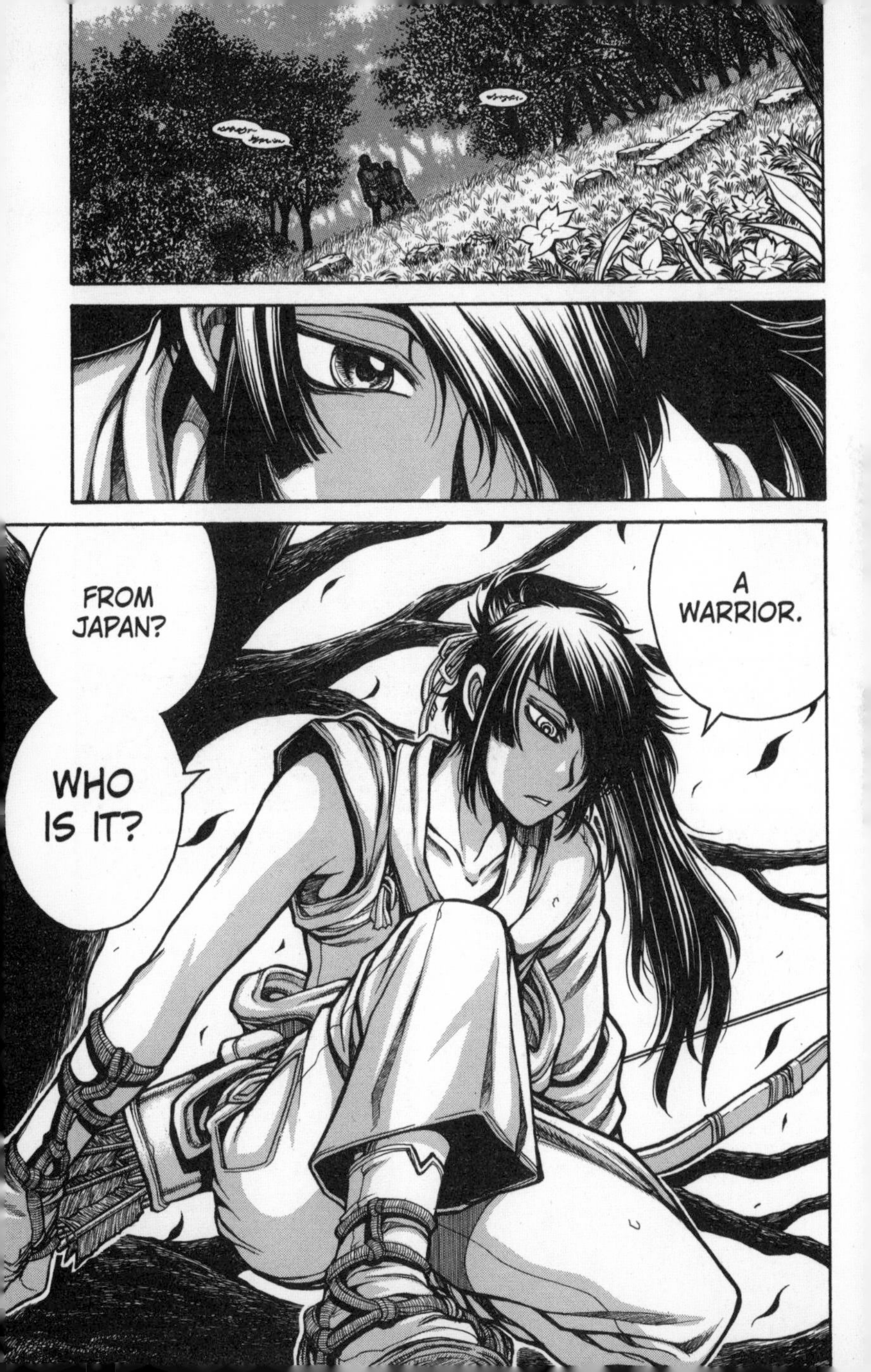
A WARRIOR.
FROM JAPAN?
WHO IS IT?

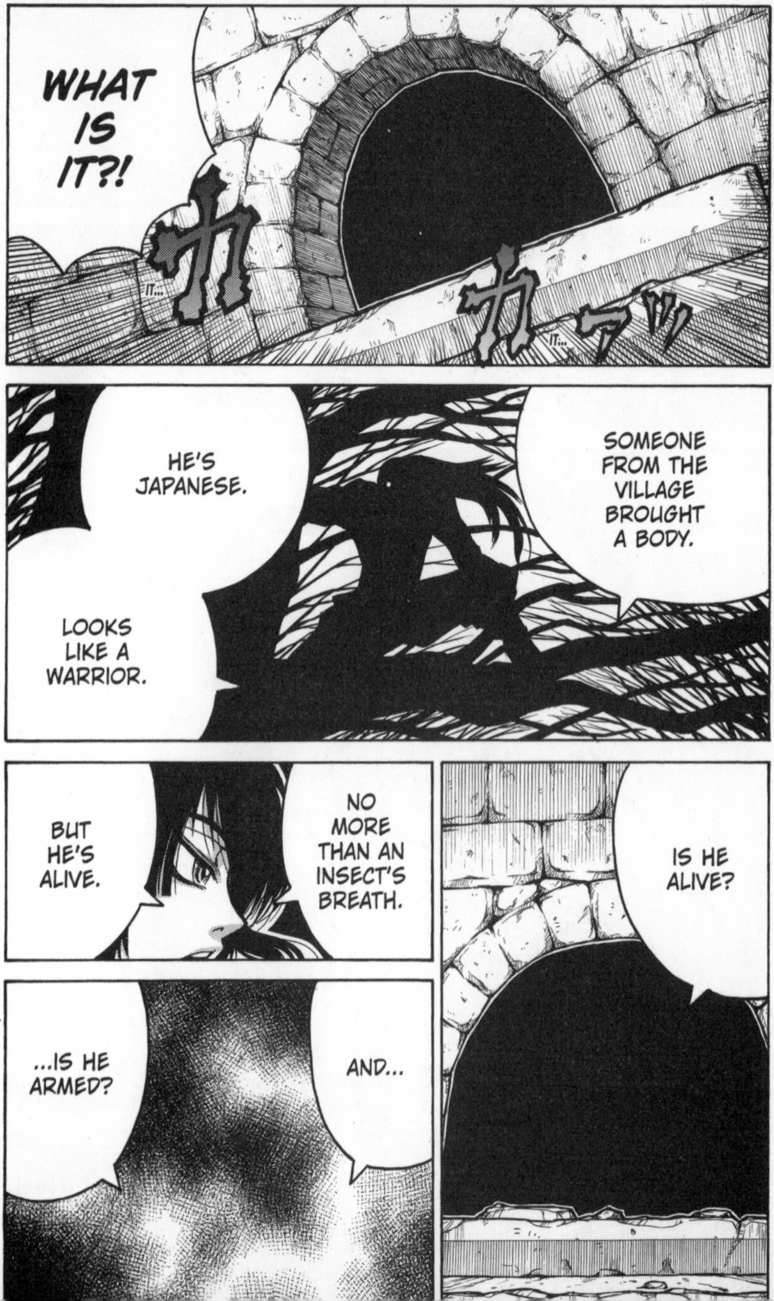
WHAT IS IT?!
IT...
IT...
SOMEONE FROM THE VILLAGE BROUGHT A BODY.
HE'S JAPANESE.
LOOKS LIKE A WARRIOR.
IS HE ALIVE?
NO MORE THAN AN INSECT'S BREATH.
BUT HE'S ALIVE.
AND...
...IS HE ARMED?

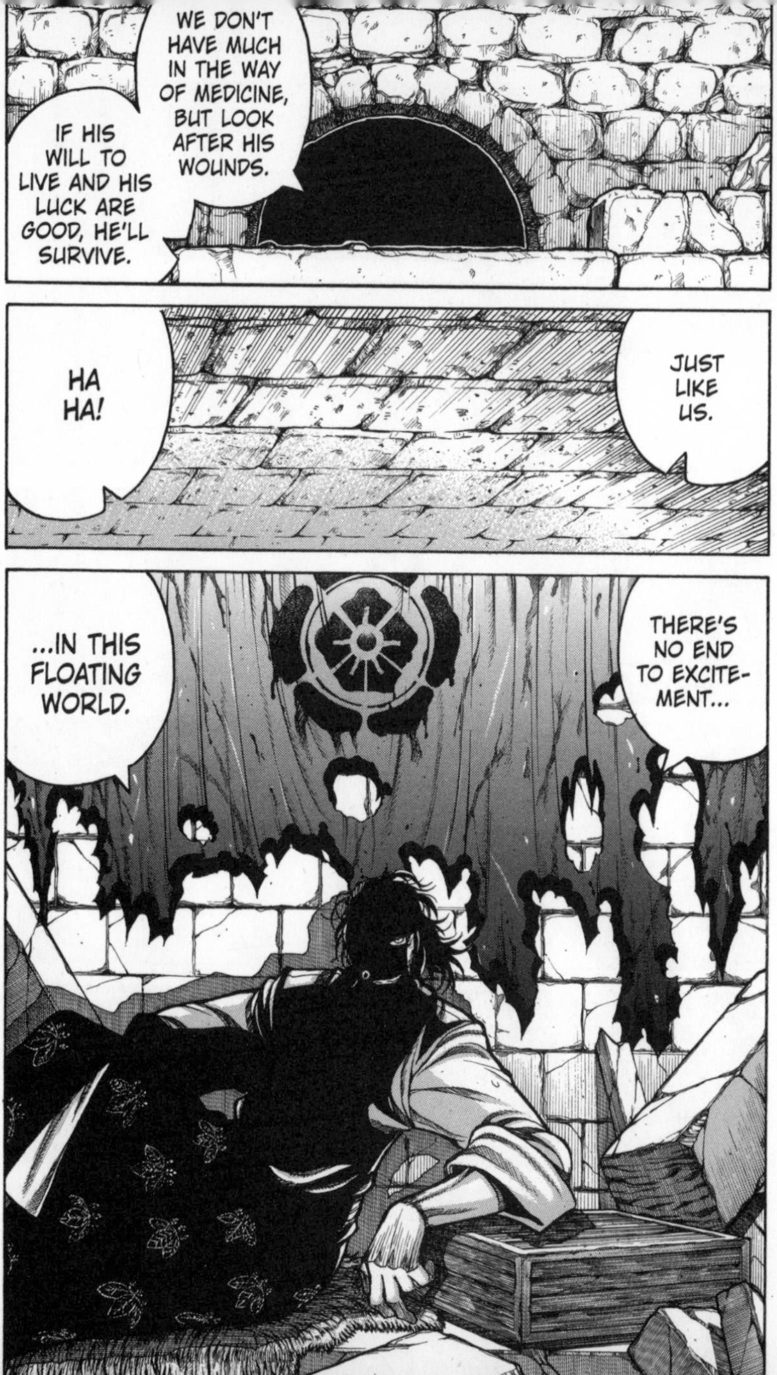
WE DON'T HAVE MUCH IN THE WAY OF MEDICINE, BUT LOOK AFTER HIS WOUNDS.
IF HIS WILL TO LIVE AND HIS LUCK ARE GOOD, HE'LL SURVIVE.
JUST LIKE US.
HA HA!
THERE'S NO END TO EXCITE-MENT...
...IN THIS FLOATING WORLD.

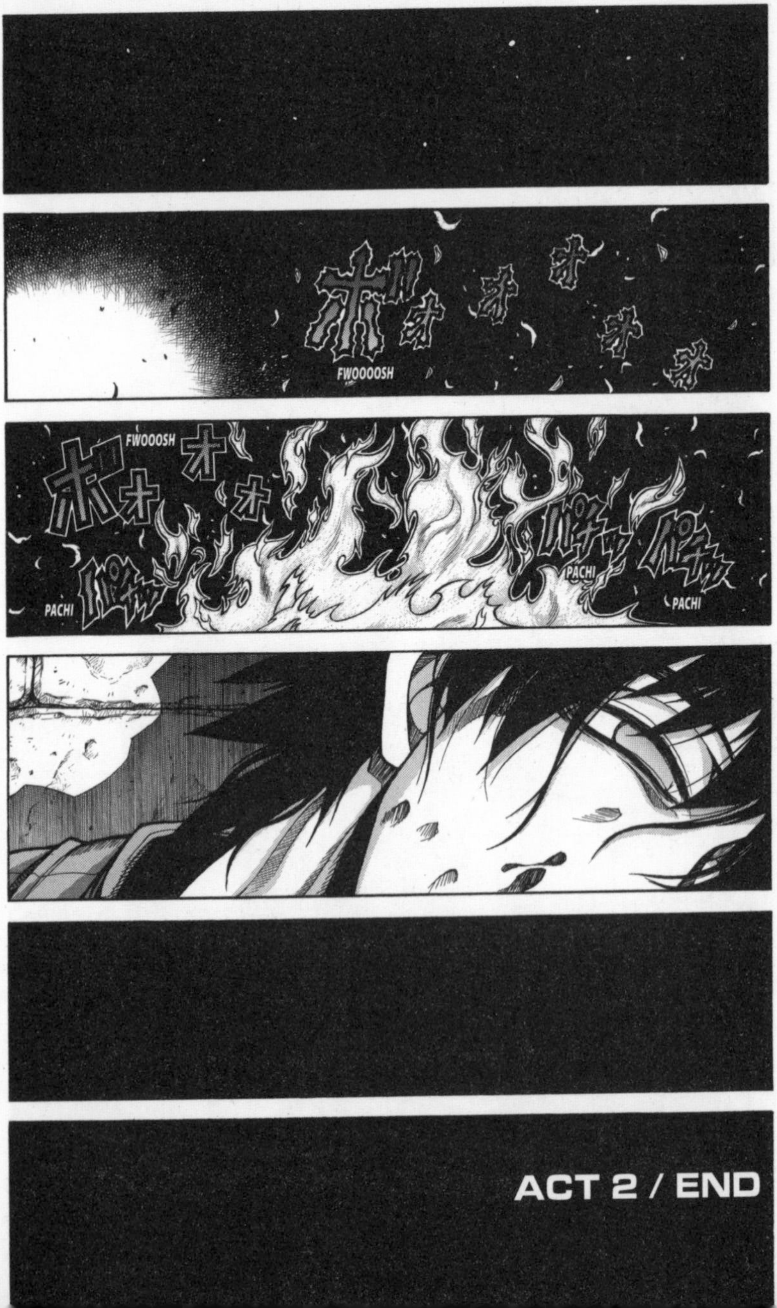
FWOOOSH
PACHI
PACHI
FWOOOSH
PACHI
ACT 2 / END

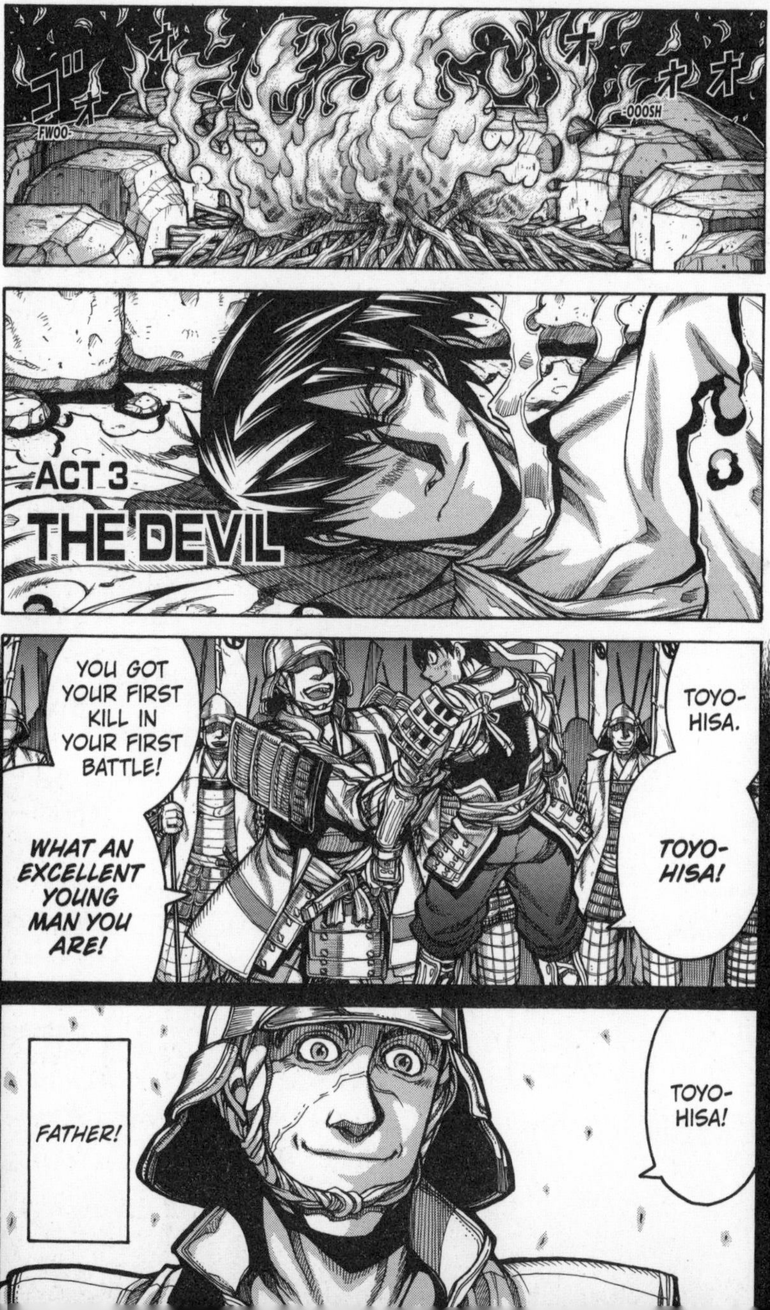
FWOO-
-OOOSH
ACT 3
THE DEVIL
TOYO-HISA.
TOYO-HISA!
YOU GOT YOUR FIRST KILL IN YOUR FIRST BATTLE!
WHAT AN EXCELLENT YOUNG MAN YOU ARE!
TOYO-HISA!
FATHER!

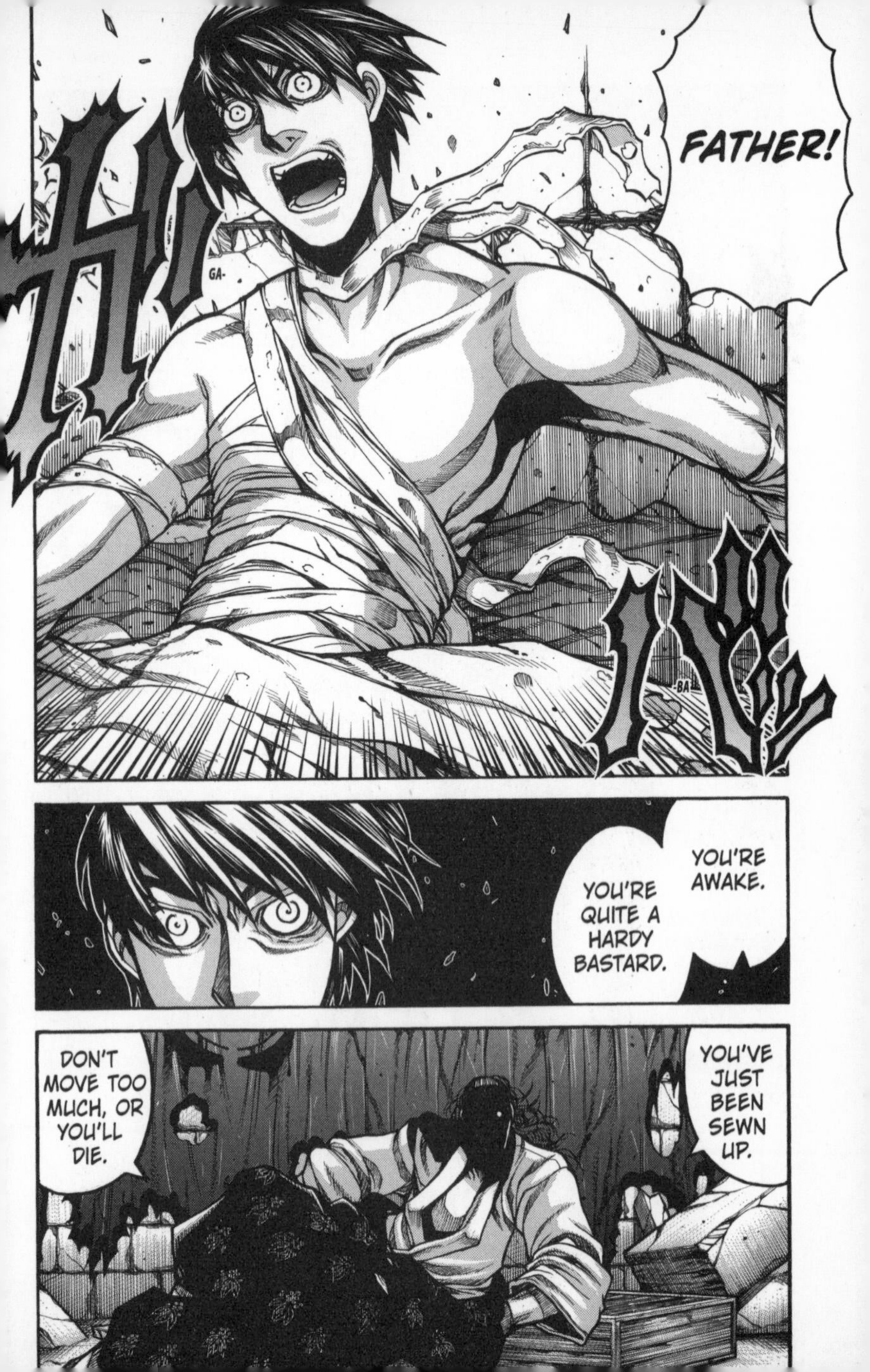
FATHER!
GA-
-BA
YOU'RE AWAKE.
YOU'RE QUITE A HARDY BASTARD.
YOU'VE JUST BEEN SEWN UP.
DON'T MOVE TOO MUCH, OR YOU'LL DIE.

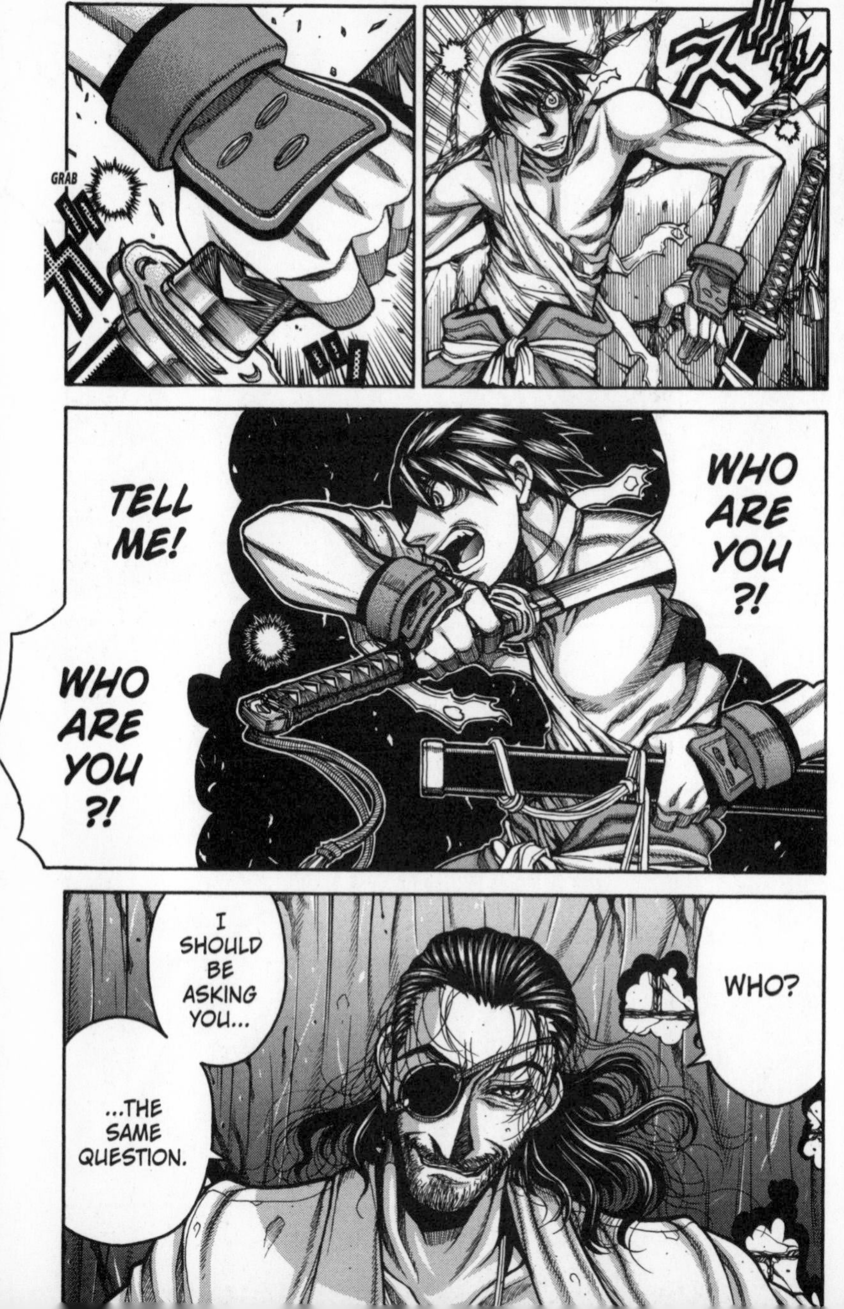
WOOSH
GRAB
WHO ARE YOU ?!
TELL ME!
WHO ARE YOU ?!
WHO?
I SHOULD BE ASKING YOU...
...THE SAME QUESTION.

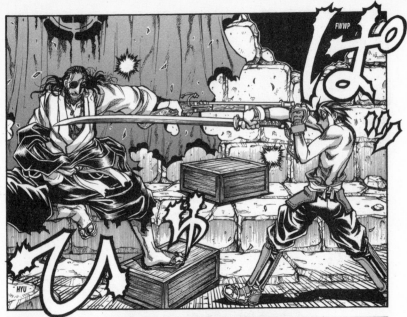

WHO ARE YOU...

...AND WHERE ARE YOU FROM?

ANSWER NOW.

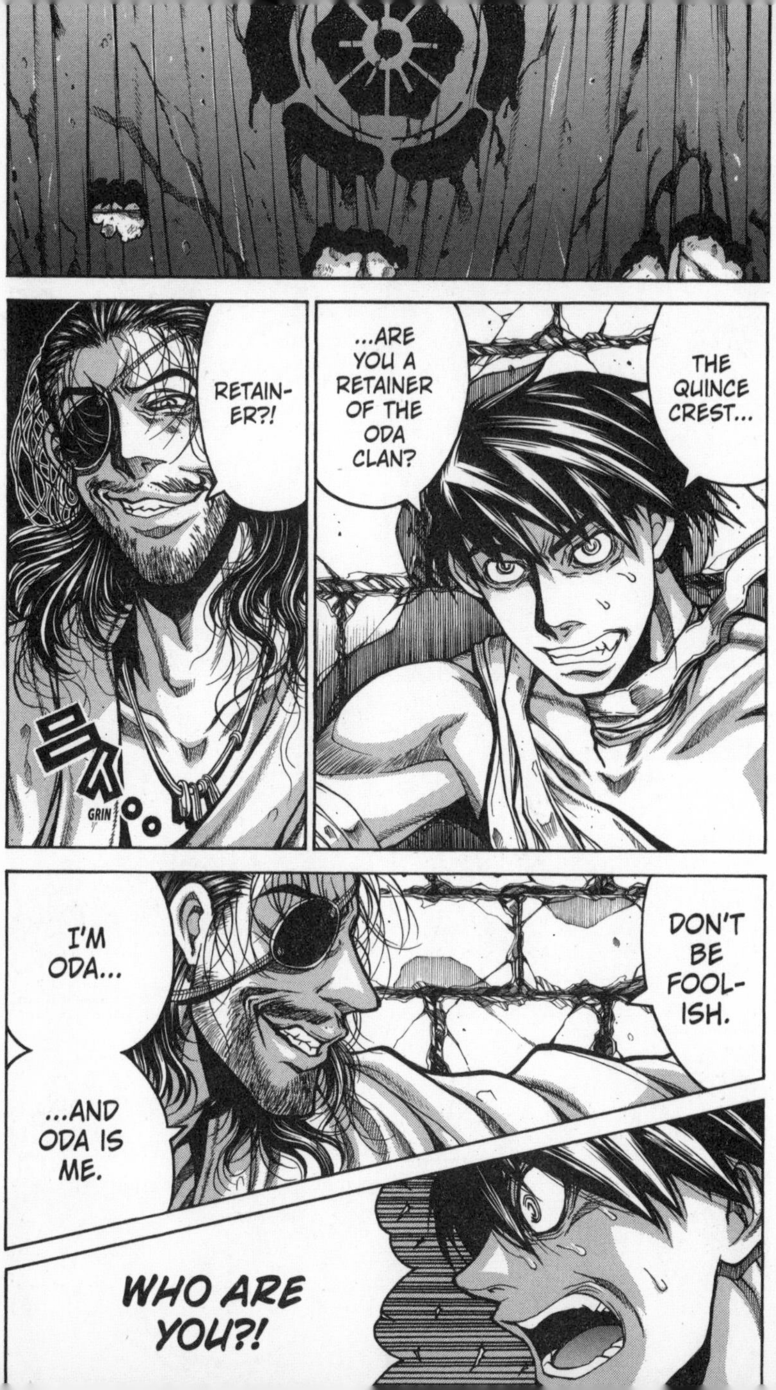
THE QUINCE CREST...
...ARE YOU A RETAINER OF THE ODA CLAN?
RETAIN-ER?!
GRIN
DON'T BE FOOL-ISH.
I'M ODA...
...AND ODA IS ME.
WHO ARE YOU?!

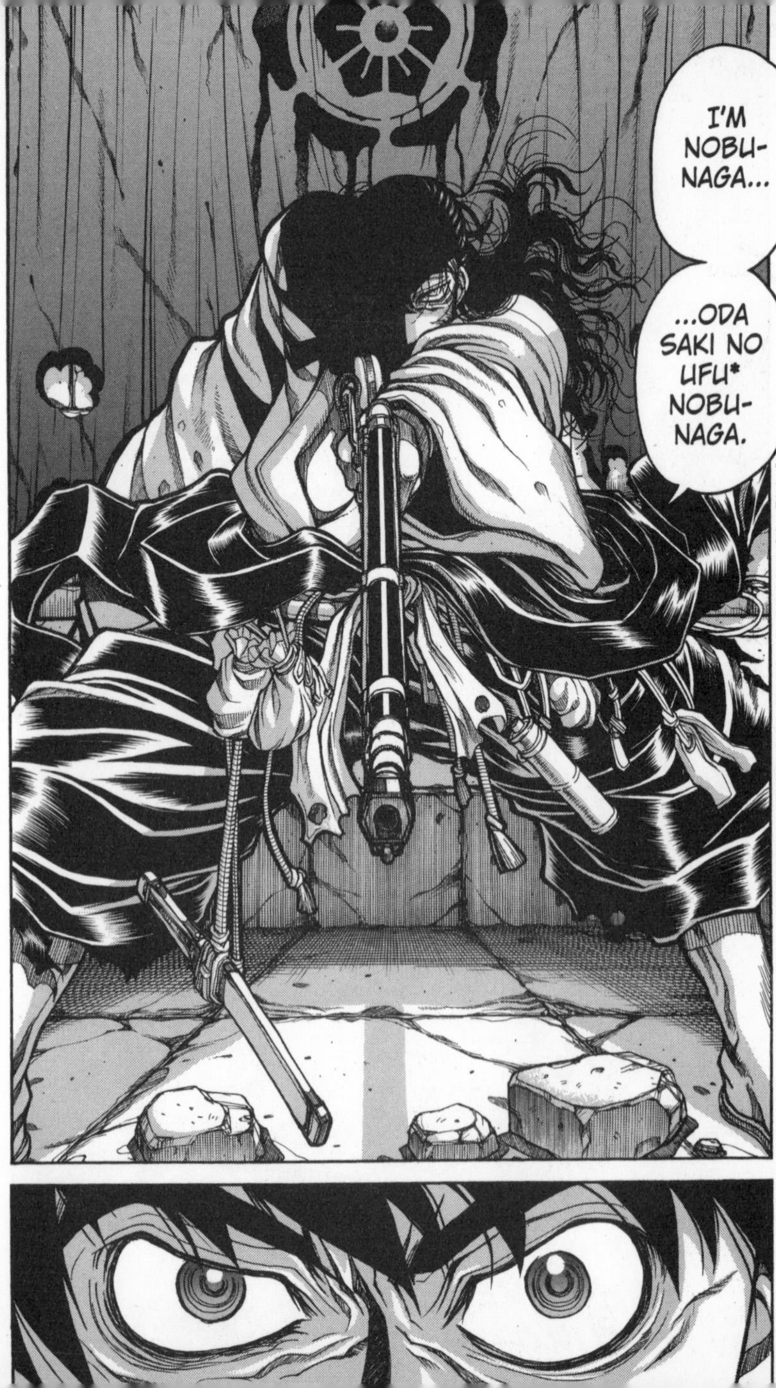
I'M NOBU-NAGA...
...ODA SAKI NO UFU* NOBU-NAGA.

**Saki No Ufu* is an imperial title akin to "the Former Minister of the Right."

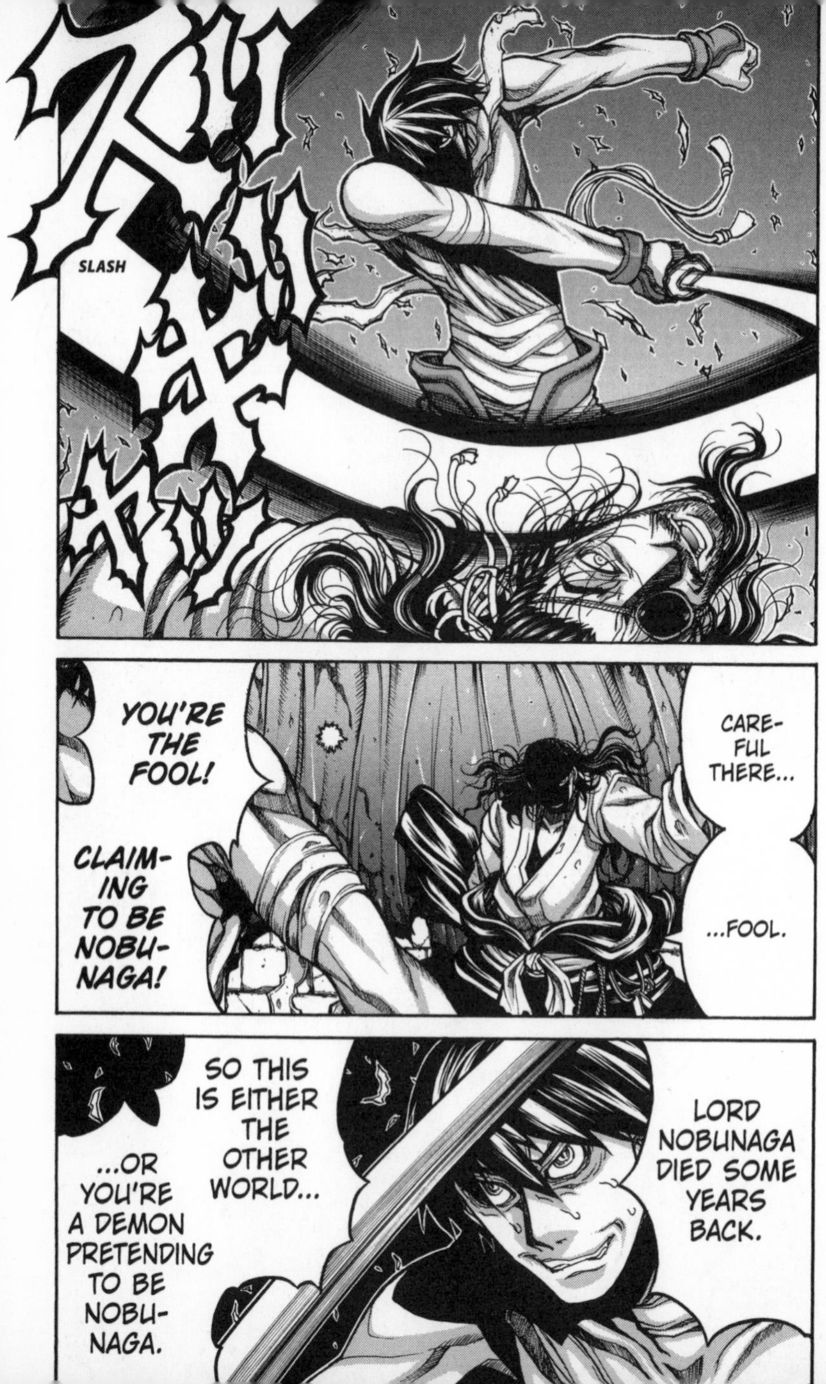
SLASH
CAREFUL THERE...
...FOOL.
YOU'RE THE FOOL!
CLAIMING TO BE NOBUNAGA!
LORD NOBUNAGA DIED SOME YEARS BACK.
SO THIS IS EITHER THE OTHER WORLD...
...OR YOU'RE A DEMON PRETENDING TO BE NOBUNAGA.

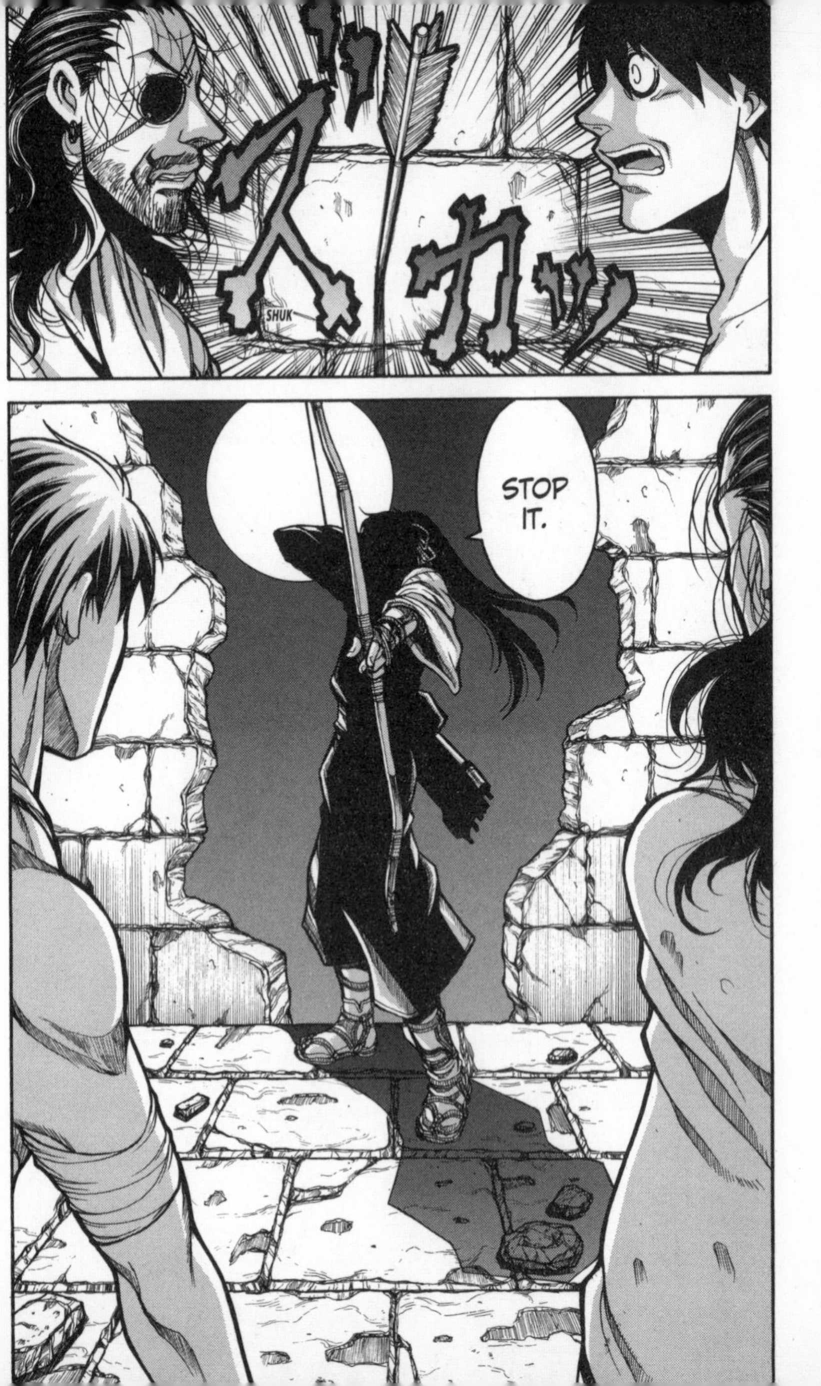
スカッ
SHUK
STOP IT.

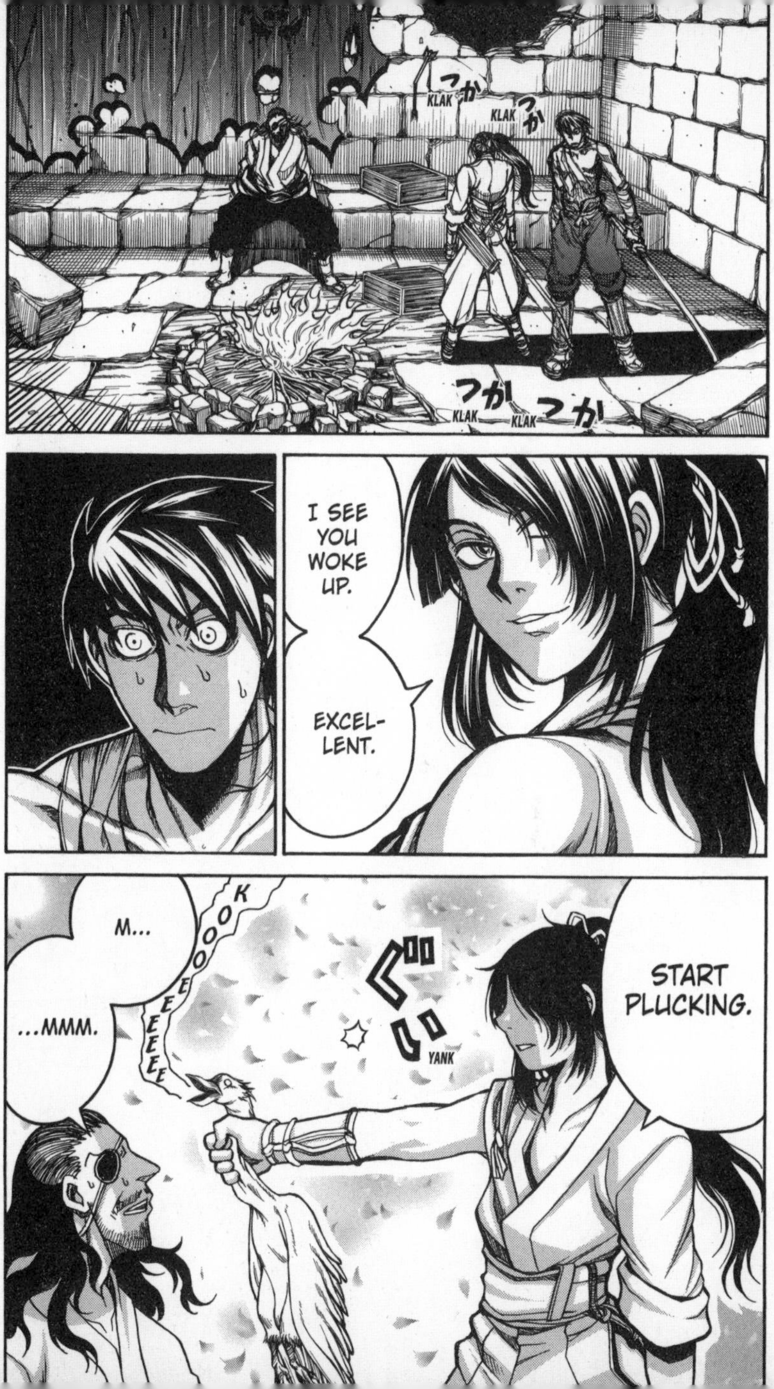

KLAK つか
KLAK つか
KLAK つか
KLAK つか
I SEE YOU WOKE UP.
EXCEL-LENT.
START PLUCKING.
YANK
EEEEEEOOOOOK
M...
...MMM.

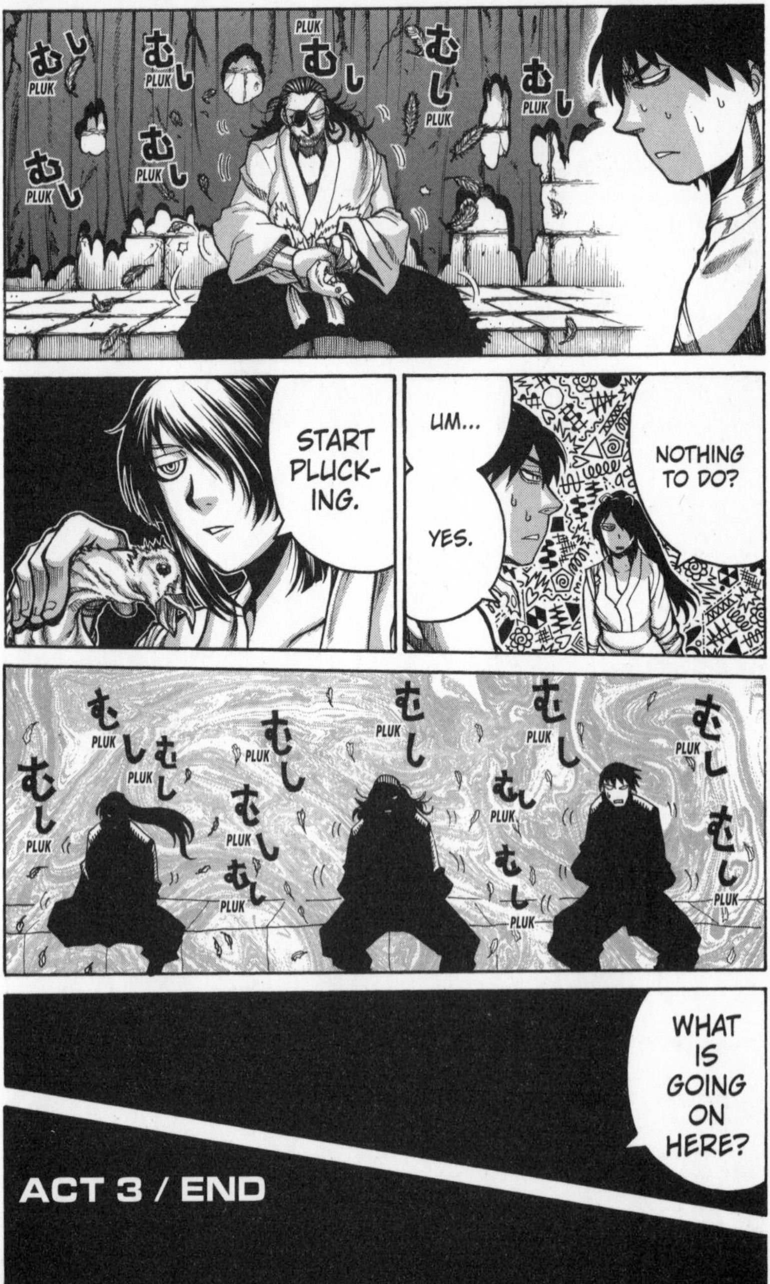
むし PLUK
むし PLUK
むし PLUK
むし PLUK
むし PLUK
むし PLUK
むし PLUK
NOTHING TO DO?
UM...
YES.
START PLUCK-ING.
むし PLUK
むし PLUK
むし PLUK
むし PLUK
むし PLUK
むし PLUK
むし PLUK
むし PLUK
むし PLUK
むし PLUK
むし PLUK
むし PLUK
WHAT IS GOING ON HERE?
ACT 3 / END

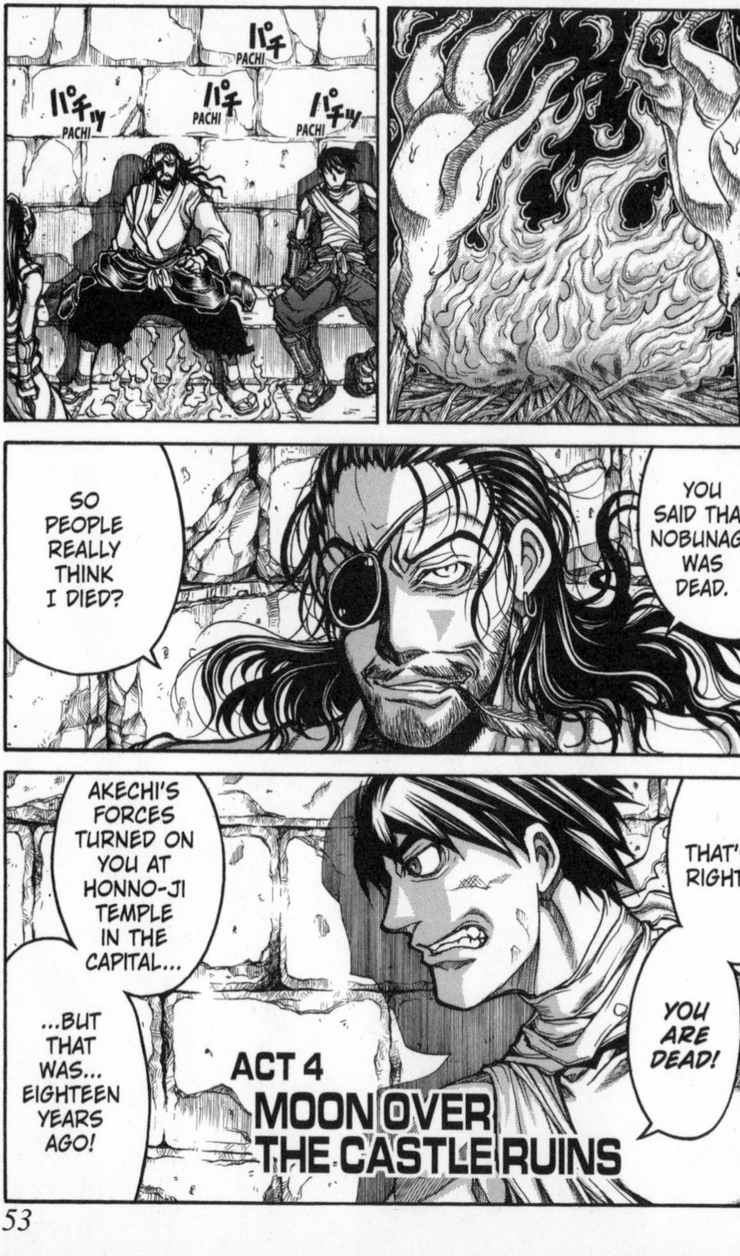
パチ
PACHI
パチッ
PACHI
パチ
PACHI
パチッ
PACHI
YOU SAID THAT NOBUNAGA WAS DEAD.
SO PEOPLE REALLY THINK I DIED?
THAT'S RIGHT!
YOU ARE DEAD!
AKECHI'S FORCES TURNED ON YOU AT HONNO-JI TEMPLE IN THE CAPITAL...
...BUT THAT WAS... EIGHTEEN YEARS AGO!
ACT 4
MOON OVER THE CASTLE RUINS

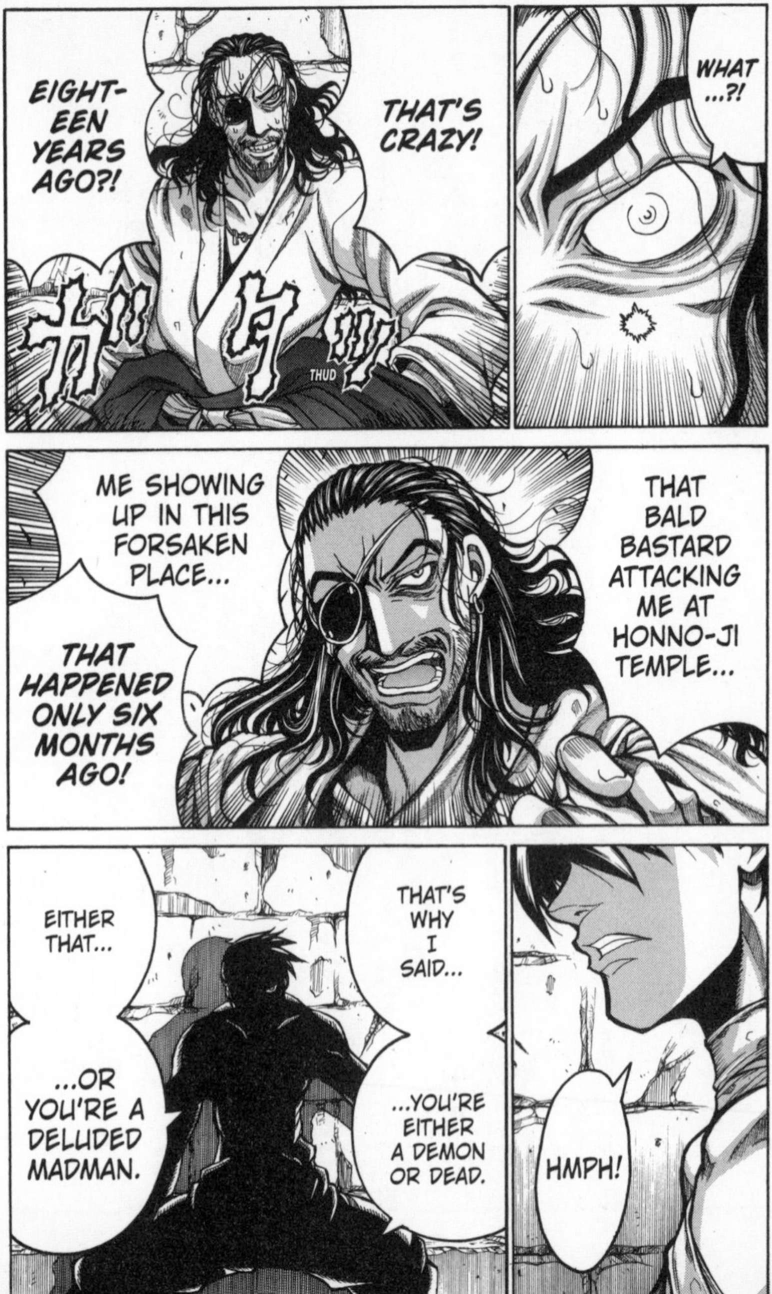
WHAT ...?!
THAT'S CRAZY!
EIGHTEEN YEARS AGO?!
THUD
THAT BALD BASTARD ATTACKING ME AT HONNO-JI TEMPLE...
ME SHOWING UP IN THIS FORSAKEN PLACE...
THAT HAPPENED ONLY SIX MONTHS AGO!
HMPH!
THAT'S WHY I SAID...
...YOU'RE EITHER A DEMON OR DEAD.
EITHER THAT...
...OR YOU'RE A DELUDED MADMAN.

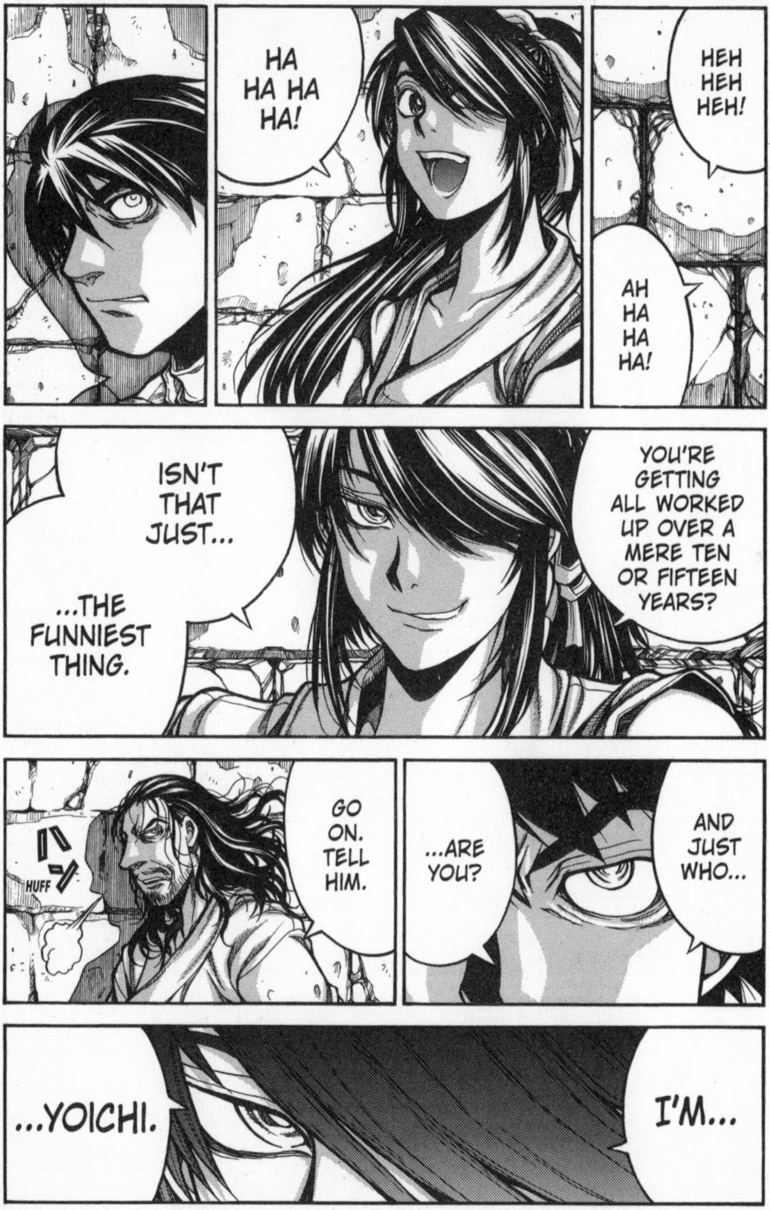
HEH HEH HEH!
AH HA HA HA!
HA HA HA HA!
YOU'RE GETTING ALL WORKED UP OVER A MERE TEN OR FIFTEEN YEARS?
ISN'T THAT JUST...
...THE FUNNIEST THING.
AND JUST WHO...
...ARE YOU?
GO ON. TELL HIM.
HUFF
I'M...
...YOICHI.

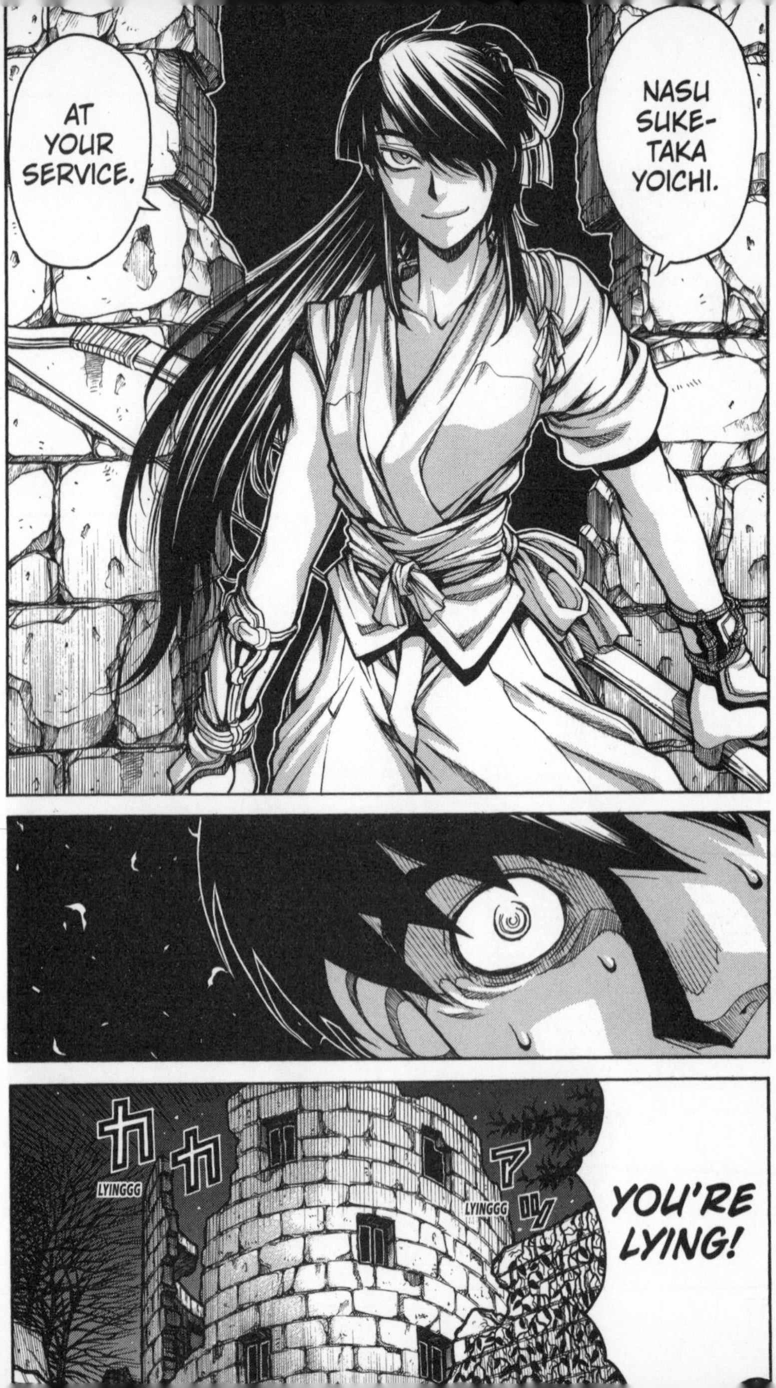
NASU SUKE-TAKA YOICHI.
AT YOUR SERVICE.
YOU'RE LYING!
LYINGGG
LYINGGG

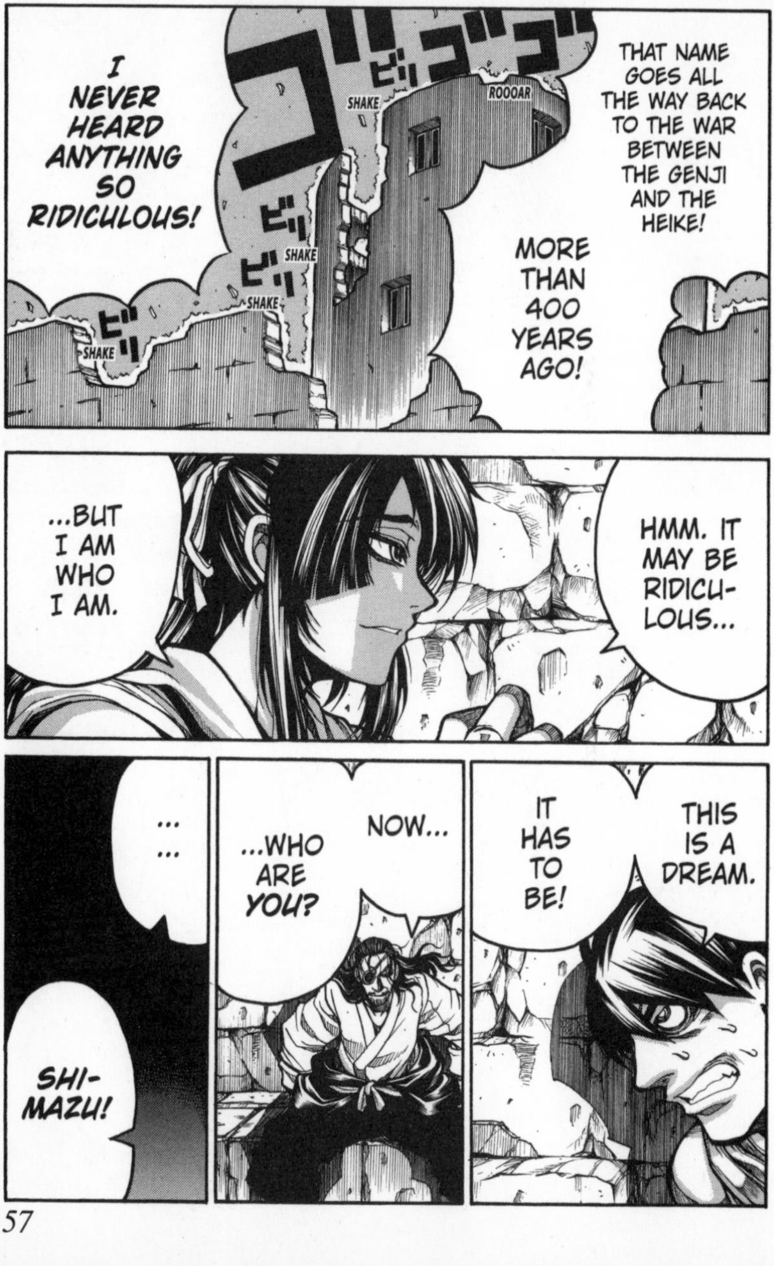
THAT NAME GOES ALL THE WAY BACK TO THE WAR BETWEEN THE GENJI AND THE HEIKE!
MORE THAN 400 YEARS AGO!
ROOOAR
SHAKE
I NEVER HEARD ANYTHING SO RIDICULOUS!
SHAKE
SHAKE
SHAKE
HMM. IT MAY BE RIDICU-LOUS...
...BUT I AM WHO I AM.
THIS IS A DREAM.
IT HAS TO BE!
NOW...
...WHO ARE YOU?
... ...
SHI-MAZU!

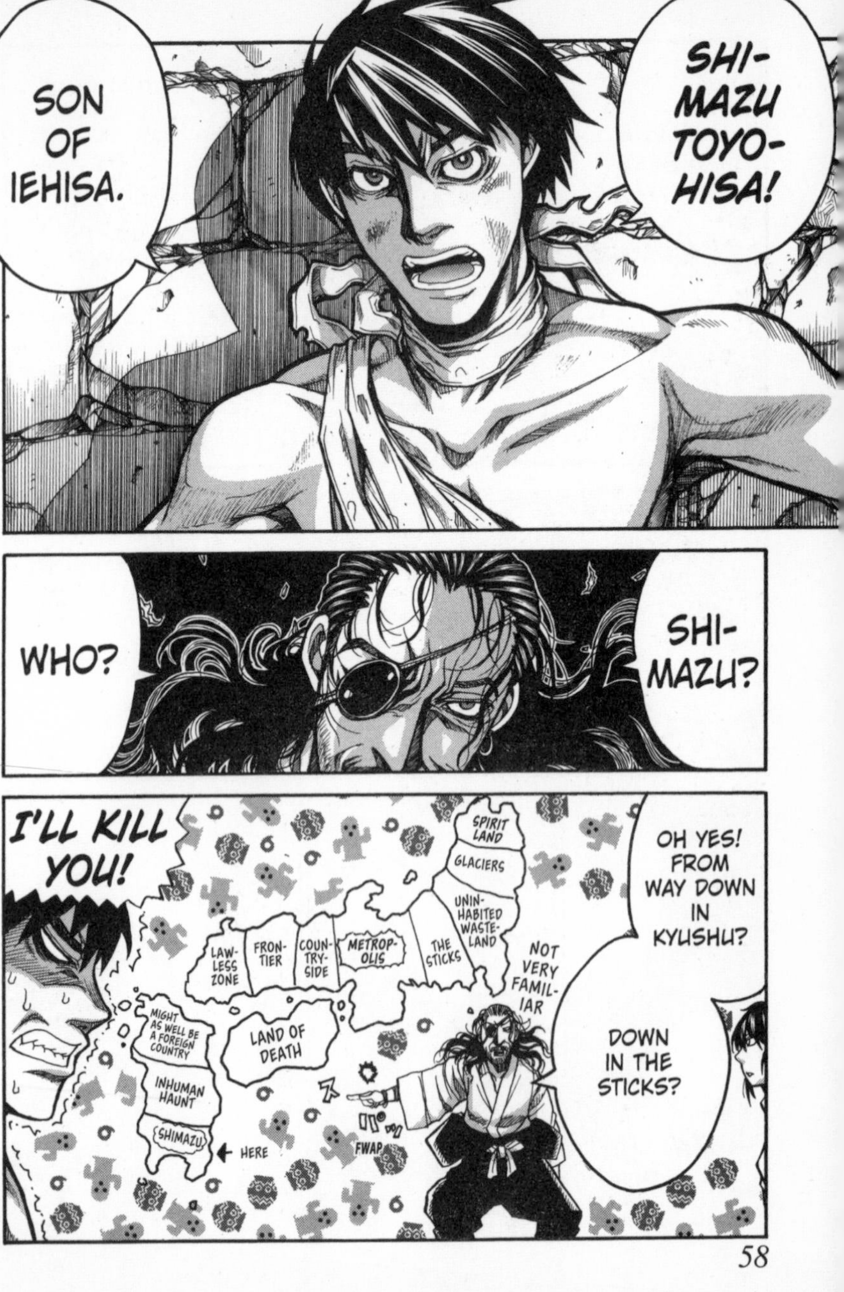
SHIMAZU TOYOHISA!
SON OF IEHISA.
SHIMAZU?
WHO?
OH YES! FROM WAY DOWN IN KYUSHU?
DOWN IN THE STICKS?
NOT VERY FAMILIAR
SPIRIT LAND
GLACIERS
UNINHABITED WASTELAND
THE STICKS
METROPOLIS
COUNTRYSIDE
FRONTIER
LAWLESS ZONE
LAND OF DEATH
MIGHT AS WELL BE A FOREIGN COUNTRY
INHUMAN HAUNT
SHIMAZU
HERE
FWAP
I'LL KILL YOU!

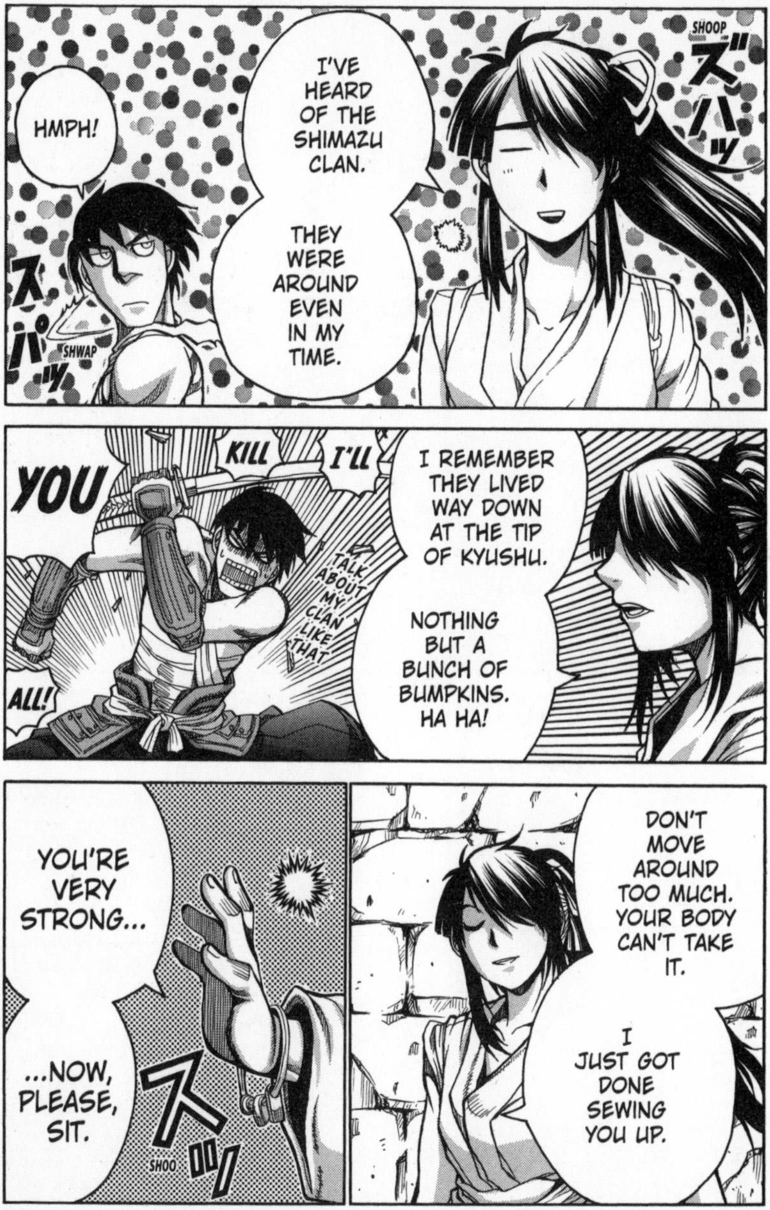
SHOOP
ズバッ
I'VE HEARD OF THE SHIMAZU CLAN.
THEY WERE AROUND EVEN IN MY TIME.
HMPH!
SHWAP
スパッ
I REMEMBER THEY LIVED WAY DOWN AT THE TIP OF KYUSHU.
NOTHING BUT A BUNCH OF BUMPKINS. HA HA!
I'LL
KILL
YOU
TALK ABOUT MY CLAN LIKE THAT
ALL!
DON'T MOVE AROUND TOO MUCH. YOUR BODY CAN'T TAKE IT.
I JUST GOT DONE SEWING YOU UP.
YOU'RE VERY STRONG...
...NOW, PLEASE, SIT.
SHOO

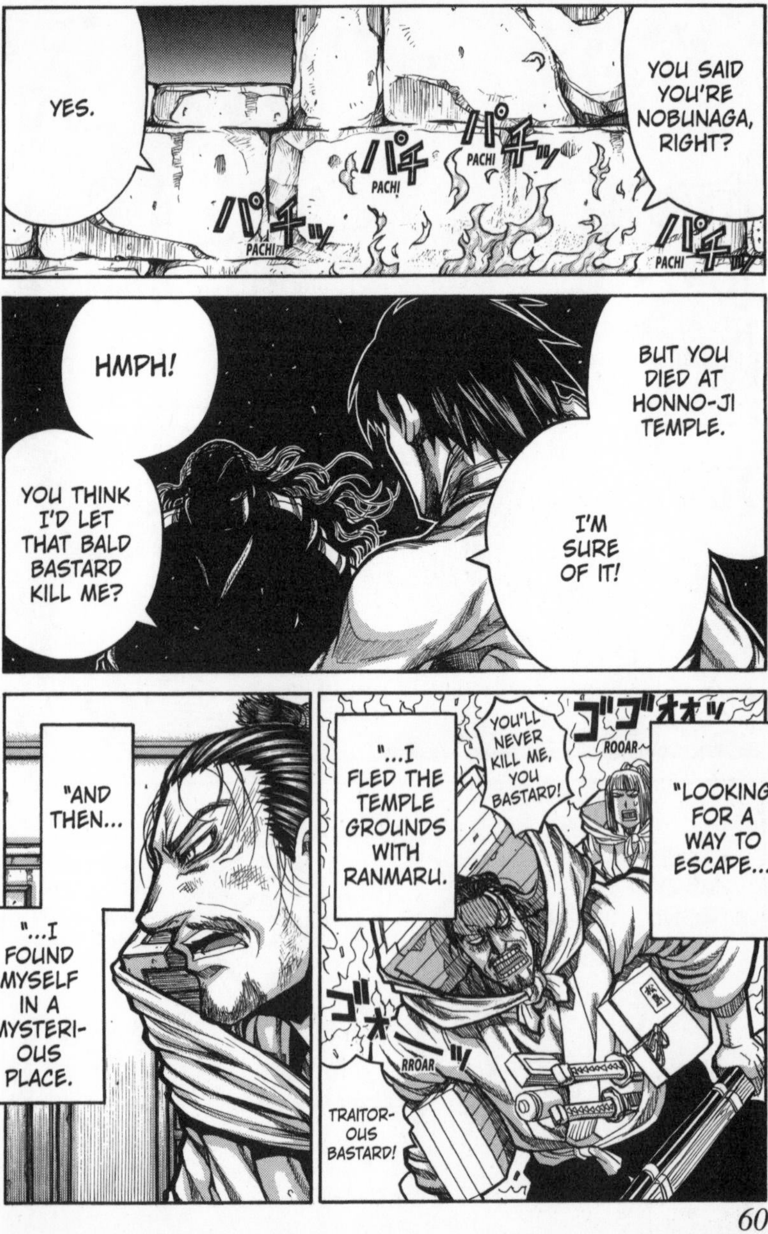
YOU SAID YOU'RE NOBUNAGA, RIGHT?
PACHI
PACHI
PACHI!
PACHI
YES.
BUT YOU DIED AT HONNO-JI TEMPLE.
I'M SURE OF IT!
HMPH!
YOU THINK I'D LET THAT BALD BASTARD KILL ME?
"LOOKING FOR A WAY TO ESCAPE...
ROOAR
YOU'LL NEVER KILL ME, YOU BASTARD!
"...I FLED THE TEMPLE GROUNDS WITH RANMARU.
RROAR
TRAITOR-OUS BASTARD!
"AND THEN...
"...I FOUND MYSELF IN A MYSTERI-OUS PLACE.

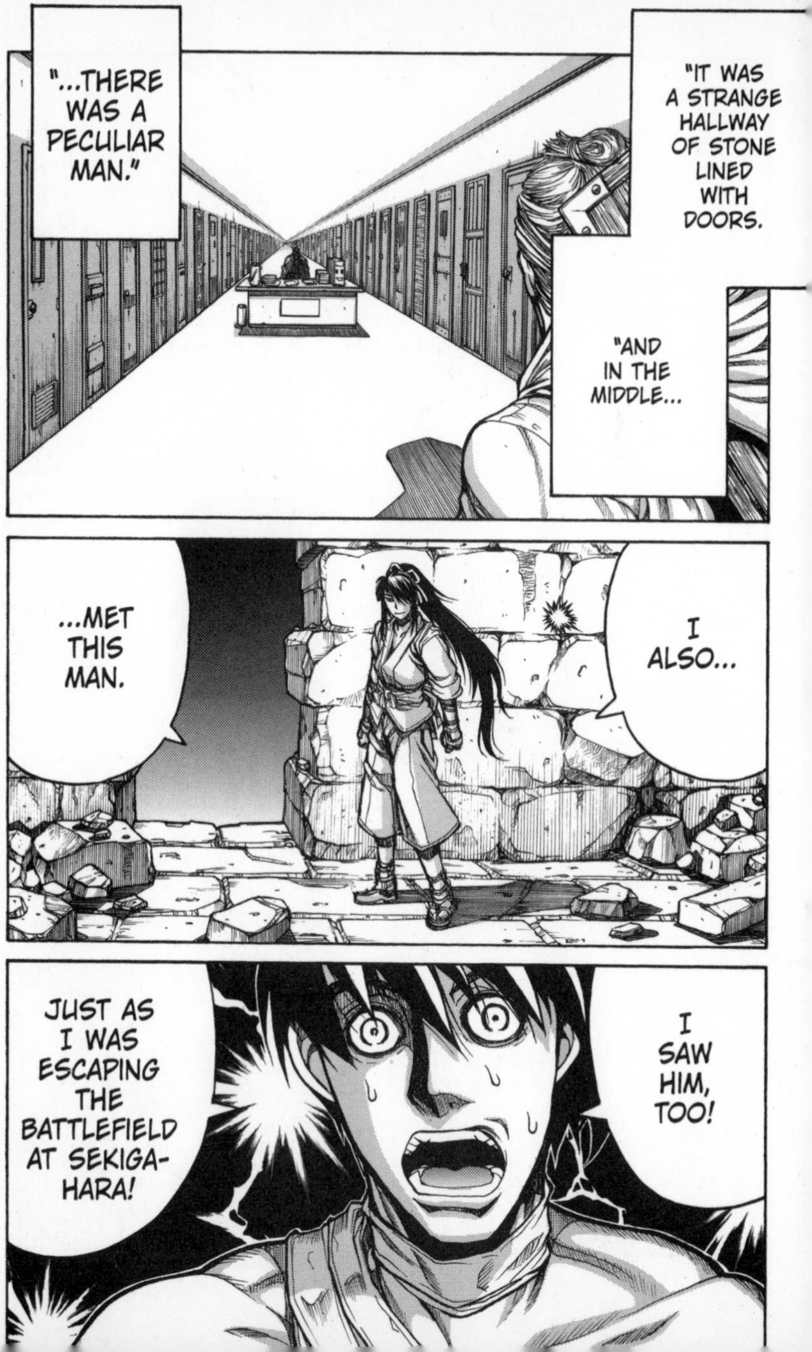
"IT WAS A STRANGE HALLWAY OF STONE LINED WITH DOORS.
"AND IN THE MIDDLE...
"...THERE WAS A PECULIAR MAN."
I ALSO...
...MET THIS MAN.
I SAW HIM, TOO!
JUST AS I WAS ESCAPING THE BATTLEFIELD AT SEKIGA-HARA!

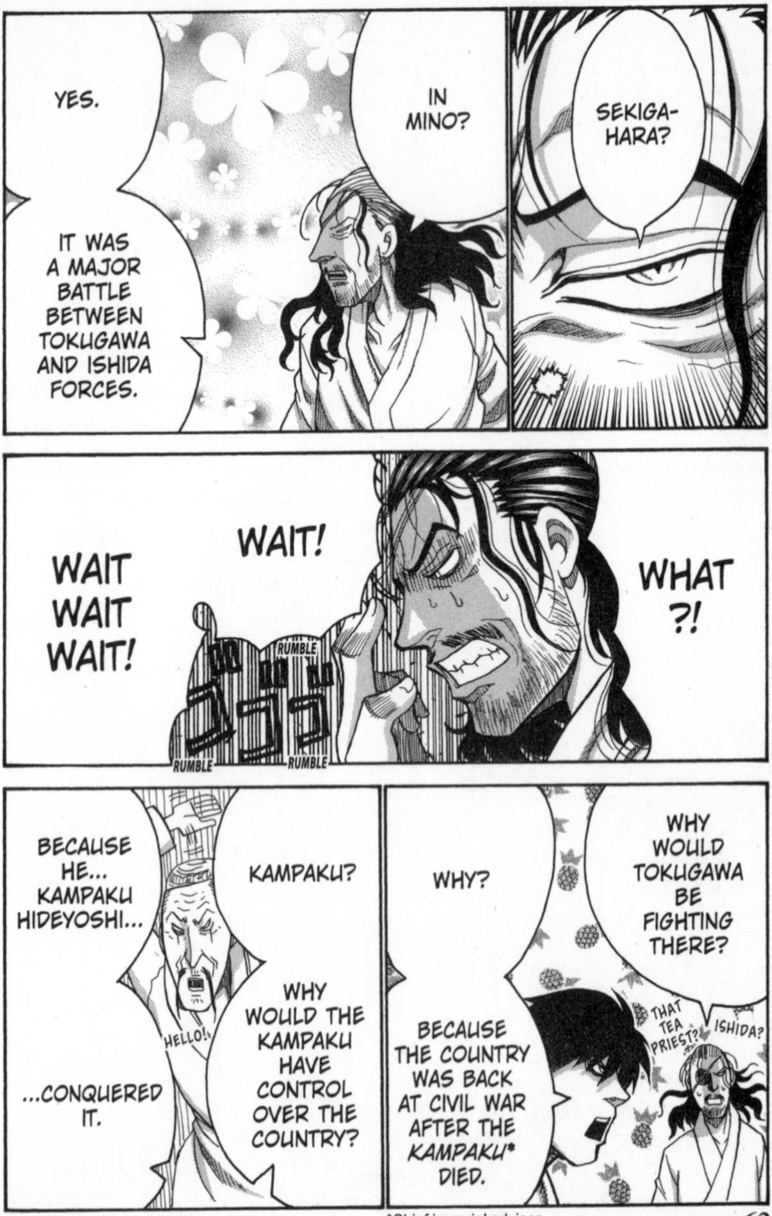
SEKIGA-HARA?
IN MINO?
YES.
IT WAS A MAJOR BATTLE BETWEEN TOKUGAWA AND ISHIDA FORCES.
WHAT ?!
WAIT!
WAIT WAIT WAIT!
RUMBLE
RUMBLE
RUMBLE
WHY WOULD TOKUGAWA BE FIGHTING THERE?
ISHIDA?
THAT TEA PRIEST?
WHY?
BECAUSE THE COUNTRY WAS BACK AT CIVIL WAR AFTER THE *KAMPAKU** DIED.
KAMPAKU?
BECAUSE HE... KAMPAKU HIDEYOSHI...
WHY WOULD THE KAMPAKU HAVE CONTROL OVER THE COUNTRY?
HELLO!
...CONQUERED IT.

*Chief imperial advisor

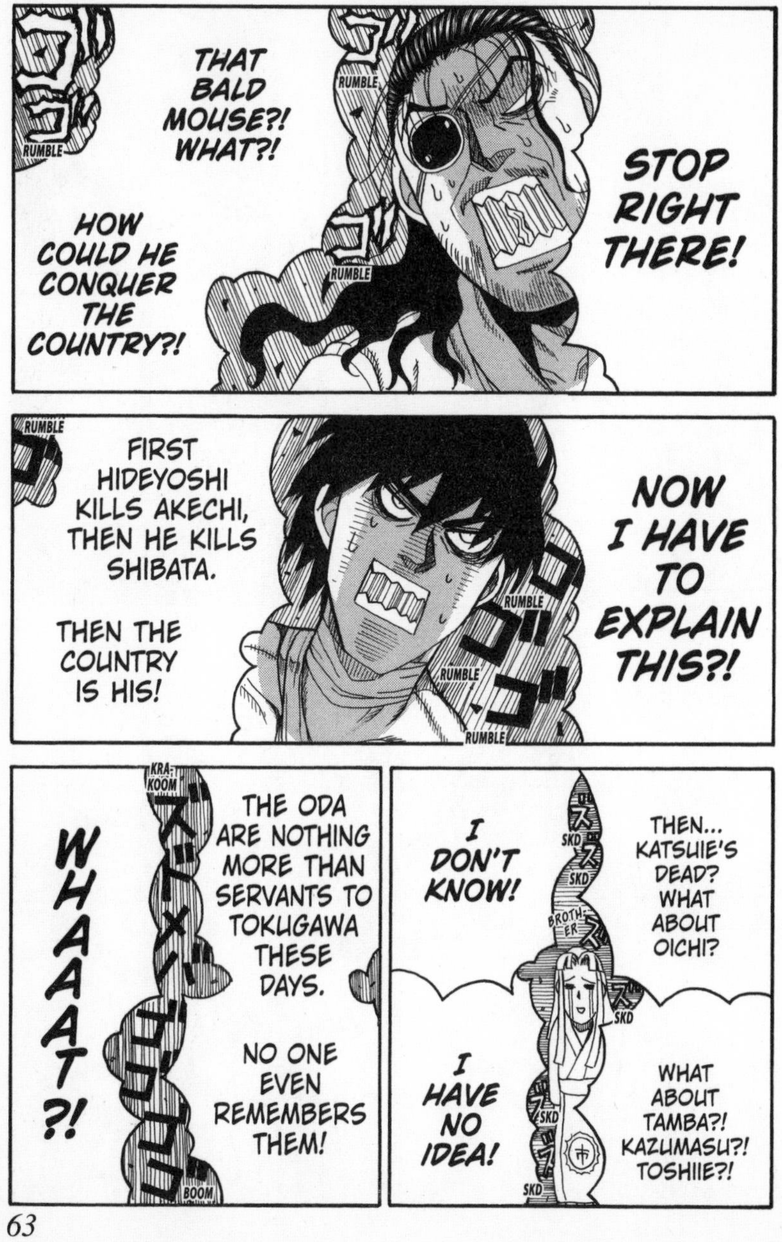
RUMBLE
STOP RIGHT THERE!
RUMBLE
THAT BALD MOUSE?! WHAT?!
RUMBLE
RUMBLE
HOW COULD HE CONQUER THE COUNTRY?!
NOW I HAVE TO EXPLAIN THIS?!
RUMBLE
RUMBLE
RUMBLE
FIRST HIDEYOSHI KILLS AKECHI, THEN HE KILLS SHIBATA.
THEN THE COUNTRY IS HIS!
RUMBLE
THEN... KATSUIE'S DEAD? WHAT ABOUT OICHI?
SKD
SKD
BROTH-ER
I DON'T KNOW!
SKD
WHAT ABOUT TAMBA?! KAZUMASU?! TOSHIIE?!
SKD
SKD
I HAVE NO IDEA!
THE ODA ARE NOTHING MORE THAN SERVANTS TO TOKUGAWA THESE DAYS.
NO ONE EVEN REMEMBERS THEM!
KRA-KOOM
WHAAAAT?!
BOOM

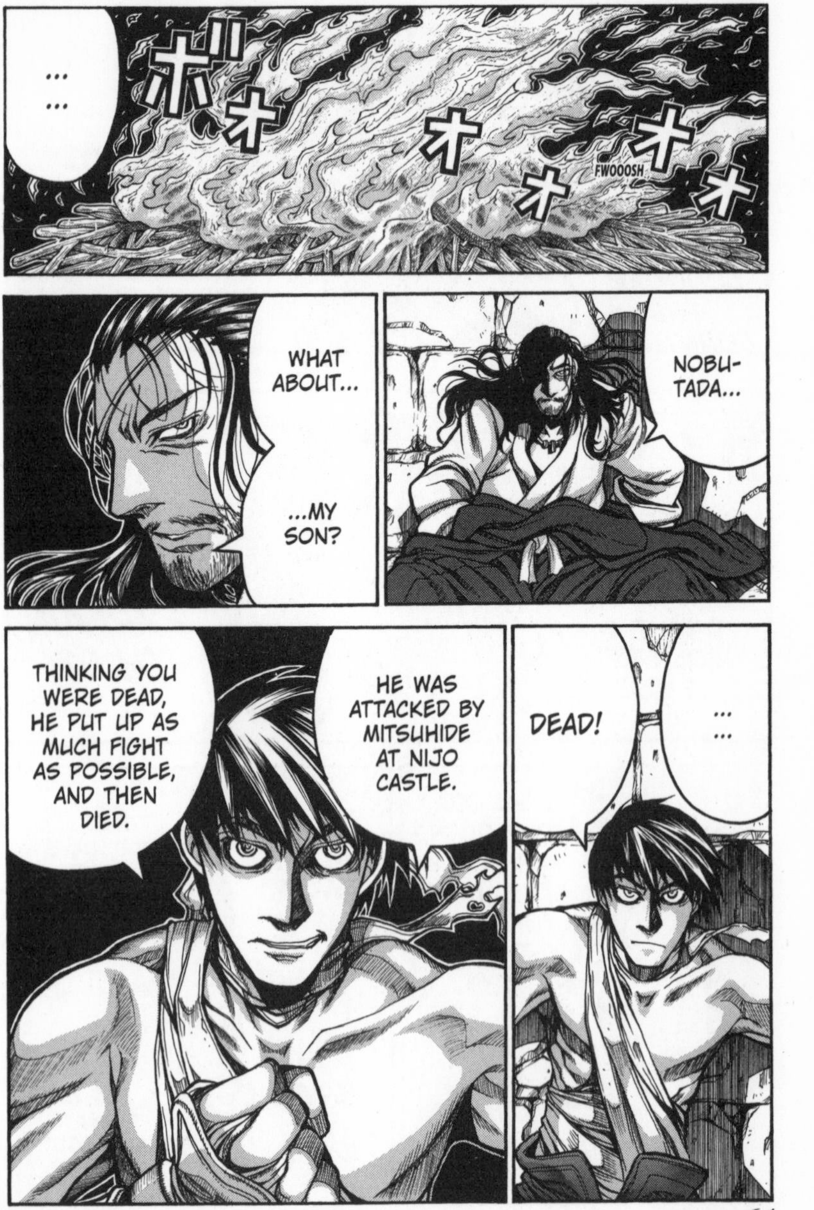
ボオオオオオ
FWOOOSH
... ...
NOBU-TADA...
WHAT ABOUT...
...MY SON?
... ...
DEAD!
HE WAS ATTACKED BY MITSUHIDE AT NIJO CASTLE.
THINKING YOU WERE DEAD, HE PUT UP AS MUCH FIGHT AS POSSIBLE, AND THEN DIED.

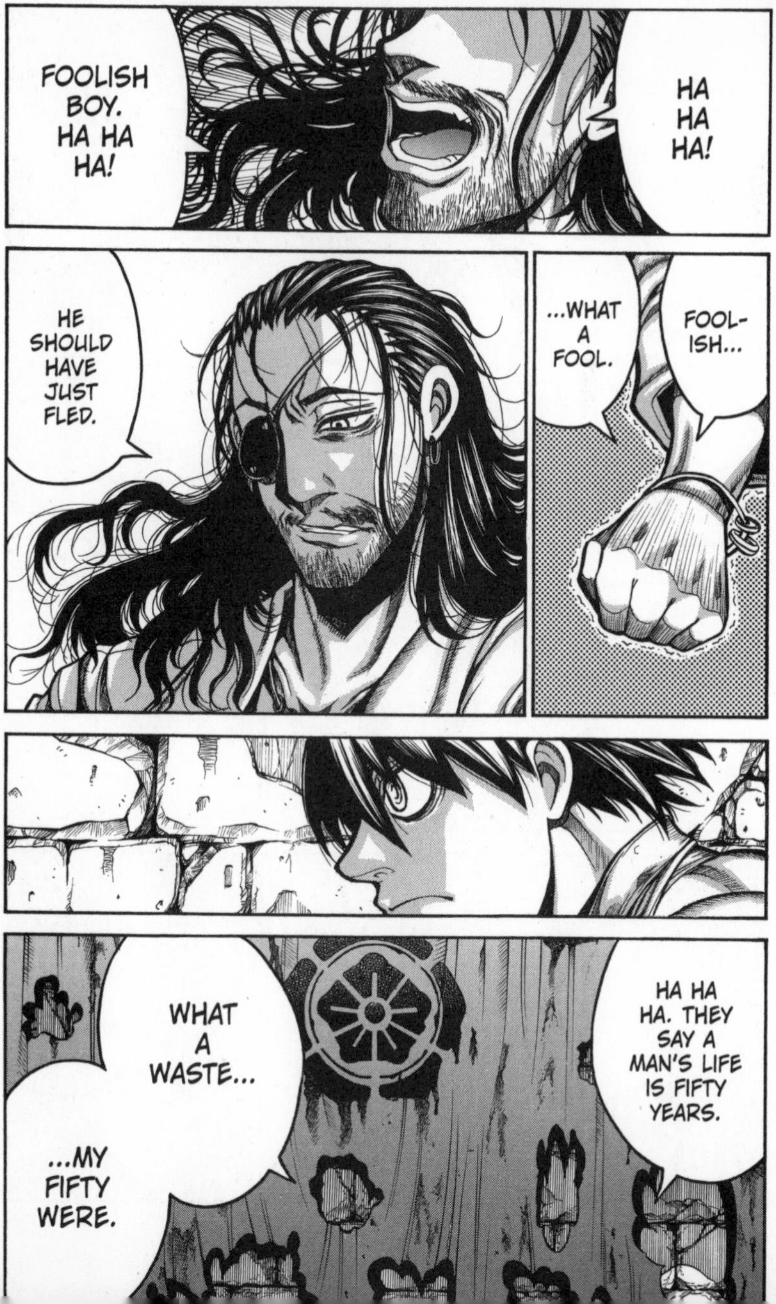
HA HA HA!
FOOLISH BOY. HA HA HA!
FOOL-ISH...
...WHAT A FOOL.
HE SHOULD HAVE JUST FLED.
HA HA HA. THEY SAY A MAN'S LIFE IS FIFTY YEARS.
WHAT A WASTE...
...MY FIFTY WERE.

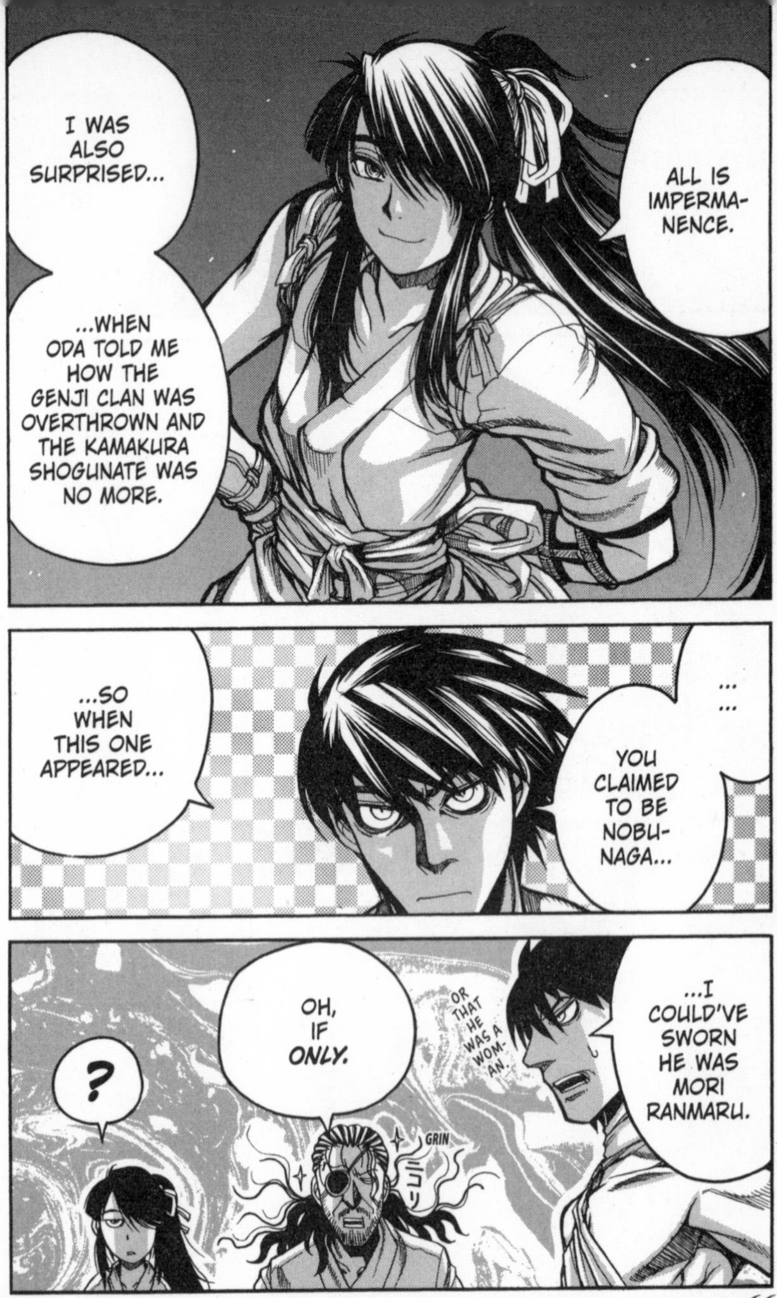
ALL IS IMPERMANENCE.
I WAS ALSO SURPRISED...
...WHEN ODA TOLD ME HOW THE GENJI CLAN WAS OVERTHROWN AND THE KAMAKURA SHOGUNATE WAS NO MORE.
... ...
YOU CLAIMED TO BE NOBUNAGA...
...SO WHEN THIS ONE APPEARED...
...I COULD'VE SWORN HE WAS MORI RANMARU.
OR THAT HE WAS A WOMAN.
GRIN
ニコリ
OH, IF *ONLY.*
?

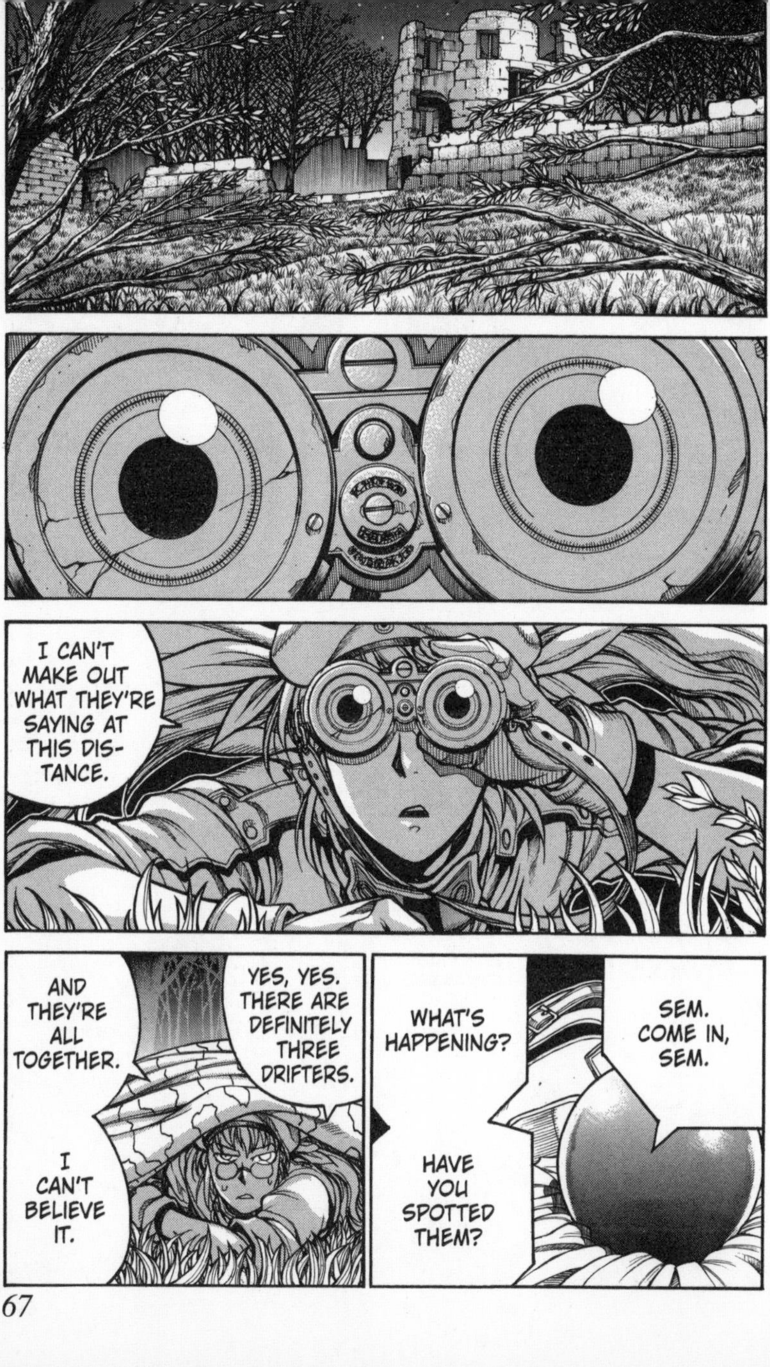
I CAN'T MAKE OUT WHAT THEY'RE SAYING AT THIS DIS-TANCE.
SEM. COME IN, SEM.
WHAT'S HAPPENING?
HAVE YOU SPOTTED THEM?
YES, YES. THERE ARE DEFINITELY THREE DRIFTERS.
AND THEY'RE ALL TOGETHER.
I CAN'T BELIEVE IT.

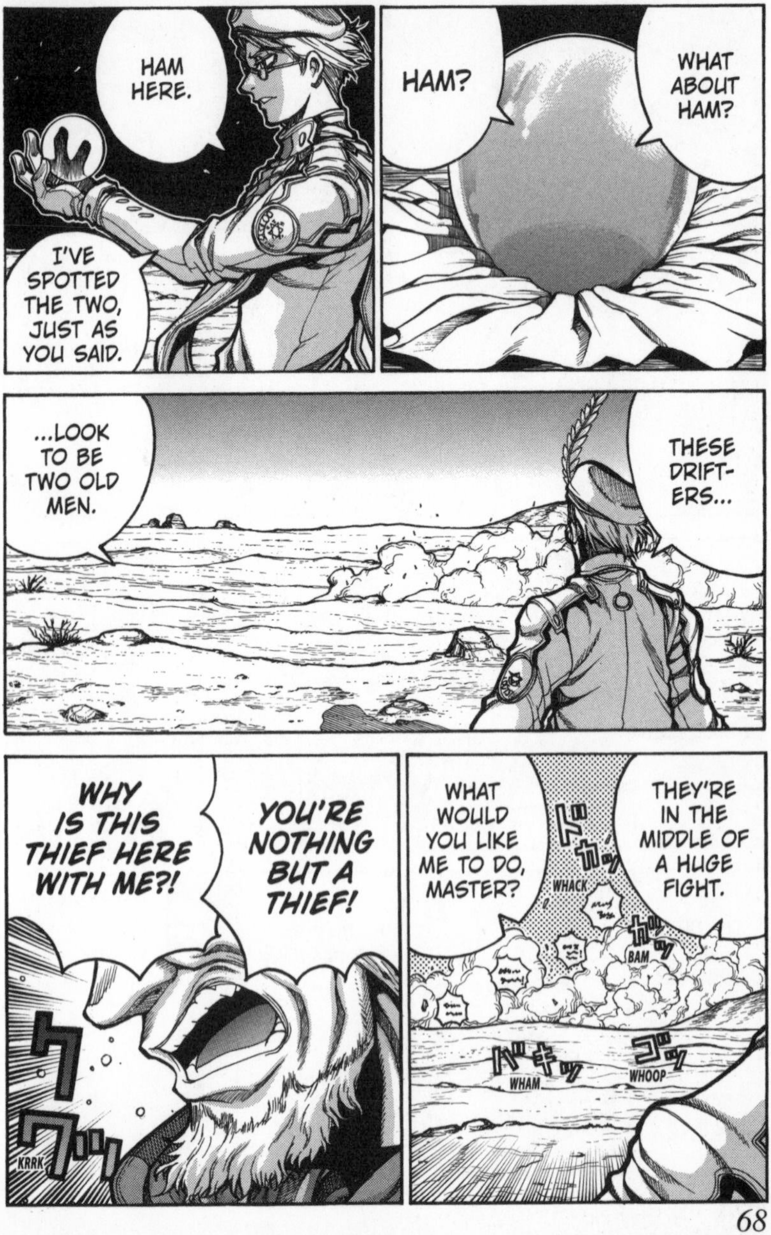

WHAT ABOUT HAM?
HAM?
HAM HERE.
I'VE SPOTTED THE TWO, JUST AS YOU SAID.
THESE DRIFTERS...
...LOOK TO BE TWO OLD MEN.
THEY'RE IN THE MIDDLE OF A HUGE FIGHT.
WHAT WOULD YOU LIKE ME TO DO, MASTER?
WHACK
BAM
WHOOP
WHAM
YOU'RE NOTHING BUT A THIEF!
WHY IS THIS THIEF HERE WITH ME?!
KRRK

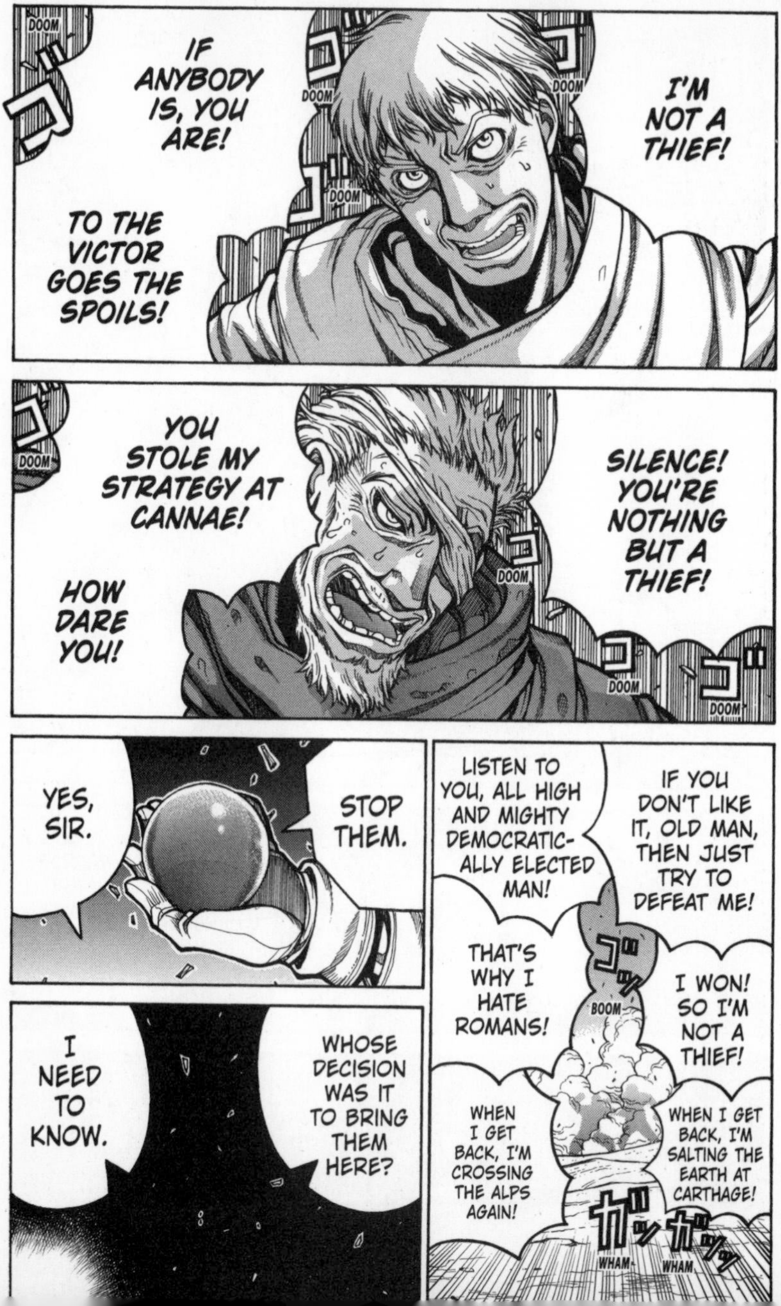
DOOM
I'M NOT A THIEF!
DOOM
DOOM
IF ANYBODY IS, YOU ARE!
DOOM
TO THE VICTOR GOES THE SPOILS!
SILENCE! YOU'RE NOTHING BUT A THIEF!
DOOM
YOU STOLE MY STRATEGY AT CANNAE!
DOOM
HOW DARE YOU!
DOOM
DOOM
IF YOU DON'T LIKE IT, OLD MAN, THEN JUST TRY TO DEFEAT ME!
LISTEN TO YOU, ALL HIGH AND MIGHTY DEMOCRATIC-ALLY ELECTED MAN!
I WON! SO I'M NOT A THIEF!
THAT'S WHY I HATE ROMANS!
BOOM
WHEN I GET BACK, I'M SALTING THE EARTH AT CARTHAGE!
WHEN I GET BACK, I'M CROSSING THE ALPS AGAIN!
WHAM
WHAM
STOP THEM.
YES, SIR.
WHOSE DECISION WAS IT TO BRING THEM HERE?
I NEED TO KNOW.

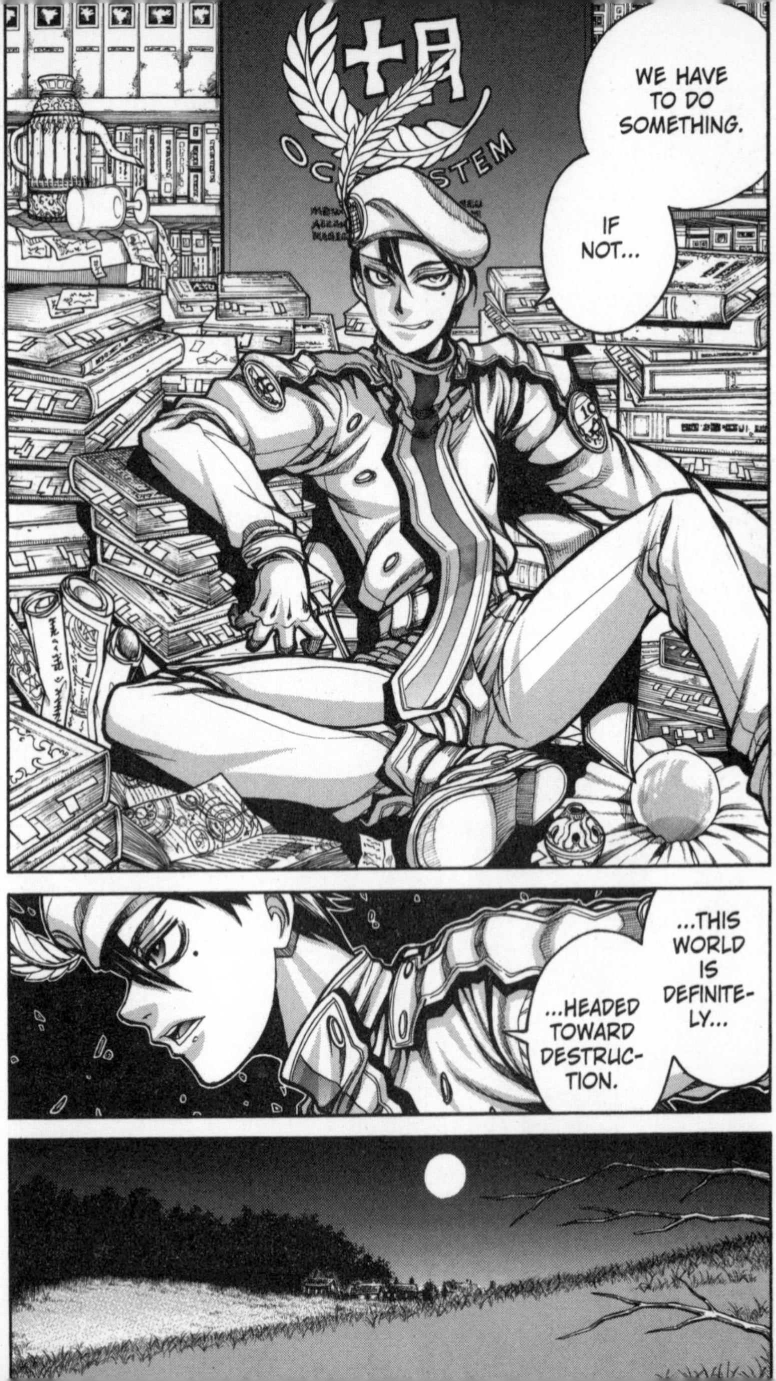
十月
WE HAVE TO DO SOMETHING.
IF NOT...
...THIS WORLD IS DEFINITE-LY...
...HEADED TOWARD DESTRUC-TION.

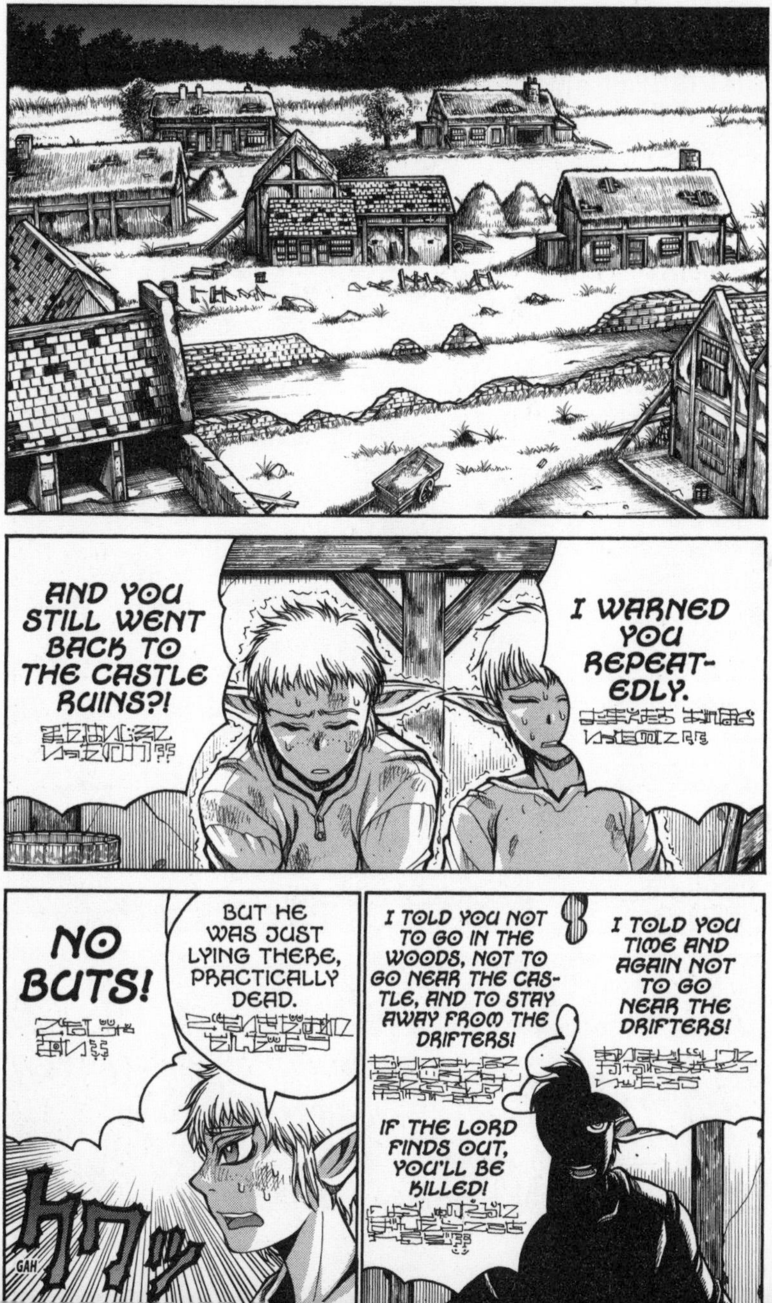
I WARNED YOU REPEATEDLY.
AND YOU STILL WENT BACK TO THE CASTLE RUINS?!
I TOLD YOU TIME AND AGAIN NOT TO GO NEAR THE DRIFTERS!
I TOLD YOU NOT TO GO IN THE WOODS, NOT TO GO NEAR THE CASTLE, AND TO STAY AWAY FROM THE DRIFTERS!
IF THE LORD FINDS OUT, YOU'LL BE KILLED!
BUT HE WAS JUST LYING THERE, PRACTICALLY DEAD.
NO BUTS!
GAH

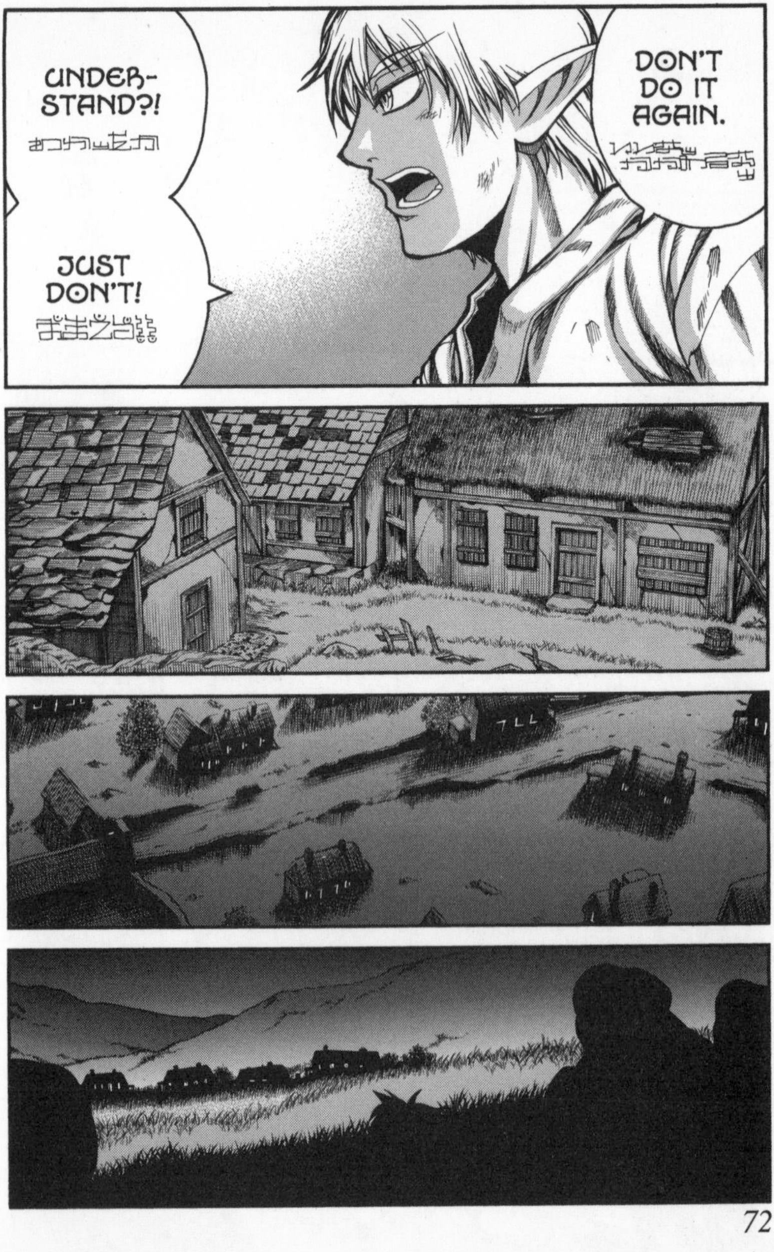
DON'T DO IT AGAIN.
UNDER-STAND?!
JUST DON'T!

GACHA
GACHA
GACHA
GACHA
SHIT! IT'S RIGHT BEFORE HARVEST.
NO MATTER.
LET'S GO!
ZA
ZA
ZA
ZA
ZA

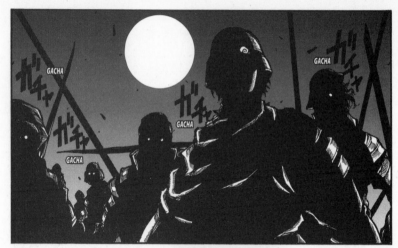

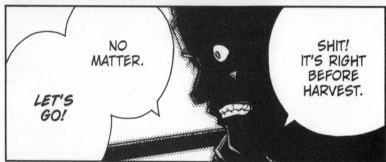

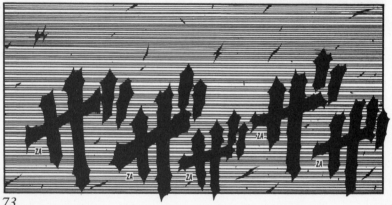

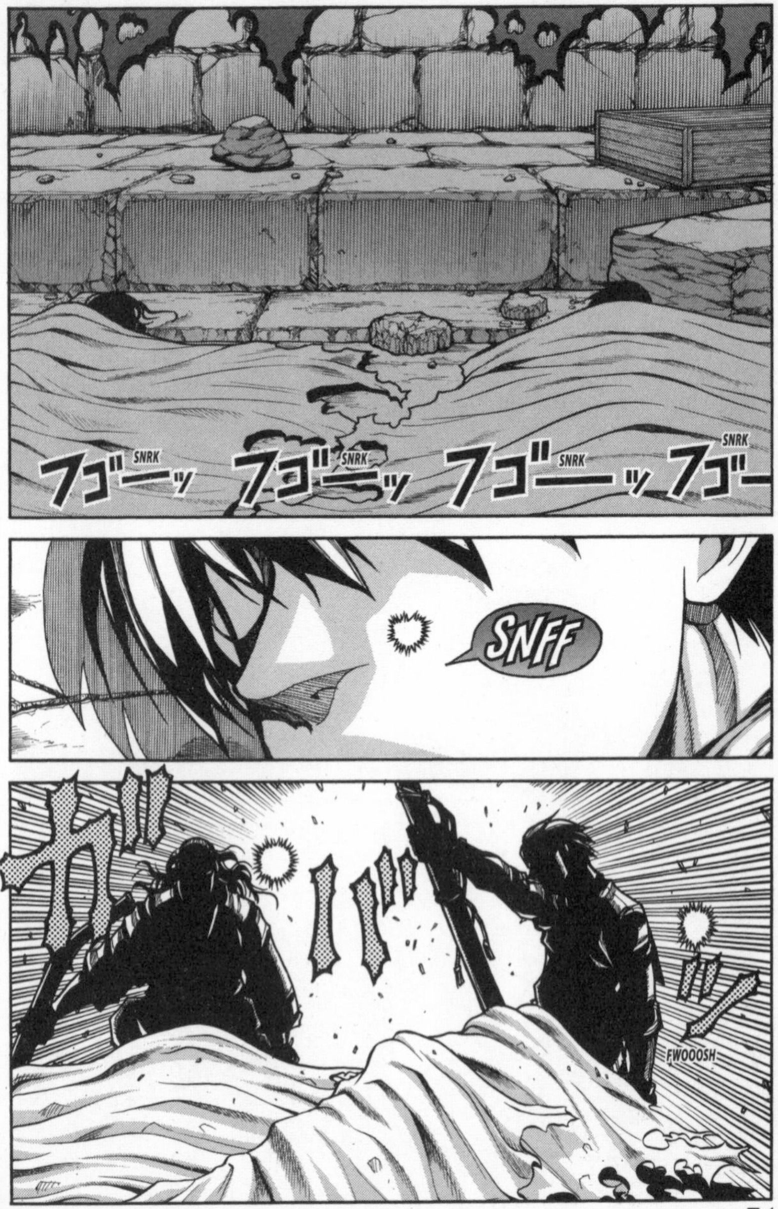
フゴー
SNRK
フゴーッ
SNRK
フゴーッ
SNRK
フゴーッ
SNRK
SNFF
FWOOOSH

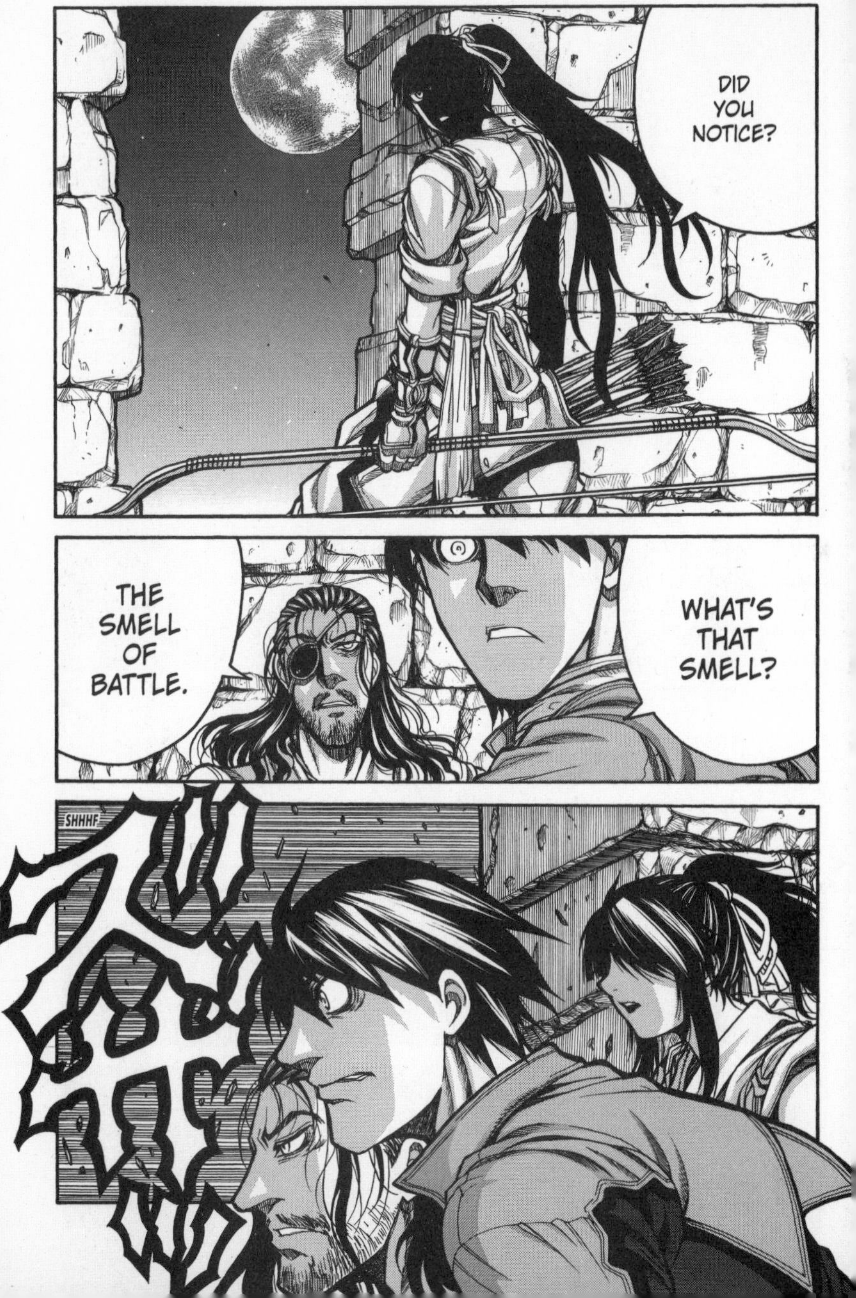
DID YOU NOTICE?
WHAT'S THAT SMELL?
THE SMELL OF BATTLE.
SHHHF

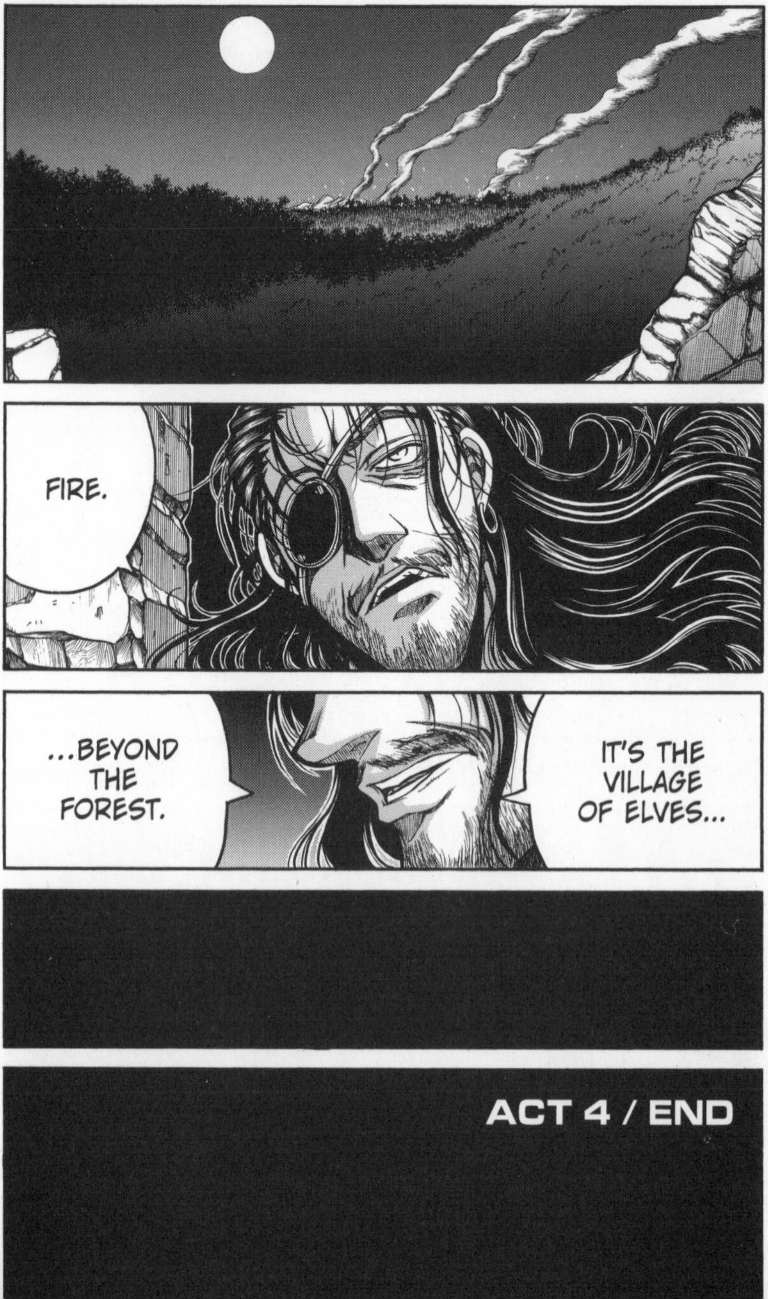
FIRE.
IT'S THE VILLAGE OF ELVES...
...BEYOND THE FOREST.
ACT 4 / END

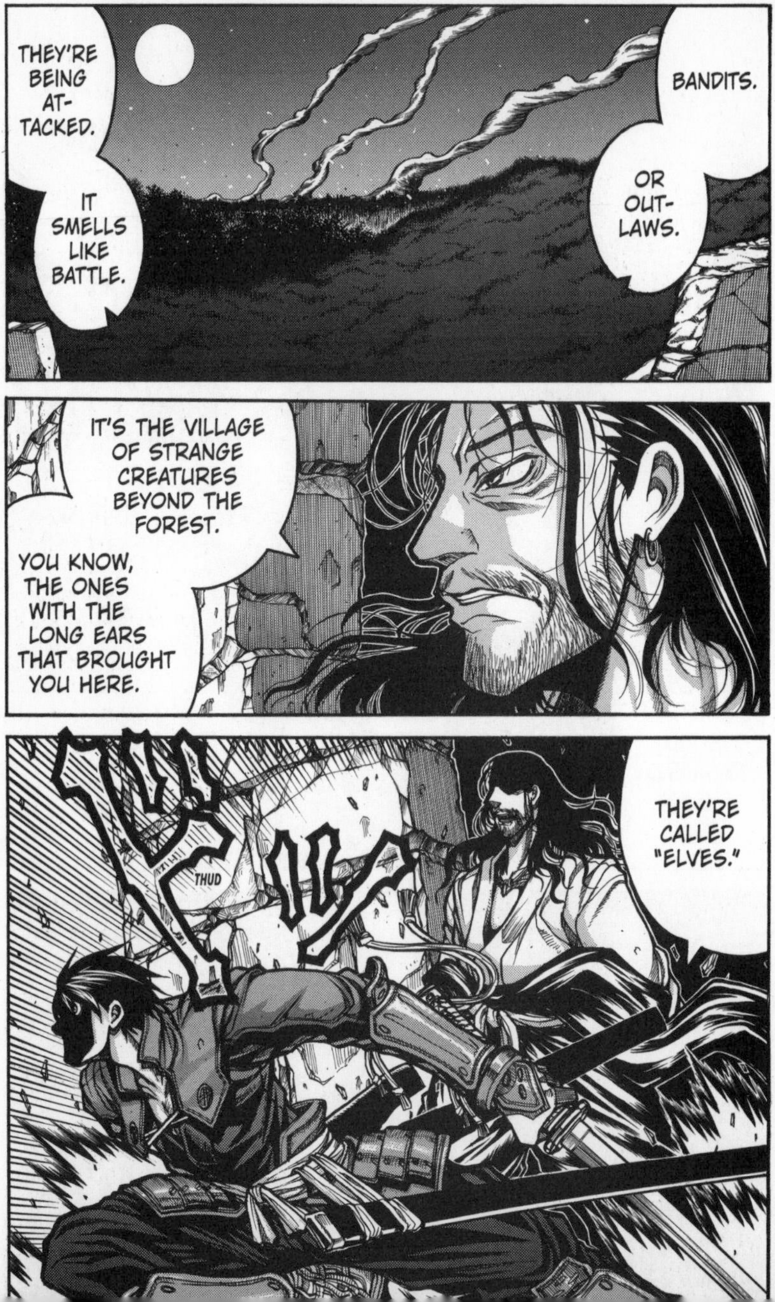
BANDITS.
OR OUT-LAWS.
THEY'RE BEING AT-TACKED.
IT SMELLS LIKE BATTLE.
IT'S THE VILLAGE OF STRANGE CREATURES BEYOND THE FOREST.
YOU KNOW, THE ONES WITH THE LONG EARS THAT BROUGHT YOU HERE.
THEY'RE CALLED "ELVES."
THUD

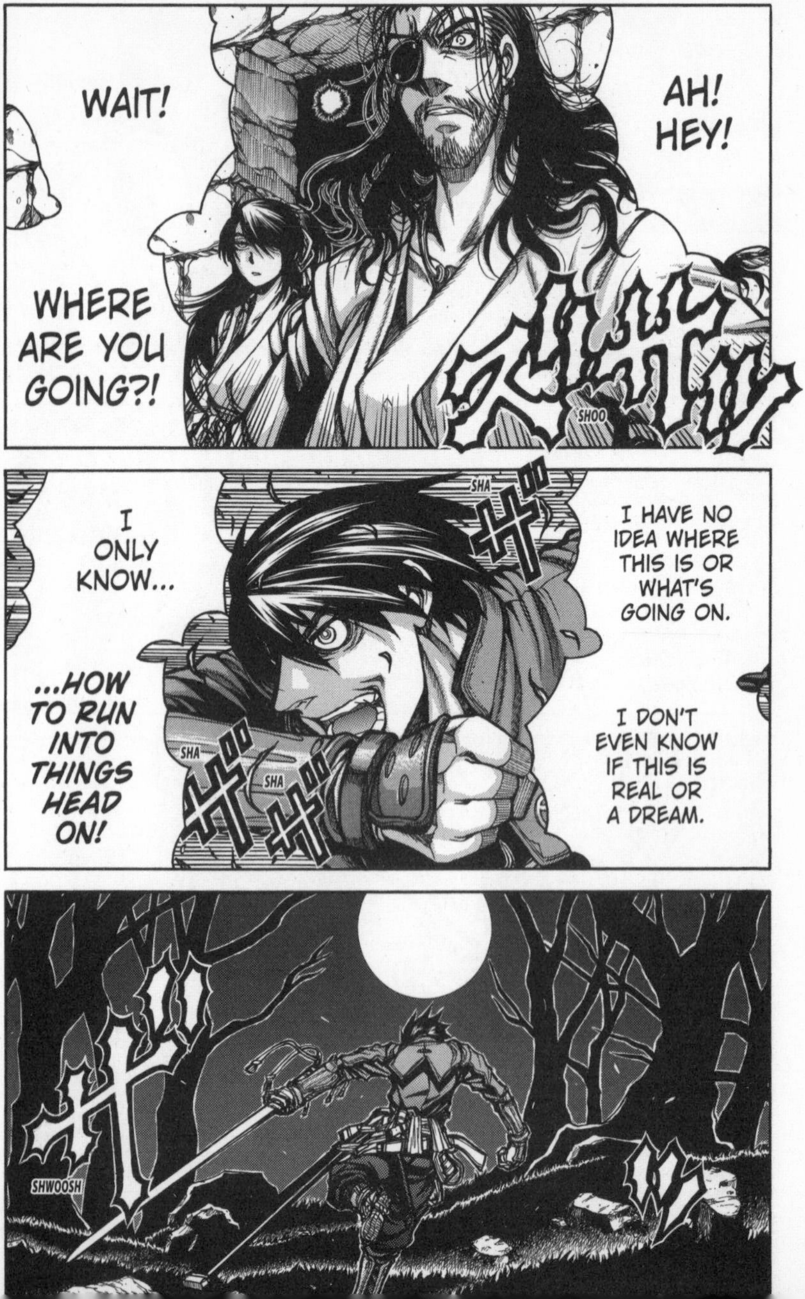
AH! HEY!
WAIT!
WHERE ARE YOU GOING?!
SHOO
SHA
I HAVE NO IDEA WHERE THIS IS OR WHAT'S GOING ON.
I DON'T EVEN KNOW IF THIS IS REAL OR A DREAM.
I ONLY KNOW...
...HOW TO RUN INTO THINGS HEAD ON!
SHA
SHA
SHWOOSH

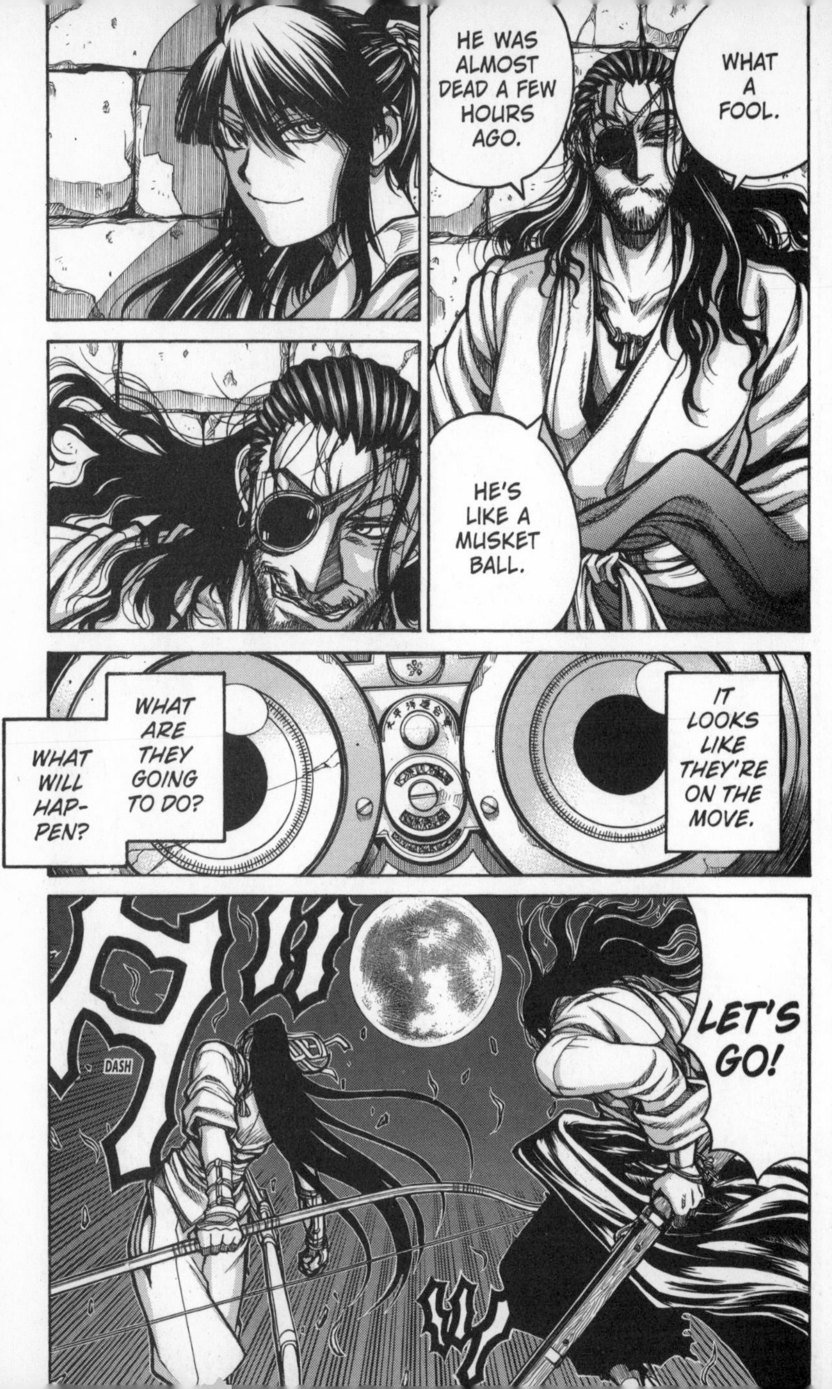
WHAT A FOOL.
HE WAS ALMOST DEAD A FEW HOURS AGO.
HE'S LIKE A MUSKET BALL.
IT LOOKS LIKE THEY'RE ON THE MOVE.
WHAT ARE THEY GOING TO DO?
WHAT WILL HAP-PEN?
LET'S GO!
DASH

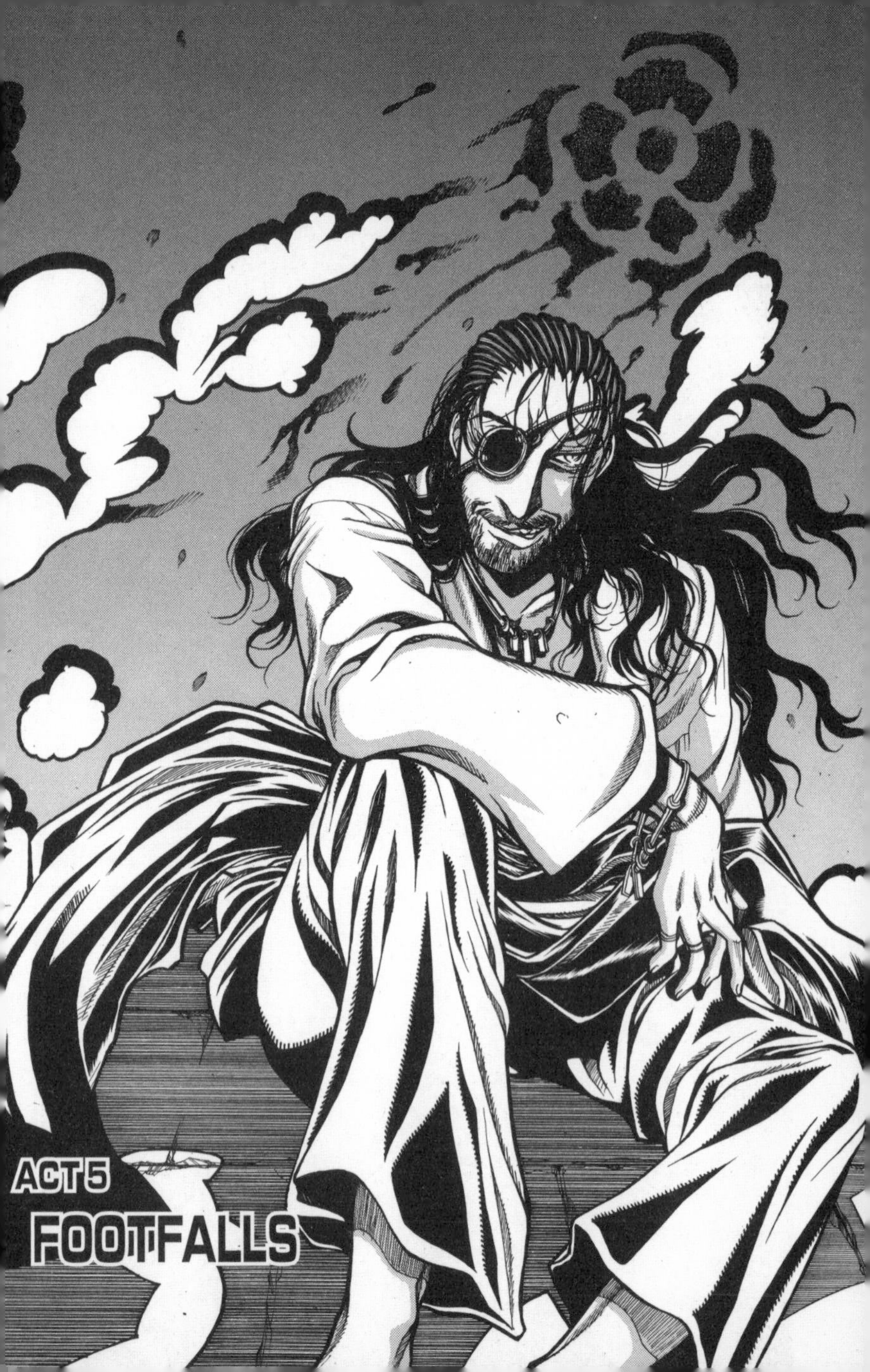
ACT 5
FOOTFALLS

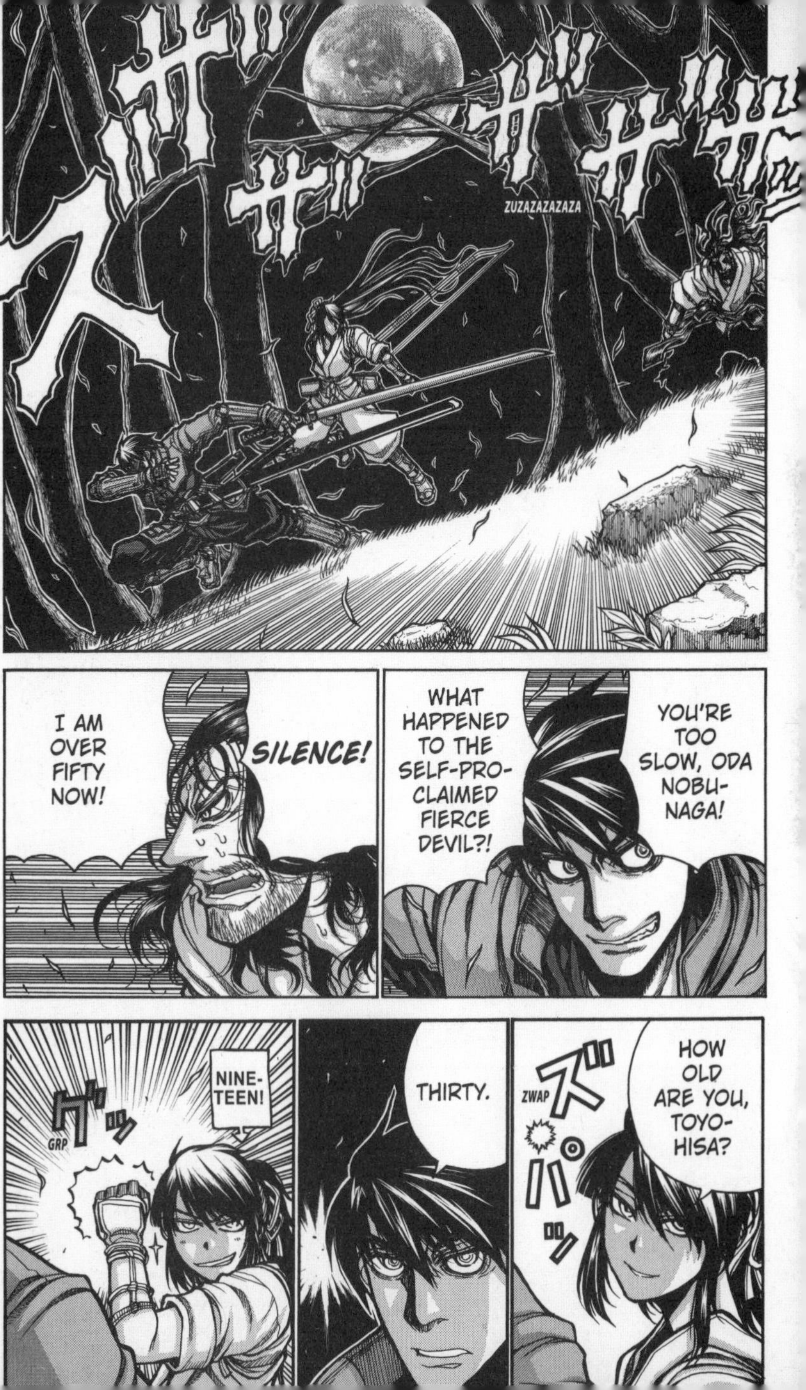
ZUZAZAZAZAZA
YOU'RE TOO SLOW, ODA NOBU-NAGA!
WHAT HAPPENED TO THE SELF-PRO-CLAIMED FIERCE DEVIL?!
SILENCE!
I AM OVER FIFTY NOW!
HOW OLD ARE YOU, TOYO-HISA?
ZWAP
THIRTY.
NINE-TEEN!
GRP

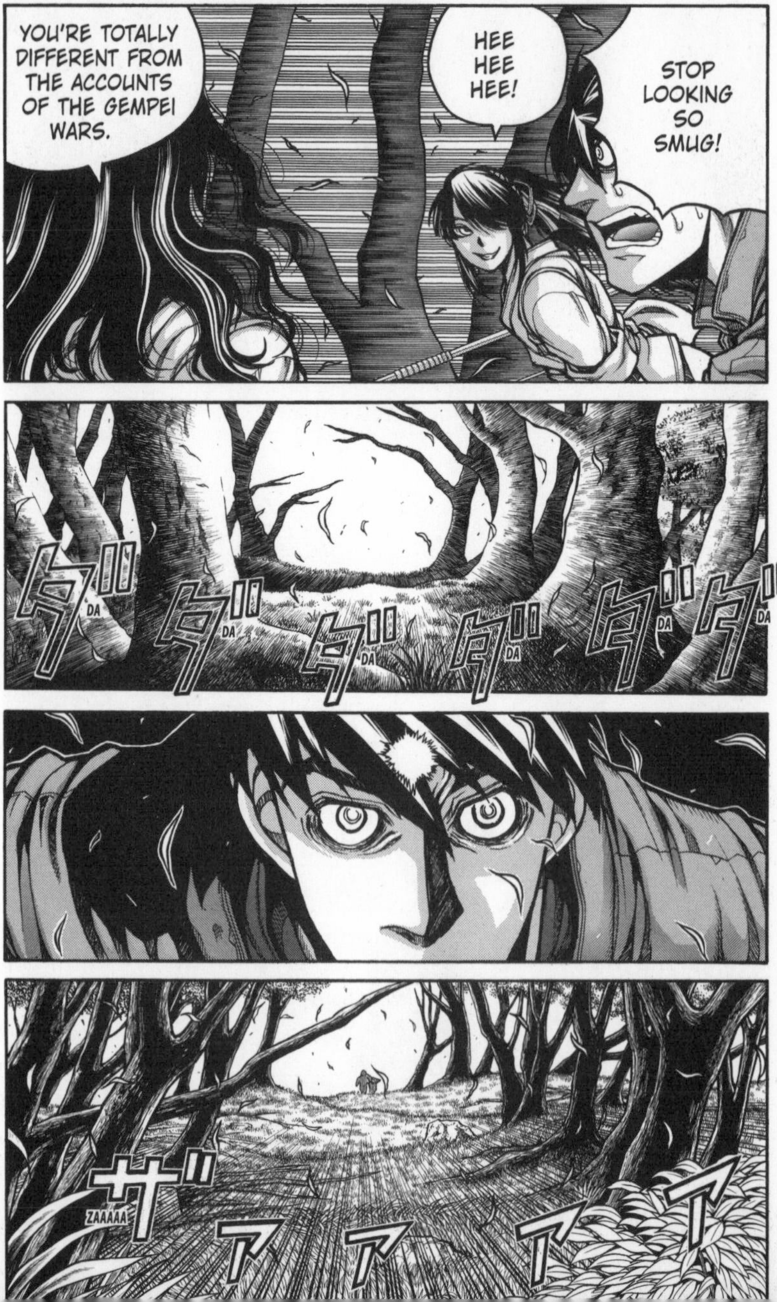
STOP LOOKING SO SMUG!
HEE HEE HEE!
YOU'RE TOTALLY DIFFERENT FROM THE ACCOUNTS OF THE GEMPEI WARS.
DA
DA
DA
DA
DA
DA
ZAAAAA

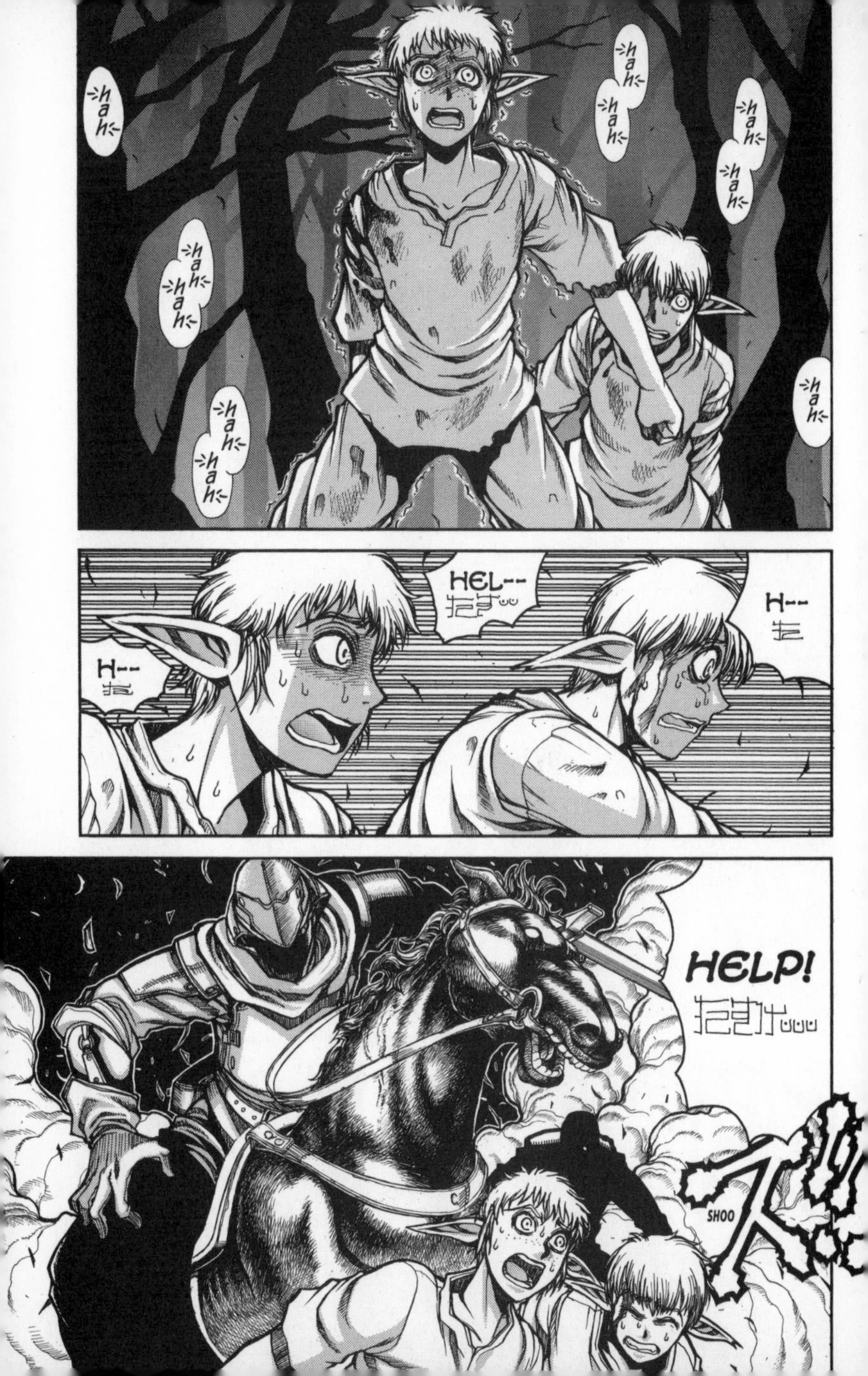
hah hah hah hah
hah hah
hah
hah
hah hah hah
hah hah hah
H--
HEL--
H--
HELP!
SHOO

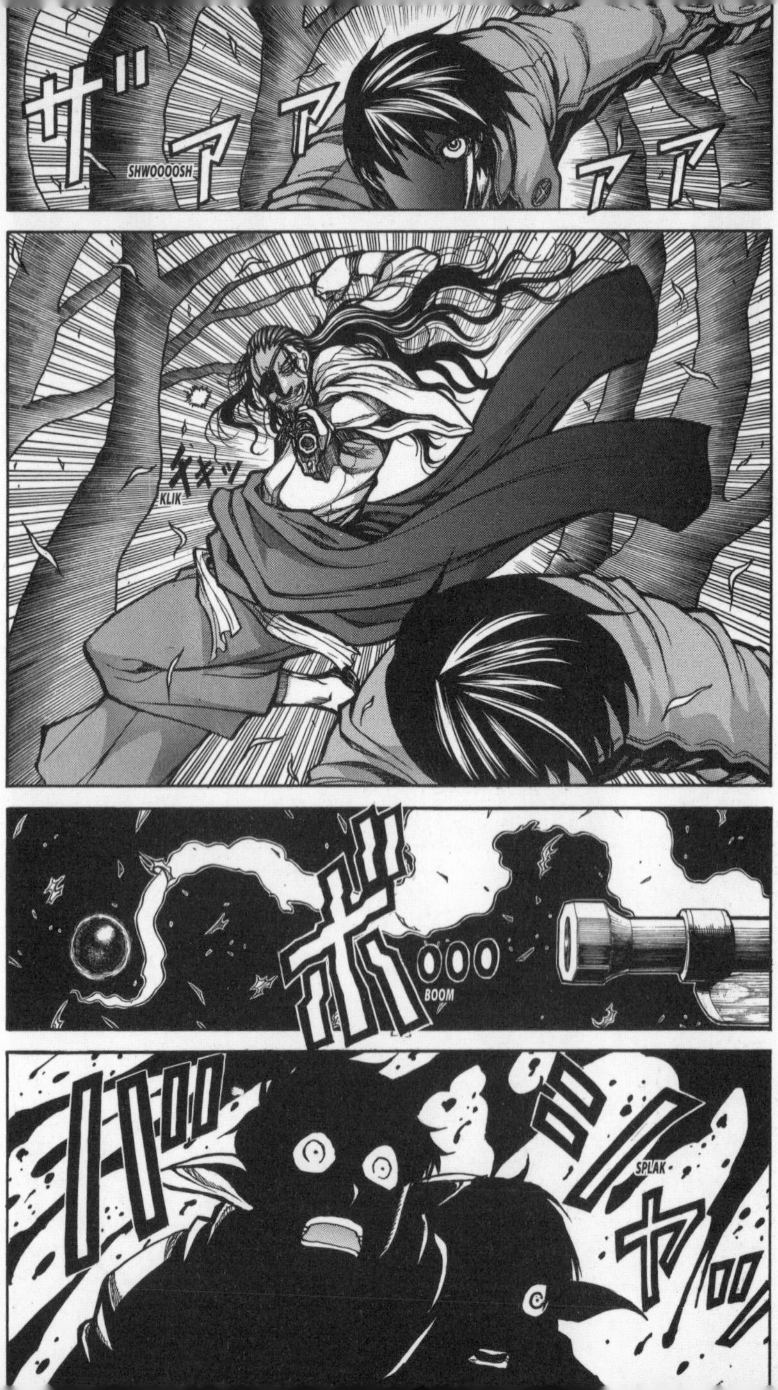
SHWOOOOSH
KLIK
BOOM
SPLAK

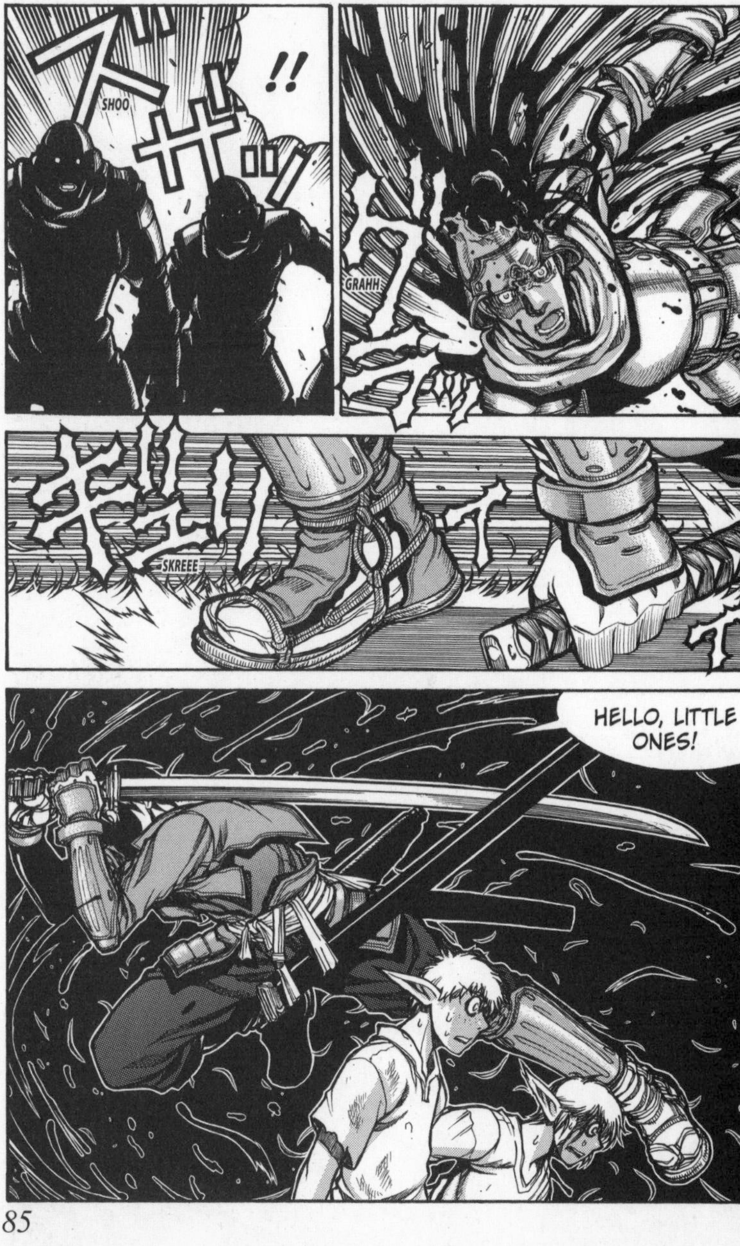
GRAHH
SHOO
!!
SKREEE
HELLO, LITTLE ONES!

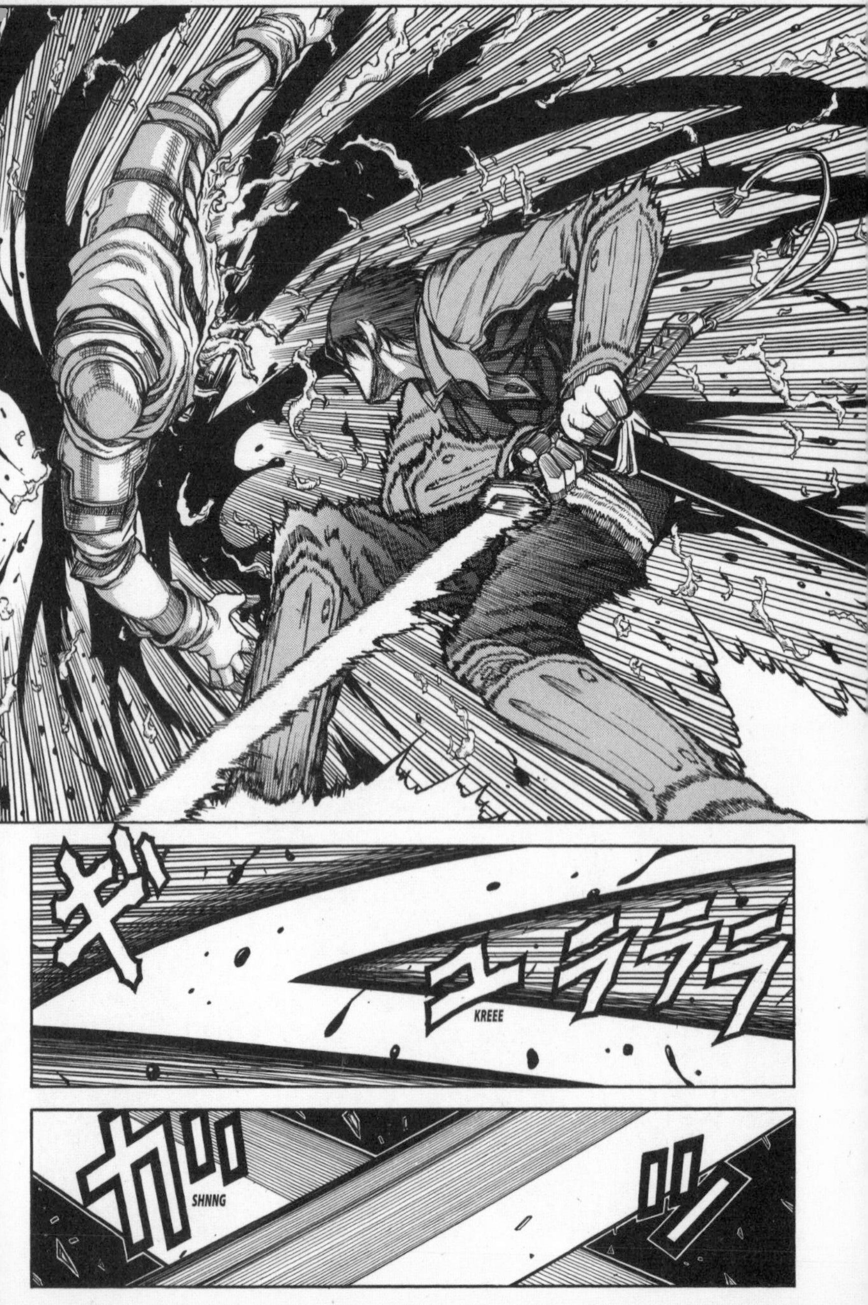
KREEE
SHNNG

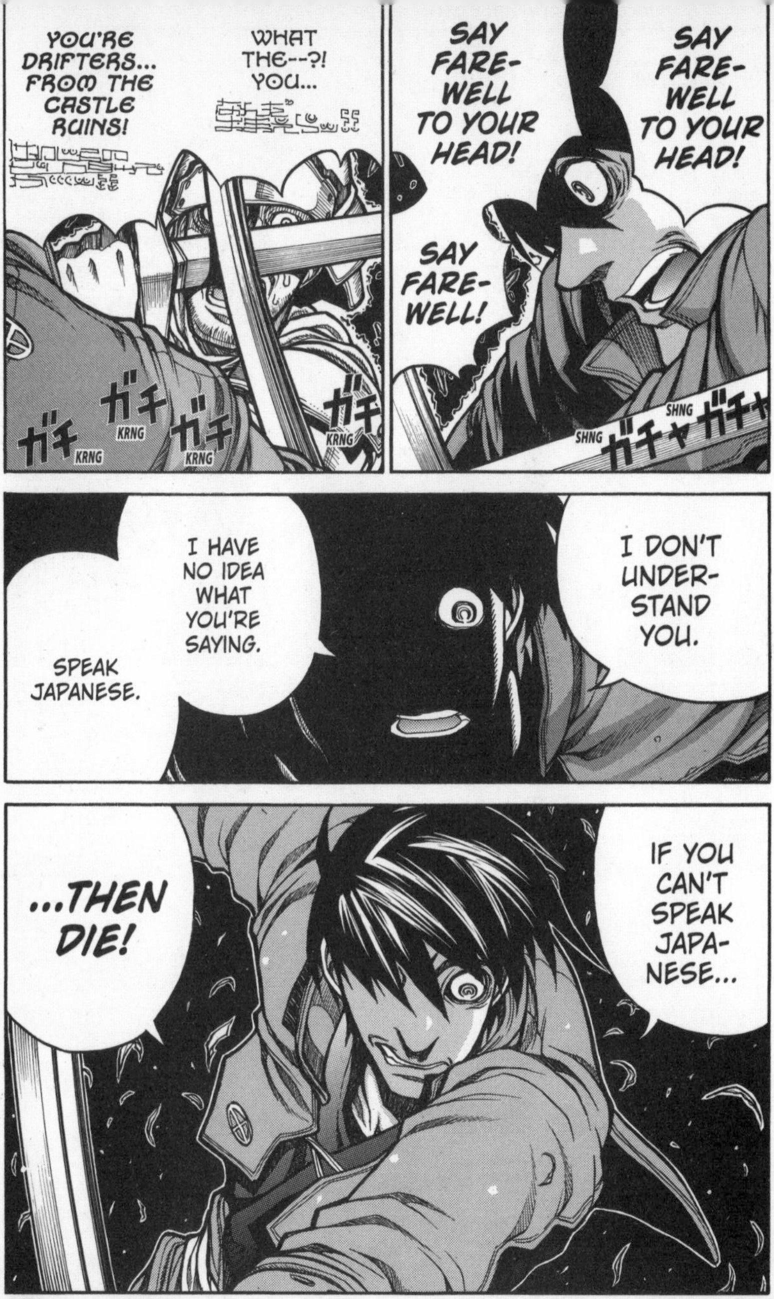
SAY FARE-WELL TO YOUR HEAD!
SAY FARE-WELL TO YOUR HEAD!
SAY FARE-WELL!
ガチャ SHNG
ガチャ SHNG
WHAT THE--?! YOU...
YOU'RE DRIFTERS... FROM THE CASTLE RUINS!
ガチ KRNG
ガチ KRNG
ガチ KRNG
ガチ KRNG
I DON'T UNDER-STAND YOU.
I HAVE NO IDEA WHAT YOU'RE SAYING.
SPEAK JAPANESE.
IF YOU CAN'T SPEAK JAPA-NESE...
...THEN DIE!

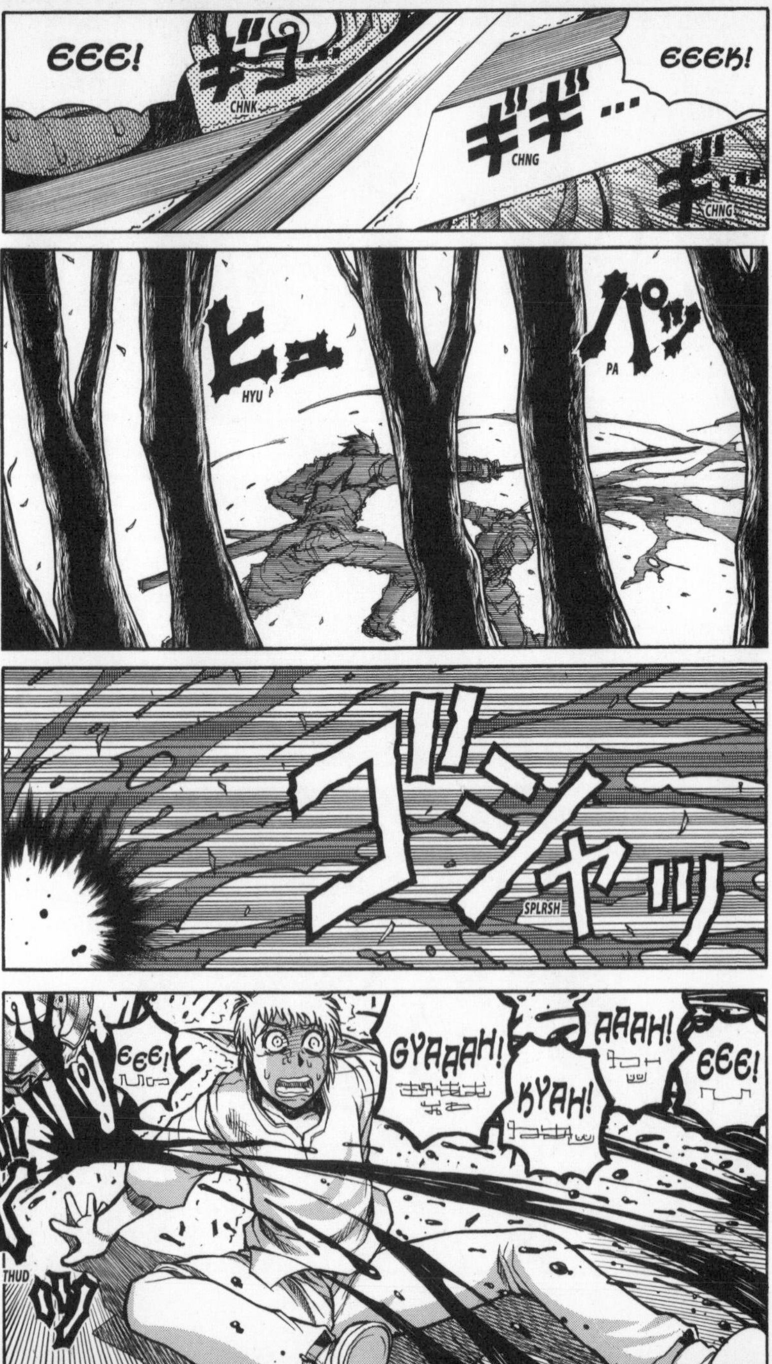
EEEK!
CHNG
CHNG
CHNK
EEE!
PA
HYU
SPLRSH
EEE!
AAAH!
KYAH!
GYAAAH!
EEE!
THUD

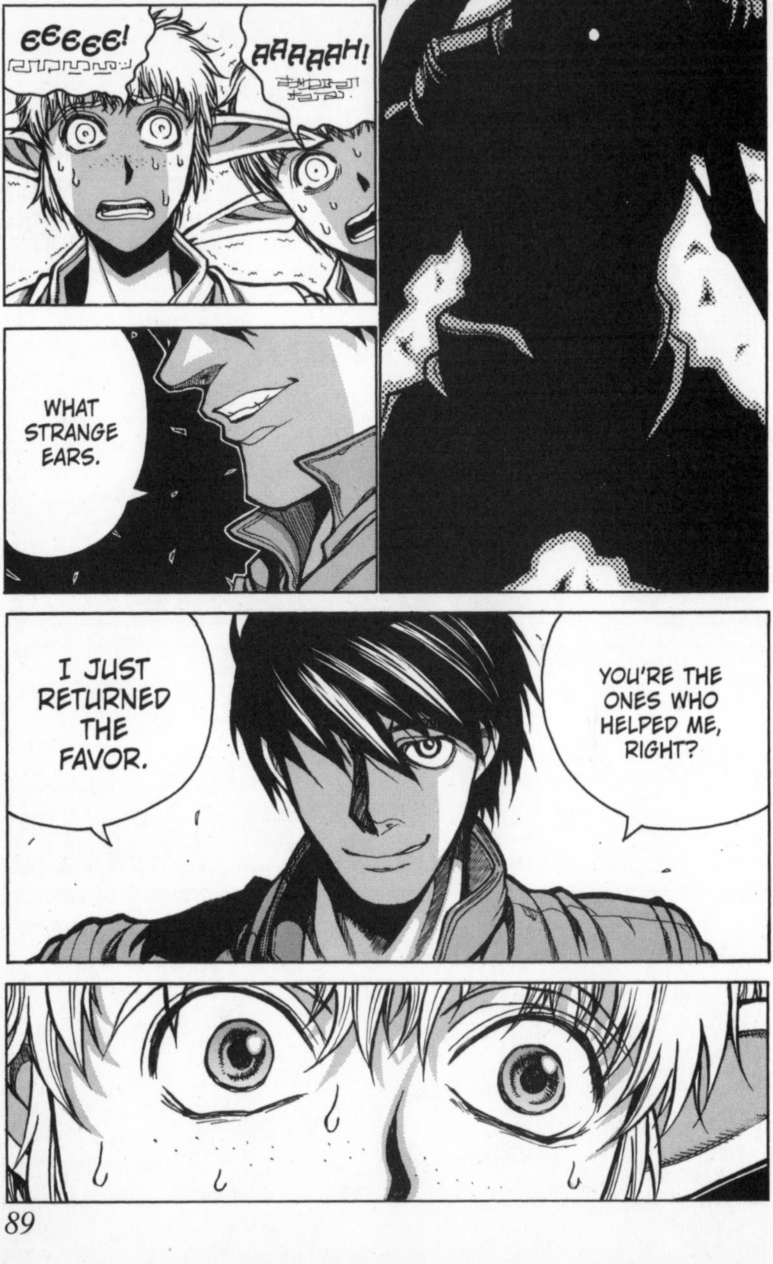
AAAAAH!
EEEEE!
WHAT STRANGE EARS.
YOU'RE THE ONES WHO HELPED ME, RIGHT?
I JUST RETURNED THE FAVOR.

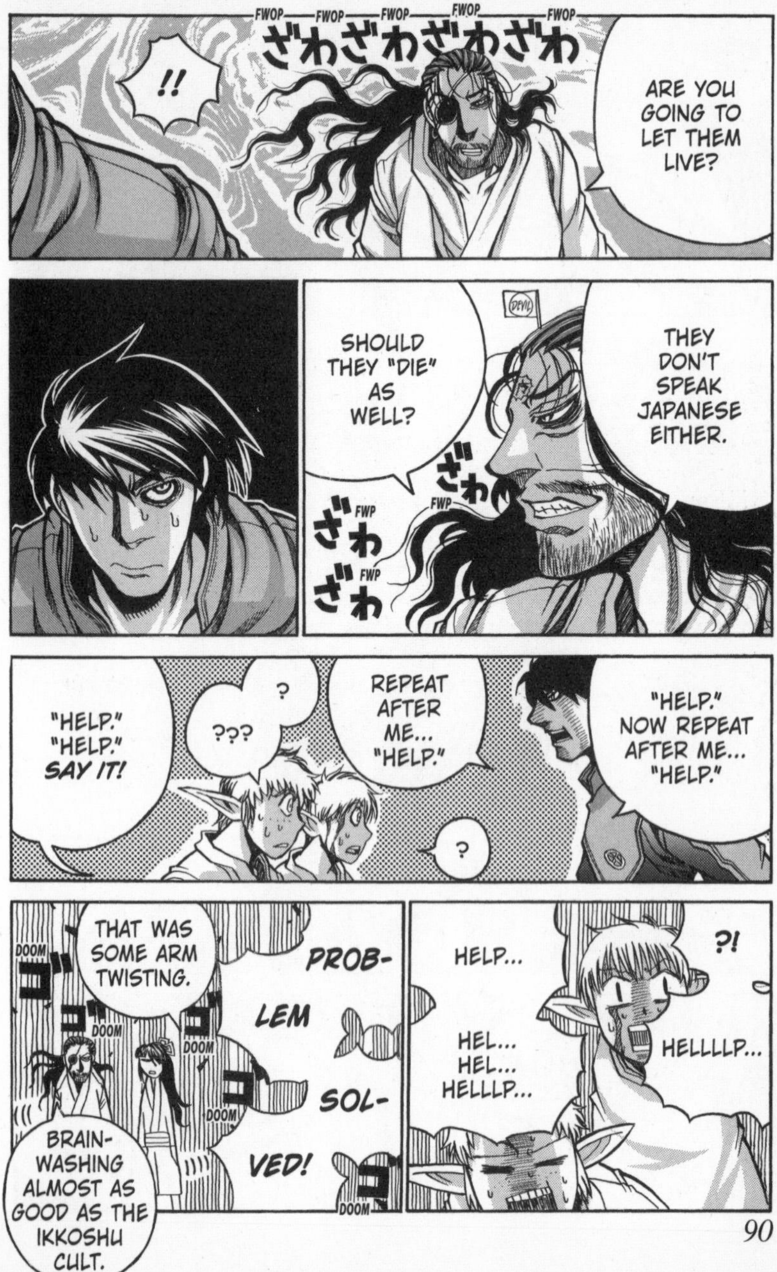
ARE YOU GOING TO LET THEM LIVE?
FWOP FWOP FWOP FWOP FWOP
ざわざわざわざわ
!!
THEY DON'T SPEAK JAPANESE EITHER.
SHOULD THEY "DIE" AS WELL?
DEVIL
ざわ FWP
ざわ FWP
ざわ FWP
"HELP." NOW REPEAT AFTER ME... "HELP."
REPEAT AFTER ME... "HELP."
?
???
"HELP." "HELP." SAY IT!
?
?!
HELP...
HELLLLP...
HEL... HEL... HELLLP...
PROB- LEM SOL- VED!
THAT WAS SOME ARM TWISTING.
DOOM
BRAIN-WASHING ALMOST AS GOOD AS THE IKKOSHU CULT.

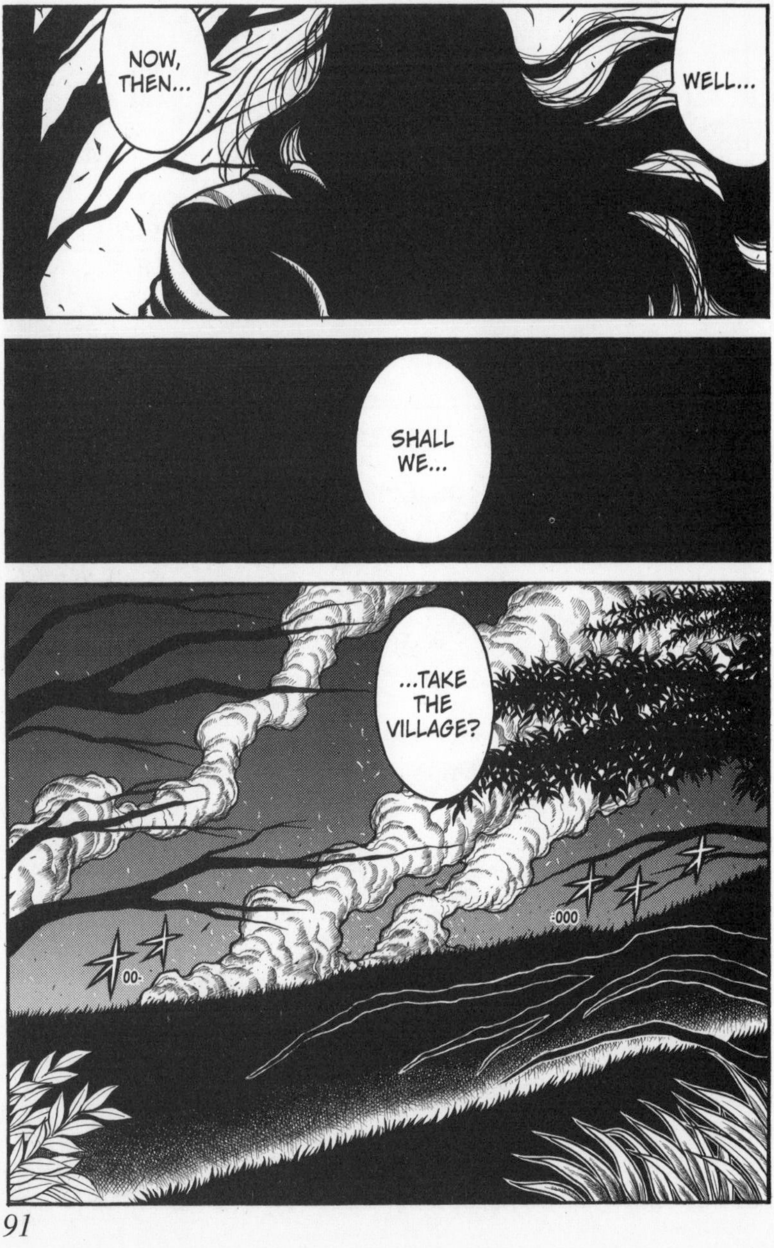
WELL...
NOW, THEN...
SHALL WE...
...TAKE THE VILLAGE?
-OOO
OO-

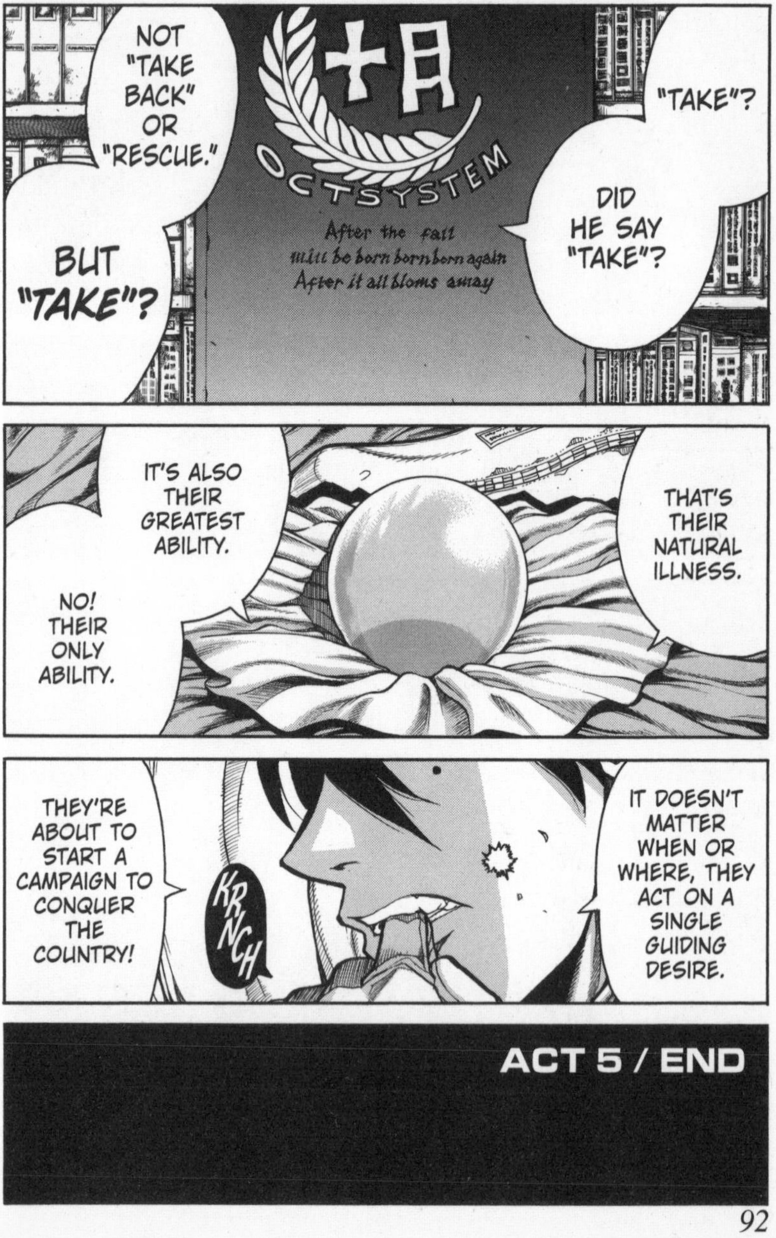
"TAKE"?
DID HE SAY "TAKE"?
十月
OCTSYSTEM
After the fall
will be born born born again
After it all blows away
NOT "TAKE BACK" OR "RESCUE."
BUT *"TAKE"*?
THAT'S THEIR NATURAL ILLNESS.
IT'S ALSO THEIR GREATEST ABILITY.
NO! THEIR ONLY ABILITY.
IT DOESN'T MATTER WHEN OR WHERE, THEY ACT ON A SINGLE GUIDING DESIRE.
KRNCH
THEY'RE ABOUT TO START A CAMPAIGN TO CONQUER THE COUNTRY!

ACT 5 / END

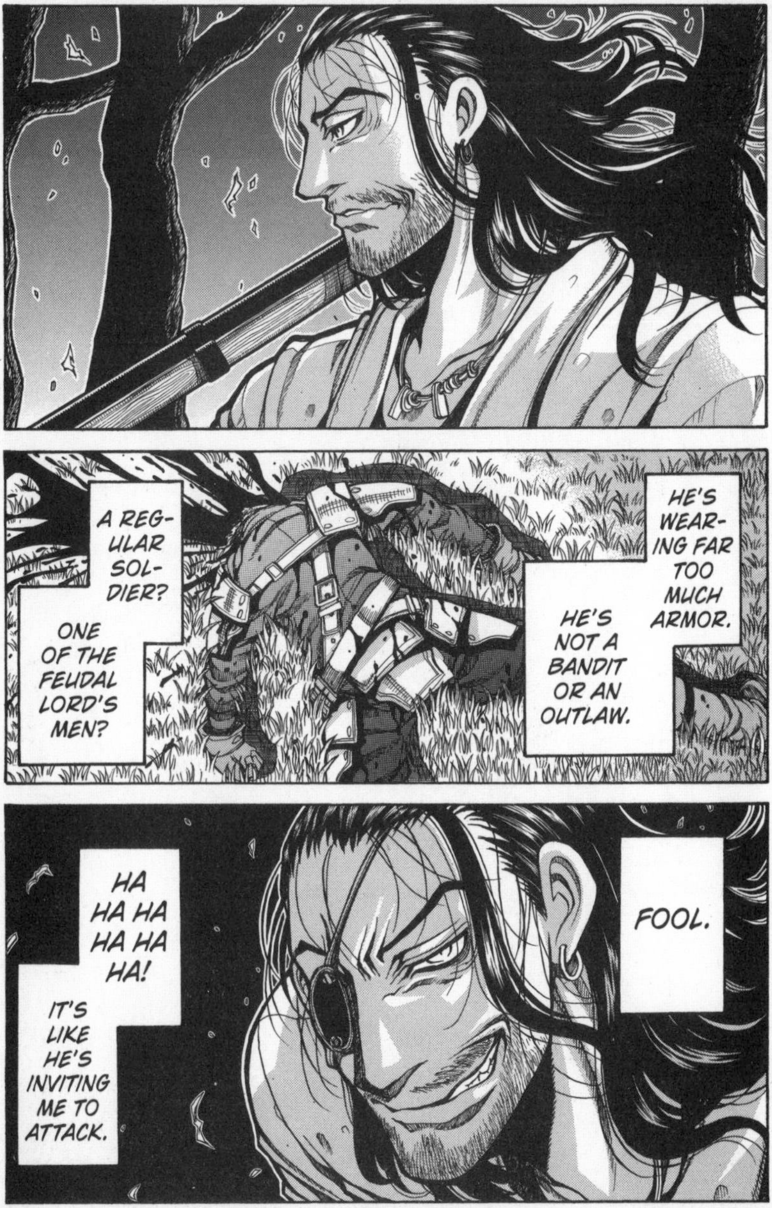
HE'S WEARING FAR TOO MUCH ARMOR.
HE'S NOT A BANDIT OR AN OUTLAW.
A REGULAR SOLDIER?
ONE OF THE FEUDAL LORD'S MEN?
FOOL.
HA HA HA HA HA HA!
IT'S LIKE HE'S INVITING ME TO ATTACK.

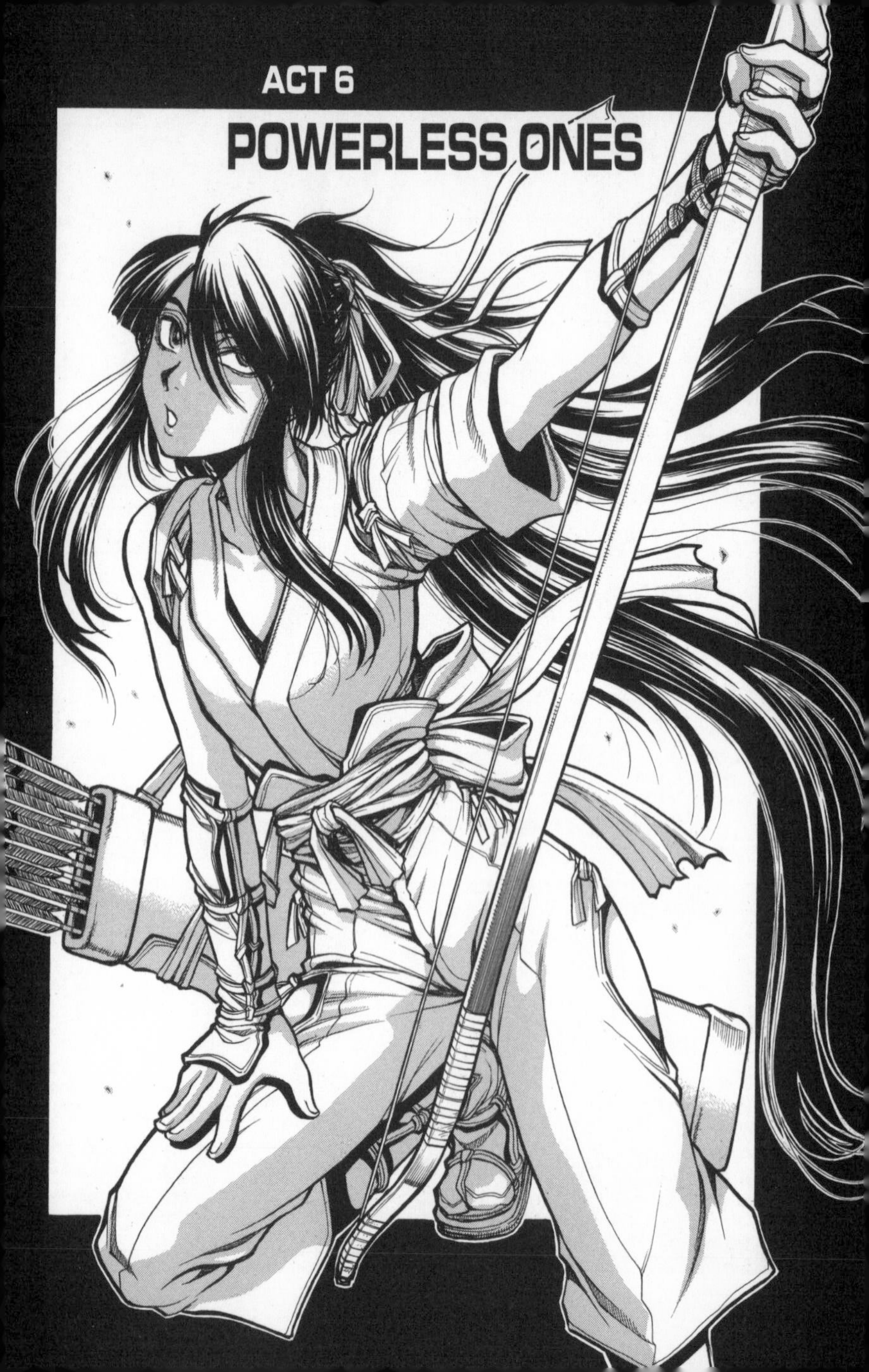
ACT 6
POWERLESS ONES

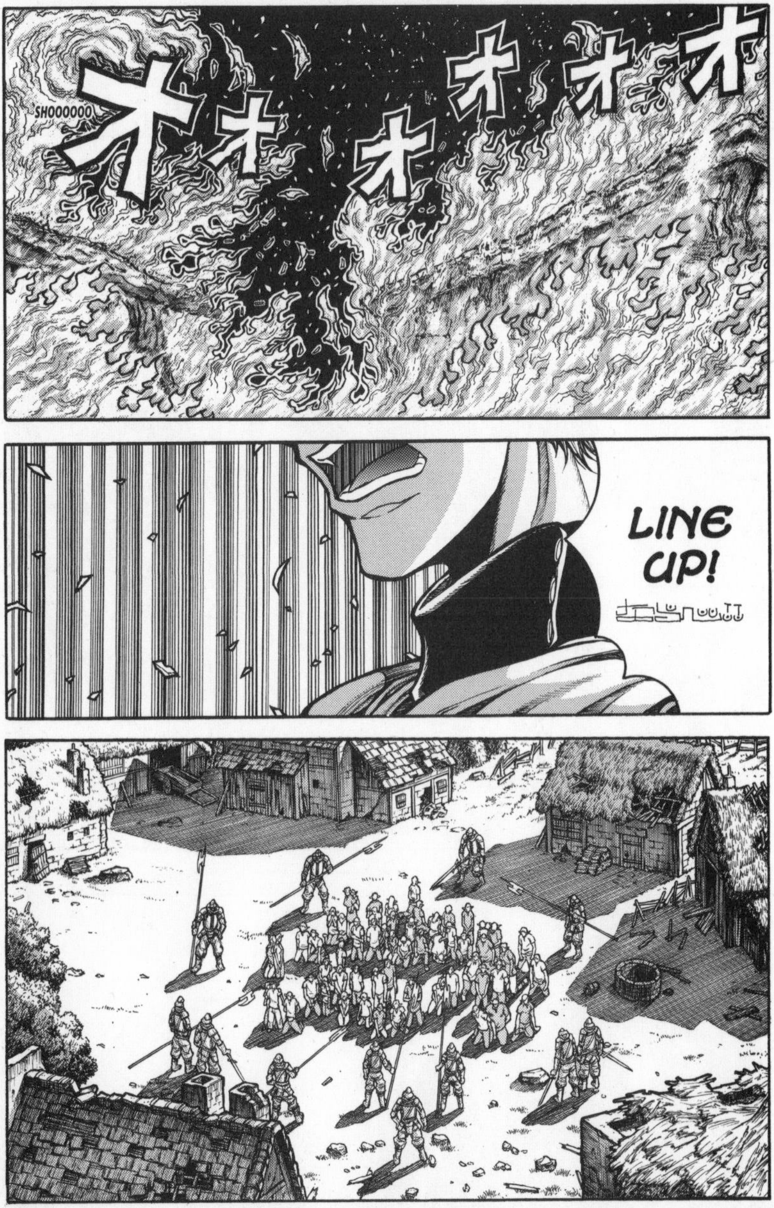
オオオオオオ
SHOOOOOO
LINE UP!

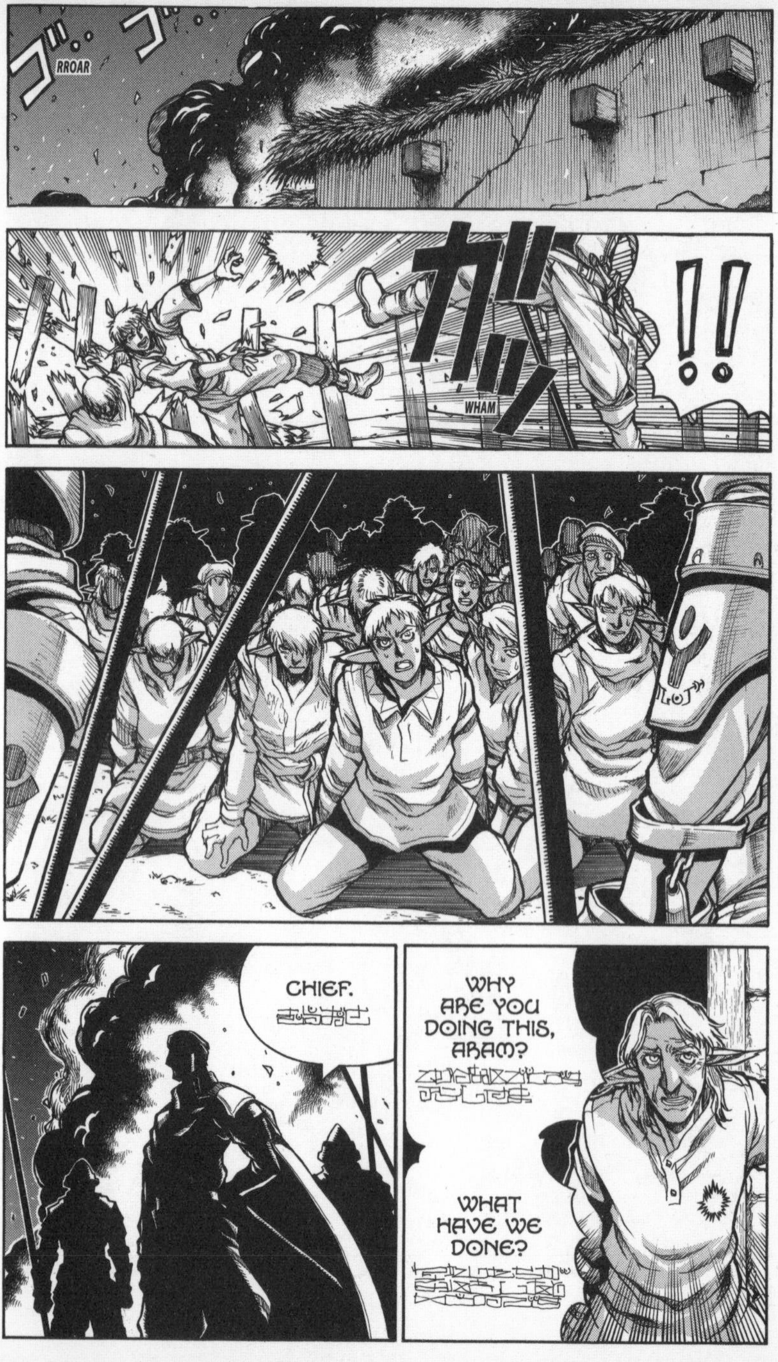

ゴ ゴ
RROAR
ガッ
WHAM
!!
WHY ARE YOU DOING THIS, ARAM?
WHAT HAVE WE DONE?
CHIEF.

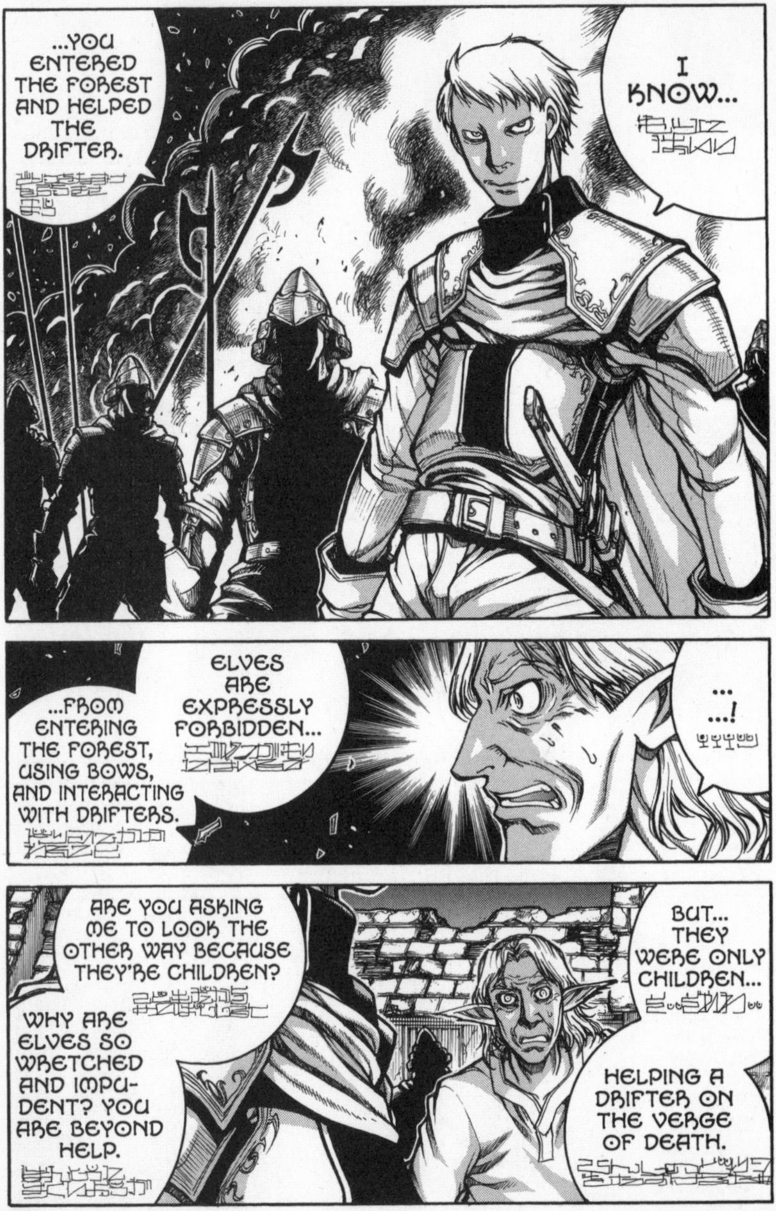
I KNOW...
...YOU ENTERED THE FOREST AND HELPED THE DRIFTER.
... ...!
ELVES ARE EXPRESSLY FORBIDDEN...
...FROM ENTERING THE FOREST, USING BOWS, AND INTERACTING WITH DRIFTERS.
BUT... THEY WERE ONLY CHILDREN...
HELPING A DRIFTER ON THE VERGE OF DEATH.
ARE YOU ASKING ME TO LOOK THE OTHER WAY BECAUSE THEY'RE CHILDREN?
WHY ARE ELVES SO WRETCHED AND IMPUDENT? YOU ARE BEYOND HELP.

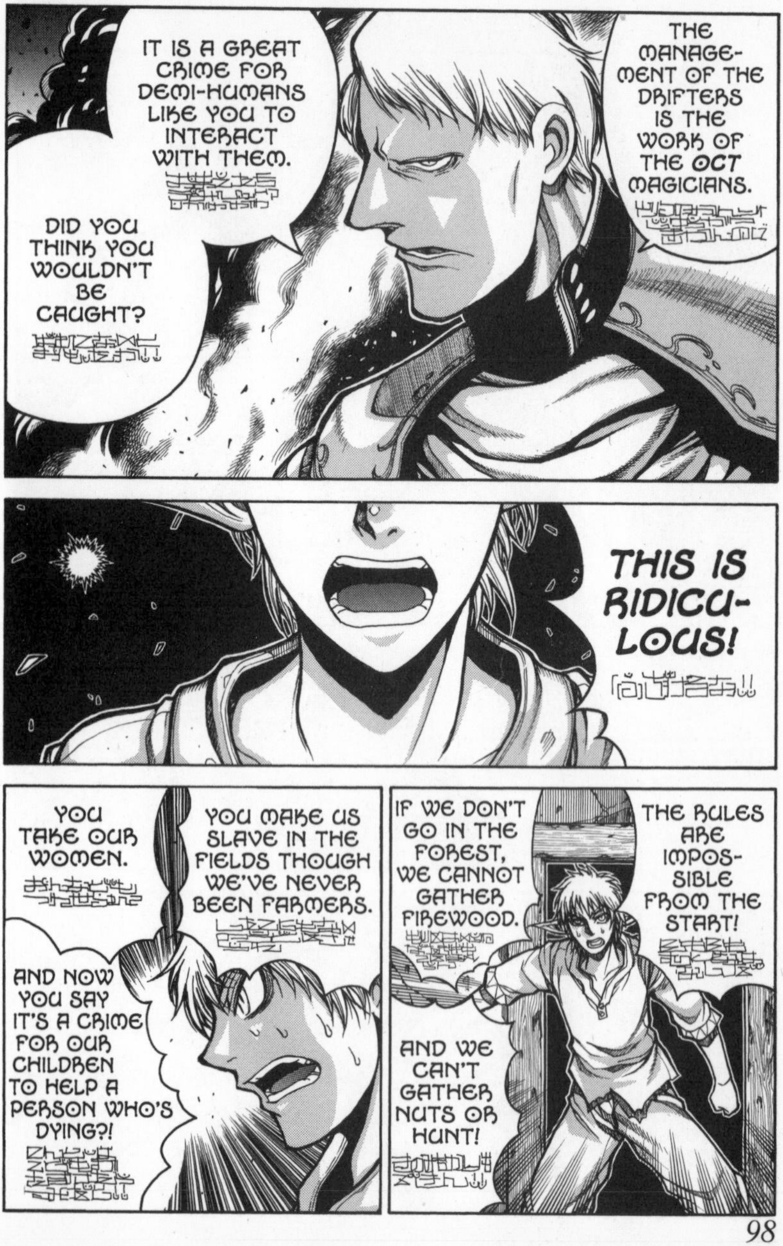
THE MANAGEMENT OF THE DRIFTERS IS THE WORK OF THE OCT MAGICIANS.
IT IS A GREAT CRIME FOR DEMI-HUMANS LIKE YOU TO INTERACT WITH THEM.
DID YOU THINK YOU WOULDN'T BE CAUGHT?
THIS IS RIDICULOUS!
THE RULES ARE IMPOSSIBLE FROM THE START!
IF WE DON'T GO IN THE FOREST, WE CANNOT GATHER FIREWOOD.
AND WE CAN'T GATHER NUTS OR HUNT!
YOU MAKE US SLAVE IN THE FIELDS THOUGH WE'VE NEVER BEEN FARMERS.
YOU TAKE OUR WOMEN.
AND NOW YOU SAY IT'S A CRIME FOR OUR CHILDREN TO HELP A PERSON WHO'S DYING?!

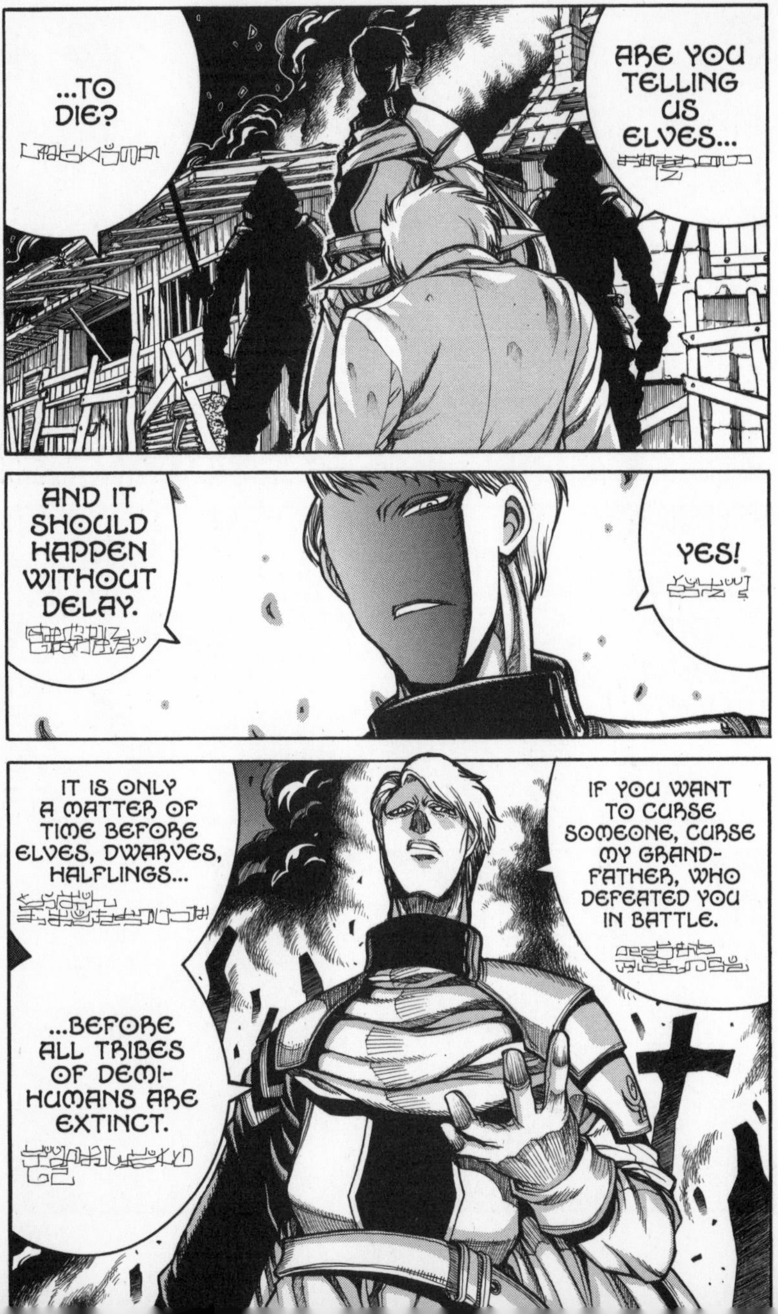
ARE YOU TELLING US ELVES...
...TO DIE?
YES!
AND IT SHOULD HAPPEN WITHOUT DELAY.
IF YOU WANT TO CURSE SOMEONE, CURSE MY GRAND-FATHER, WHO DEFEATED YOU IN BATTLE.
IT IS ONLY A MATTER OF TIME BEFORE ELVES, DWARVES, HALFLINGS...
...BEFORE ALL TRIBES OF DEMI-HUMANS ARE EXTINCT.

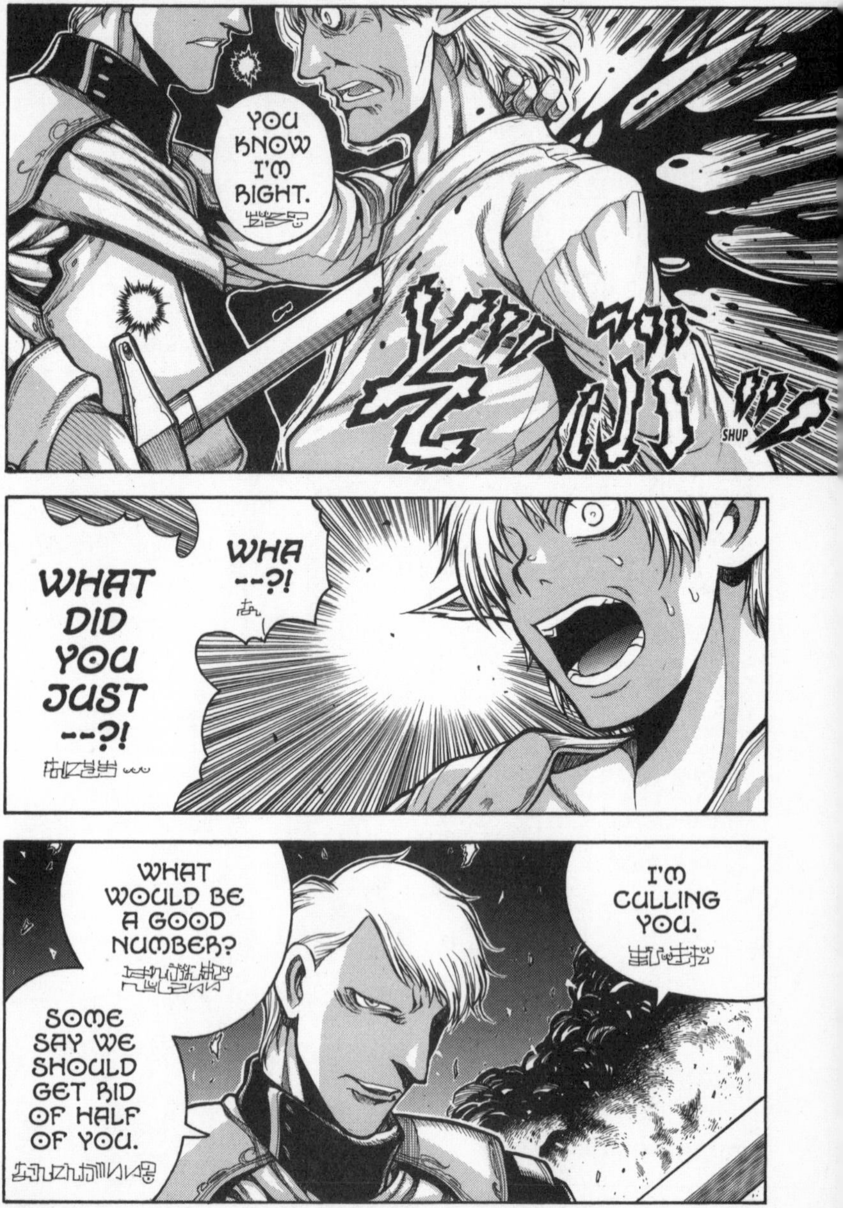
YOU KNOW I'M RIGHT.
SHUP
WHA --?!
WHAT DID YOU JUST --?!
I'M CULLING YOU.
WHAT WOULD BE A GOOD NUMBER?
SOME SAY WE SHOULD GET RID OF HALF OF YOU.

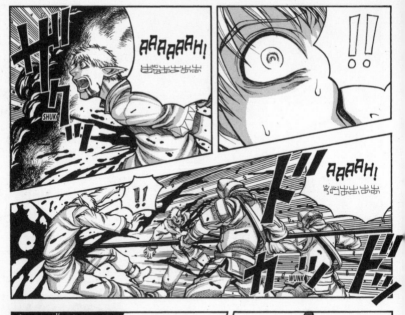

ARAAAAH!

SHUK

!!

AAAAH!

!!

WUNK

YOU ARE
STILL
YOUNG.

YOU NEED
TO TAKE
CARE OF
YOURSELF.

YOU
HAVE A
FUTURE.

ALBEIT
ONE SLAVING
IN THE
FIELDS.

KILL ME!
ME!

STOP!

NO.

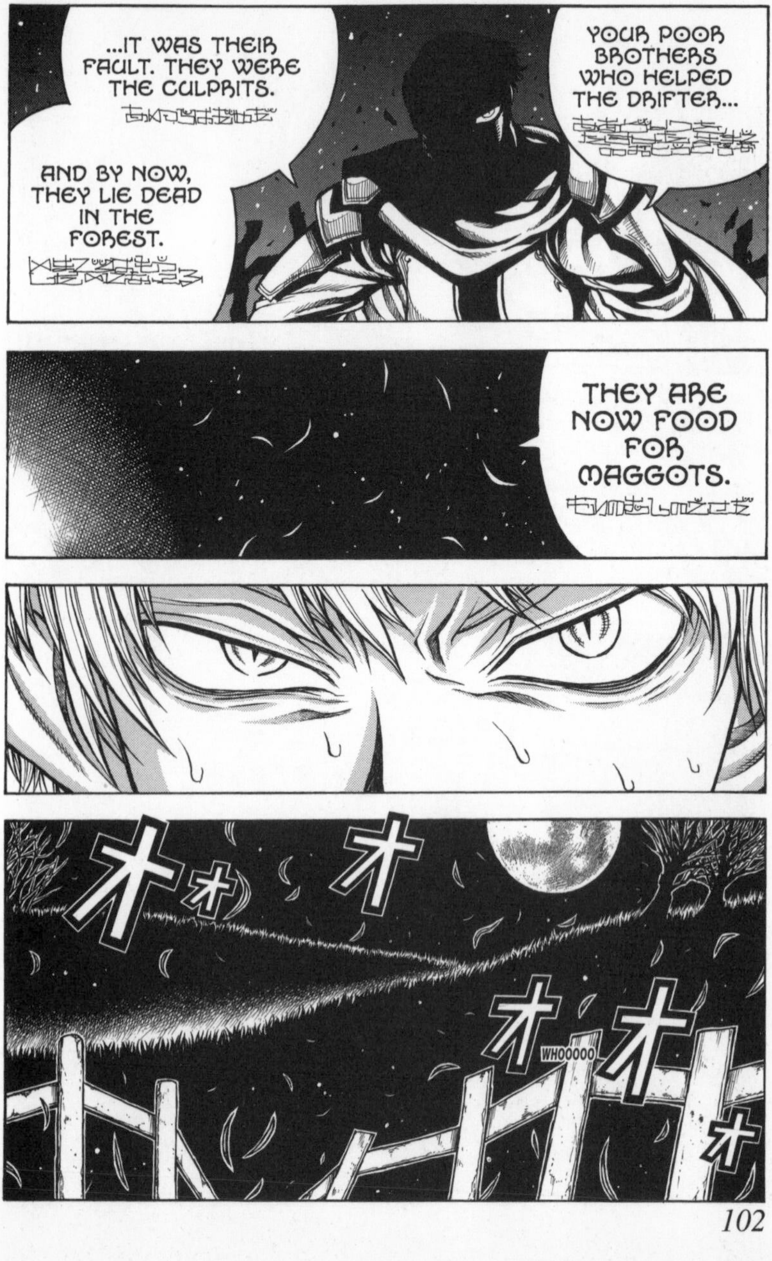
YOUR POOR BROTHERS WHO HELPED THE DRIFTER...
...IT WAS THEIR FAULT. THEY WERE THE CULPRITS.
AND BY NOW, THEY LIE DEAD IN THE FOREST.
THEY ARE NOW FOOD FOR MAGGOTS.
オォオ
オオォ
WHOOOOO

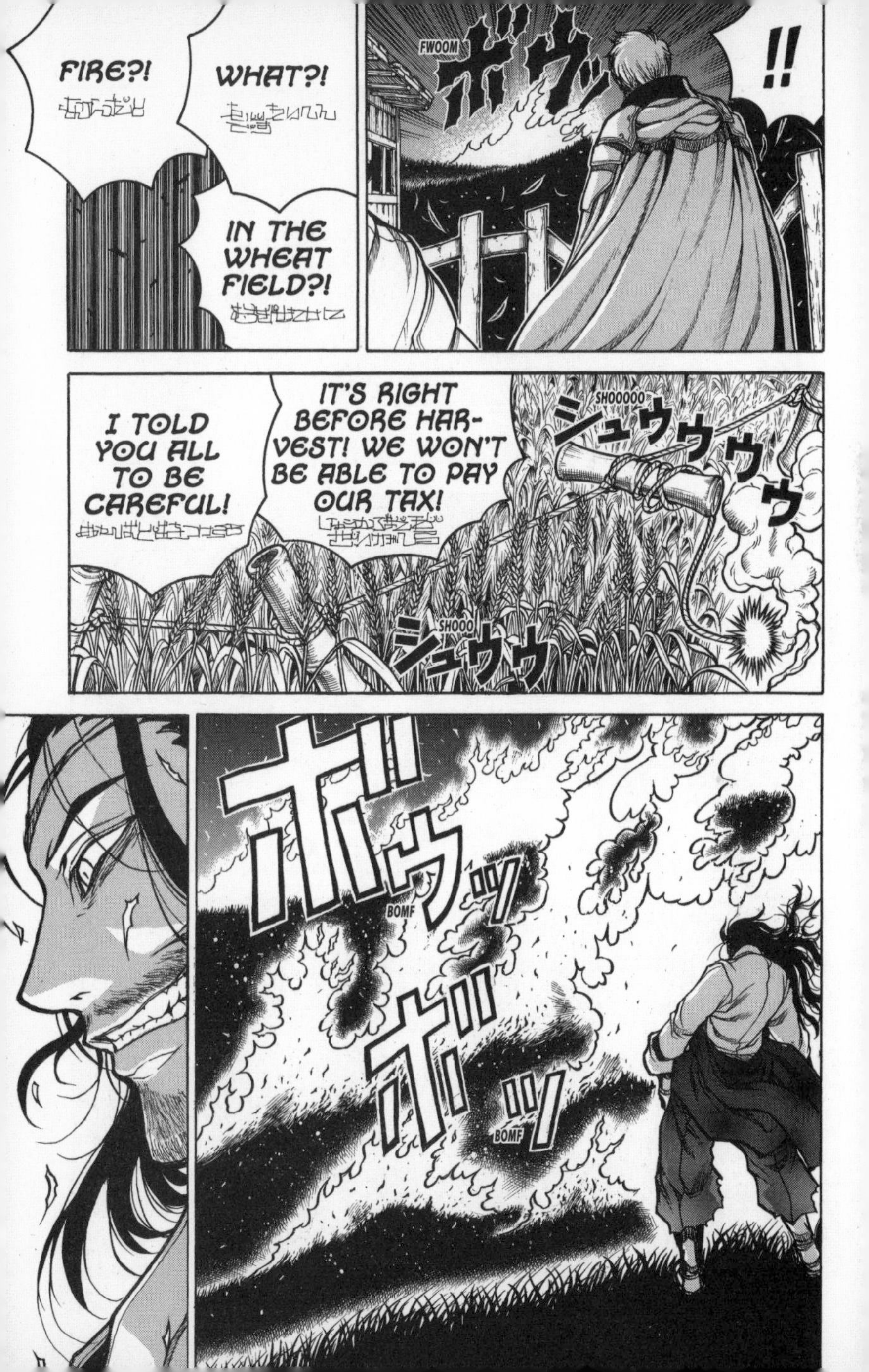
FWOOM
!!
WHAT?!
FIRE?!
IN THE WHEAT FIELD?!
SHOOOOO
IT'S RIGHT BEFORE HAR-VEST! WE WON'T BE ABLE TO PAY OUR TAX!
I TOLD YOU ALL TO BE CAREFUL!
SHOOO
BOMF
BOMF

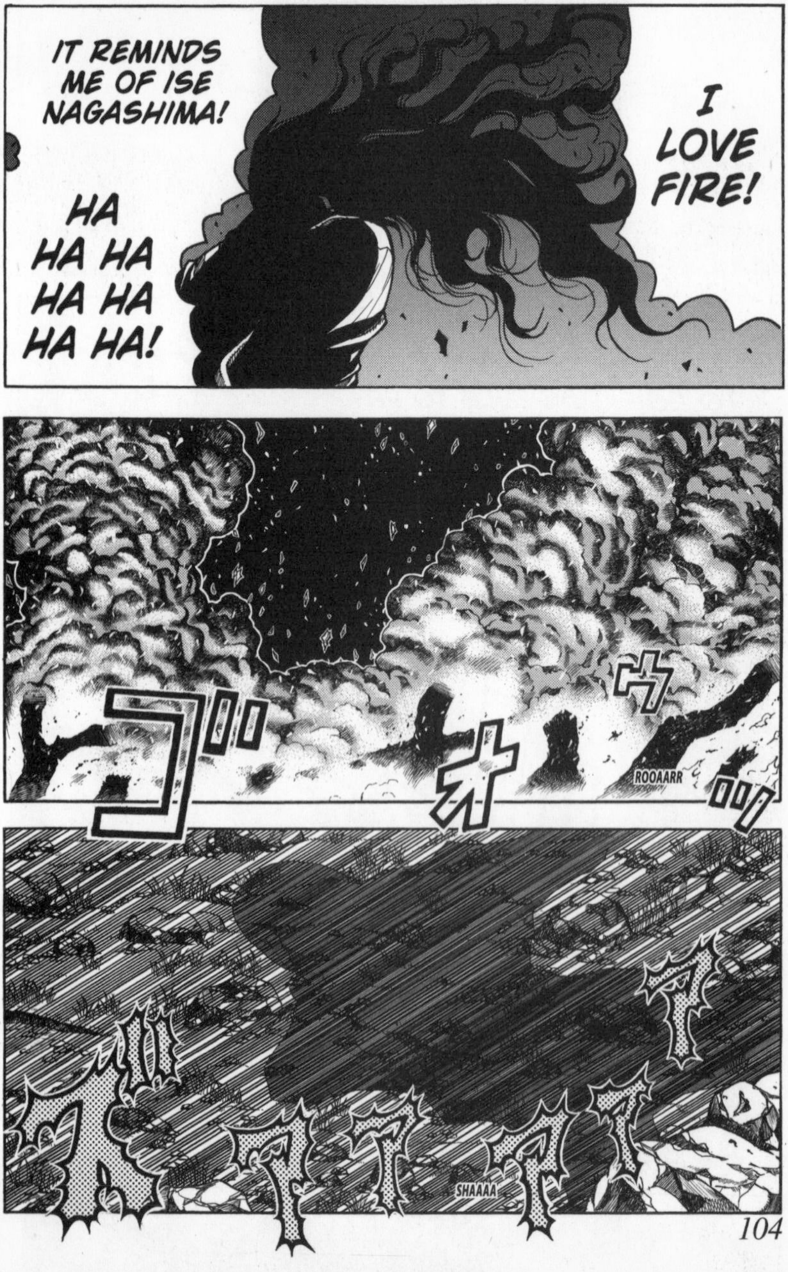
I LOVE FIRE!
IT REMINDS ME OF ISE NAGASHIMA!
HA HA HA HA HA HA HA!
ROOAARR
SHAAAA

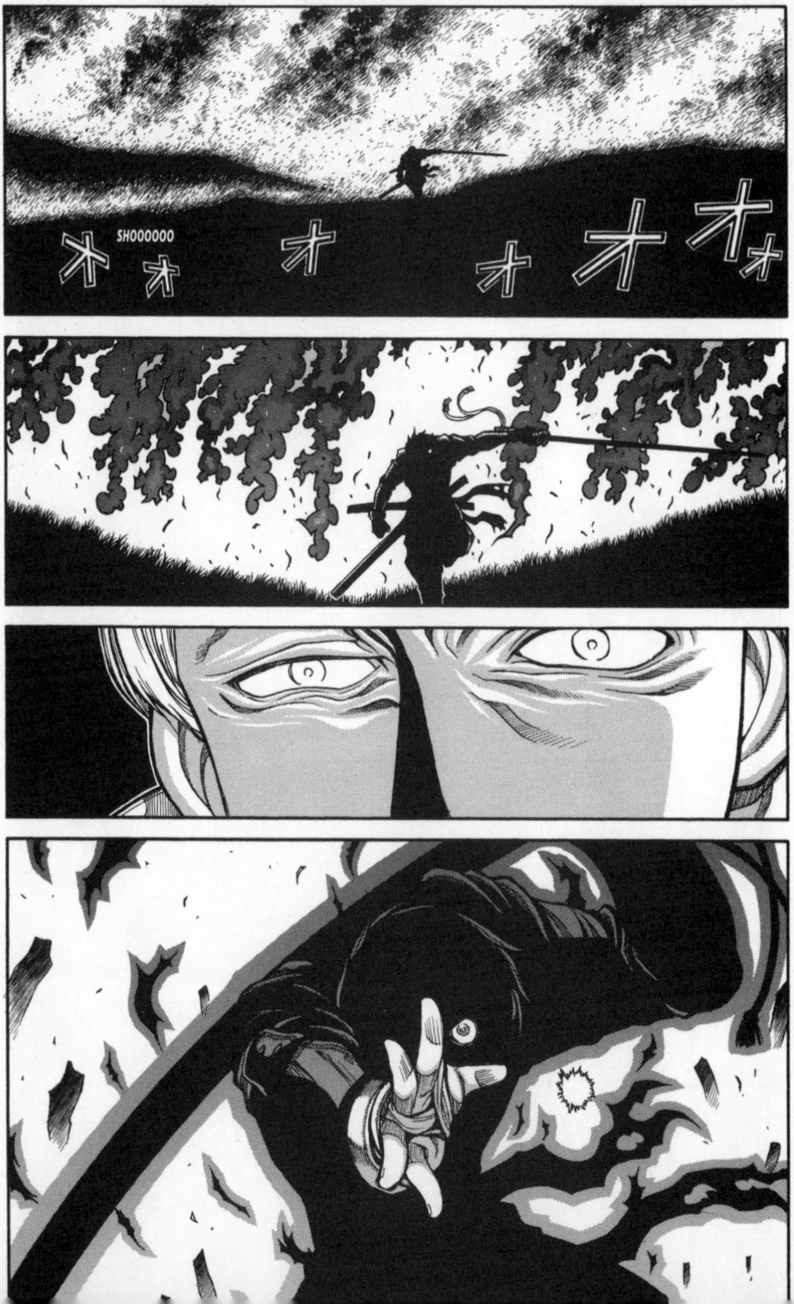
オォオォオオォ
SHOOOOOO

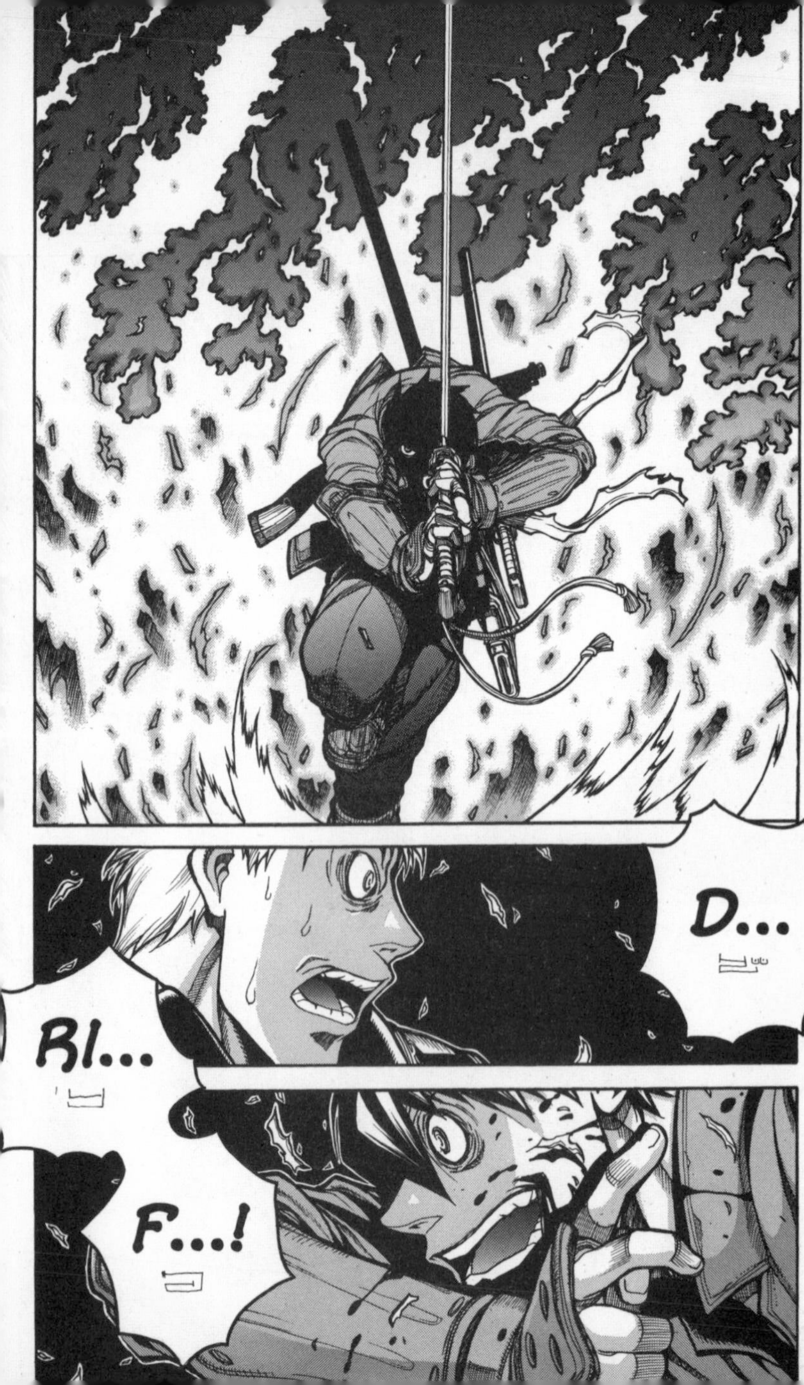
D...
Bl...
F...!

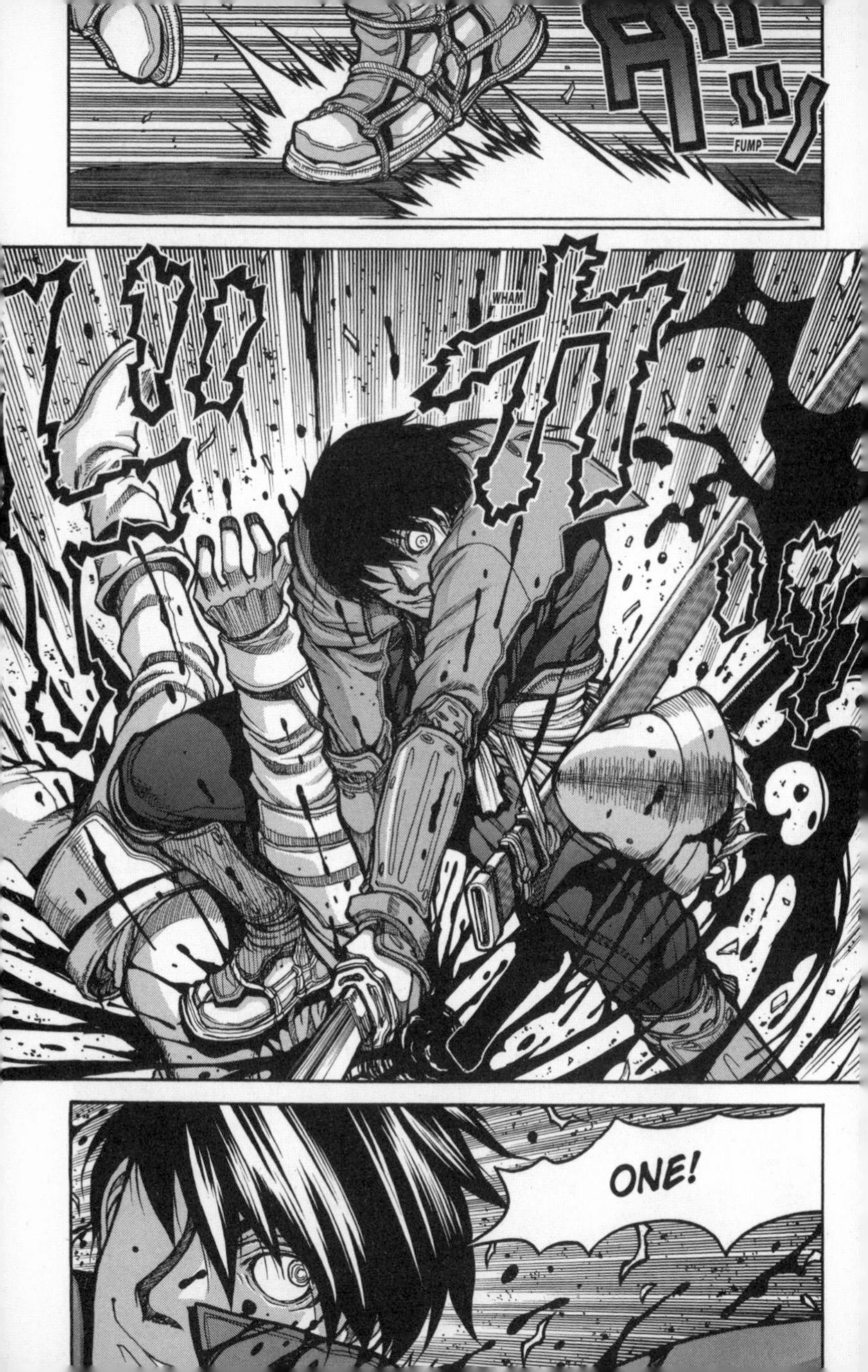
FUMP
WHAM
ONE!

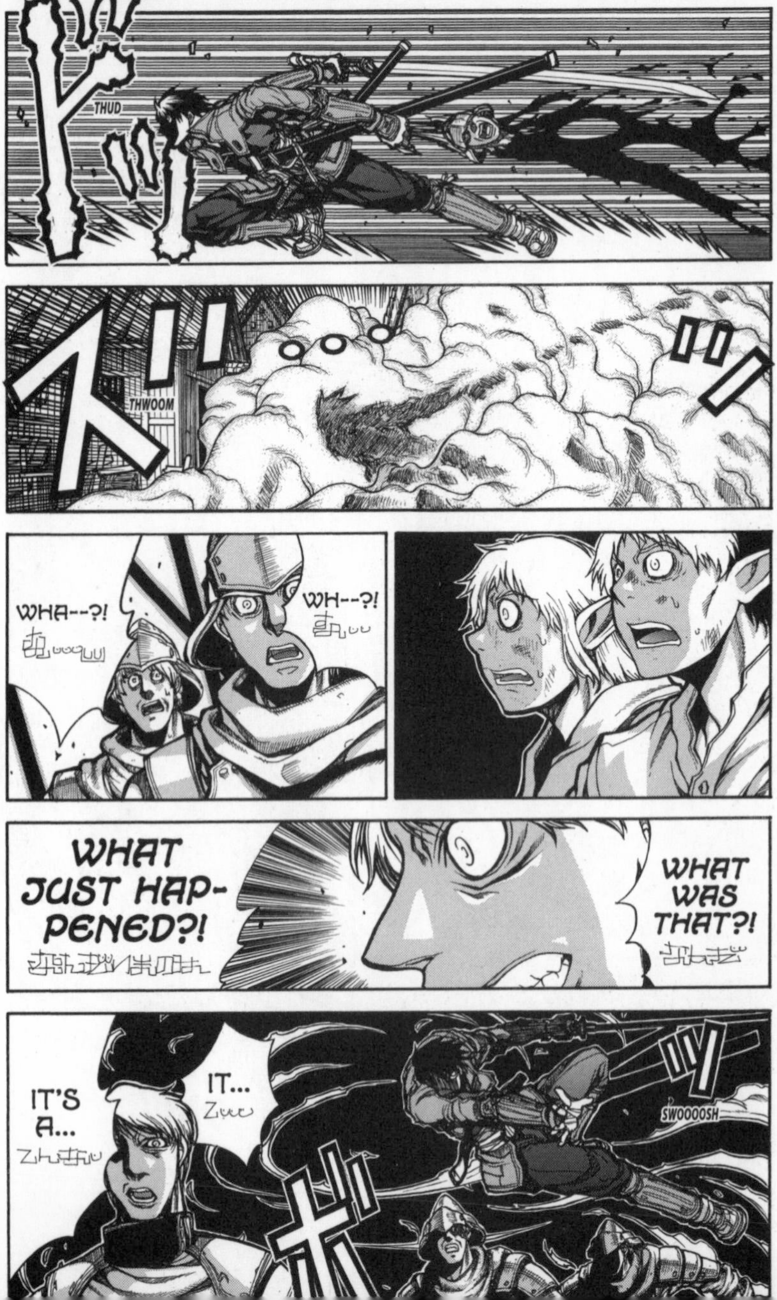
THUD
THWOOM
WH--?!
WHA--?!
WHAT WAS THAT?!
WHAT JUST HAP-PENED?!
SWOOOOSH
IT...
IT'S A...

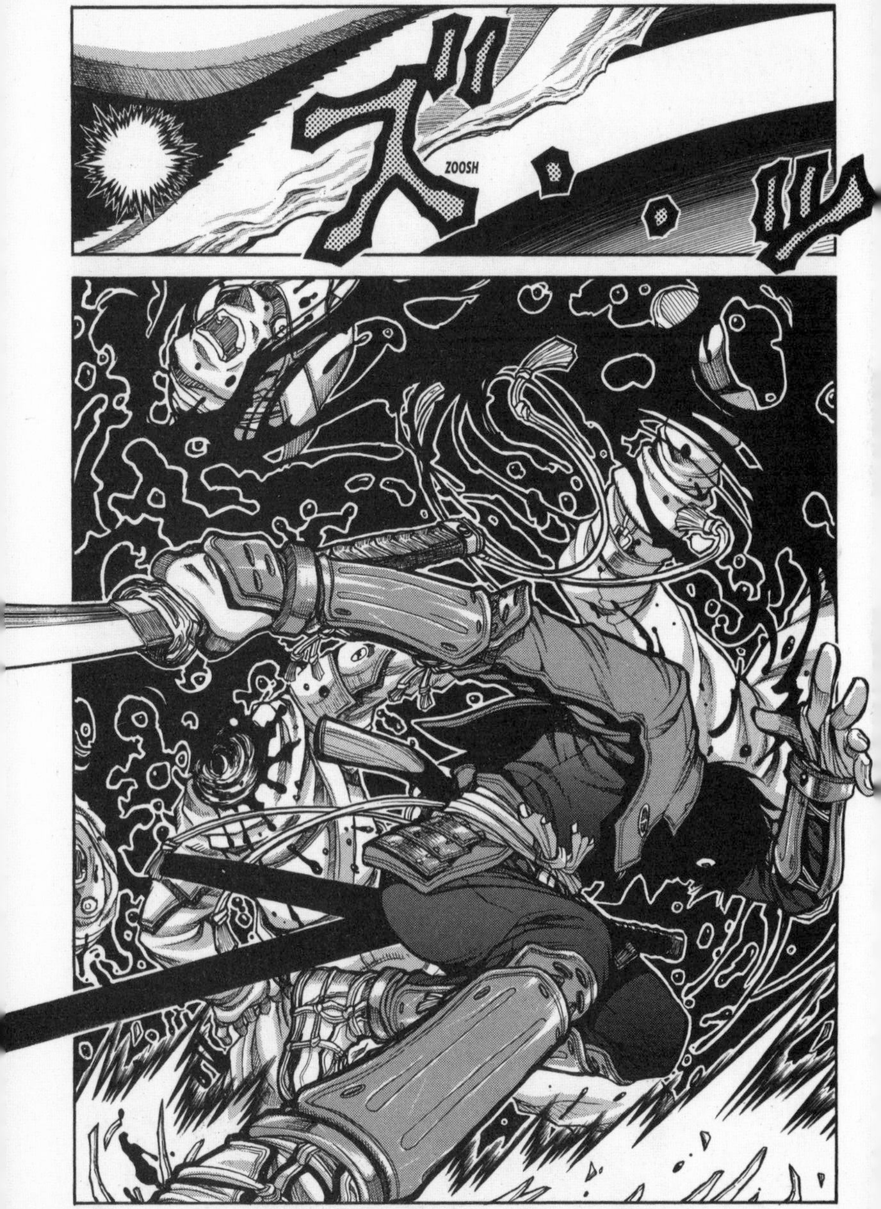
ズ・・ッ
ZOOSH

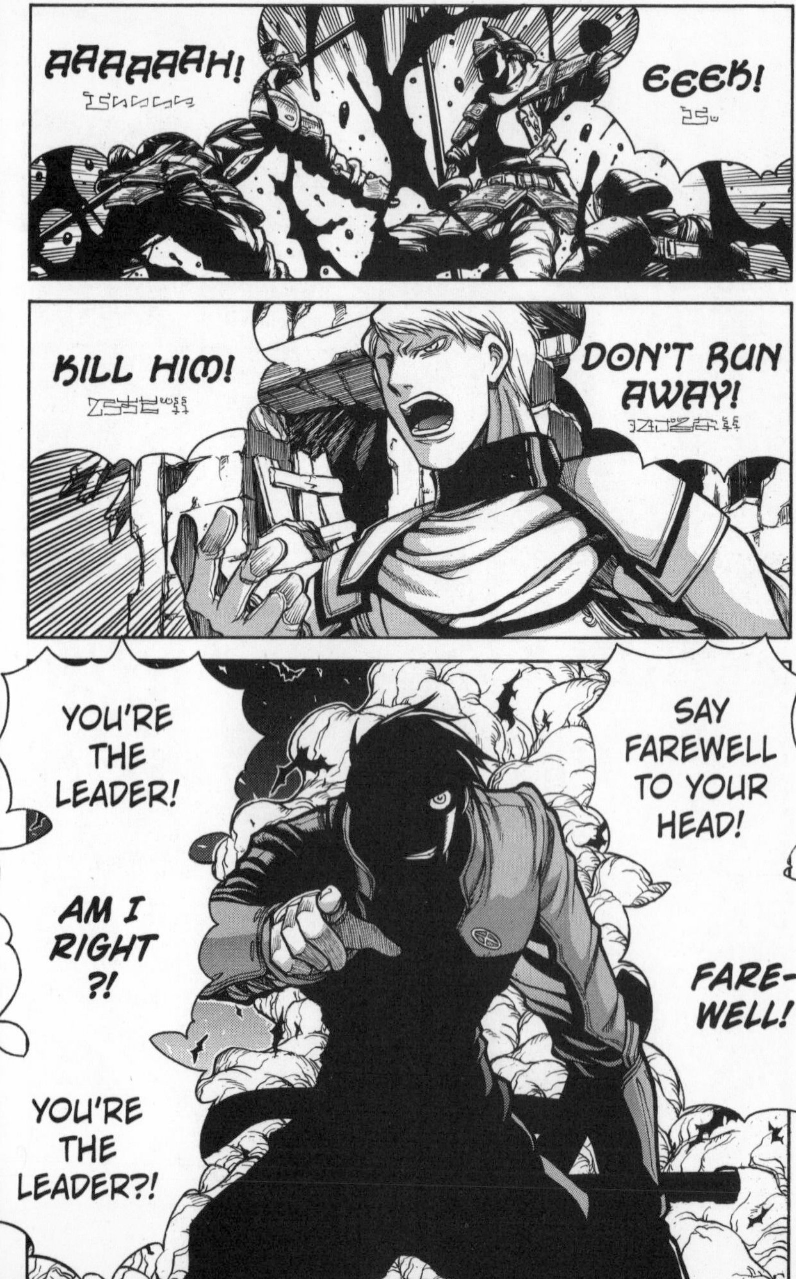
EEEK!
AAAAAAH!
DON'T RUN AWAY!
KILL HIM!
SAY FAREWELL TO YOUR HEAD!
FARE-WELL!
YOU'RE THE LEADER!
AM I RIGHT?!
YOU'RE THE LEADER?!

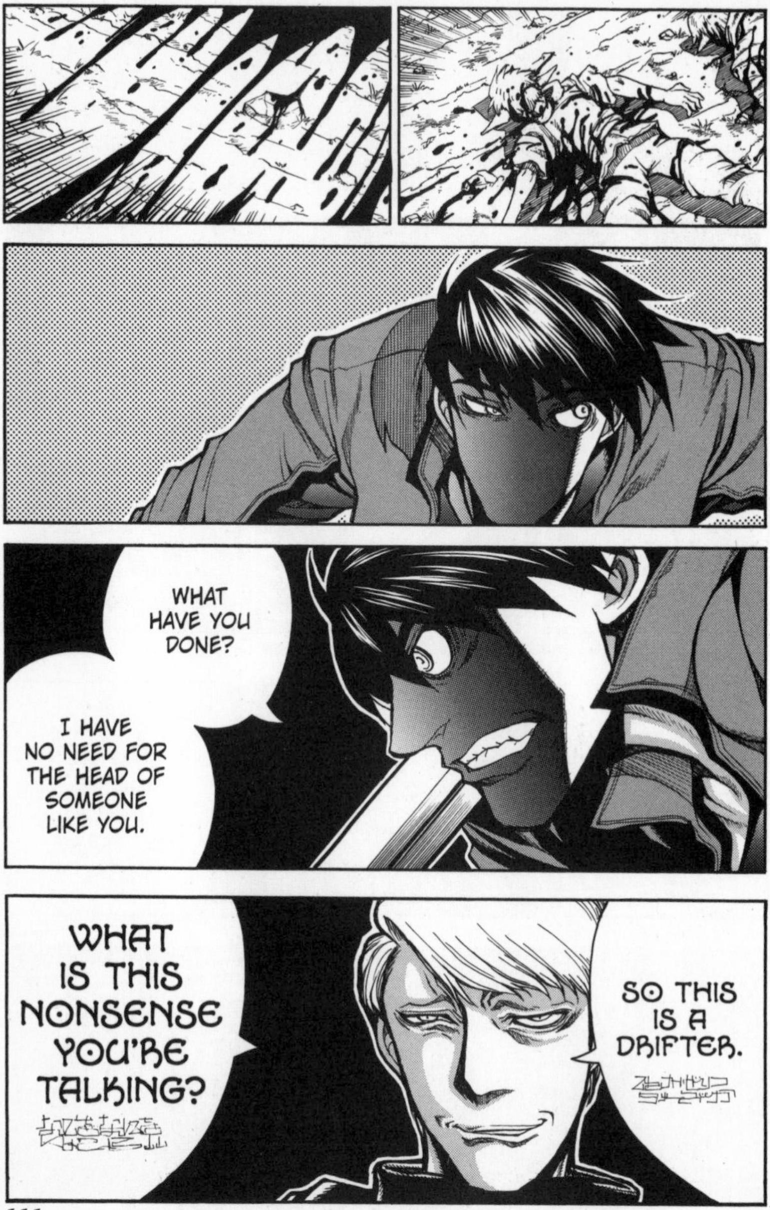
WHAT HAVE YOU DONE?
I HAVE NO NEED FOR THE HEAD OF SOMEONE LIKE YOU.
SO THIS IS A DRIFTER.
WHAT IS THIS NONSENSE YOU'RE TALKING?

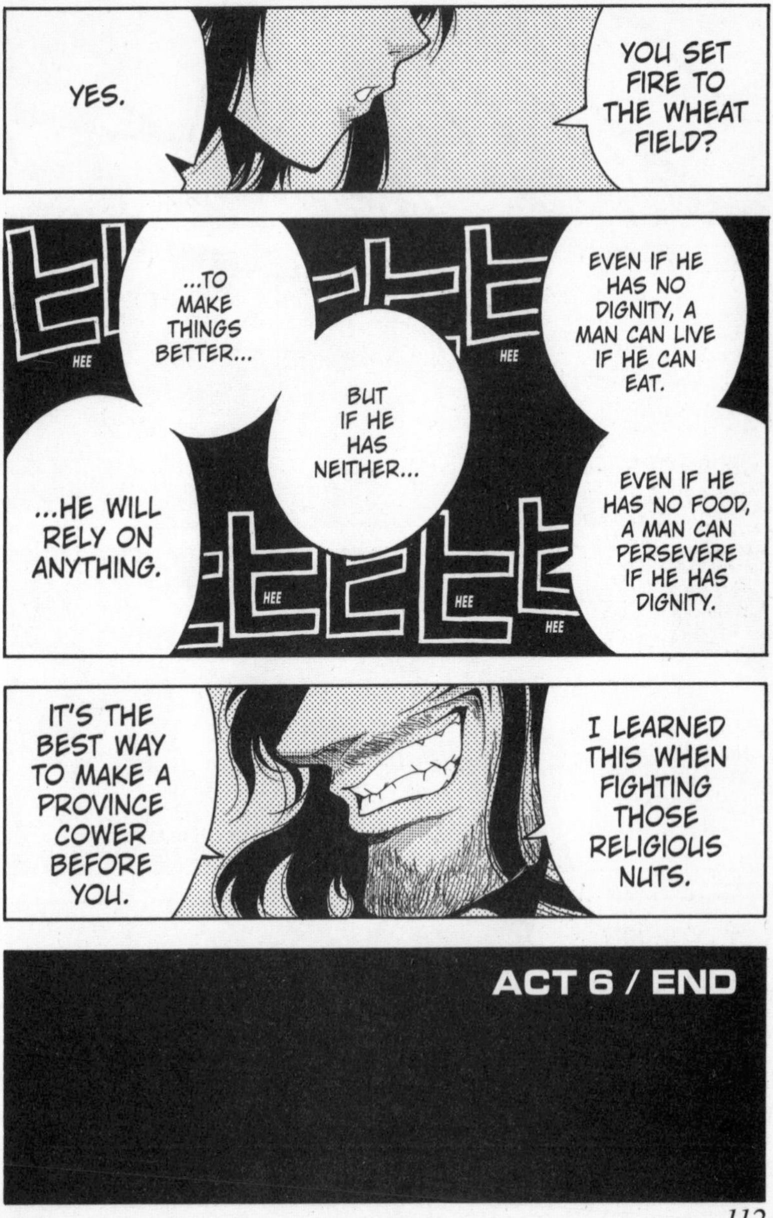
YOU SET FIRE TO THE WHEAT FIELD?
YES.
EVEN IF HE HAS NO DIGNITY, A MAN CAN LIVE IF HE CAN EAT.
HEE
EVEN IF HE HAS NO FOOD, A MAN CAN PERSEVERE IF HE HAS DIGNITY.
HEE
BUT IF HE HAS NEITHER...
HEE
HEE
...TO MAKE THINGS BETTER...
HEE
...HE WILL RELY ON ANYTHING.
I LEARNED THIS WHEN FIGHTING THOSE RELIGIOUS NUTS.
IT'S THE BEST WAY TO MAKE A PROVINCE COWER BEFORE YOU.
ACT 6 / END

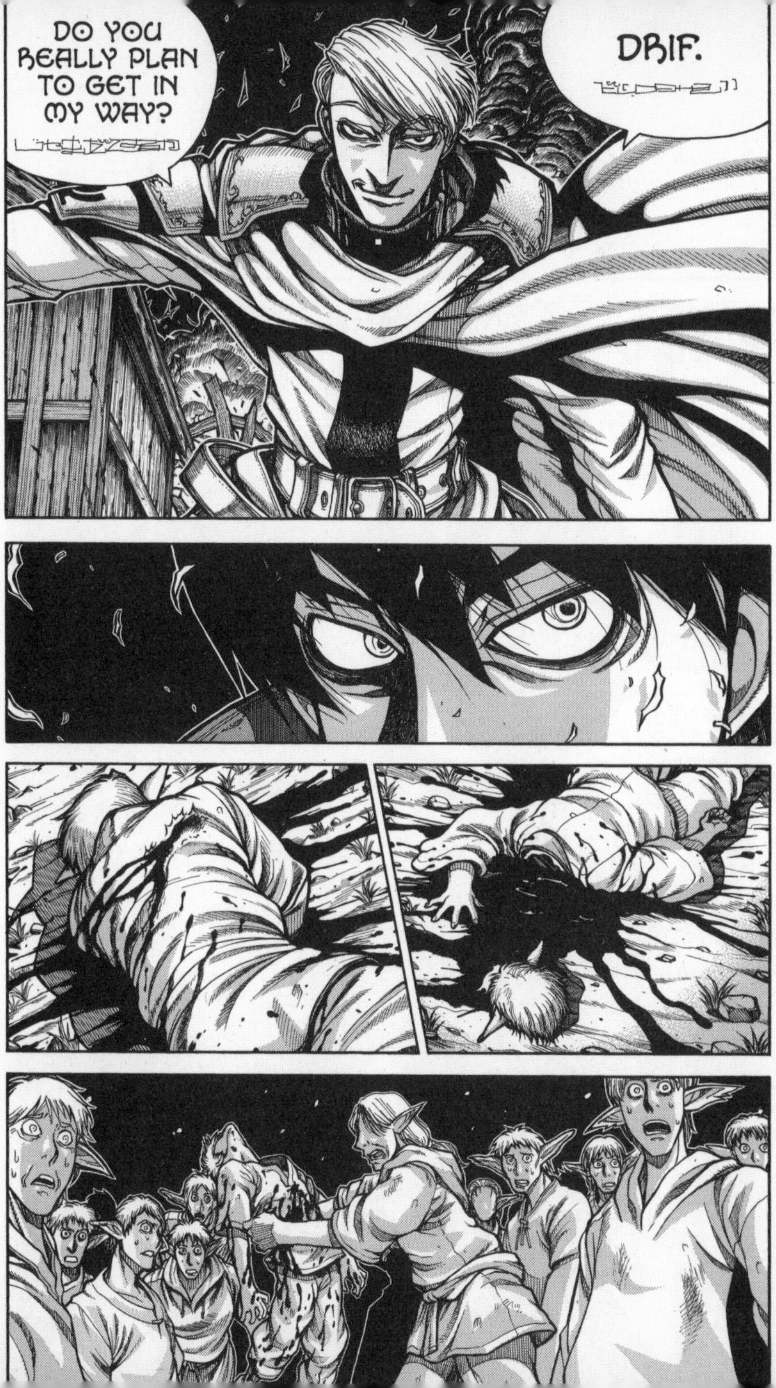
DRIF.
DO YOU REALLY PLAN TO GET IN MY WAY?

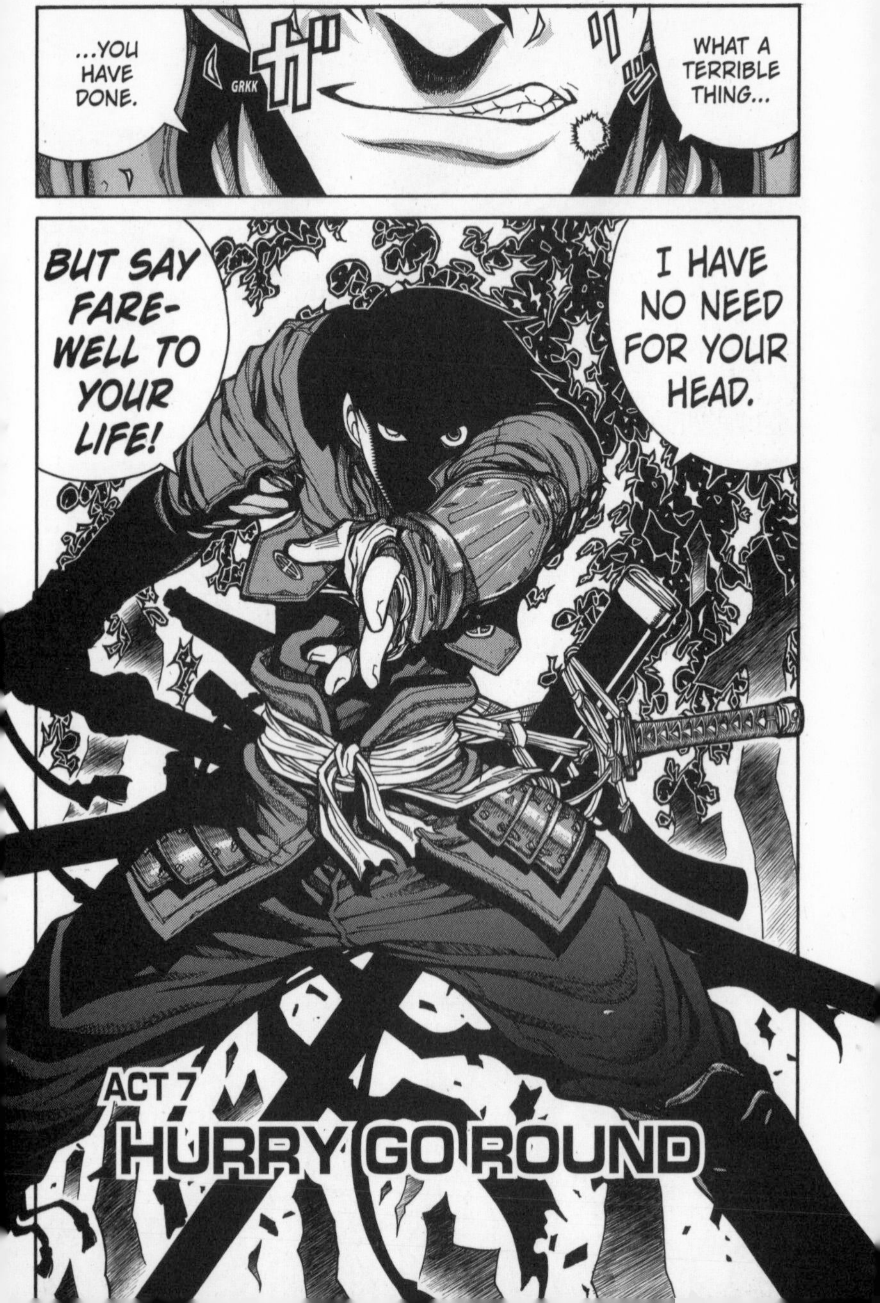
WHAT A TERRIBLE THING...
ガ
GRKK
...YOU HAVE DONE.
I HAVE NO NEED FOR YOUR HEAD.
BUT SAY FARE-WELL TO YOUR LIFE!
ACT 7
HURRY GO ROUND

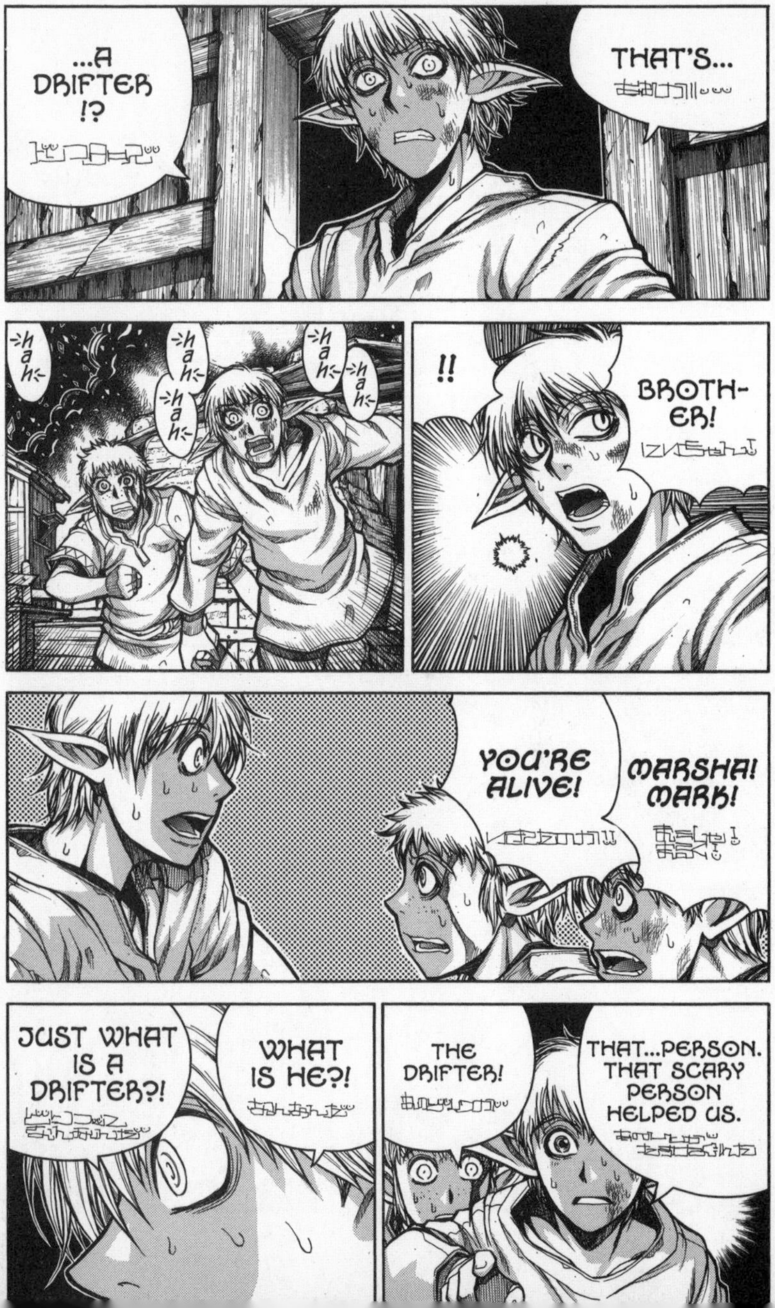
THAT'S...
...A DRIFTER!?
BROTHER!
!!
hah hah
hah hah
hah hah
hah hah
MARSHA! MARK!
YOU'RE ALIVE!
THAT...PERSON. THAT SCARY PERSON HELPED US.
THE DRIFTER!
WHAT IS HE?!
JUST WHAT IS A DRIFTER?!

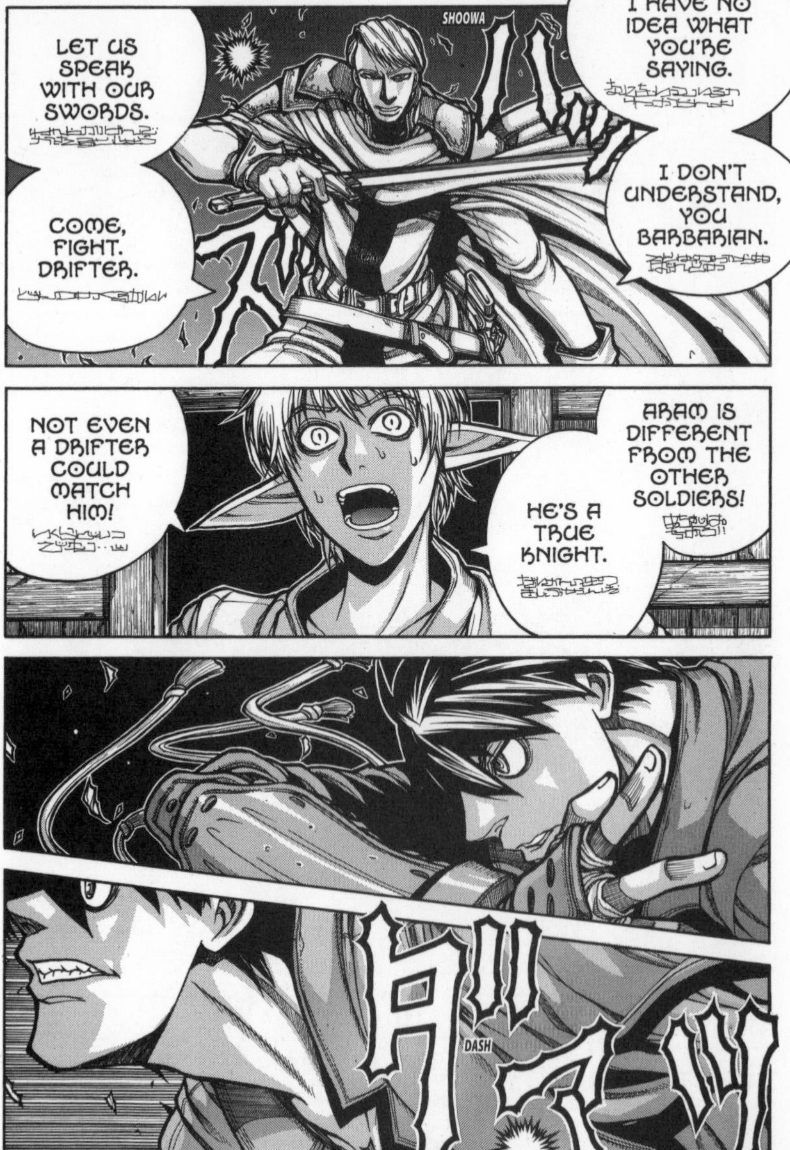
I HAVE NO IDEA WHAT YOU'RE SAYING.
I DON'T UNDERSTAND, YOU BARBARIAN.
SHOOWA
LET US SPEAK WITH OUR SWORDS.
COME, FIGHT. DRIFTER.
ARAM IS DIFFERENT FROM THE OTHER SOLDIERS!
HE'S A TRUE KNIGHT.
NOT EVEN A DRIFTER COULD MATCH HIM!
DASH

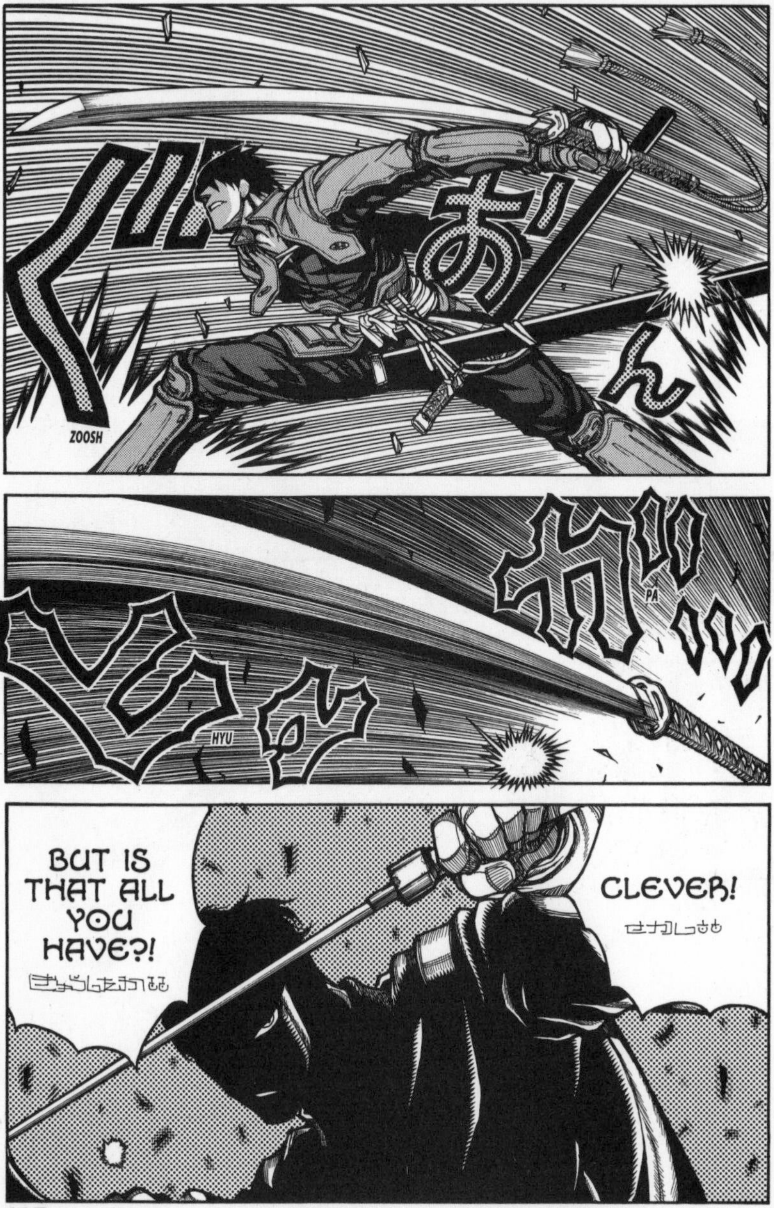
ZOOSH
PA
HYU
CLEVER!
BUT IS THAT ALL YOU HAVE?!

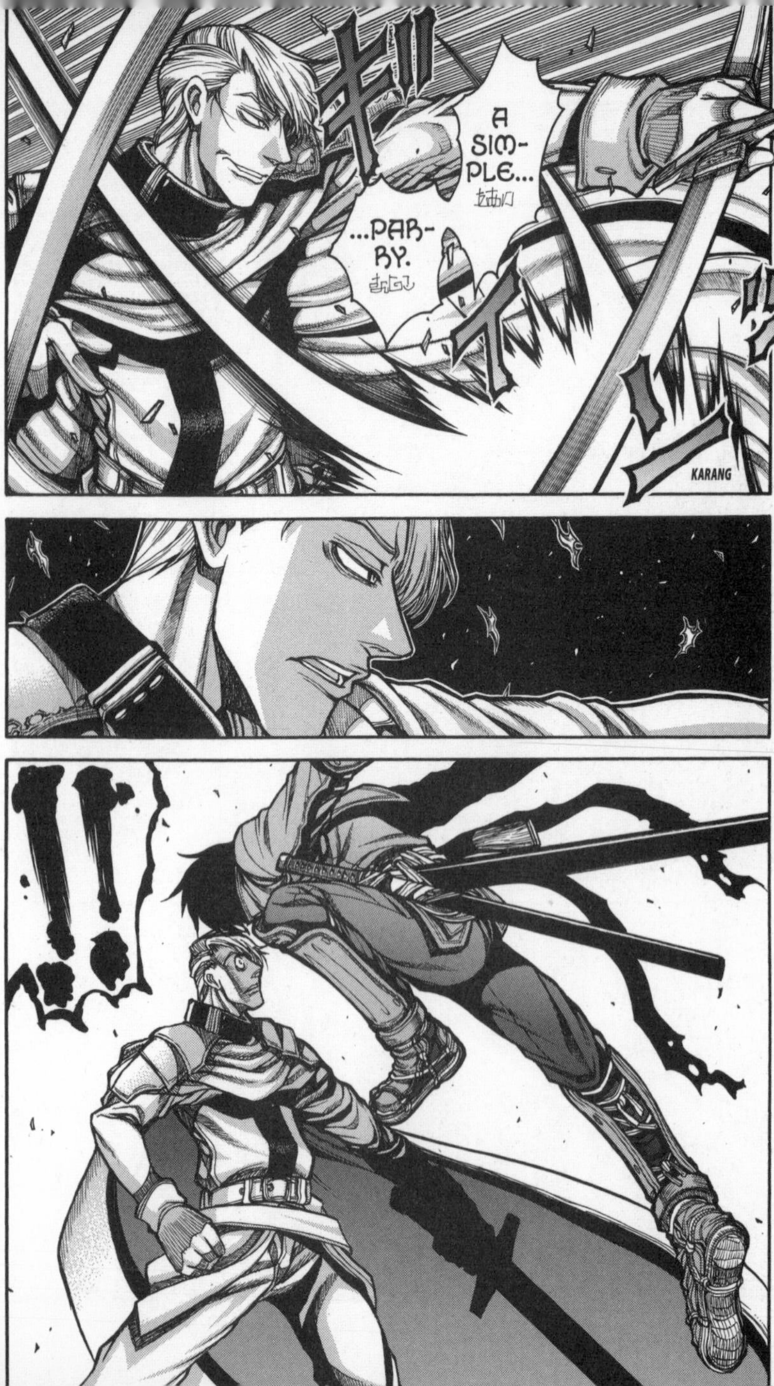
A SIMPLE...
...PARRY.
KARANG

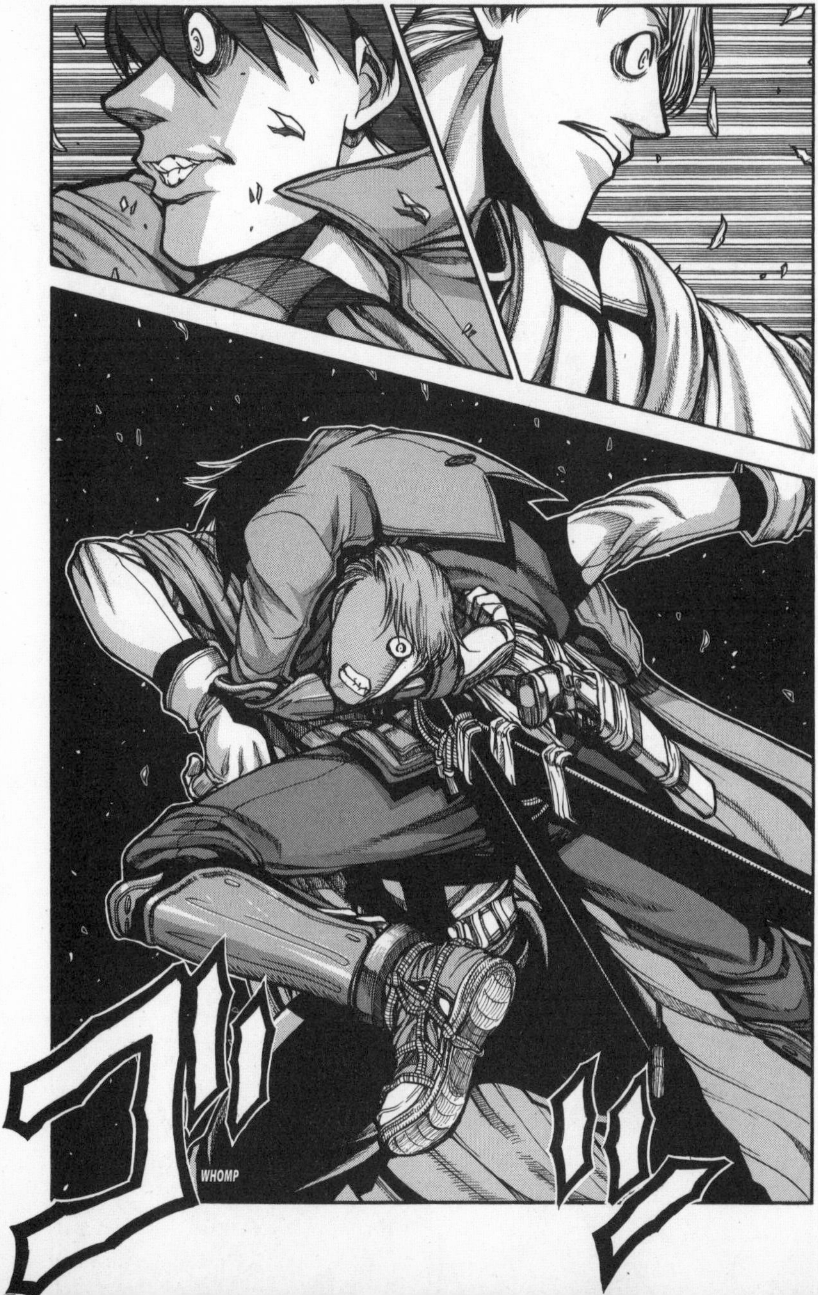
WHOMP

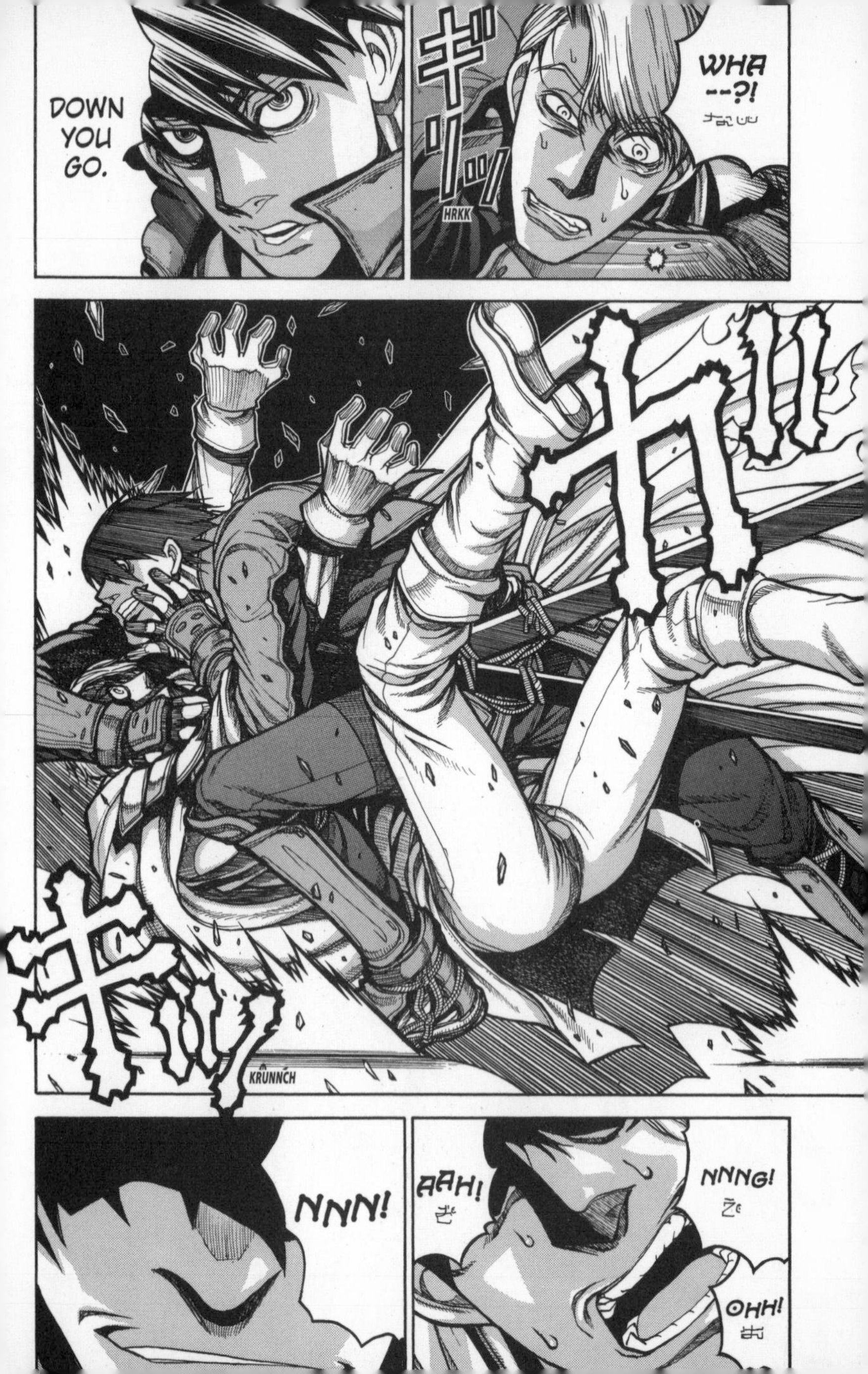
WHA --?!
HRKK
DOWN YOU GO.
KRUNNCH
NNNG!
AAH!
OHH!
NNN!

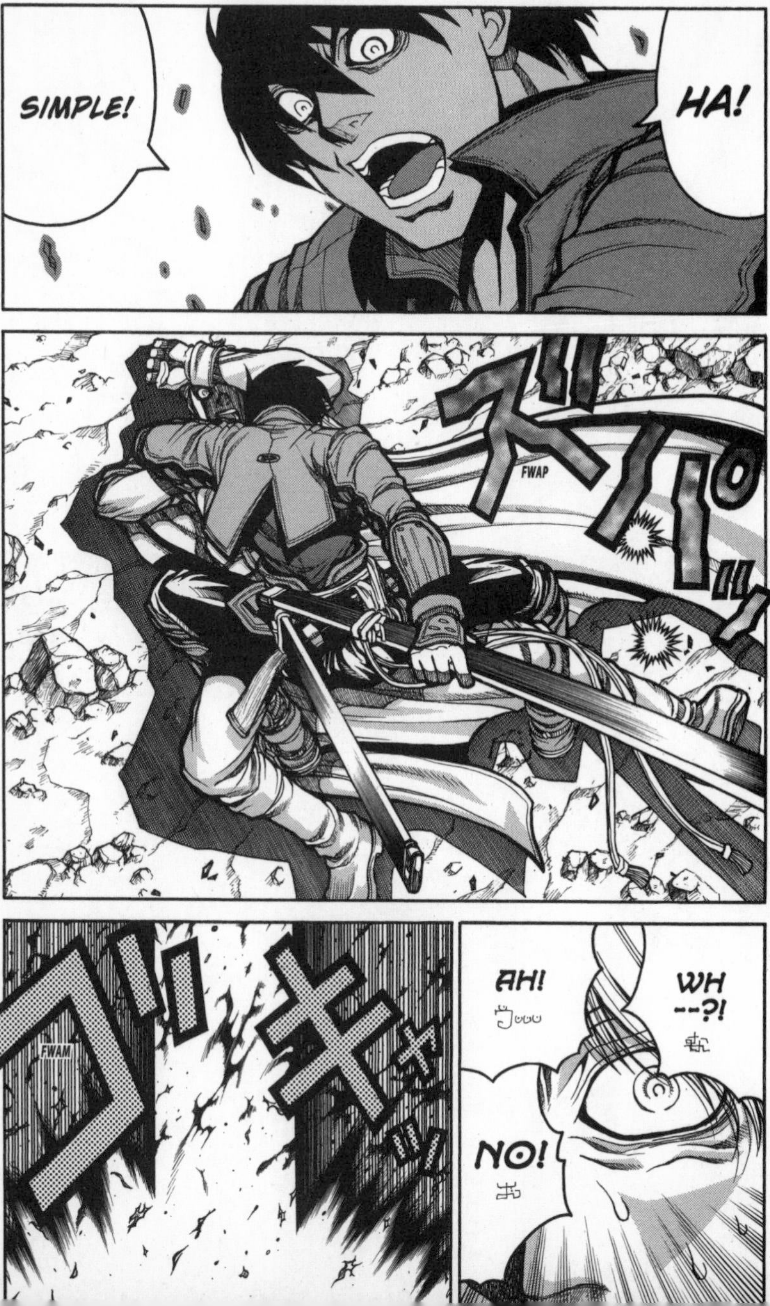
HA!
SIMPLE!
FWAP
WH--?!
AH!
NO!
FWAM

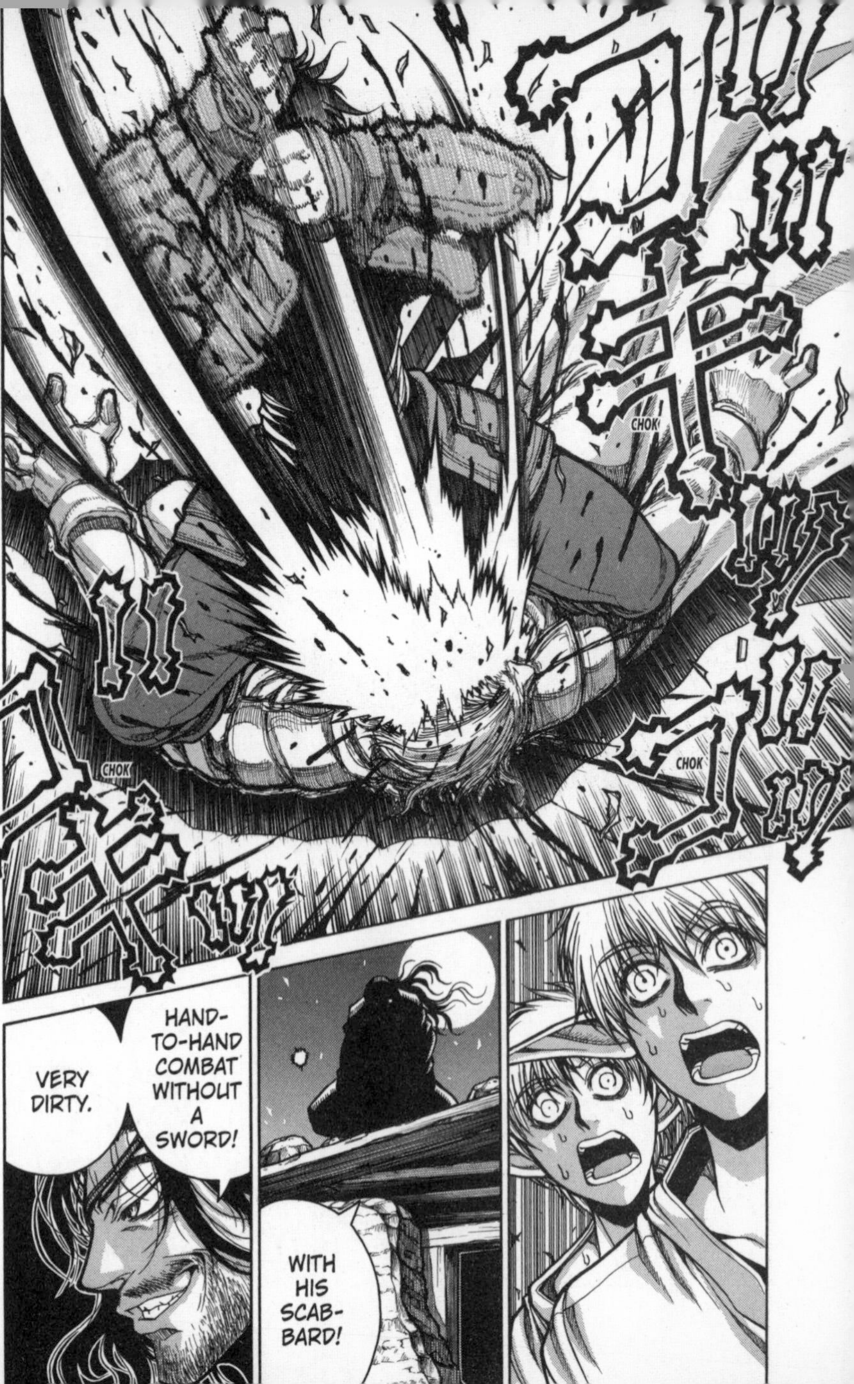
CHOK
CHOK
CHOK
WITH HIS SCAB-BARD!
HAND-TO-HAND COMBAT WITHOUT A SWORD!
VERY DIRTY.

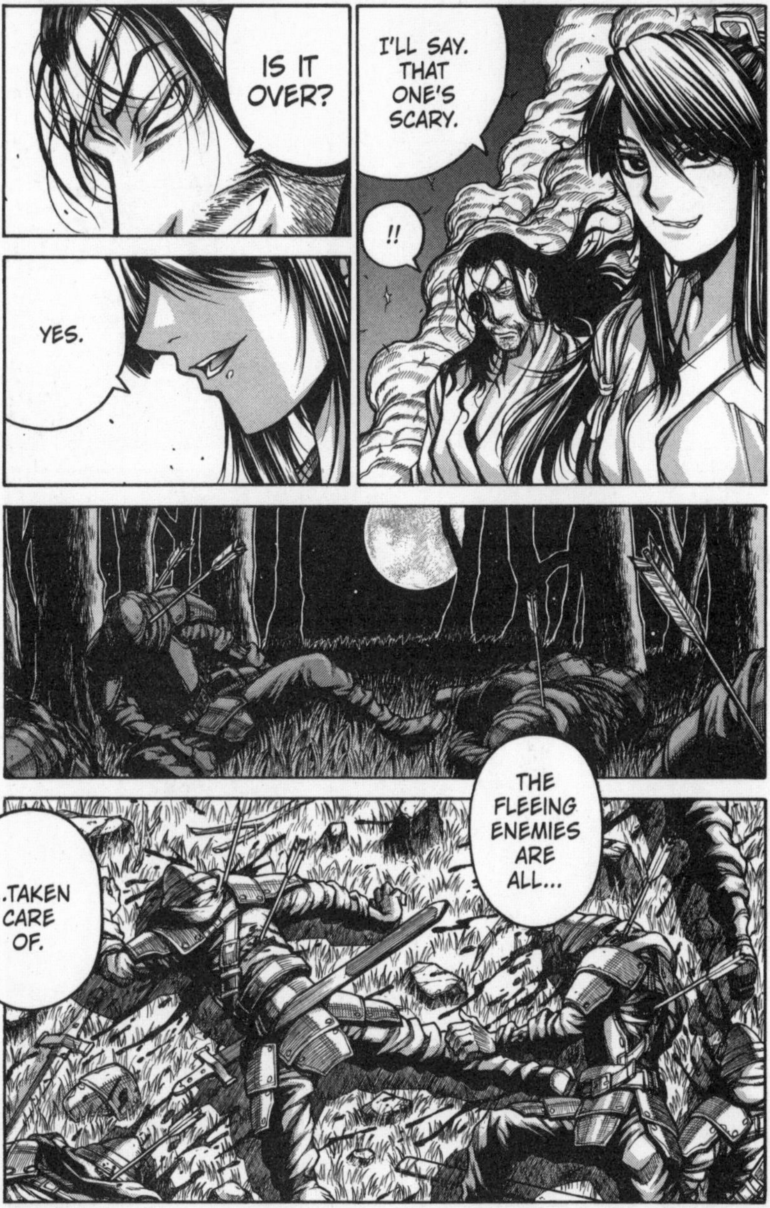
I'LL SAY. THAT ONE'S SCARY.
!!
IS IT OVER?
YES.
THE FLEEING ENEMIES ARE ALL...
...TAKEN CARE OF.

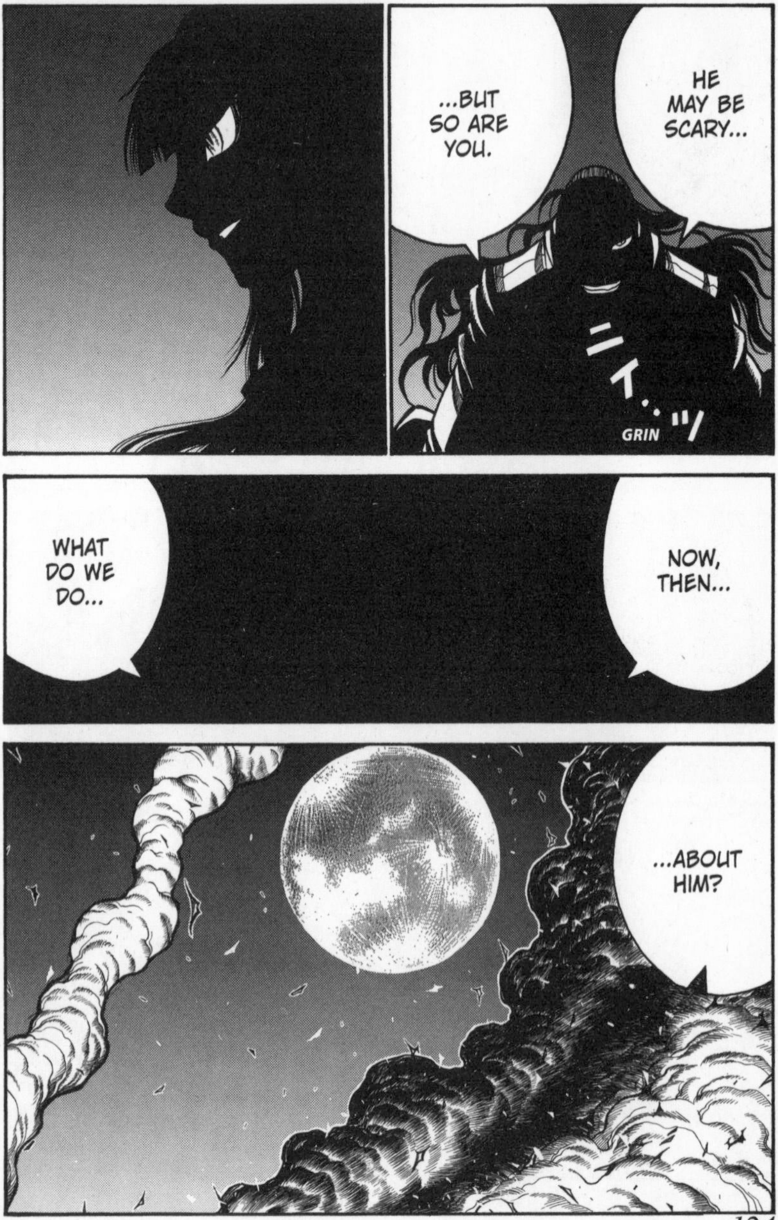
HE MAY BE SCARY...
...BUT SO ARE YOU.
GRIN
NOW, THEN...
WHAT DO WE DO...
...ABOUT HIM?

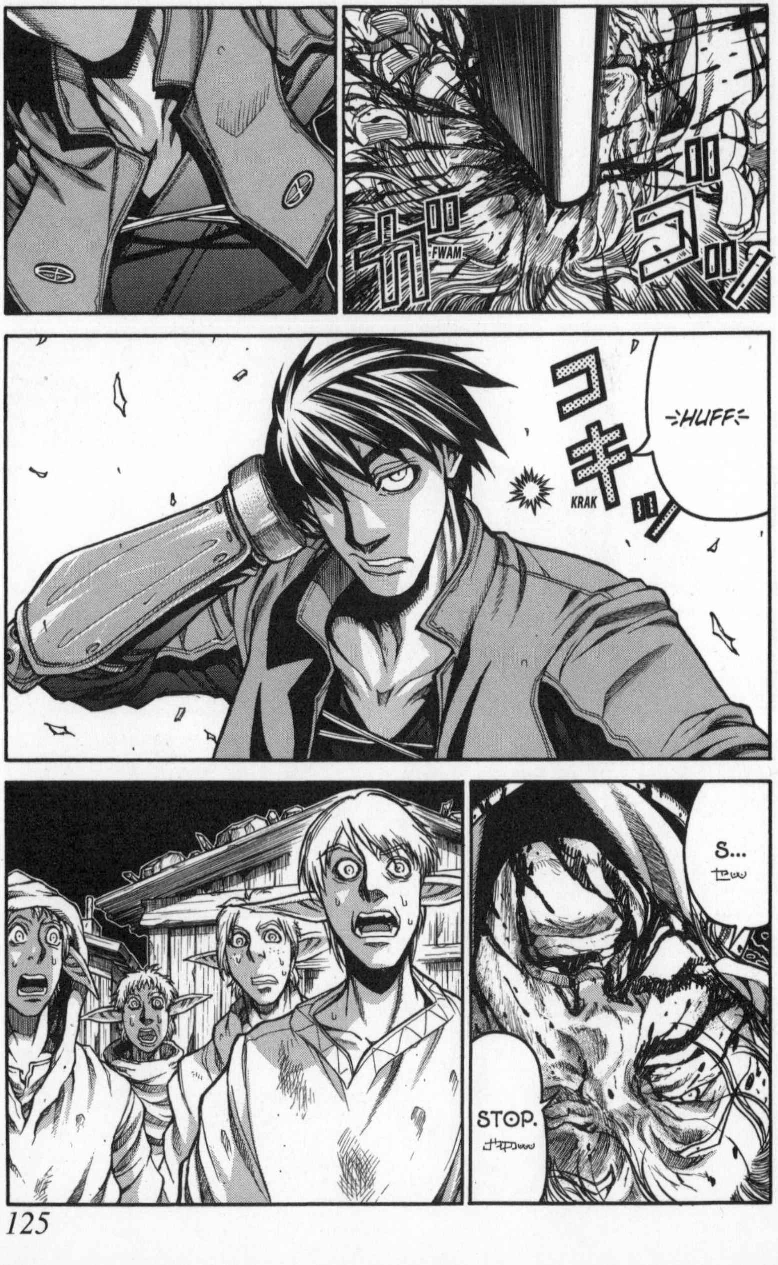
FWAM
HUFF
KRAK
S...
STOP.

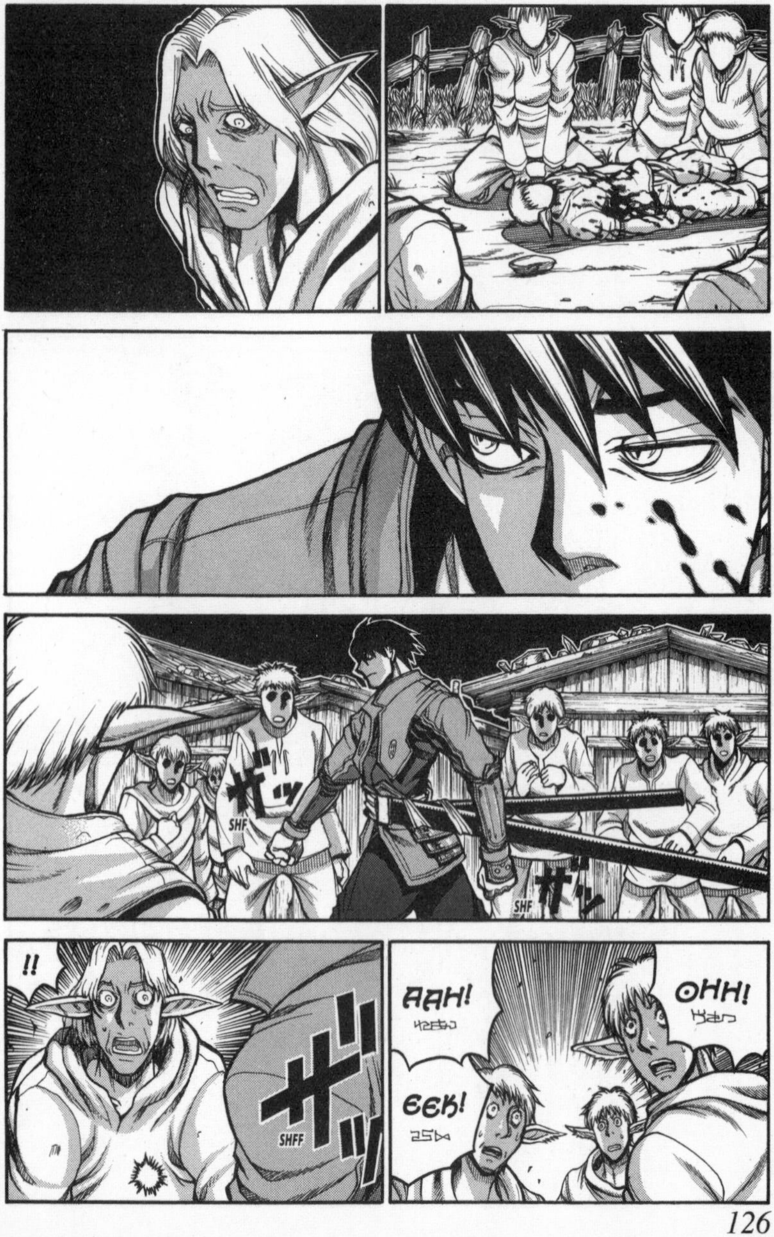
SHF
SHF
OHH!
AAH!
EEK!
!!
SHFF

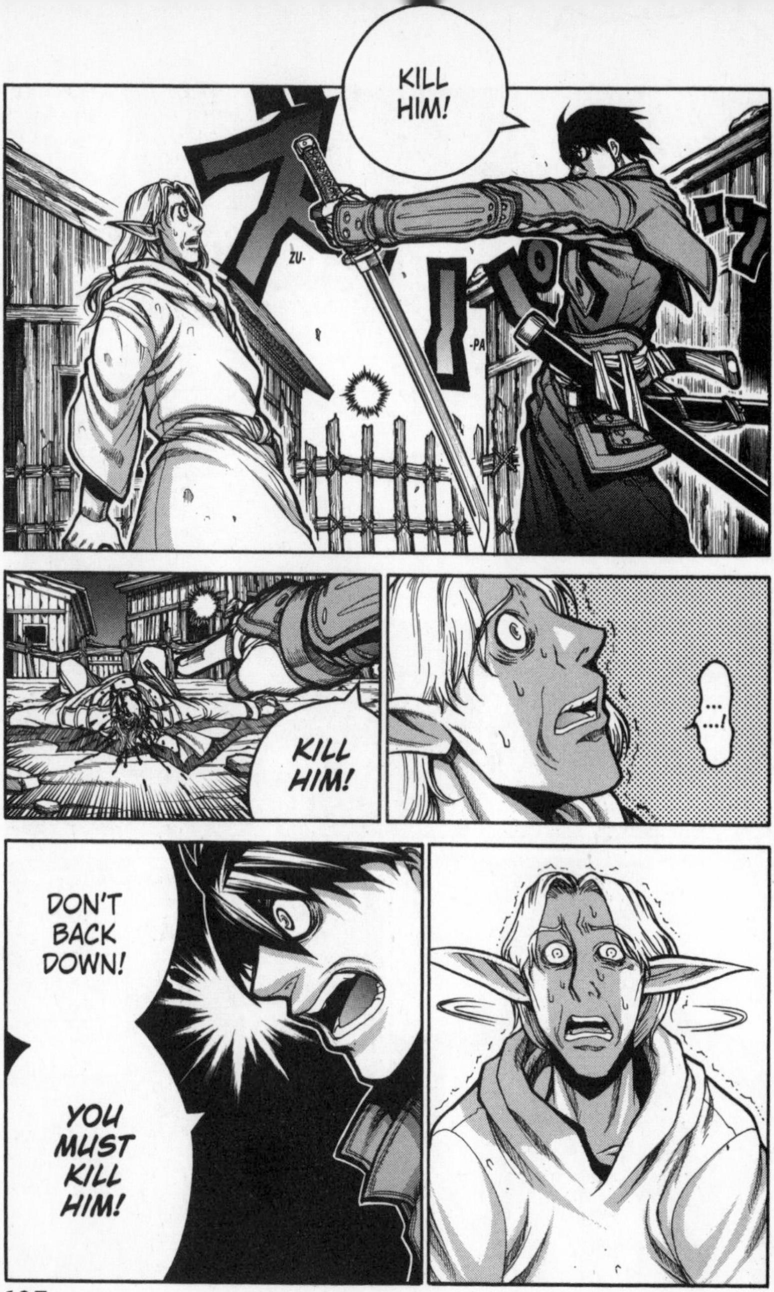

KILL HIM!
ZU-
-PA
......!
KILL HIM!
DON'T BACK DOWN!
YOU MUST KILL HIM!

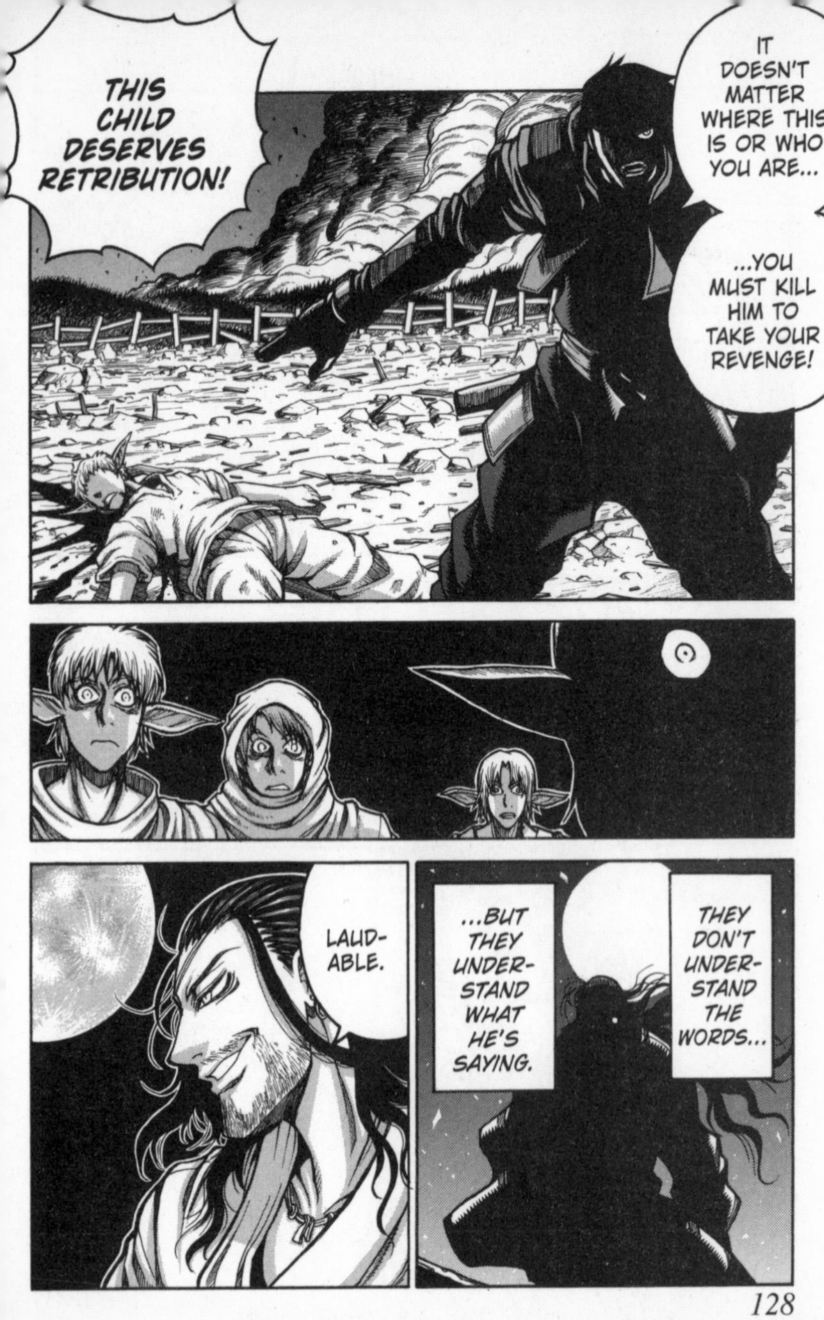
IT DOESN'T MATTER WHERE THIS IS OR WHO YOU ARE...
...YOU MUST KILL HIM TO TAKE YOUR REVENGE!
THIS CHILD DESERVES RETRIBUTION!
THEY DON'T UNDER-STAND THE WORDS...
...BUT THEY UNDER-STAND WHAT HE'S SAYING.
LAUD-ABLE.

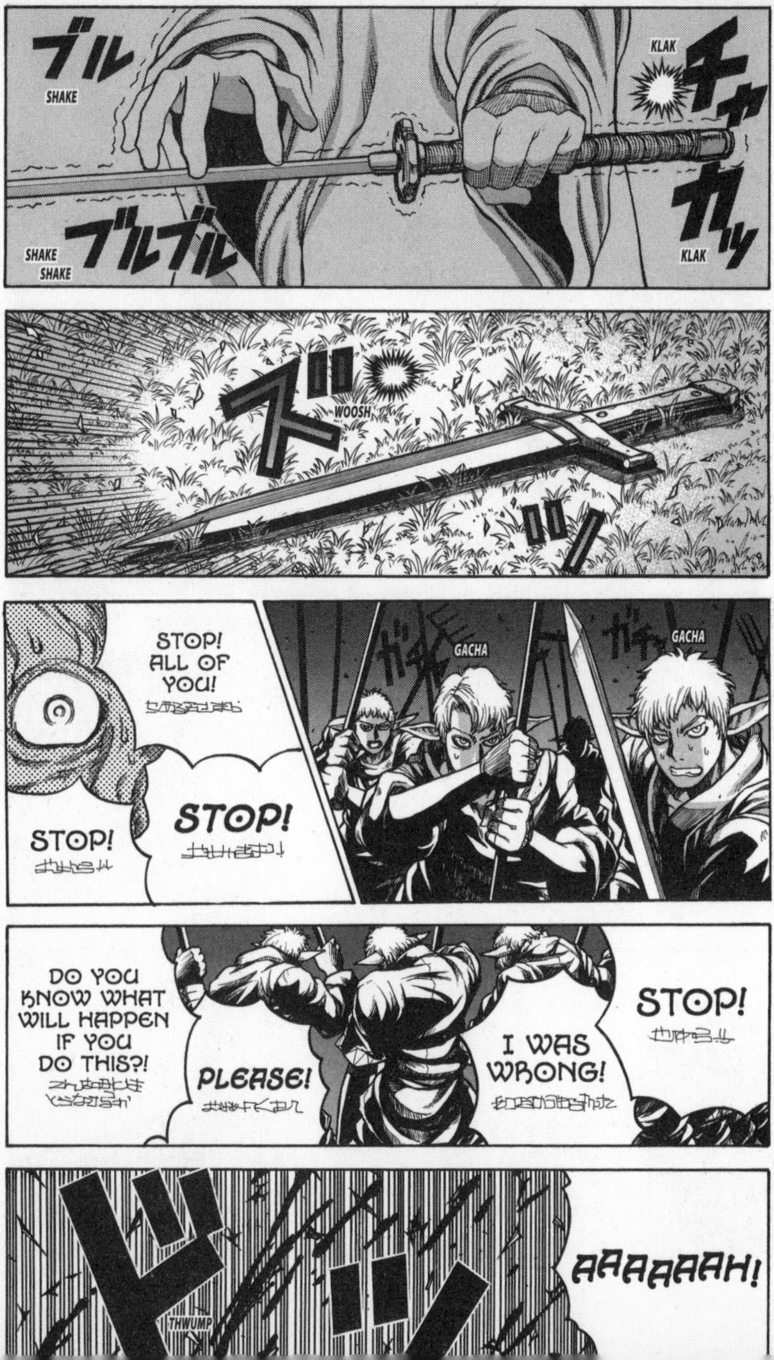
KLAK
KLAK
SHAKE
SHAKE SHAKE
WOOSH
GACHA
GACHA
STOP! ALL OF YOU!
STOP!
STOP!
STOP!
I WAS WRONG!
PLEASE!
DO YOU KNOW WHAT WILL HAPPEN IF YOU DO THIS?!
AAAAAAH!
THWUMP

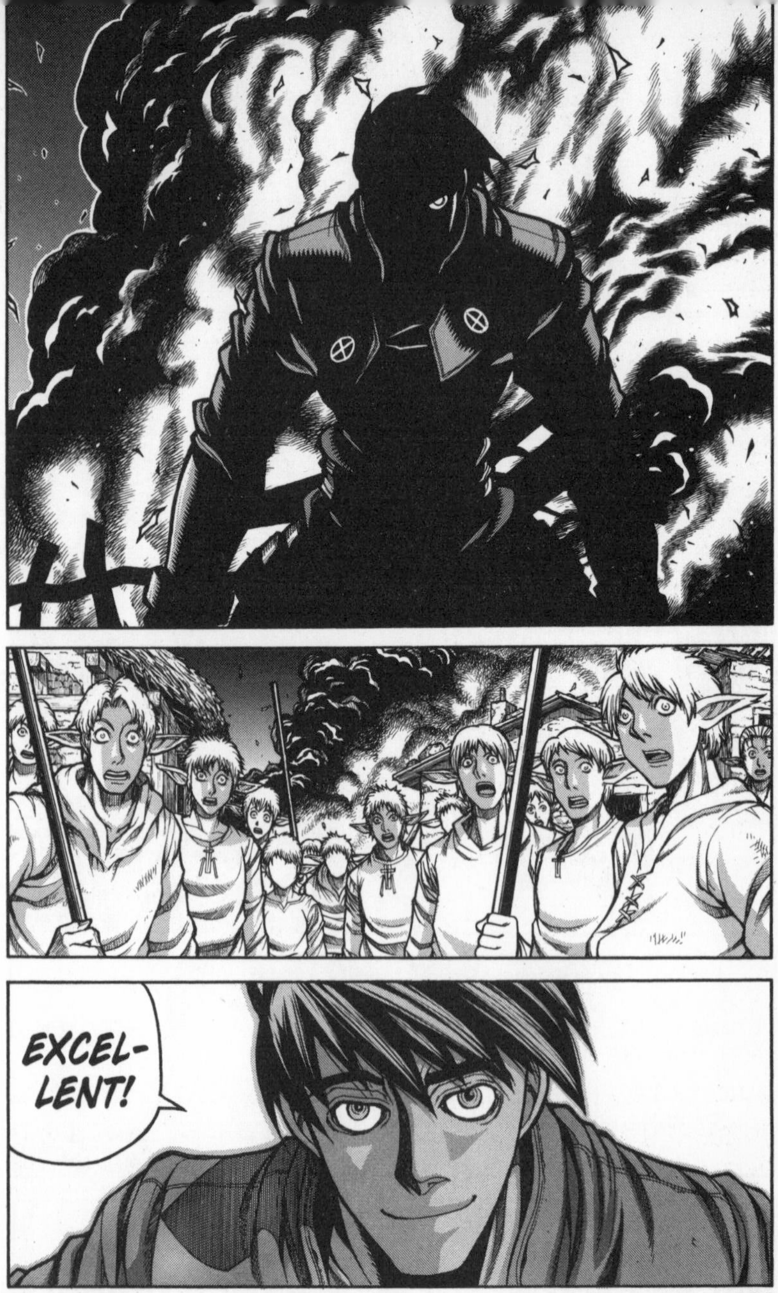
EXCEL-LENT!

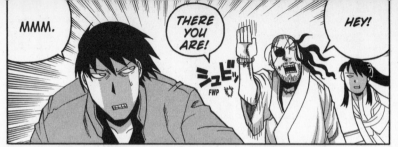

HEY!
THERE YOU ARE!
シュビッ
FWP
MMM.
WHERE HAVE YOU BEEN?
I'M STILL RECOVER-ING.
WE'VE BEEN TAKING CARE OF THINGS.
ゴ
DO
YES. THINGS.
ゴゴゴ
DO DO DO
YOU MUST BE TIRED.
TAKE A SEAT.
フラフラ
FLT
FLT
フラ
FLT
I WAS THINKING OF TAK-ING A REST.
ギラリ
SHNG
YOU SHOULD AS WELL.
?
"THIS IS TERRIBLE. JUST TERRIBLE.
"MASTER. THEY...
"THEY--!"

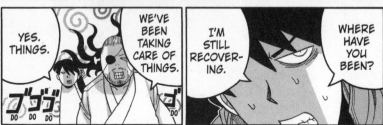

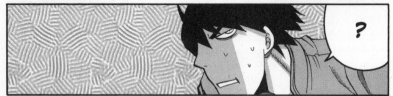

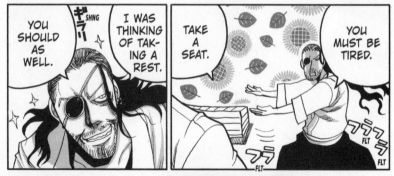

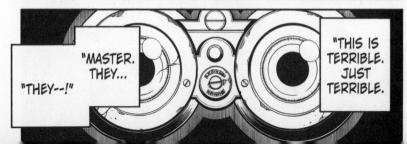

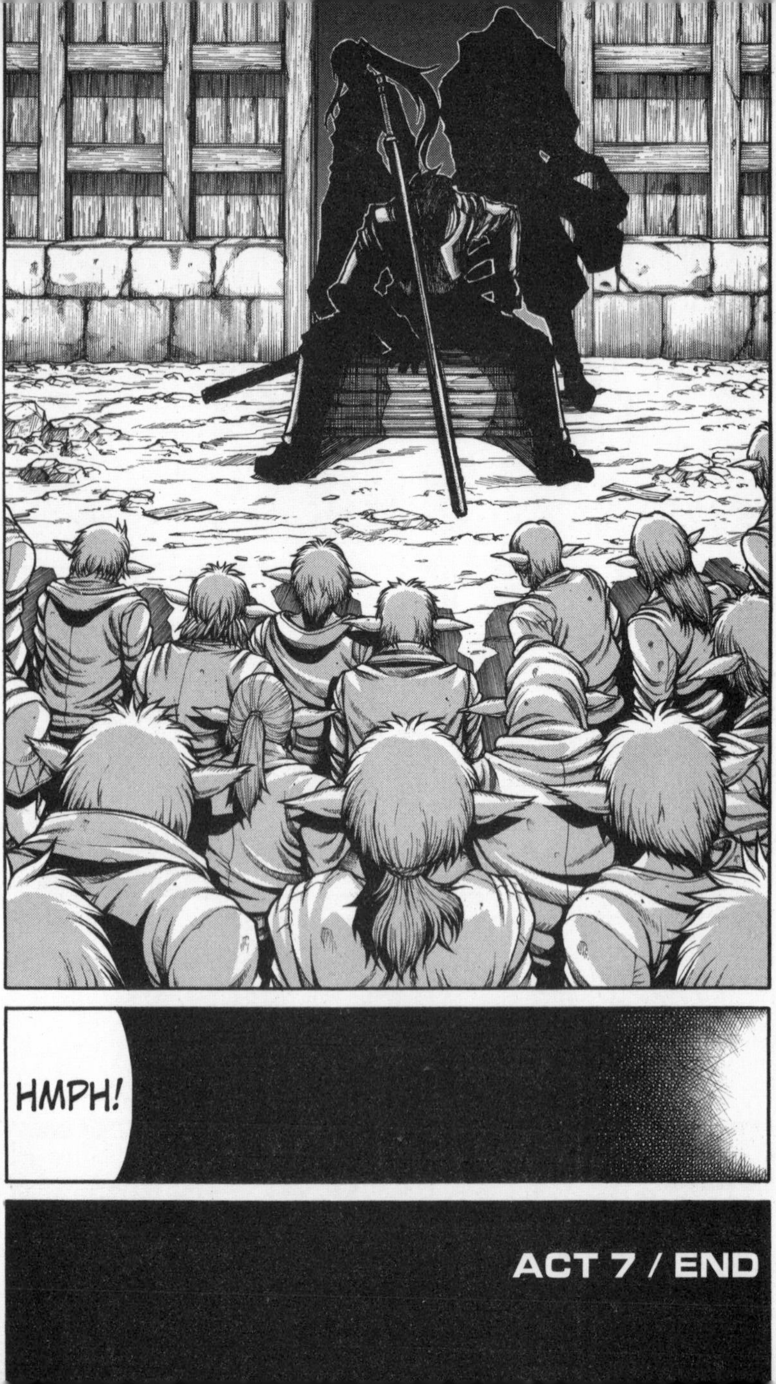
HMPH!
ACT 7 / END

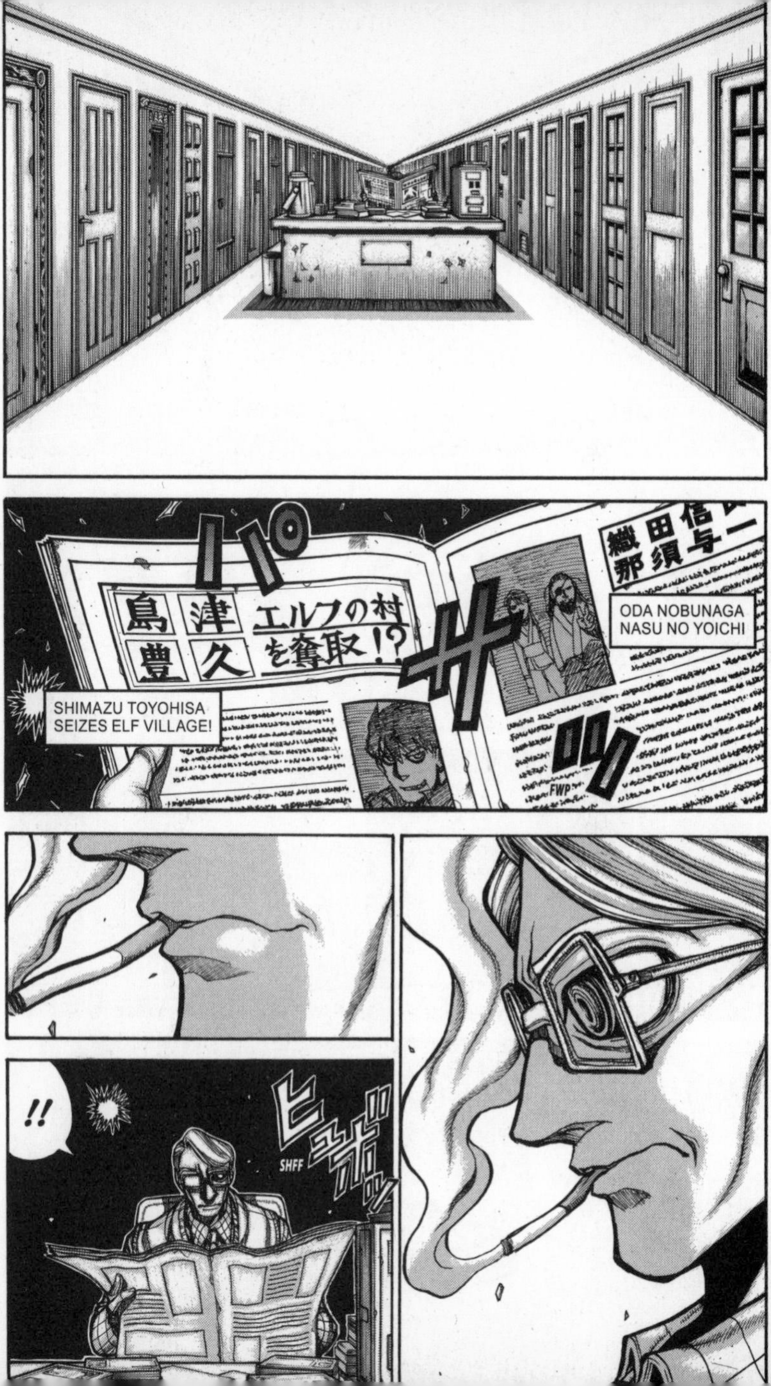
織田信
那須与一
ODA NOBUNAGA
NASU NO YOICHI
パサッ
FWP
島津豊久 エルフの村を奪取!?
SHIMAZU TOYOHISA
SEIZES ELF VILLAGE!
ヒュボッ
SHFF
!!

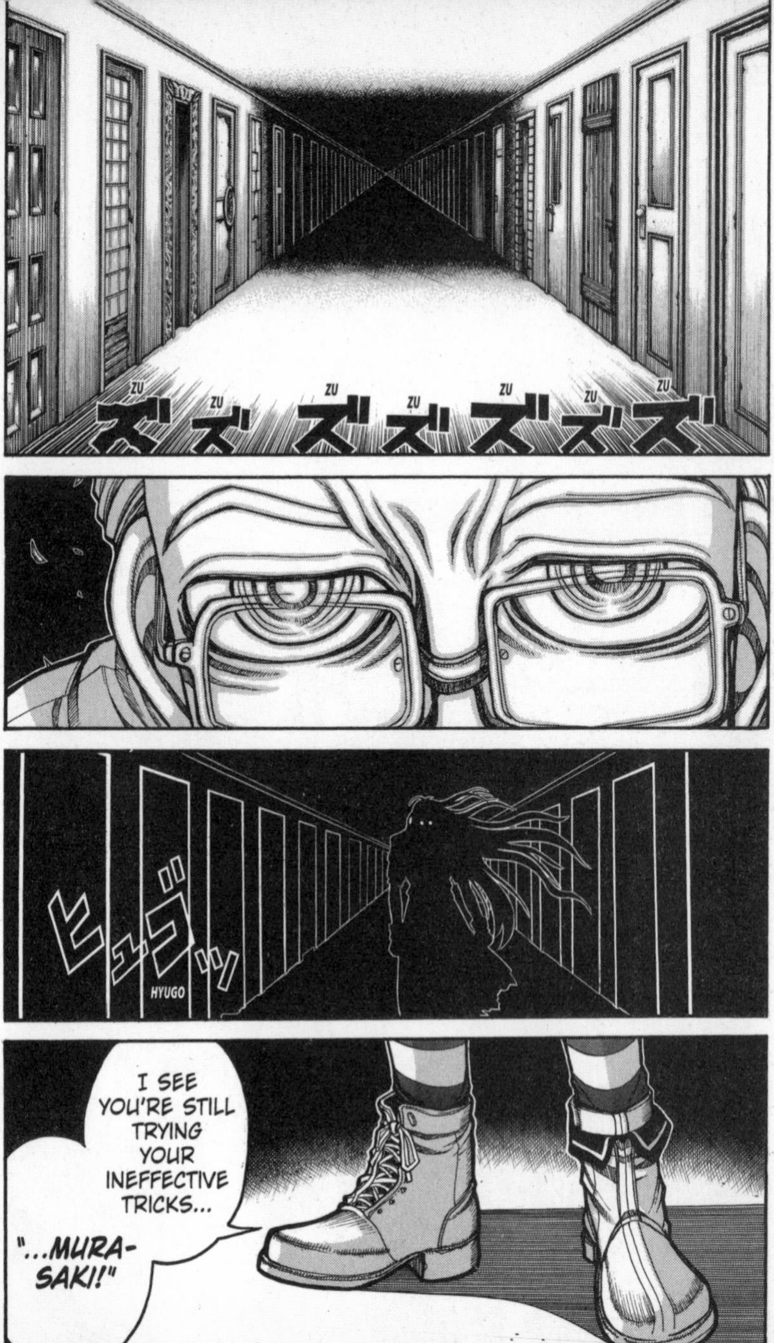
ZU ZU ZU ZU ZU ZU ZU
ズズズズズズズ
ヒュゴッ
HYUGO
I SEE YOU'RE STILL TRYING YOUR INEFFECTIVE TRICKS...
"...MURA-SAKI!"

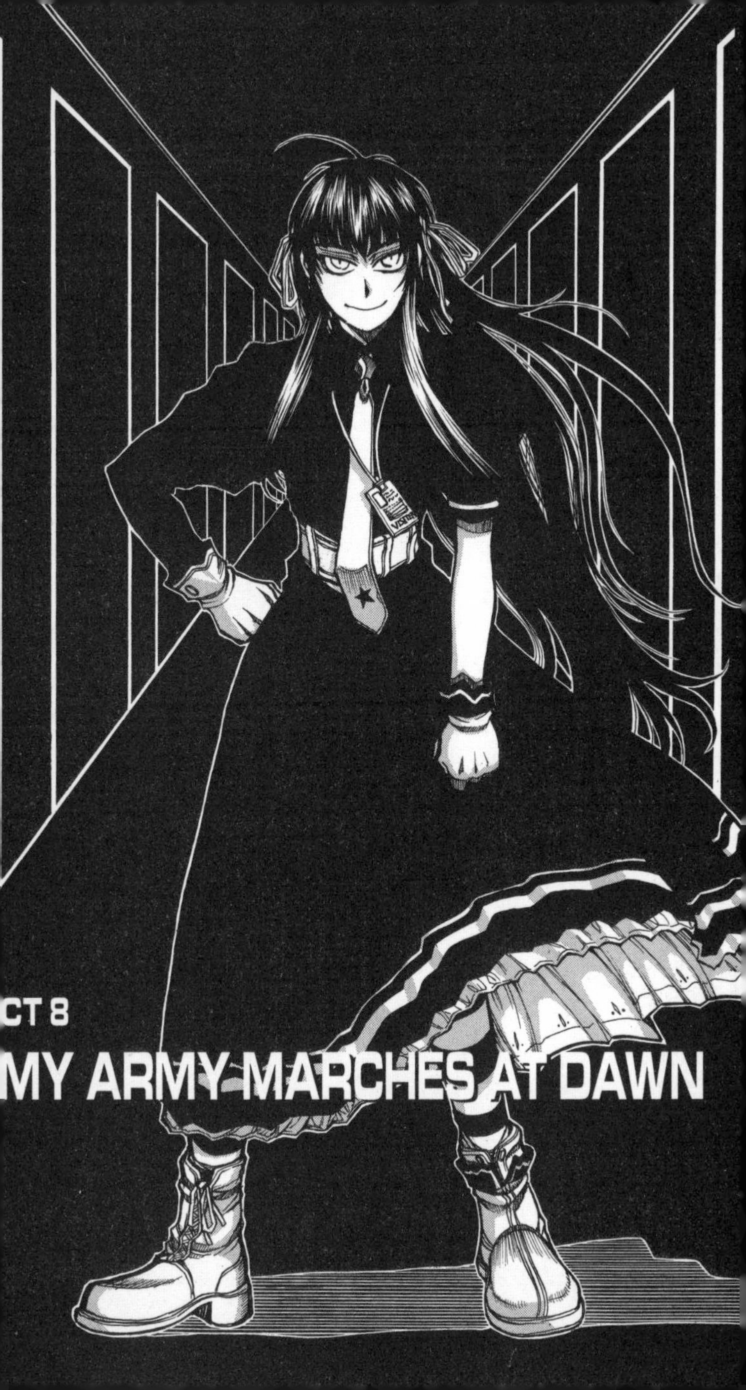
CT 8
MY ARMY MARCHES AT DAWN

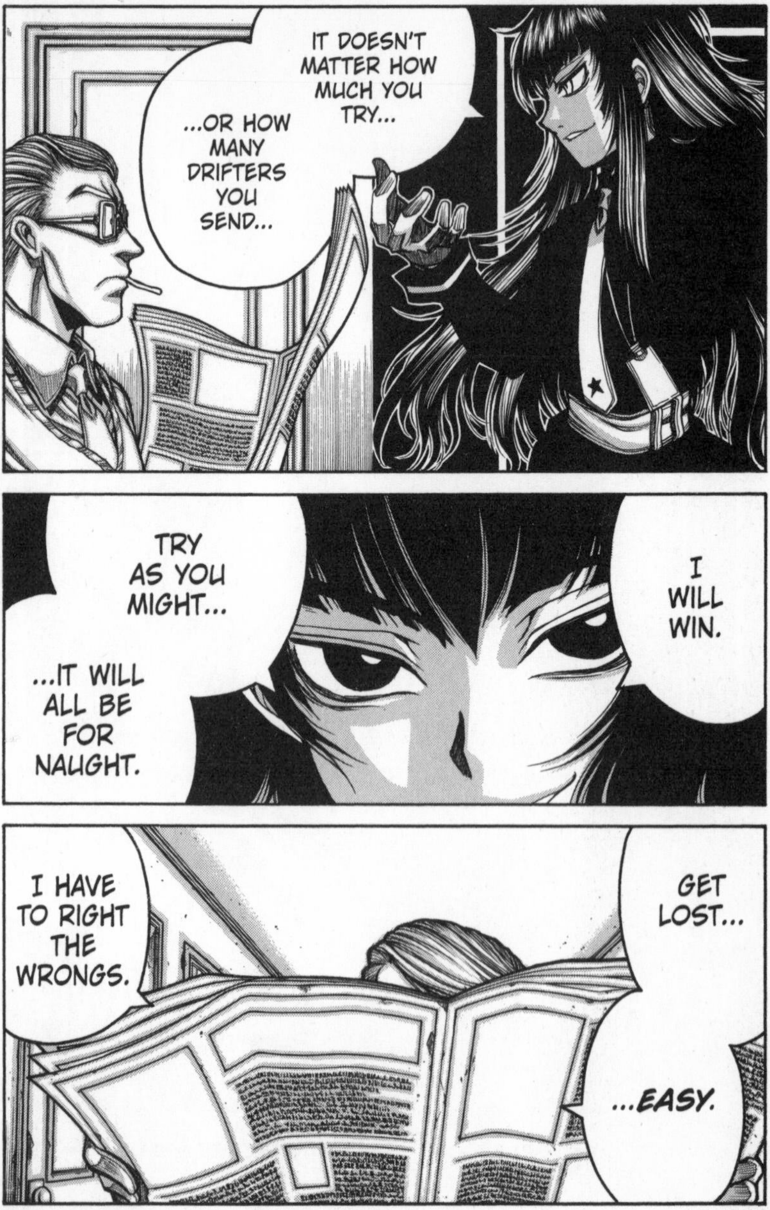
IT DOESN'T MATTER HOW MUCH YOU TRY...
...OR HOW MANY DRIFTERS YOU SEND...
I WILL WIN.
TRY AS YOU MIGHT...
...IT WILL ALL BE FOR NAUGHT.
GET LOST...
...EASY.
I HAVE TO RIGHT THE WRONGS.

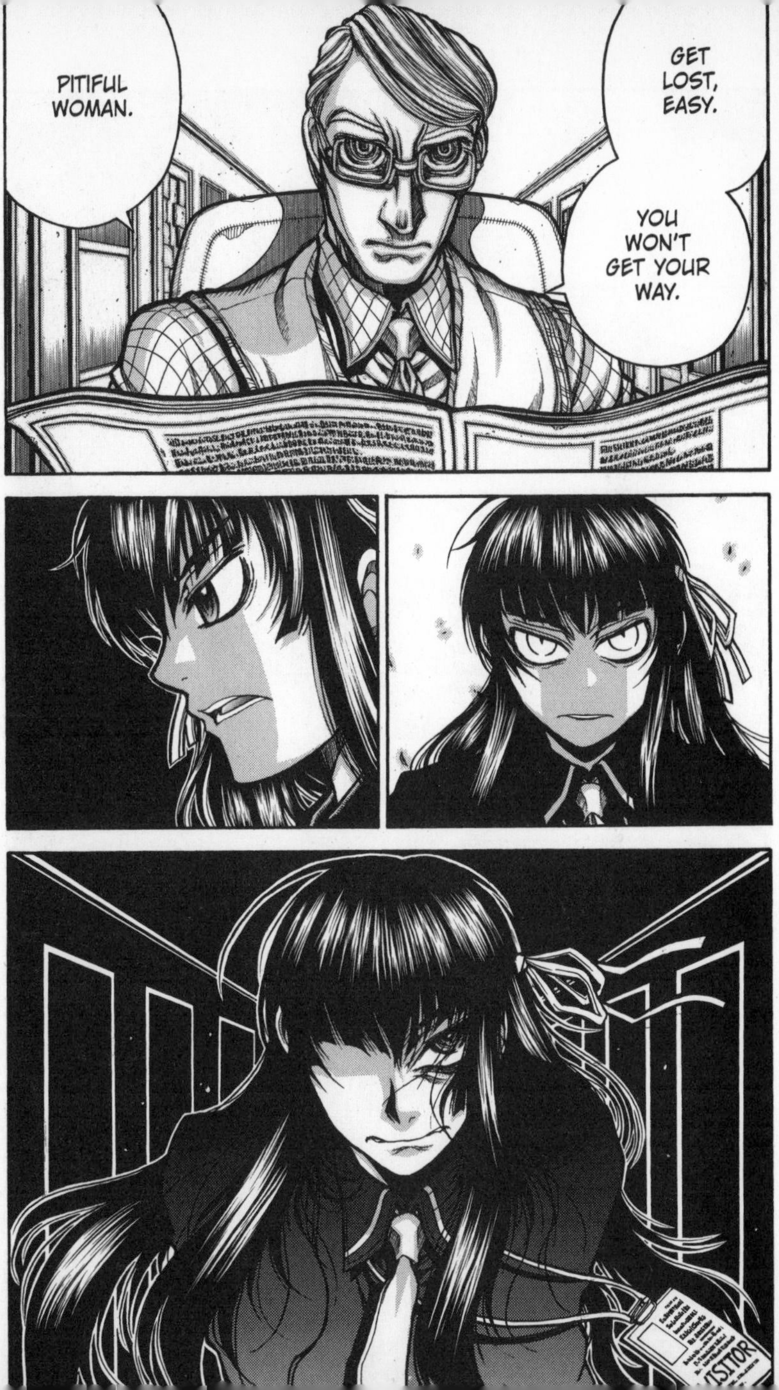
GET LOST, EASY.
YOU WON'T GET YOUR WAY.
PITIFUL WOMAN.
VISITOR

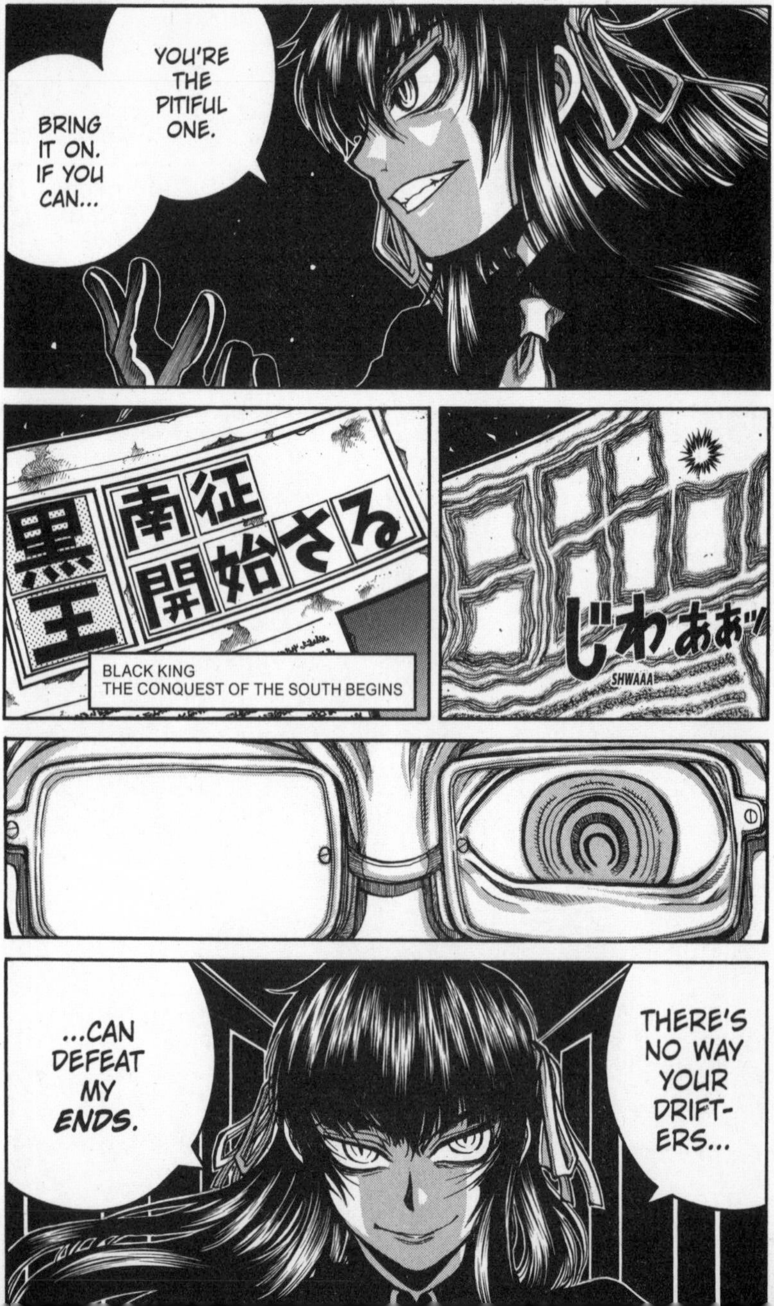
YOU'RE THE PITIFUL ONE.
BRING IT ON. IF YOU CAN...
じわぁぁッ
SHWAAA
黒王 南征開始さる
BLACK KING THE CONQUEST OF THE SOUTH BEGINS
THERE'S NO WAY YOUR DRIFTERS...
...CAN DEFEAT MY ENDS.

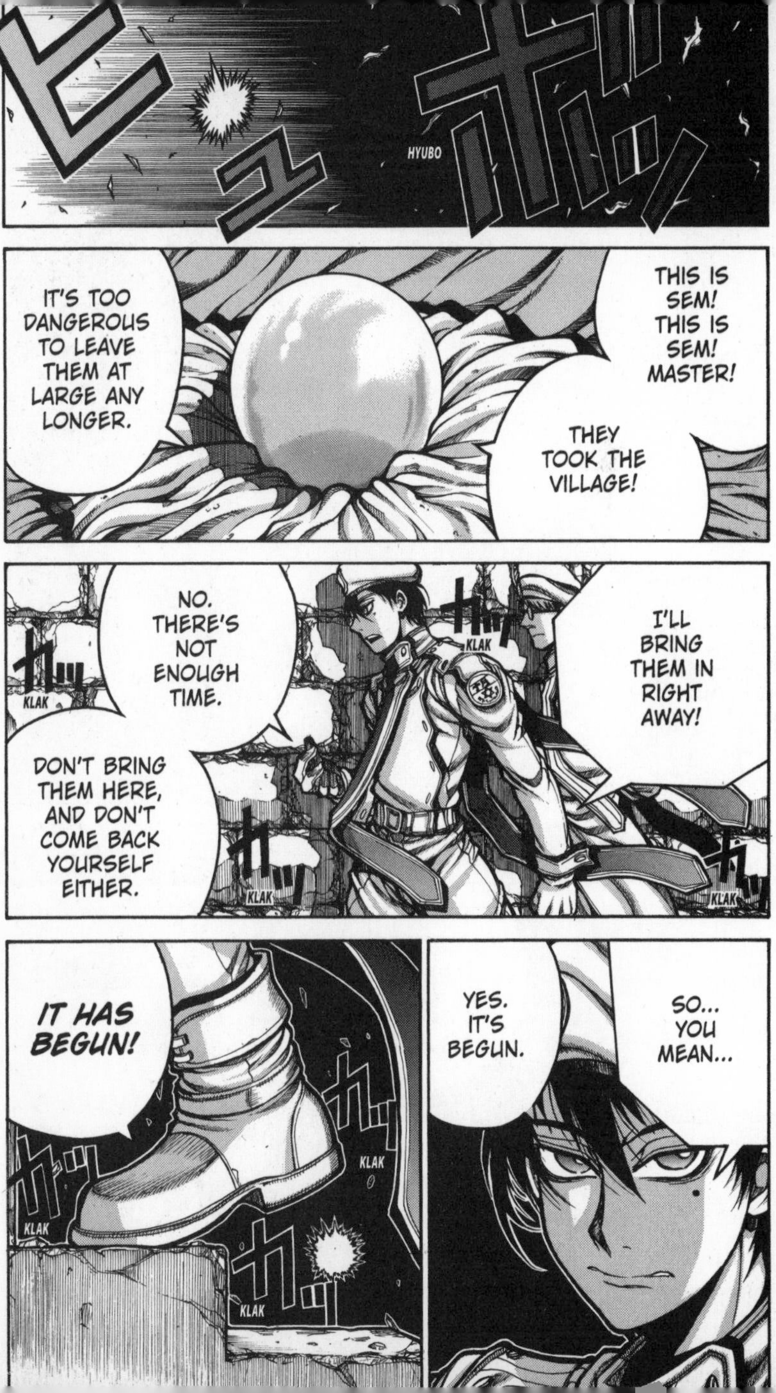
HYUBO
THIS IS SEM! THIS IS SEM! MASTER!
THEY TOOK THE VILLAGE!
IT'S TOO DANGEROUS TO LEAVE THEM AT LARGE ANY LONGER.
I'LL BRING THEM IN RIGHT AWAY!
KLAK
KLAK
NO. THERE'S NOT ENOUGH TIME.
KLAK
DON'T BRING THEM HERE, AND DON'T COME BACK YOURSELF EITHER.
KLAK
SO... YOU MEAN...
YES. IT'S BEGUN.
IT HAS BEGUN!
KLAK
KLAK
KLAK

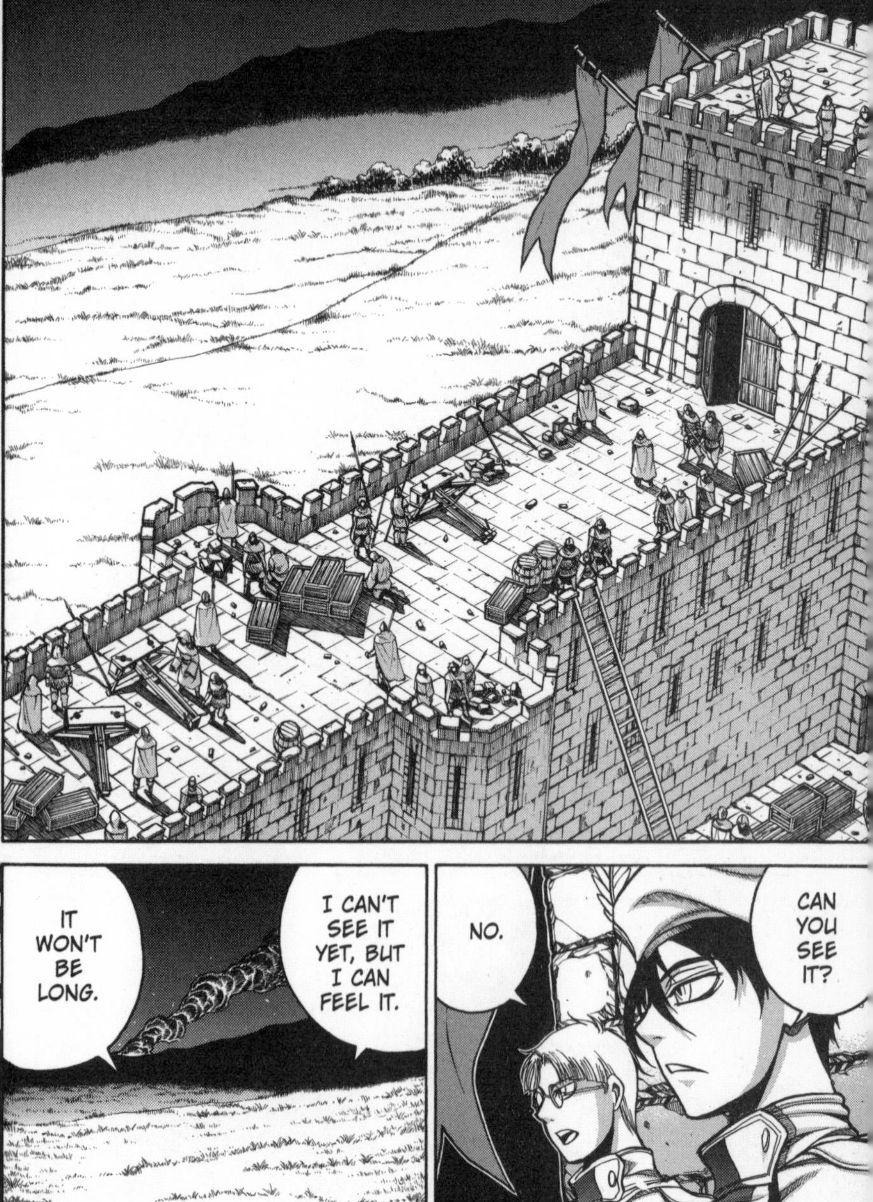
CAN YOU SEE IT?
NO.
I CAN'T SEE IT YET, BUT I CAN FEEL IT.
IT WON'T BE LONG.

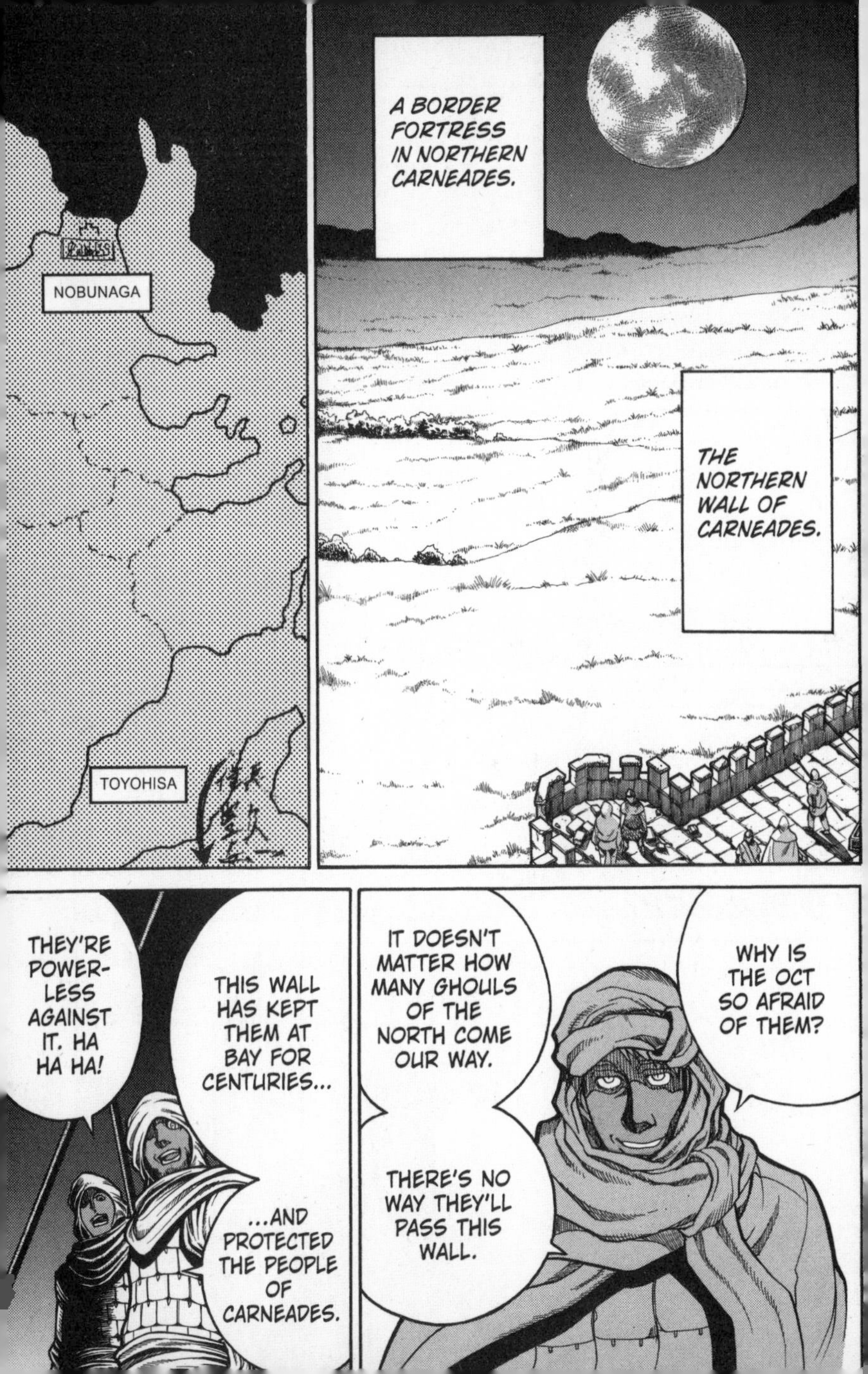
A BORDER FORTRESS IN NORTHERN CARNEADES.
THE NORTHERN WALL OF CARNEADES.
NOBUNAGA
TOYOHISA
WHY IS THE OCT SO AFRAID OF THEM?
IT DOESN'T MATTER HOW MANY GHOULS OF THE NORTH COME OUR WAY.
THERE'S NO WAY THEY'LL PASS THIS WALL.
THIS WALL HAS KEPT THEM AT BAY FOR CENTURIES...
...AND PROTECTED THE PEOPLE OF CARNEADES.
THEY'RE POWER-LESS AGAINST IT. HA HA HA!

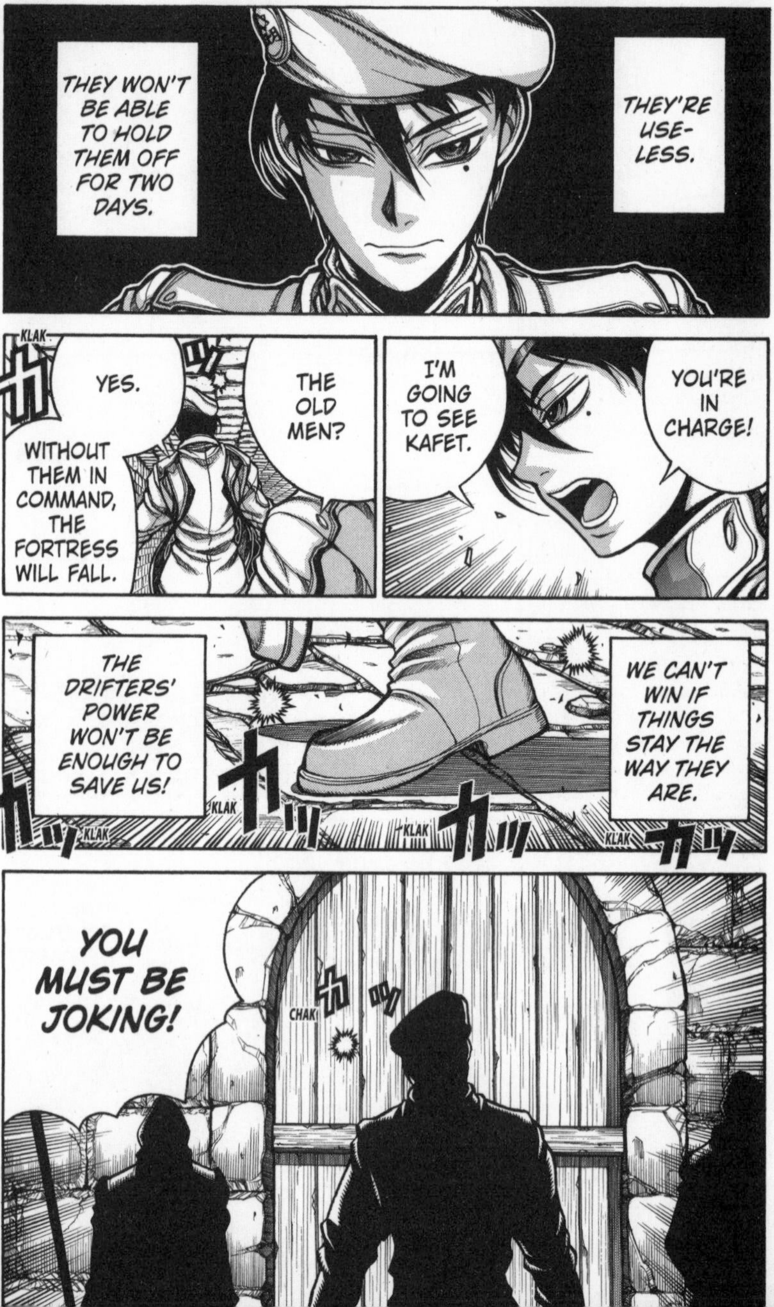
THEY'RE USE-LESS.
THEY WON'T BE ABLE TO HOLD THEM OFF FOR TWO DAYS.
YOU'RE IN CHARGE!
I'M GOING TO SEE KAFET.
THE OLD MEN?
KLAK
YES.
WITHOUT THEM IN COMMAND, THE FORTRESS WILL FALL.
WE CAN'T WIN IF THINGS STAY THE WAY THEY ARE.
KLAK
KLAK
KLAK
KLAK
THE DRIFTERS' POWER WON'T BE ENOUGH TO SAVE US!
CHAK
YOU MUST BE JOKING!

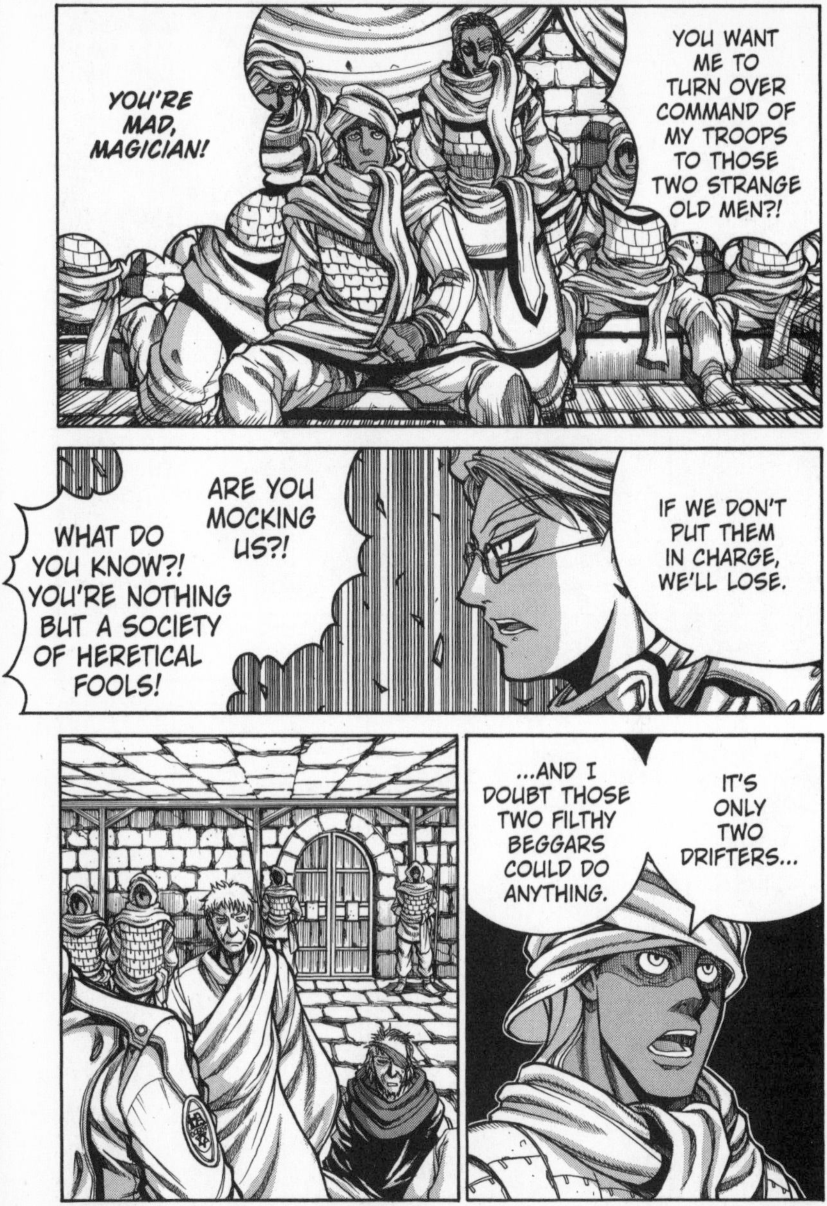
YOU WANT ME TO TURN OVER COMMAND OF MY TROOPS TO THOSE TWO STRANGE OLD MEN?!
YOU'RE MAD, MAGICIAN!
IF WE DON'T PUT THEM IN CHARGE, WE'LL LOSE.
ARE YOU MOCKING US?!
WHAT DO YOU KNOW?! YOU'RE NOTHING BUT A SOCIETY OF HERETICAL FOOLS!
IT'S ONLY TWO DRIFTERS...
...AND I DOUBT THOSE TWO FILTHY BEGGARS COULD DO ANYTHING.

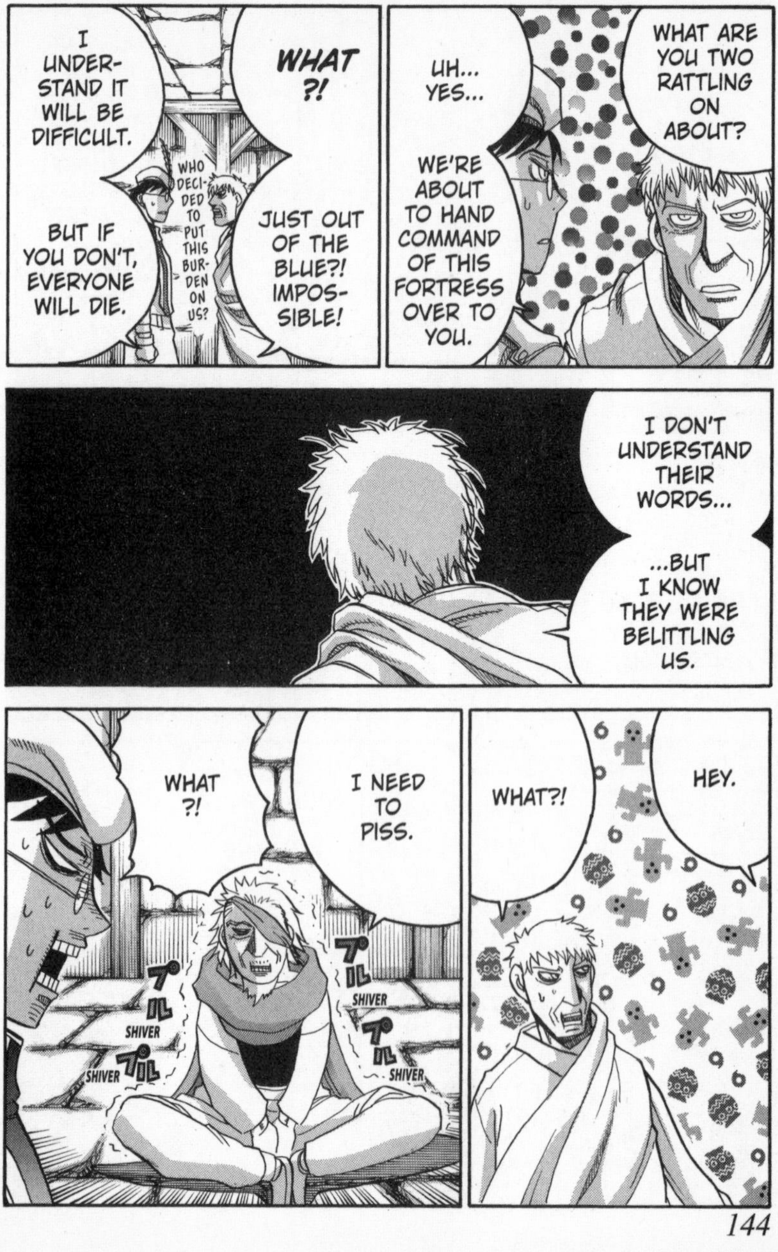
WHAT ARE YOU TWO RATTLING ON ABOUT?
UH... YES...
WE'RE ABOUT TO HAND COMMAND OF THIS FORTRESS OVER TO YOU.
WHAT ?!
JUST OUT OF THE BLUE?! IMPOSSIBLE!
WHO DECIDED TO PUT THIS BURDEN ON US?
I UNDERSTAND IT WILL BE DIFFICULT.
BUT IF YOU DON'T, EVERYONE WILL DIE.
I DON'T UNDERSTAND THEIR WORDS...
...BUT I KNOW THEY WERE BELITTLING US.
HEY.
WHAT?!
I NEED TO PISS.
WHAT ?!
プル SHIVER
プル SHIVER
プル SHIVER
プル SHIVER

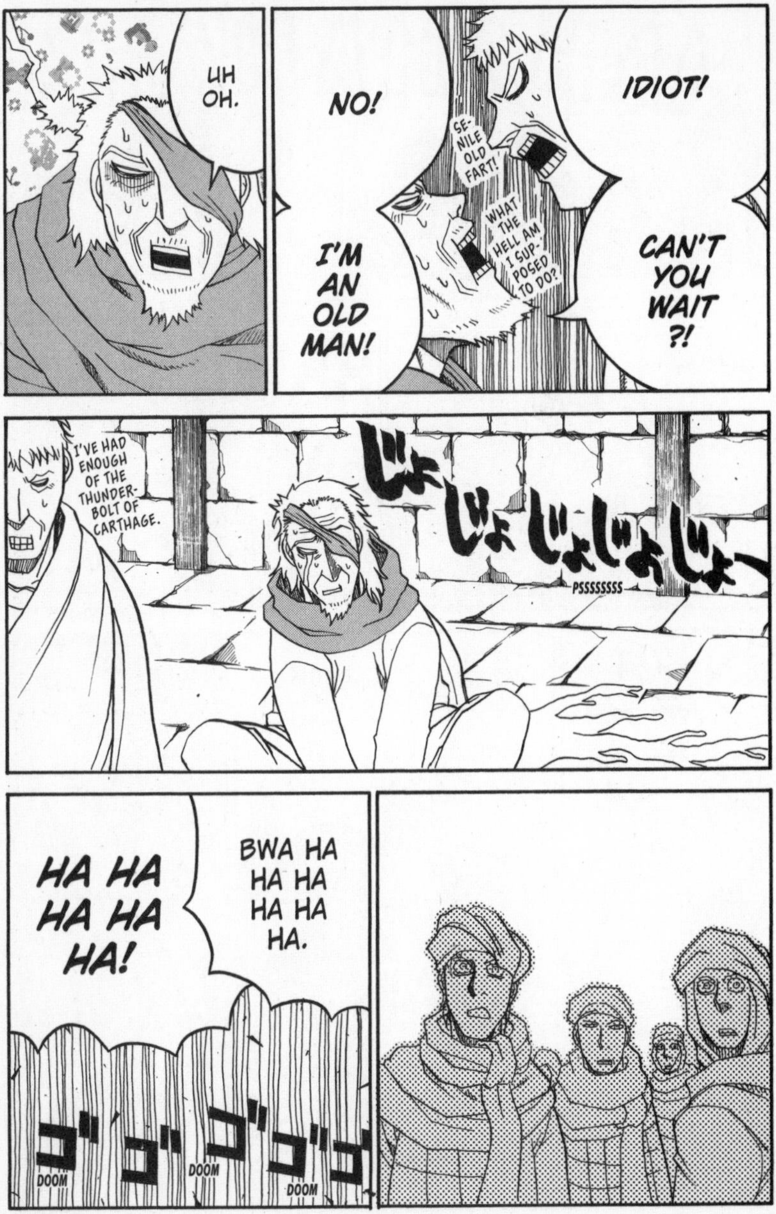
IDIOT!
CAN'T YOU WAIT ?!
SE-NILE OLD FART!
WHAT THE HELL AM I SUP-POSED TO DO?
NO!
I'M AN OLD MAN!
UH OH.
じょじょじょじょじょじょー
PSSSSSSSS
I'VE HAD ENOUGH OF THE THUNDER-BOLT OF CARTHAGE.
BWA HA HA HA HA HA HA.
HA HA HA HA HA!
ゴゴゴゴゴ
DOOM
DOOM
DOOM

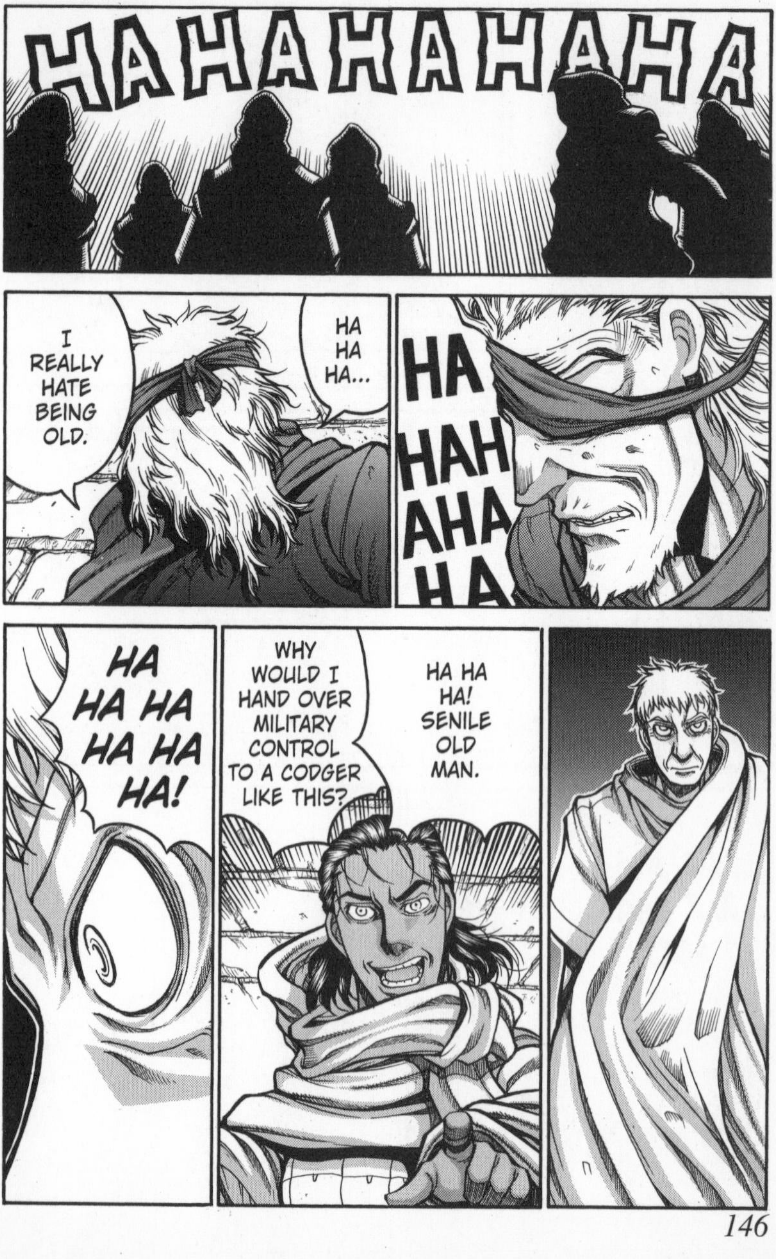
HAHAHAHAHA
HA HAH AHA HA
HA HA HA...
I REALLY HATE BEING OLD.
HA HA HA! SENILE OLD MAN.
WHY WOULD I HAND OVER MILITARY CONTROL TO A CODGER LIKE THIS?
HA HA HA HA HA HA HA!

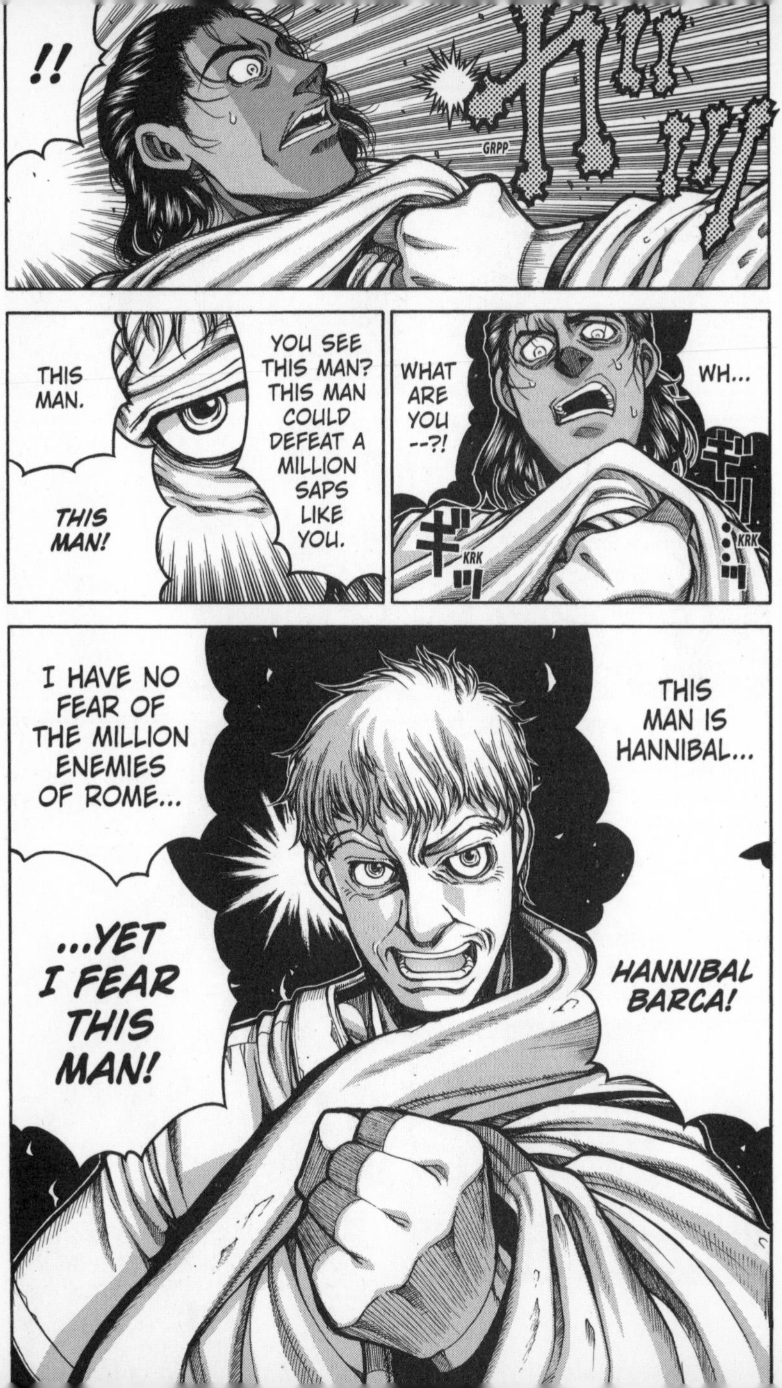
!!
GRPP
WH...
WHAT ARE YOU --?!
KRK
KRK
YOU SEE THIS MAN? THIS MAN COULD DEFEAT A MILLION SAPS LIKE YOU.
THIS MAN.
THIS MAN!
THIS MAN IS HANNIBAL...
I HAVE NO FEAR OF THE MILLION ENEMIES OF ROME...
HANNIBAL BARCA!
...YET I FEAR THIS MAN!

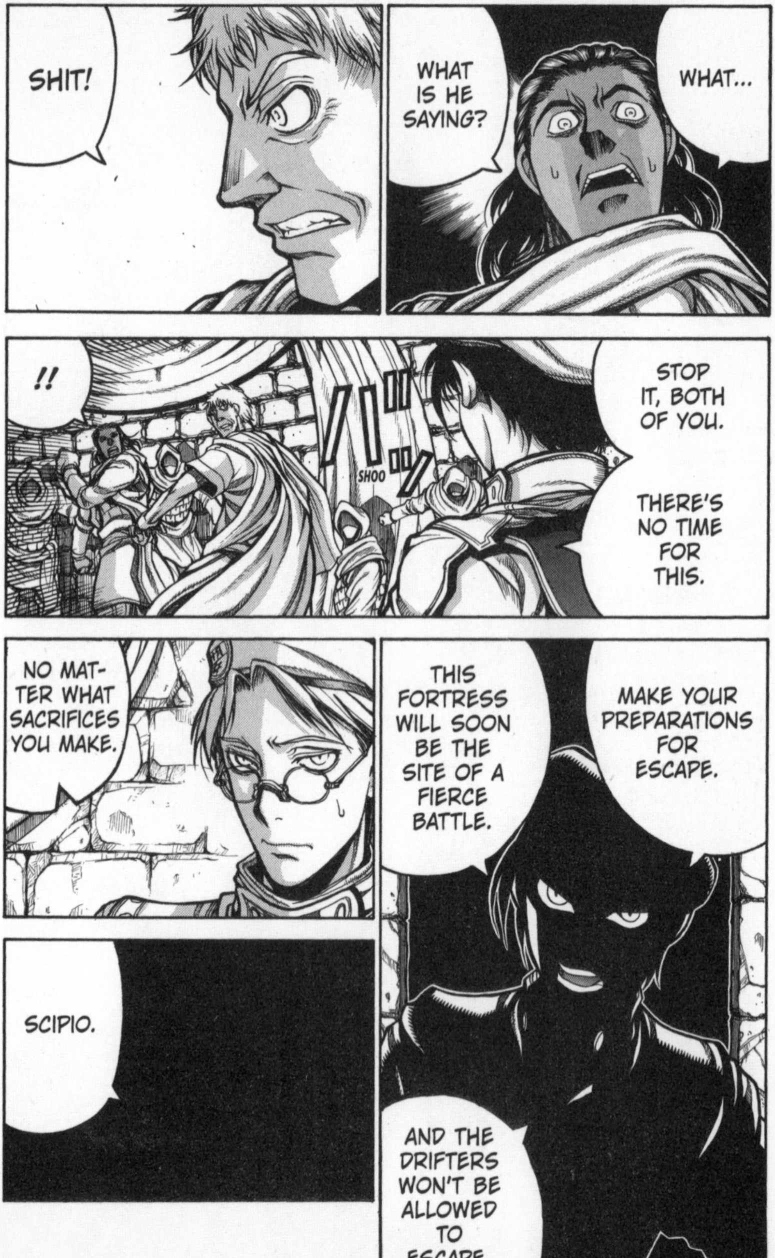
WHAT...
WHAT IS HE SAYING?
SHIT!
STOP IT, BOTH OF YOU.
THERE'S NO TIME FOR THIS.
SHOO
!!
MAKE YOUR PREPARATIONS FOR ESCAPE.
THIS FORTRESS WILL SOON BE THE SITE OF A FIERCE BATTLE.
AND THE DRIFTERS WON'T BE ALLOWED TO ESCAPE.
NO MAT-TER WHAT SACRIFICES YOU MAKE.
SCIPIO.

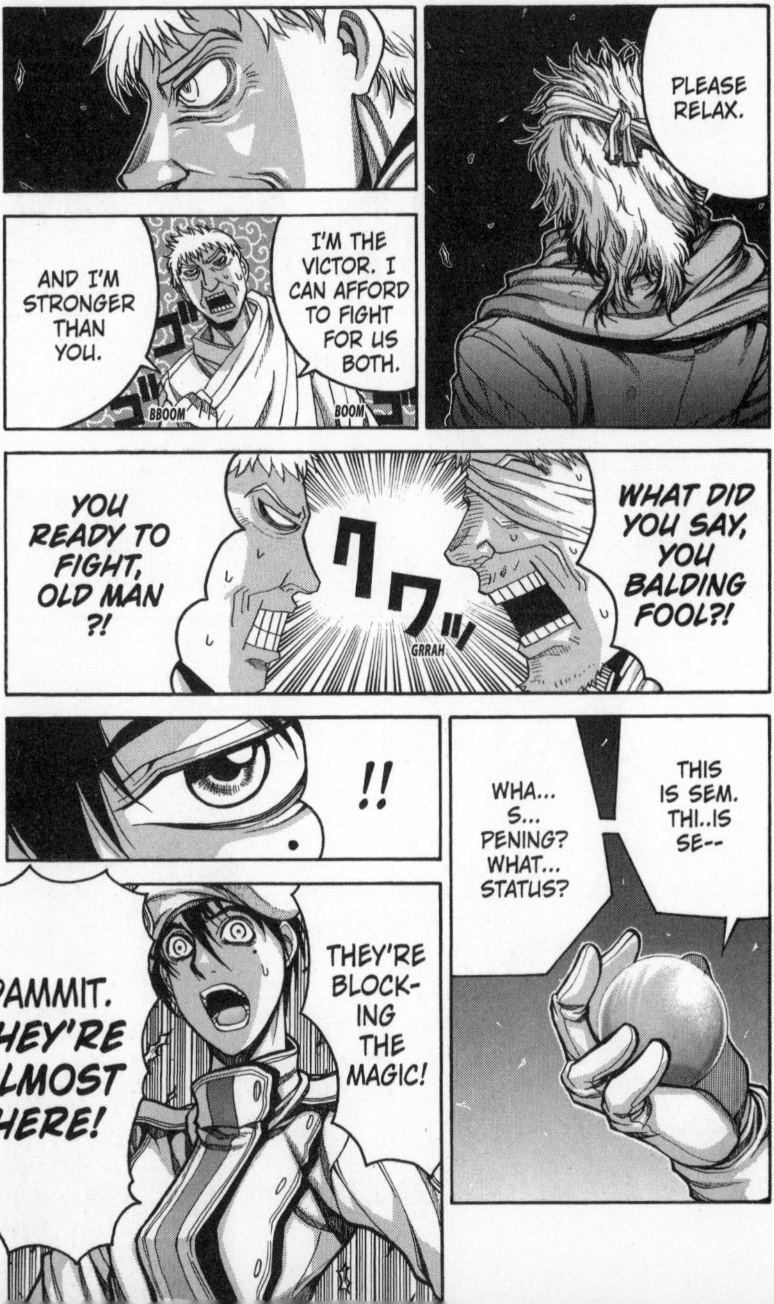
PLEASE RELAX.
I'M THE VICTOR. I CAN AFFORD TO FIGHT FOR US BOTH.
AND I'M STRONGER THAN YOU.
BOOM
BBOOM
WHAT DID YOU SAY, YOU BALDING FOOL?!
クワッ
GRRAH
YOU READY TO FIGHT, OLD MAN ?!
THIS IS SEM. THI..IS SE--
WHA... S... PENING? WHAT... STATUS?
!!
THEY'RE BLOCK-ING THE MAGIC!
DAMMIT. THEY'RE ALMOST HERE!

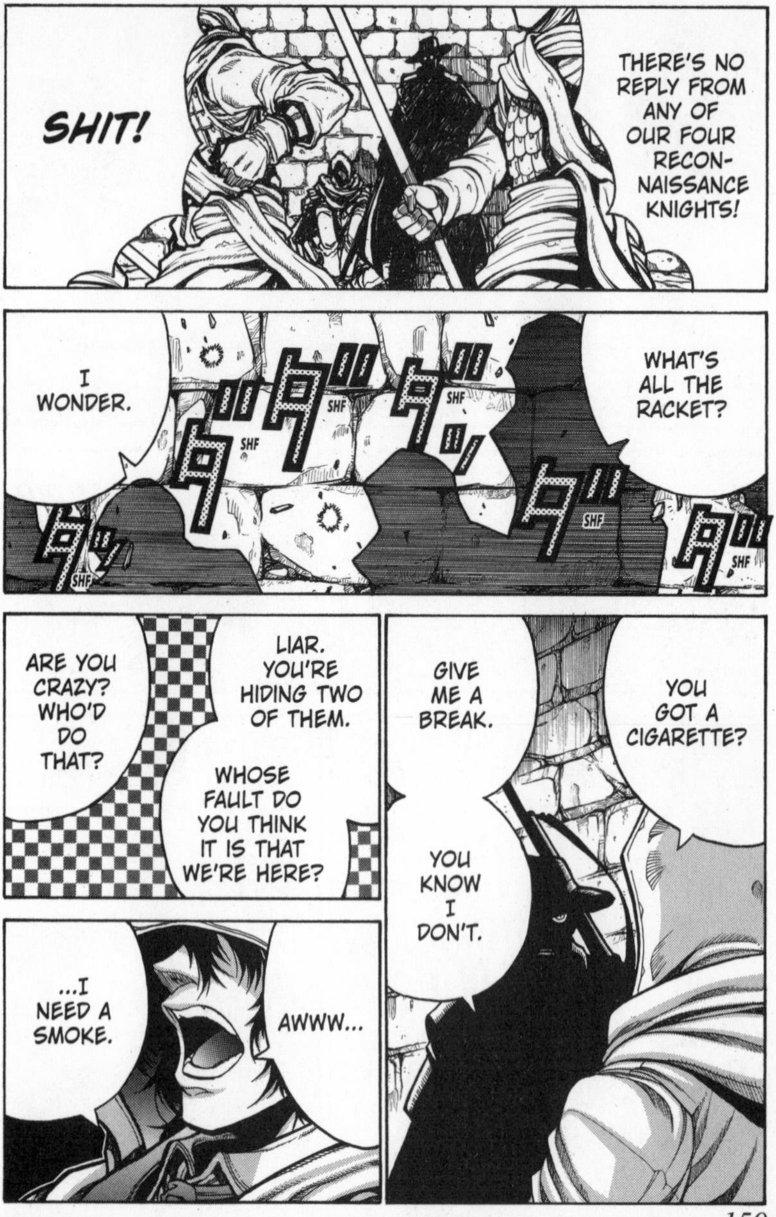
THERE'S NO REPLY FROM ANY OF OUR FOUR RECON-NAISSANCE KNIGHTS!
SHIT!
WHAT'S ALL THE RACKET?
SHF
SHF
SHF
SHF
I WONDER.
SHF
YOU GOT A CIGARETTE?
GIVE ME A BREAK.
YOU KNOW I DON'T.
LIAR. YOU'RE HIDING TWO OF THEM.
ARE YOU CRAZY? WHO'D DO THAT?
WHOSE FAULT DO YOU THINK IT IS THAT WE'RE HERE?
AWWW...
...I NEED A SMOKE.

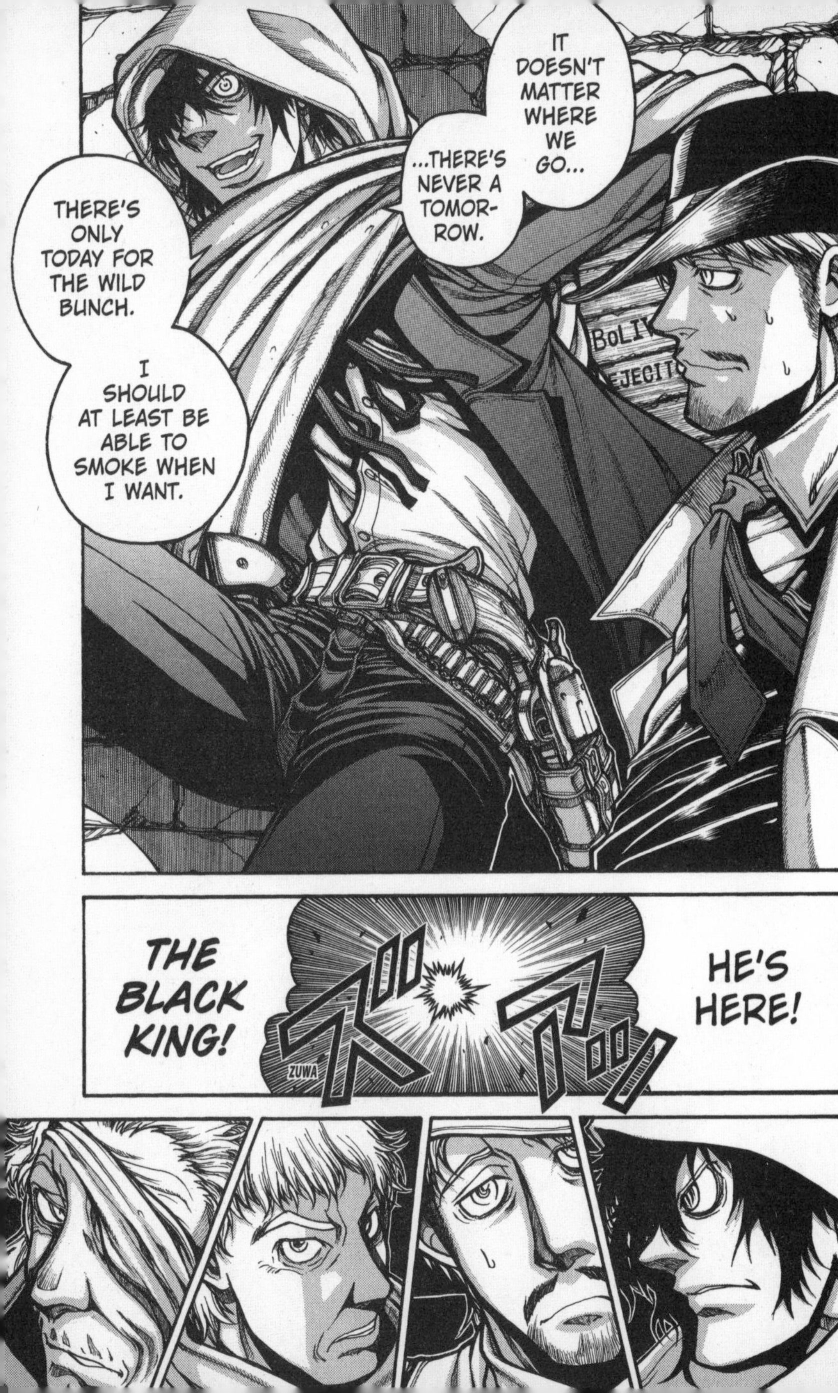
IT DOESN'T MATTER WHERE WE GO...
...THERE'S NEVER A TOMOR-ROW.
THERE'S ONLY TODAY FOR THE WILD BUNCH.
I SHOULD AT LEAST BE ABLE TO SMOKE WHEN I WANT.
HE'S HERE!
ZUWA
THE BLACK KING!

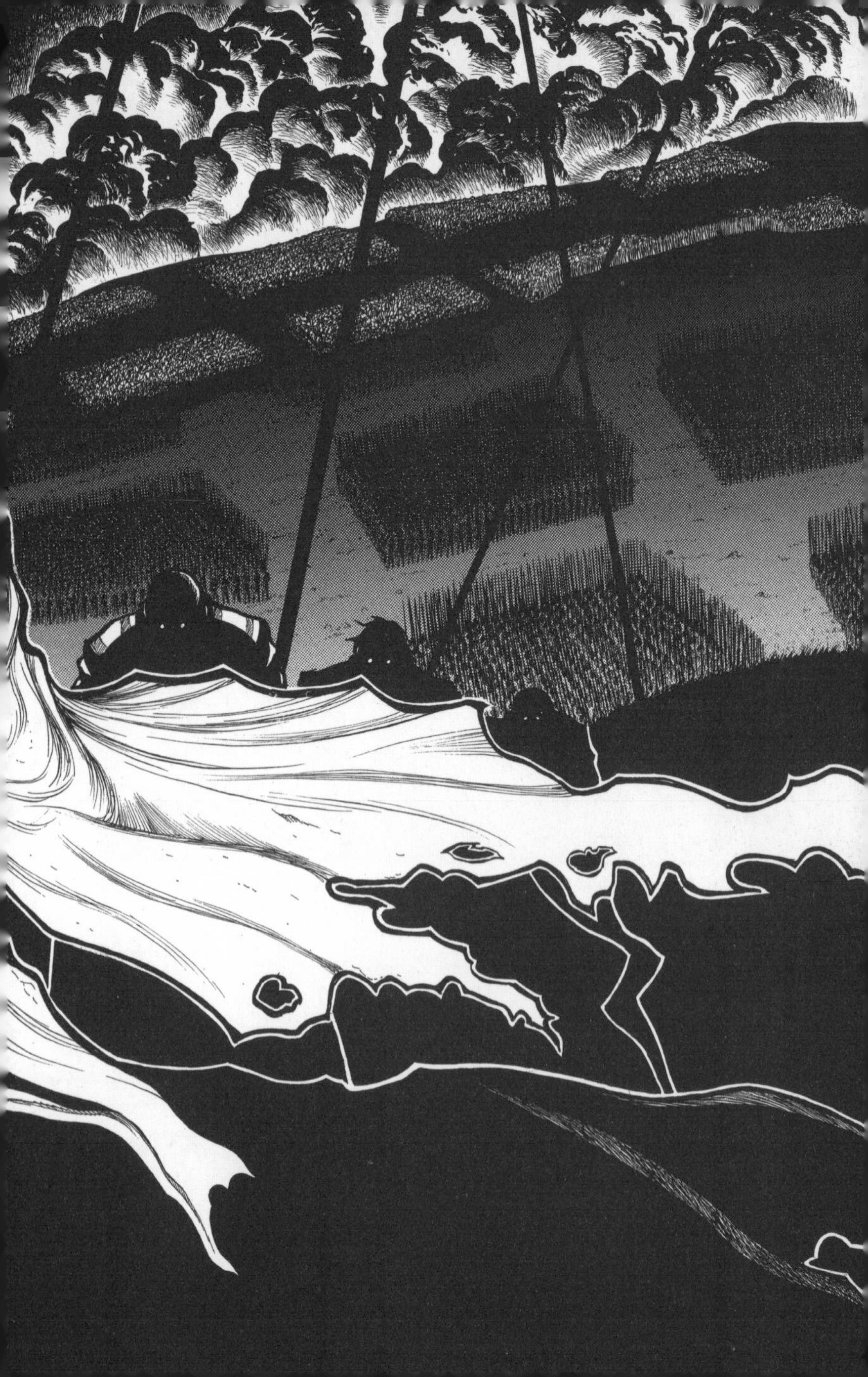

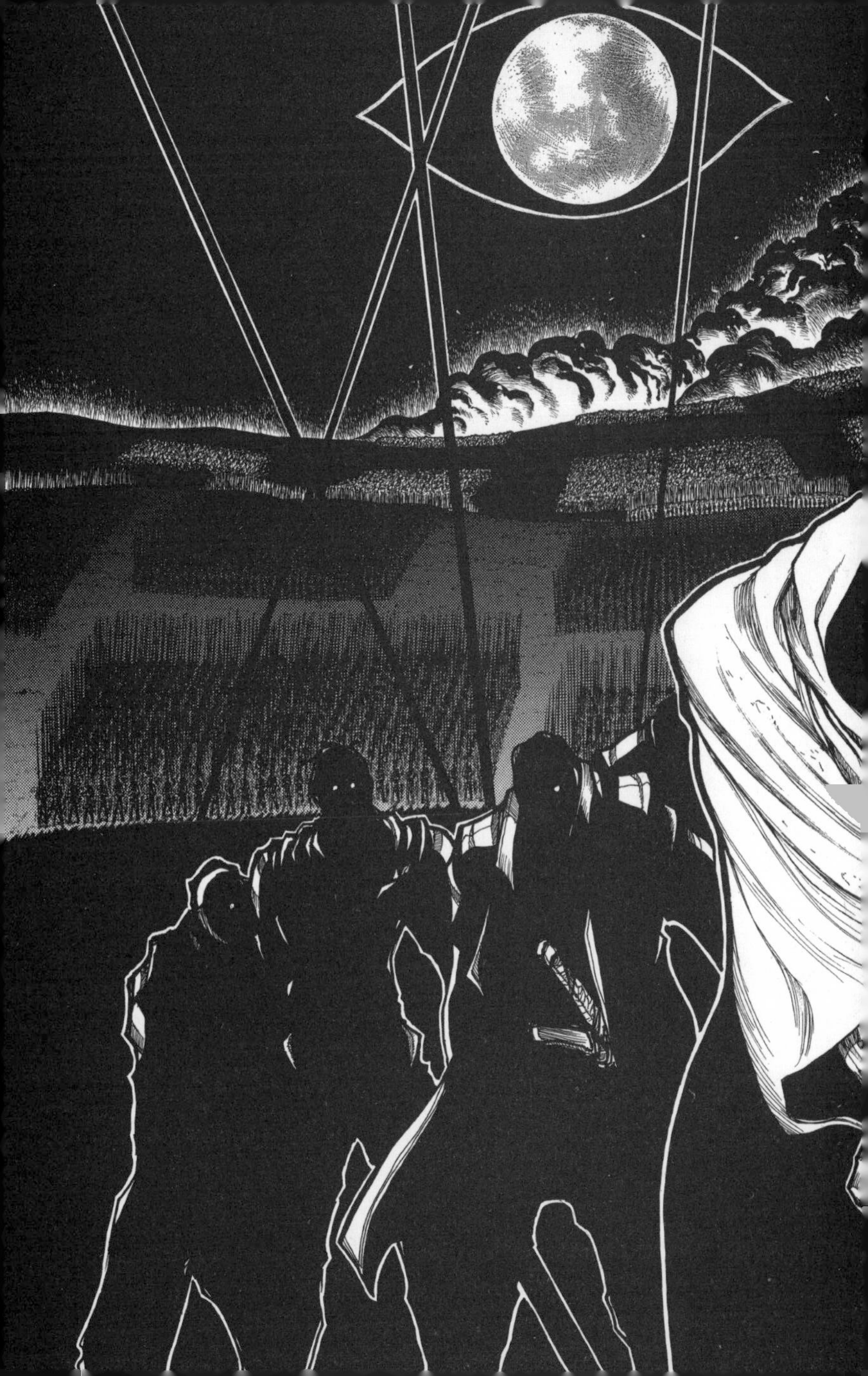

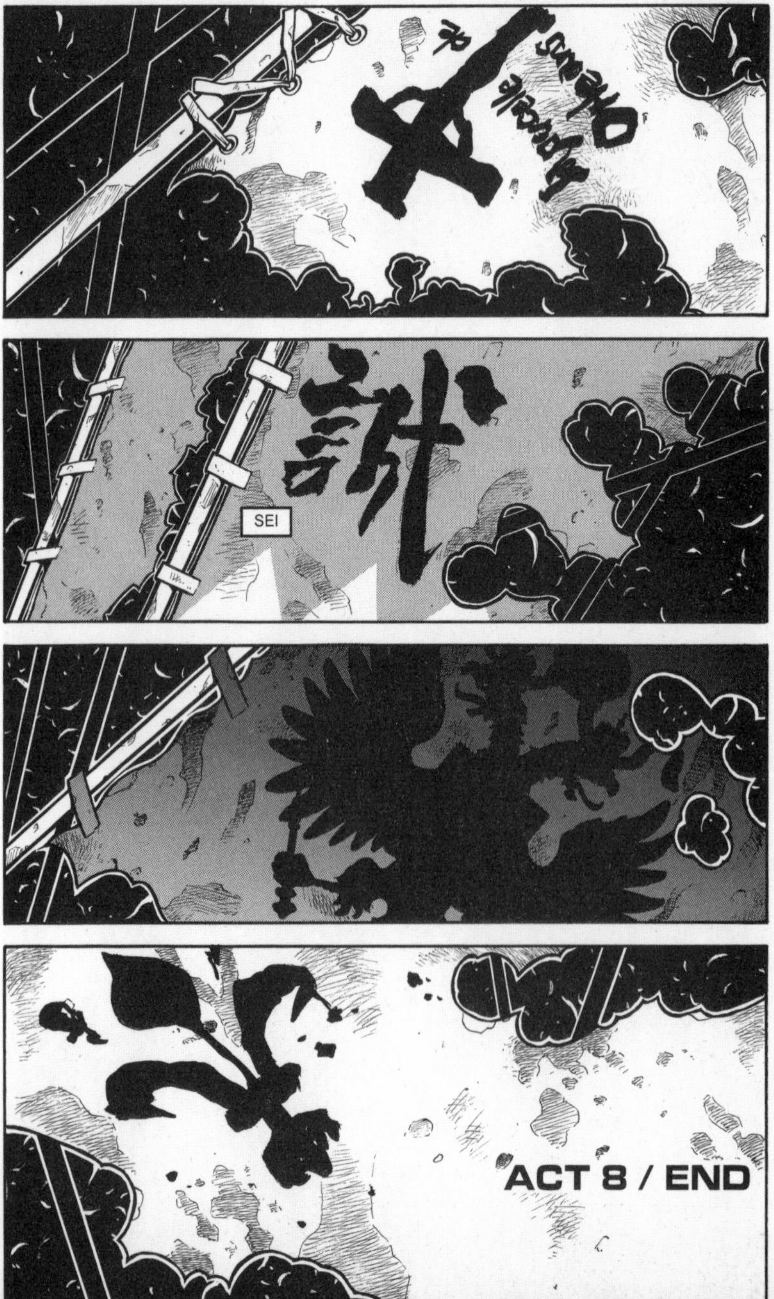
SEI
ACT 8 / END

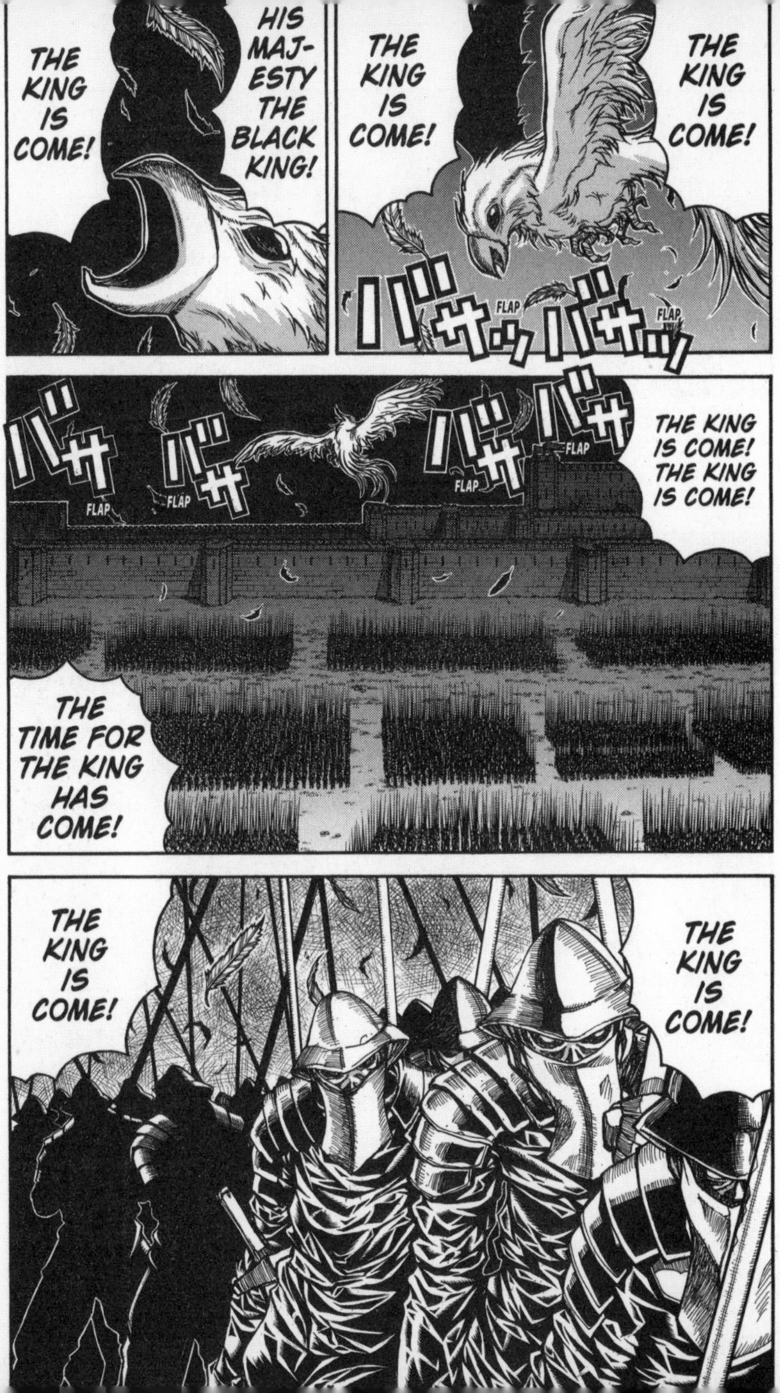
THE KING IS COME!
THE KING IS COME!
バサッ
FLAP
バサッ
FLAP
HIS MAJESTY THE BLACK KING!
THE KING IS COME!
THE KING IS COME! THE KING IS COME!
バサ
FLAP
バサ
FLAP
バサ
FLAP
バサ
FLAP
THE TIME FOR THE KING HAS COME!
THE KING IS COME!
THE KING IS COME!

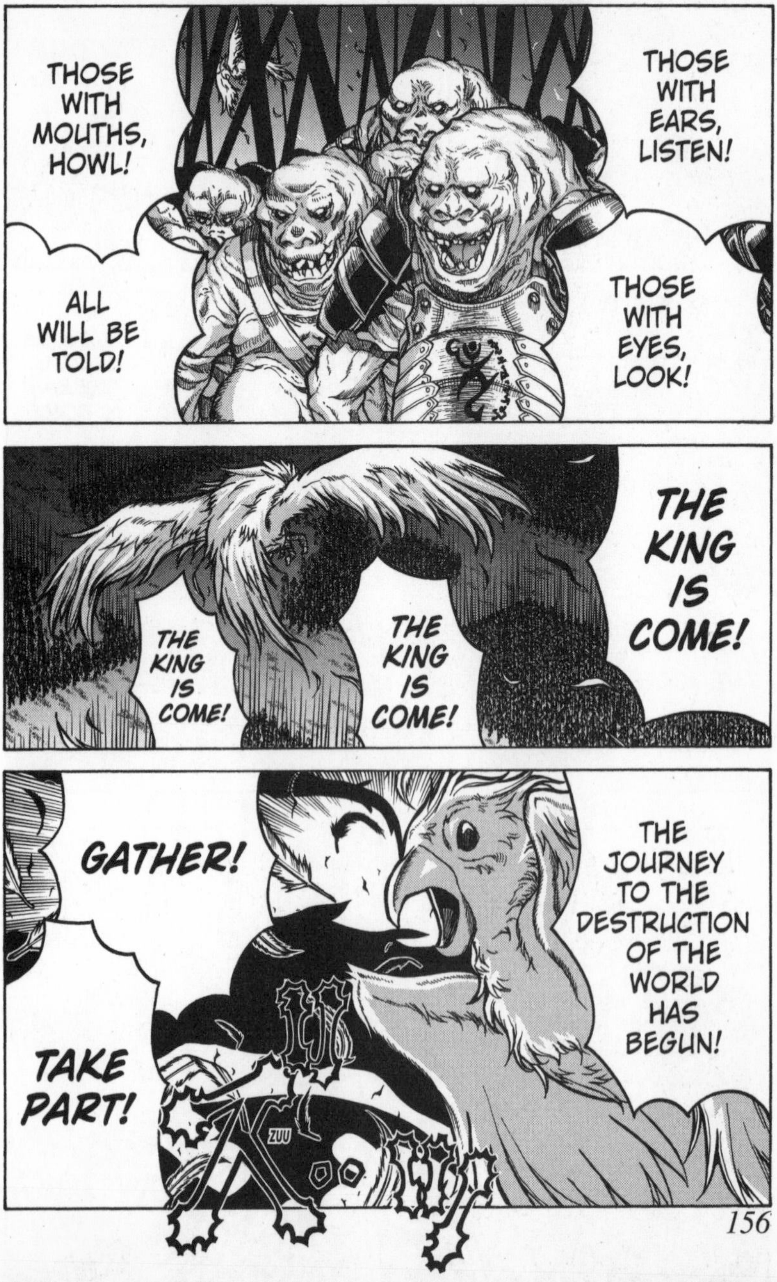
THOSE WITH EARS, LISTEN!
THOSE WITH MOUTHS, HOWL!
THOSE WITH EYES, LOOK!
ALL WILL BE TOLD!
THE KING IS COME!
THE KING IS COME!
THE KING IS COME!
THE JOURNEY TO THE DESTRUCTION OF THE WORLD HAS BEGUN!
GATHER!
TAKE PART!
ZUU

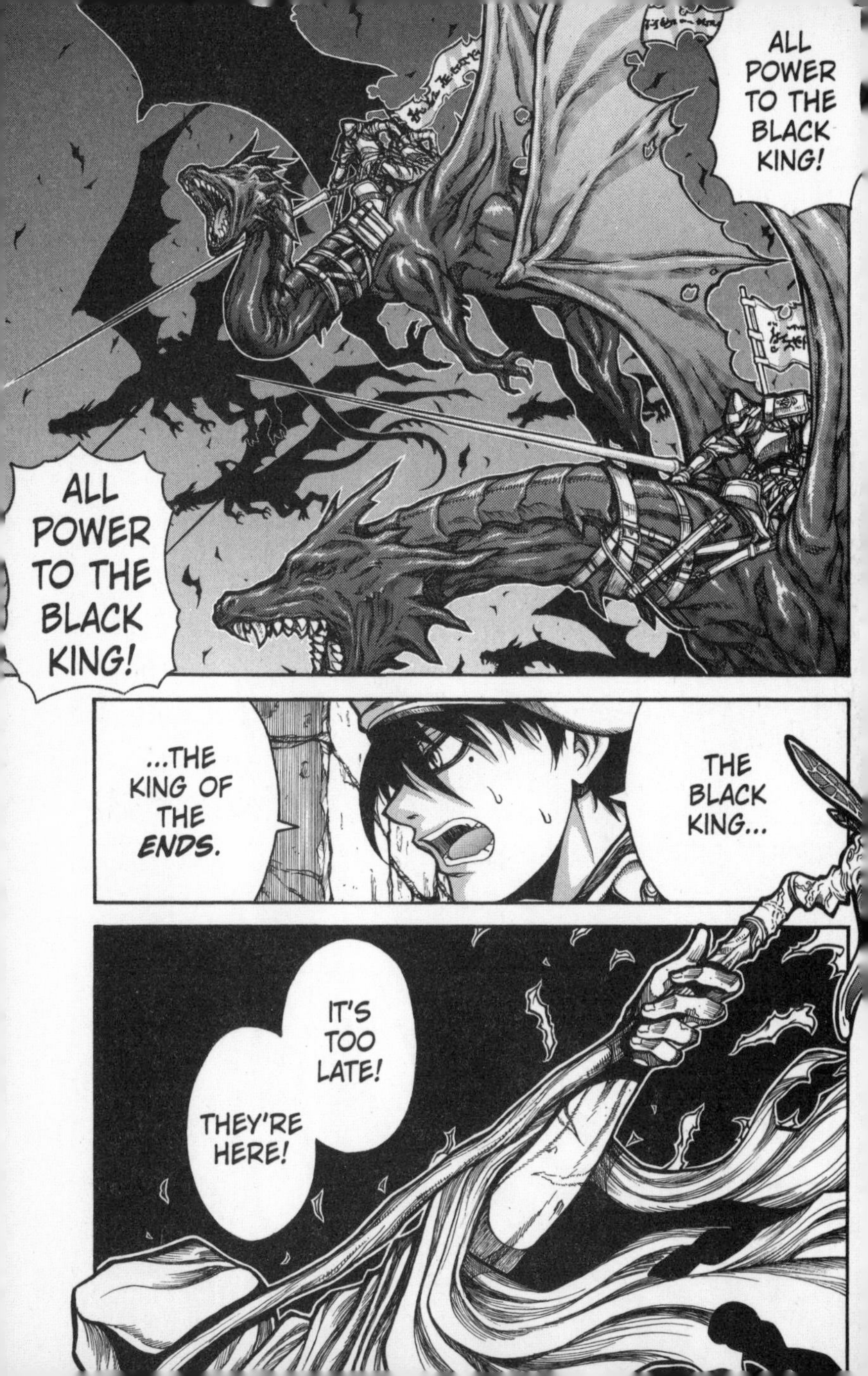
ALL POWER TO THE BLACK KING!
ALL POWER TO THE BLACK KING!
THE BLACK KING...
...THE KING OF THE *ENDS*.
IT'S TOO LATE!
THEY'RE HERE!

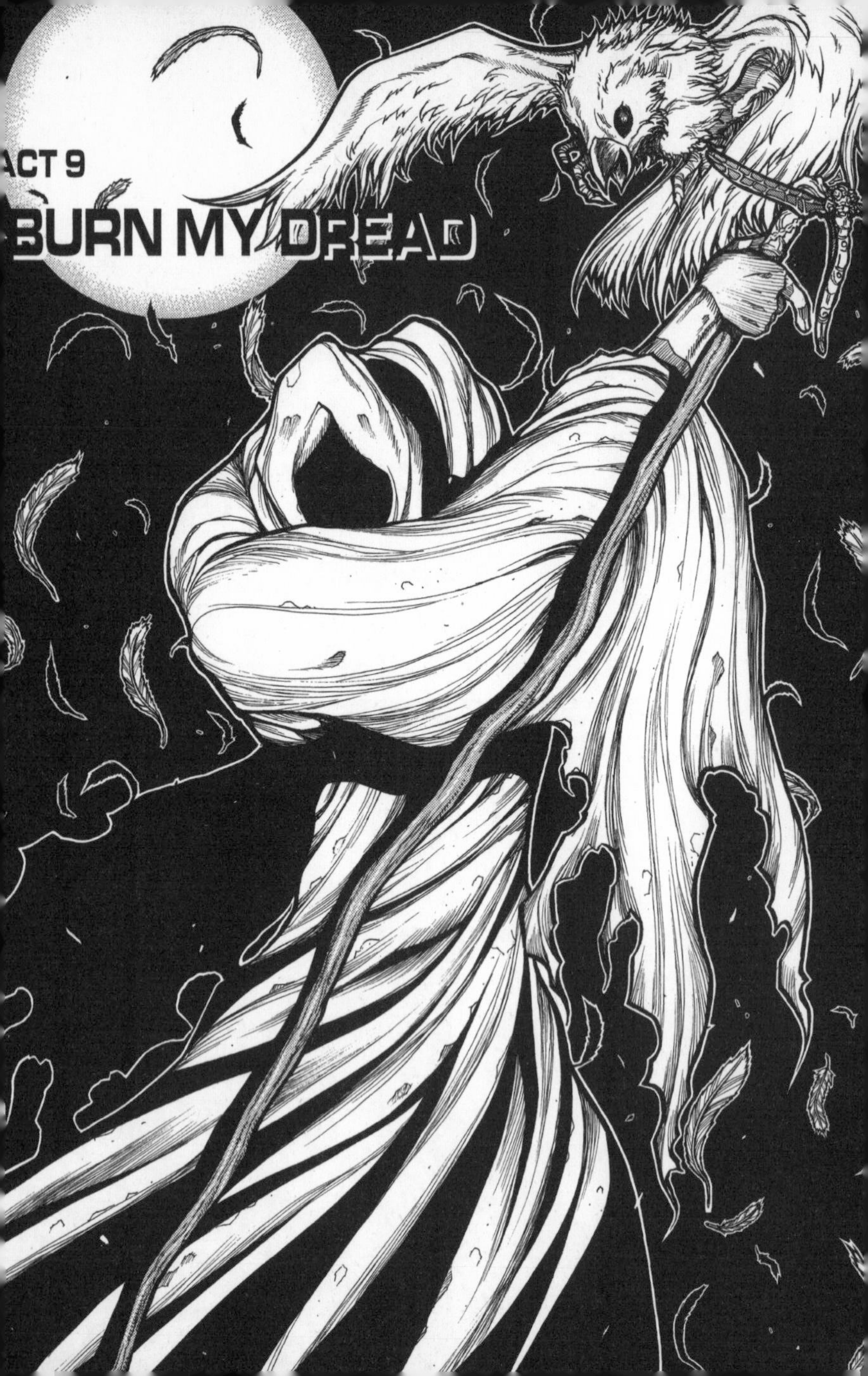
ACT 9
BURN MY DREAD

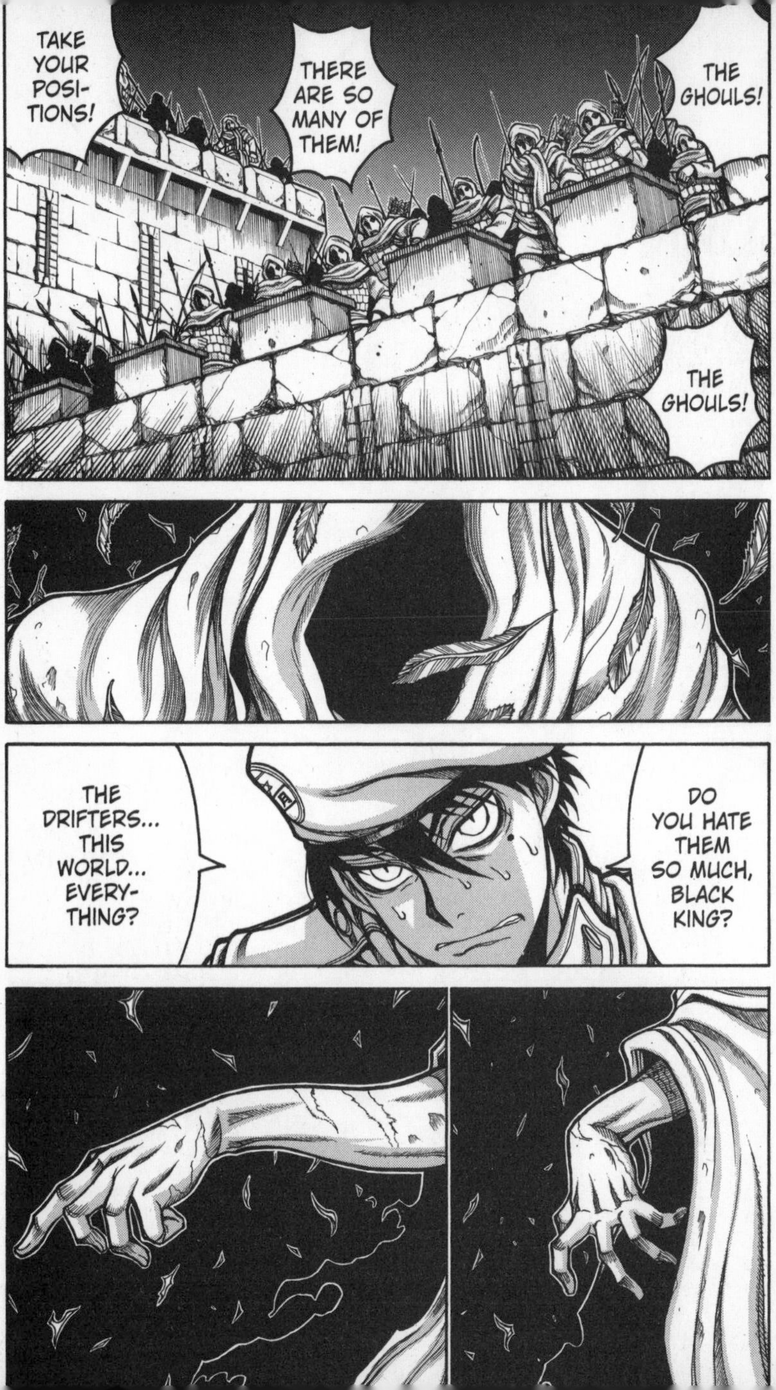
THE GHOULS!
THE GHOULS!
THERE ARE SO MANY OF THEM!
TAKE YOUR POSI-TIONS!
DO YOU HATE THEM SO MUCH, BLACK KING?
THE DRIFTERS... THIS WORLD... EVERY-THING?

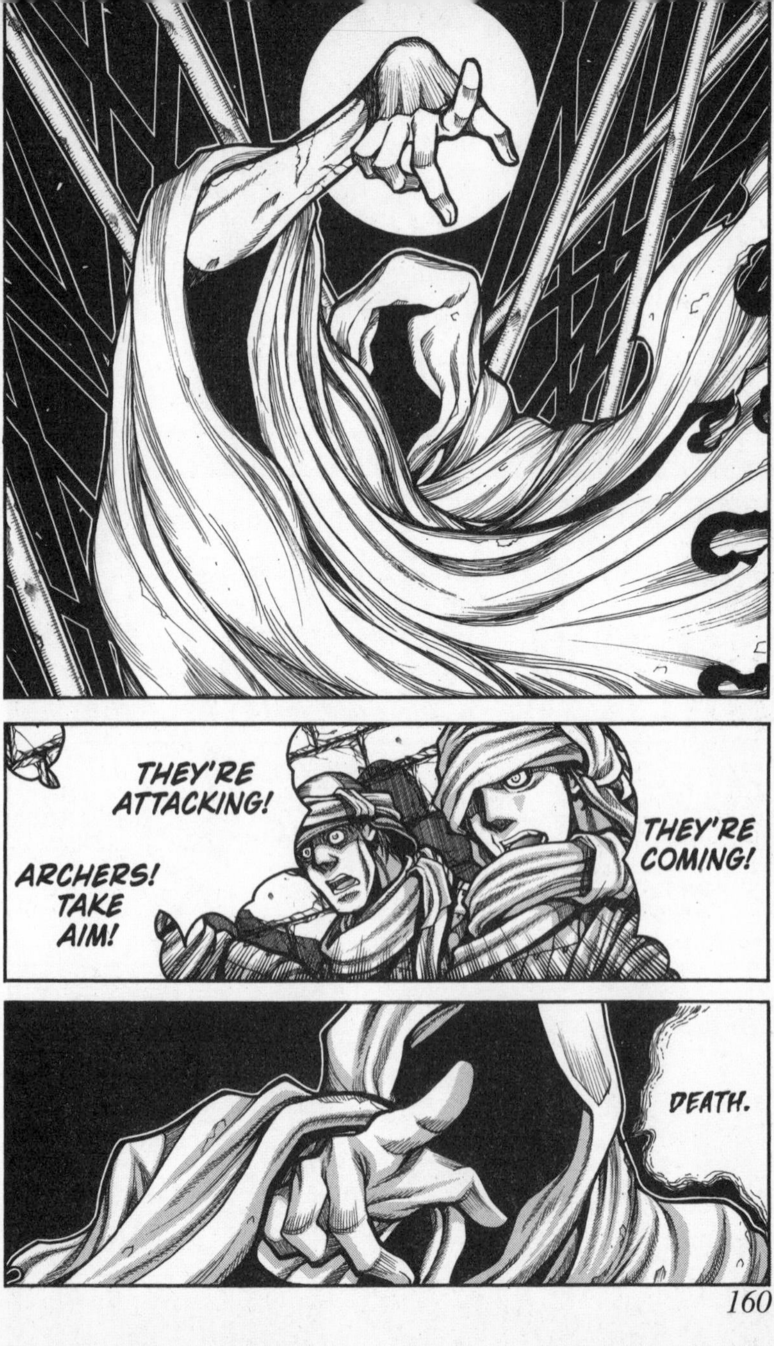
THEY'RE COMING!
THEY'RE ATTACKING!
ARCHERS! TAKE AIM!
DEATH.

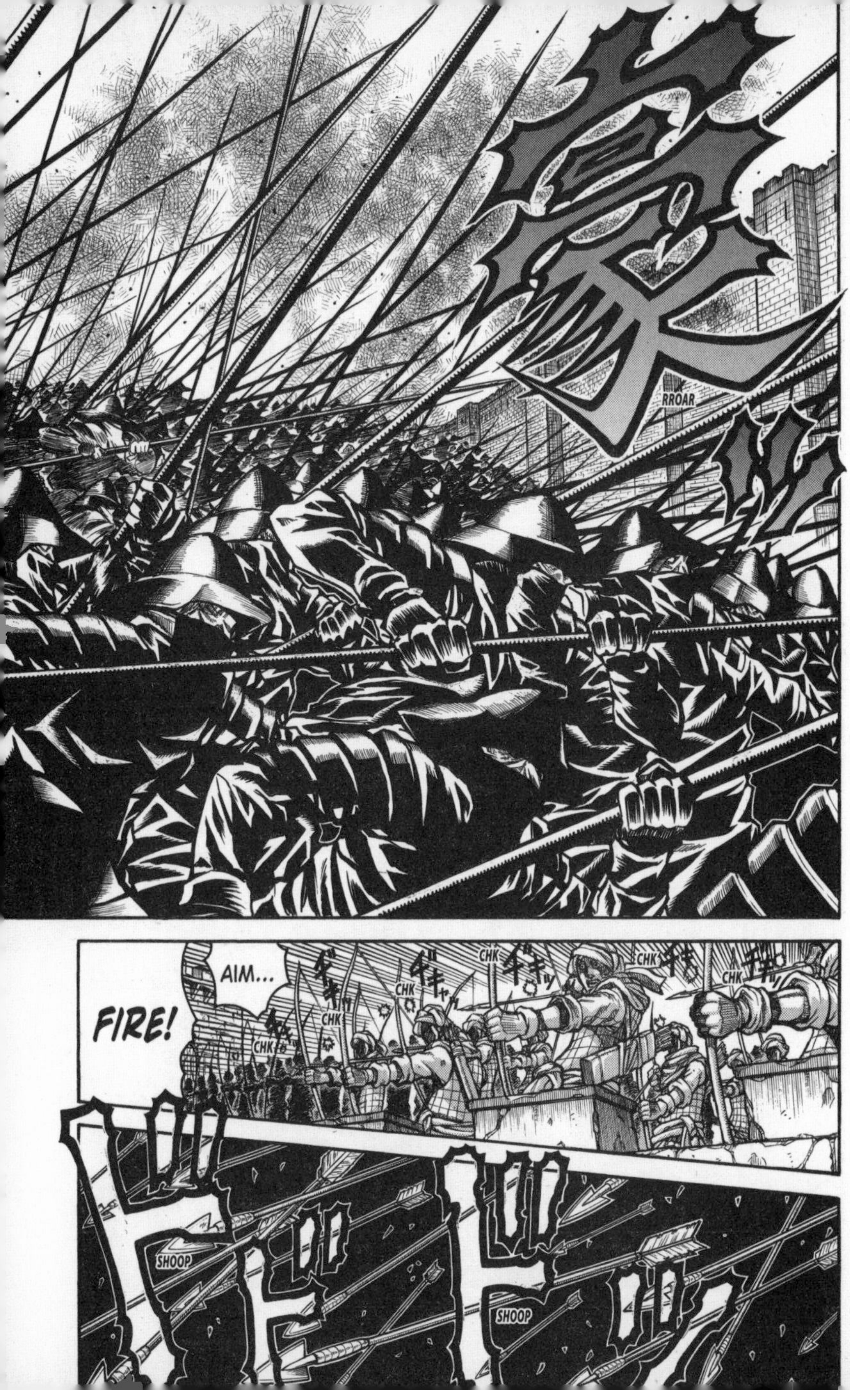
RROAR
CHK
CHK
CHK
CHK
CHK
CHK
AIM...
FIRE!
SHOOP
SHOOP

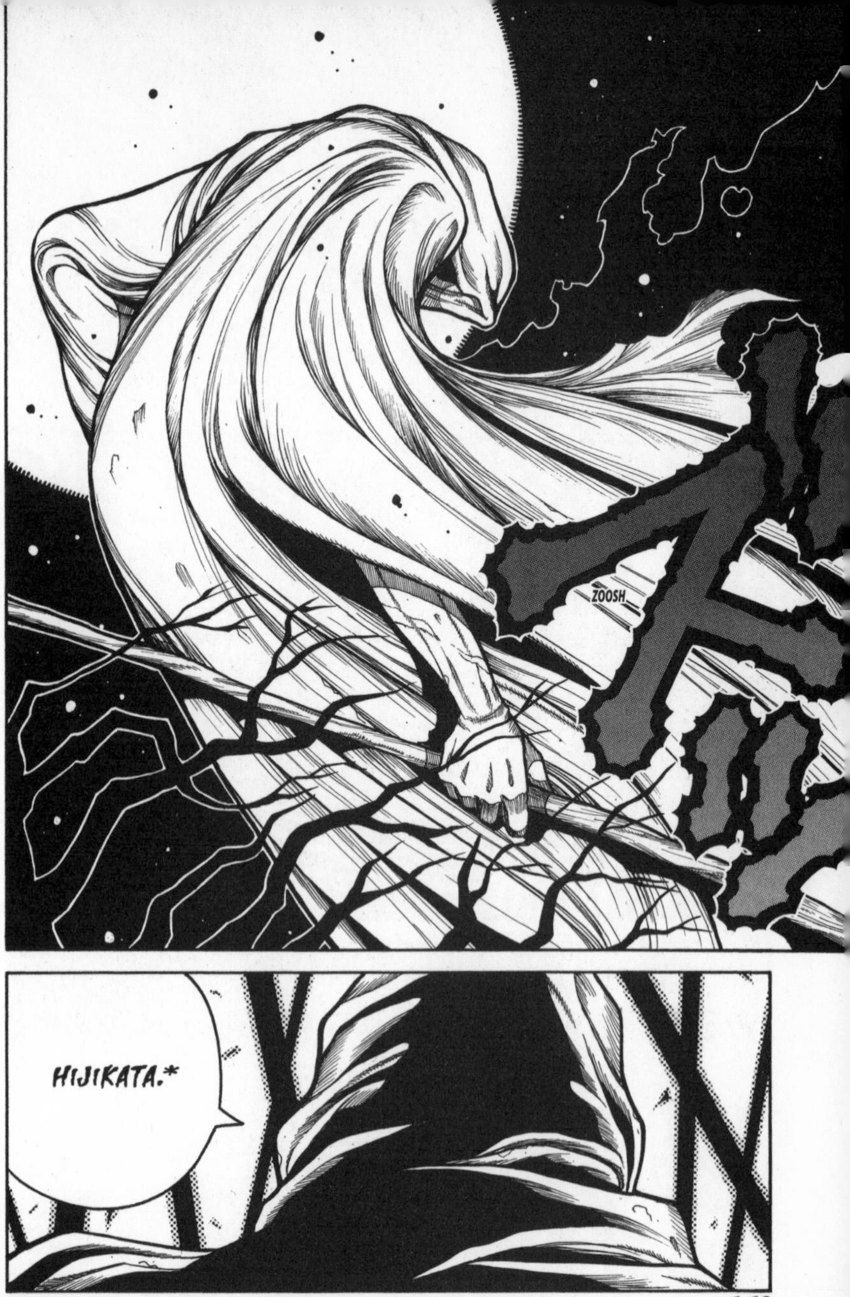
ZOOSH
HIJIKATA.*

*Hijikata Toshizo, leader of the Shinsengumi

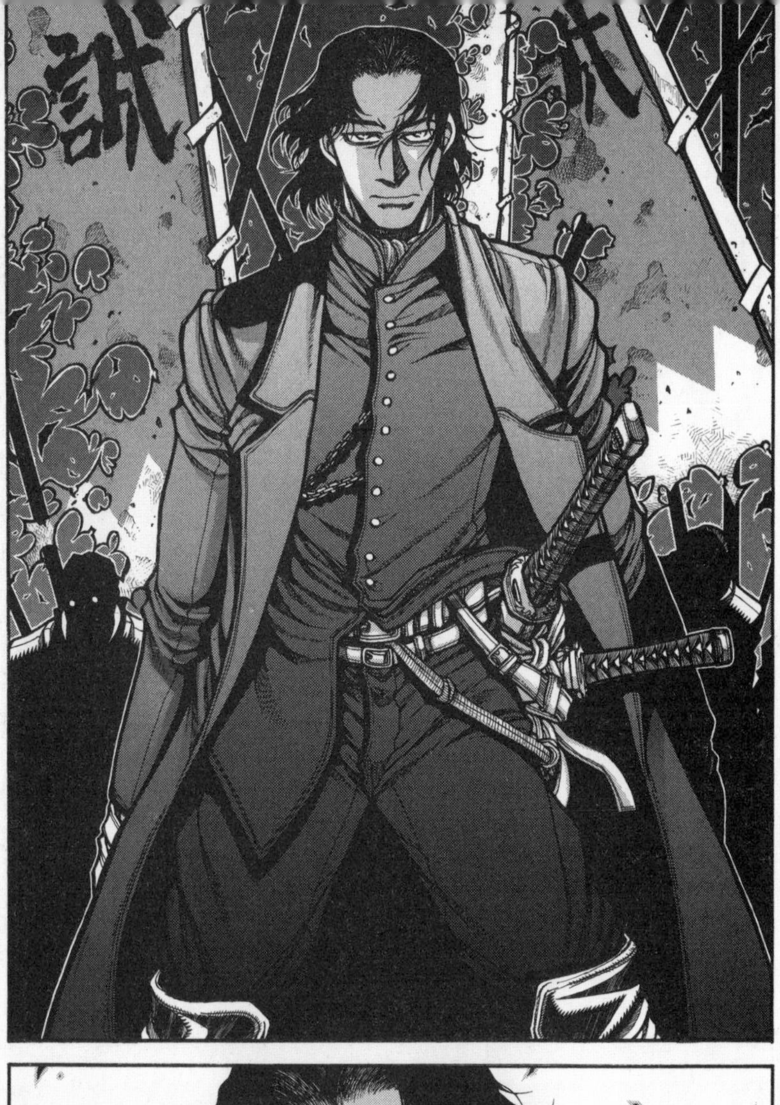

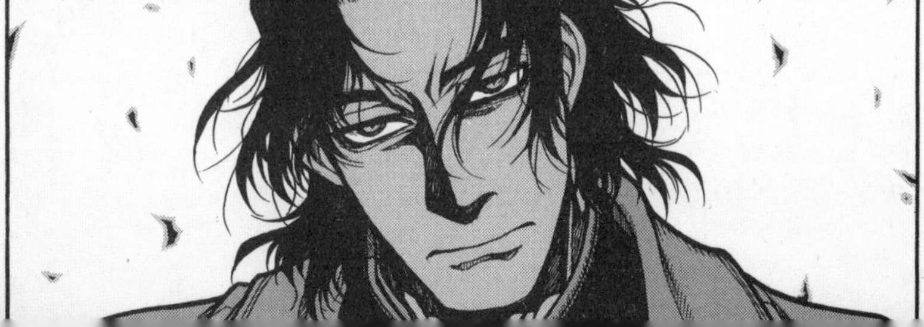

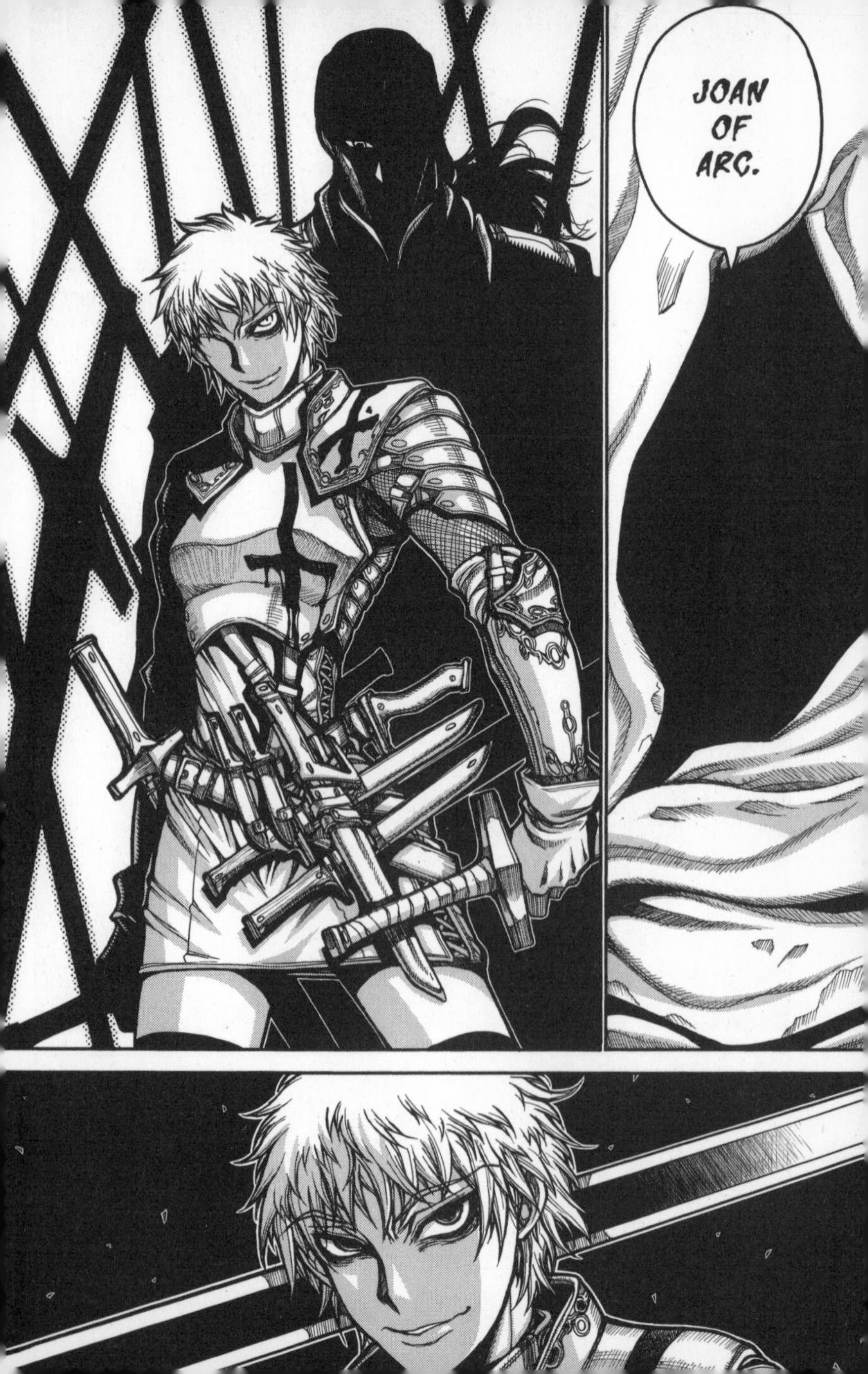
JOAN OF ARC.

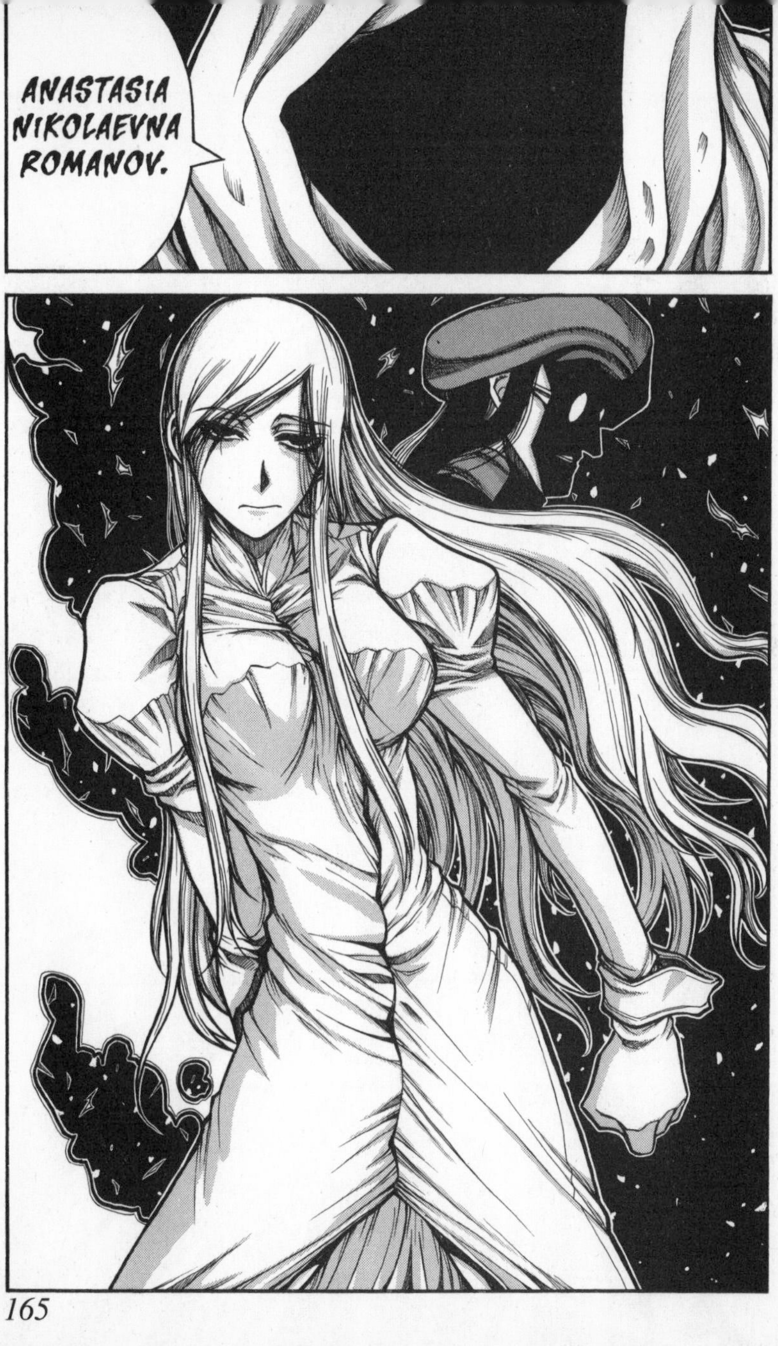
ANASTASIA NIKOLAEVNA ROMANOV.

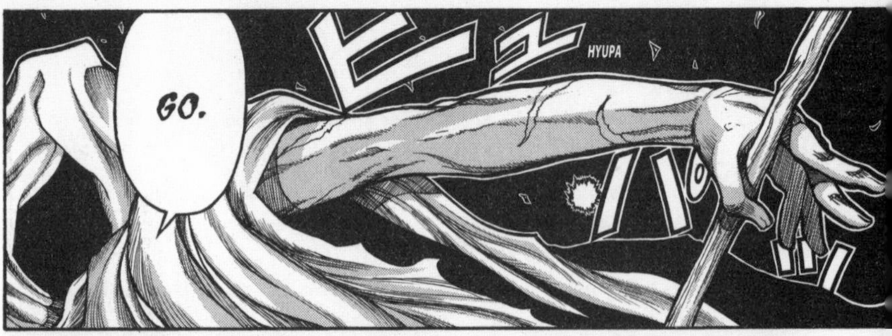
GO.
HYUPA
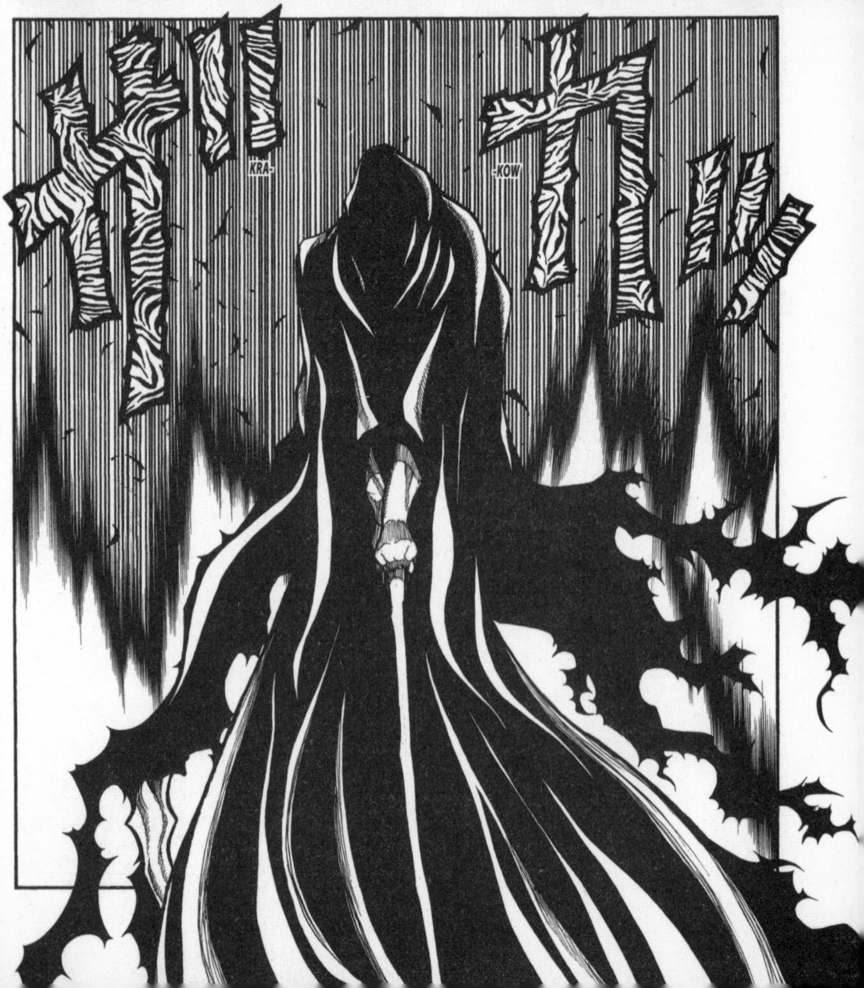
KRA-
-KOW

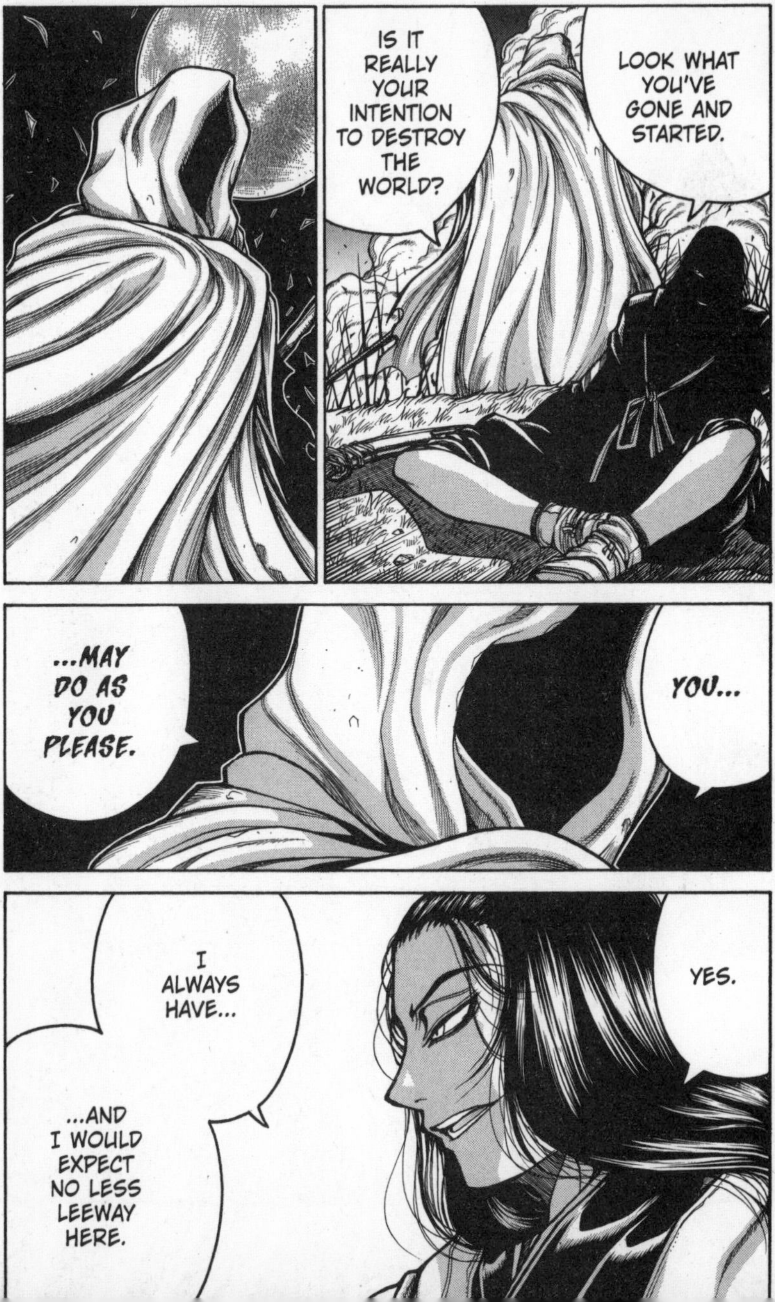
LOOK WHAT YOU'VE GONE AND STARTED.
IS IT REALLY YOUR INTENTION TO DESTROY THE WORLD?
YOU...
...MAY DO AS YOU PLEASE.
YES.
I ALWAYS HAVE...
...AND I WOULD EXPECT NO LESS LEEWAY HERE.

*Hogan is an imperial title. It translatles roughly into "Imperial Guard."

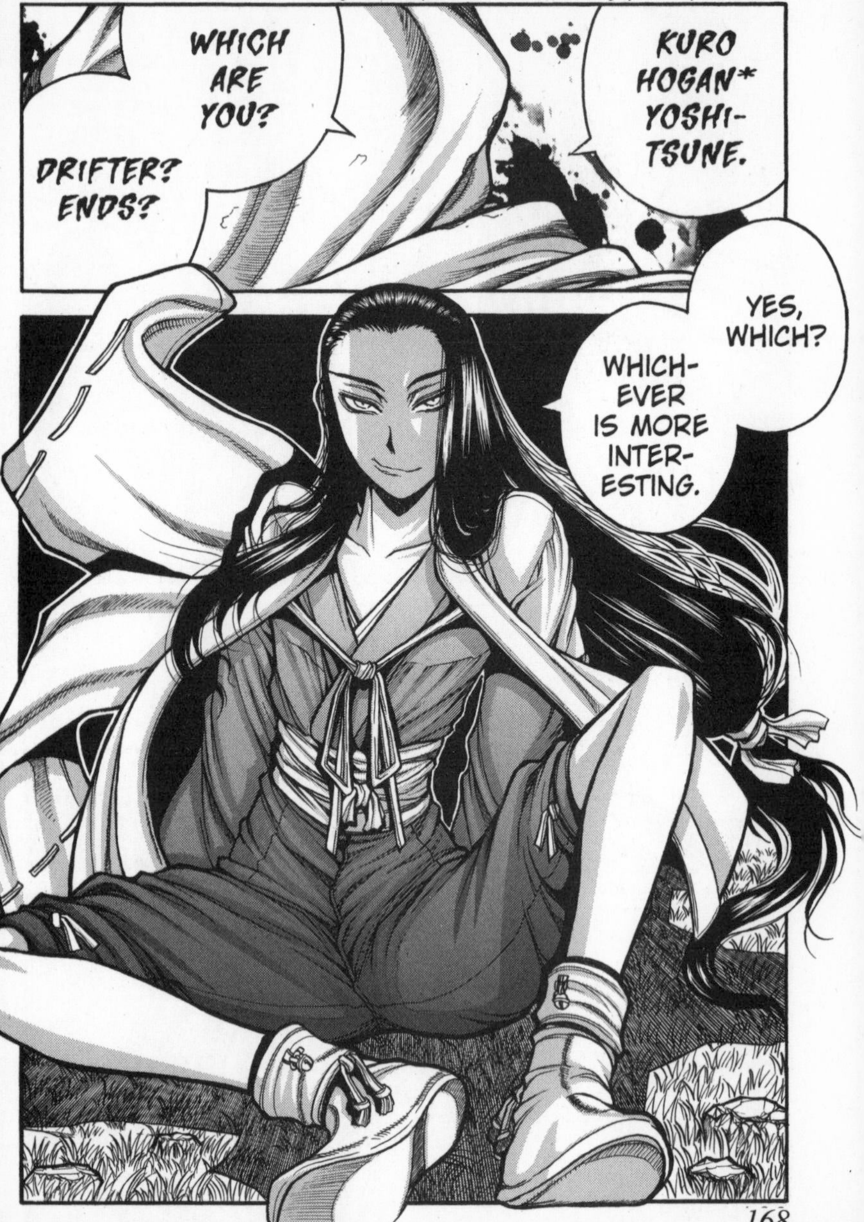
KURO HOGAN* YOSHI-TSUNE.
WHICH ARE YOU?
DRIFTER? ENDS?
YES, WHICH?
WHICH-EVER IS MORE INTER-ESTING.

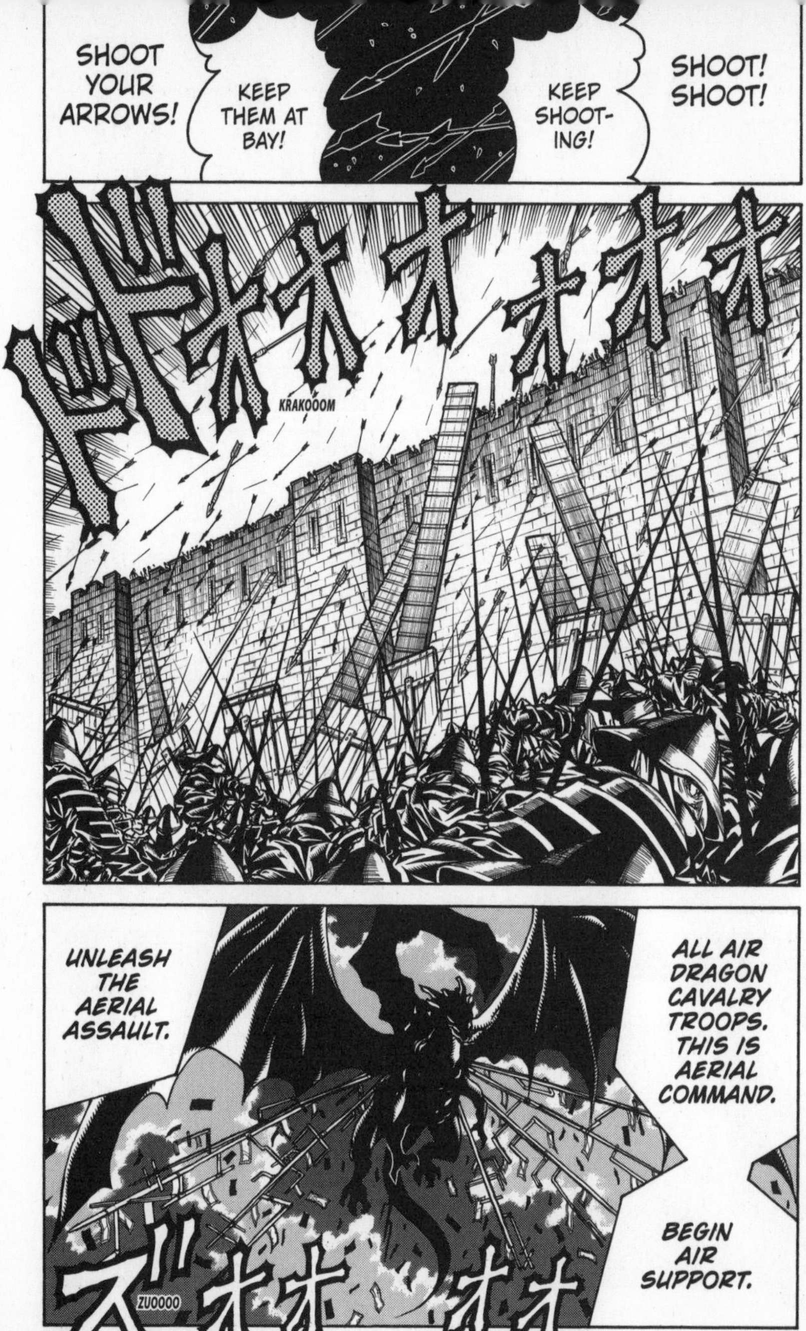
SHOOT! SHOOT!
KEEP SHOOT-ING!
KEEP THEM AT BAY!
SHOOT YOUR ARROWS!
KRAKOOOM
ALL AIR DRAGON CAVALRY TROOPS. THIS IS AERIAL COMMAND.
UNLEASH THE AERIAL ASSAULT.
BEGIN AIR SUPPORT.
ZUOOOO

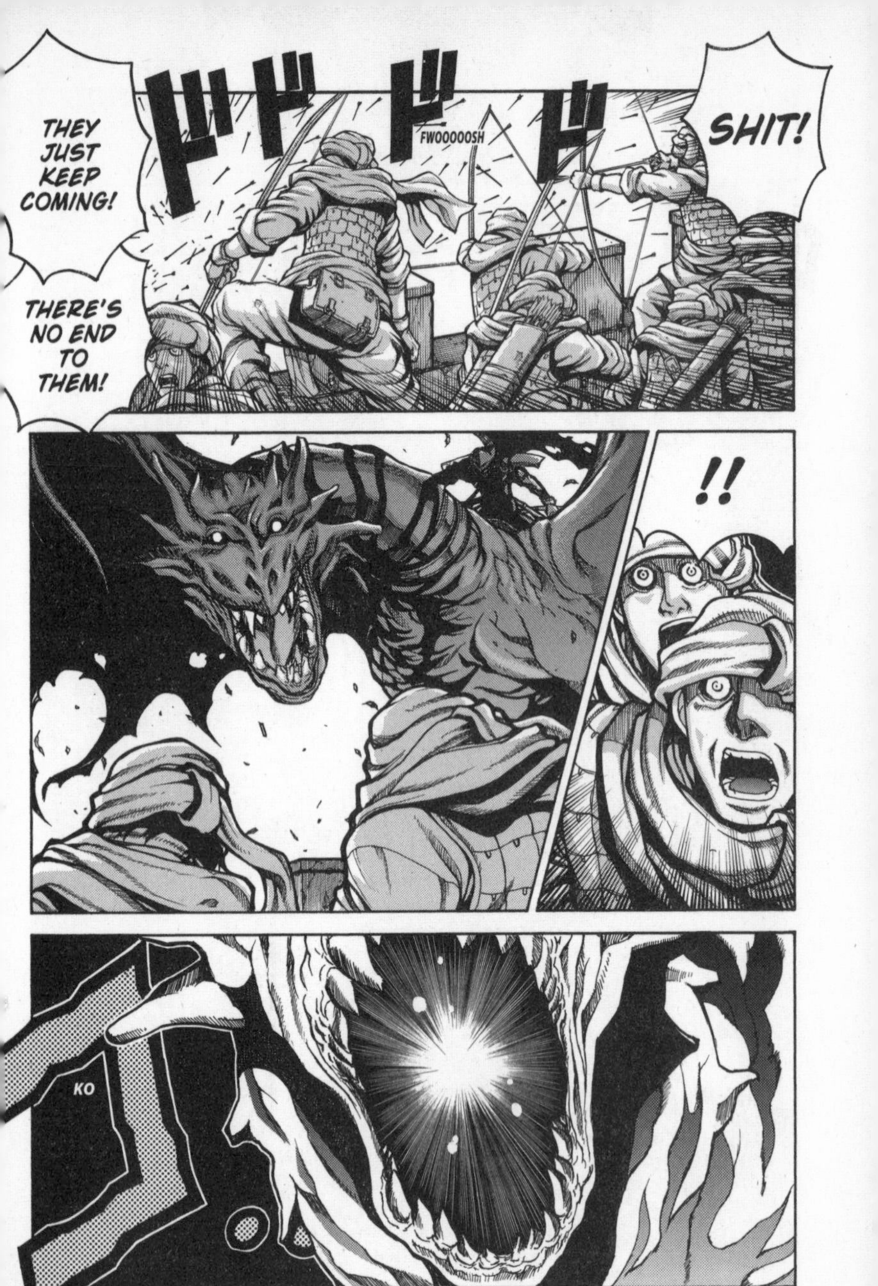
SHIT!
ドドドド
FWOOOOOSH
THEY JUST KEEP COMING!
THERE'S NO END TO THEM!
!!
KO

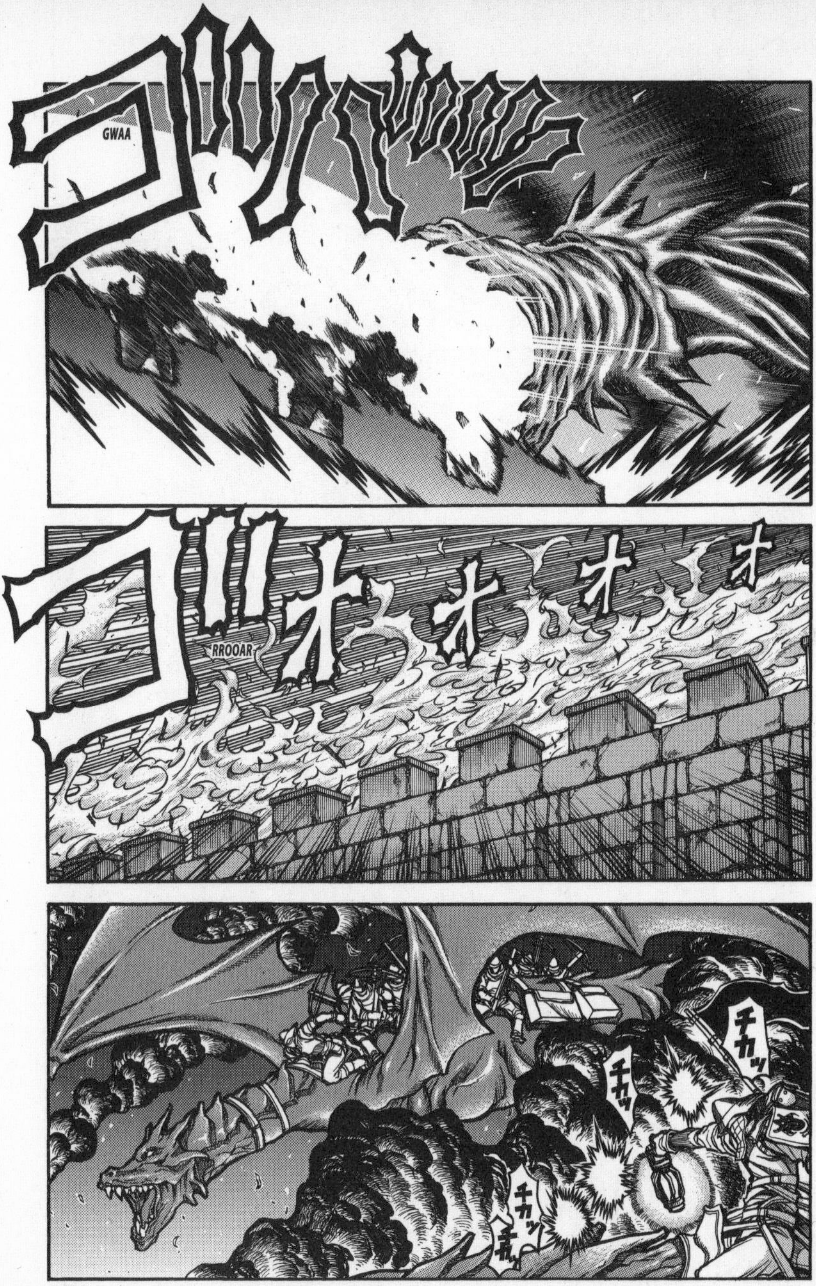
GWAA
RROOAR
チカッ
チカッ
チカッ

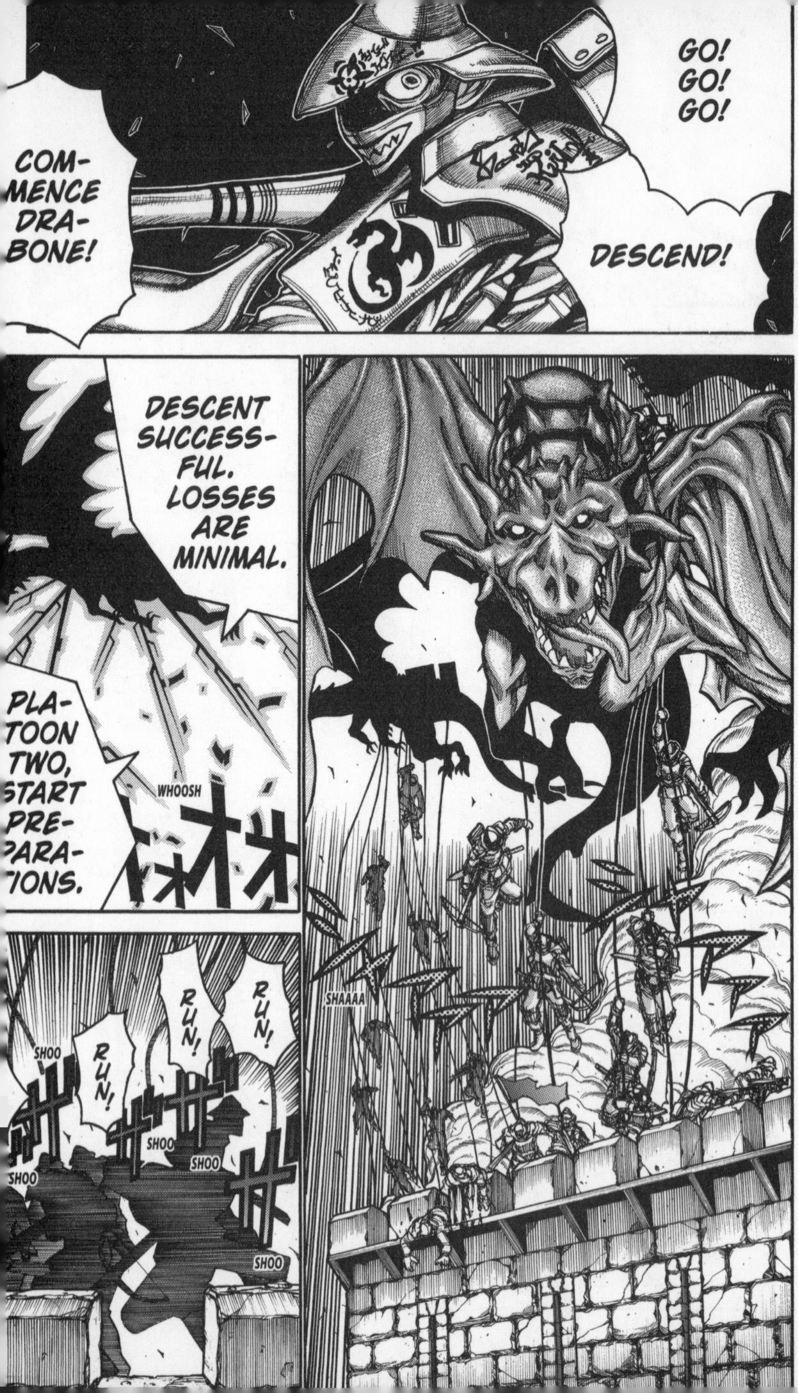
GO! GO! GO!
DESCEND!
COMMENCE DRABONE!
SHAAAA
DESCENT SUCCESSFUL. LOSSES ARE MINIMAL.
PLATOON TWO, START PREPARATIONS.
WHOOSH
RUN!
RUN!
RUN!
SHOO
SHOO
SHOO
SHOO
SHOO

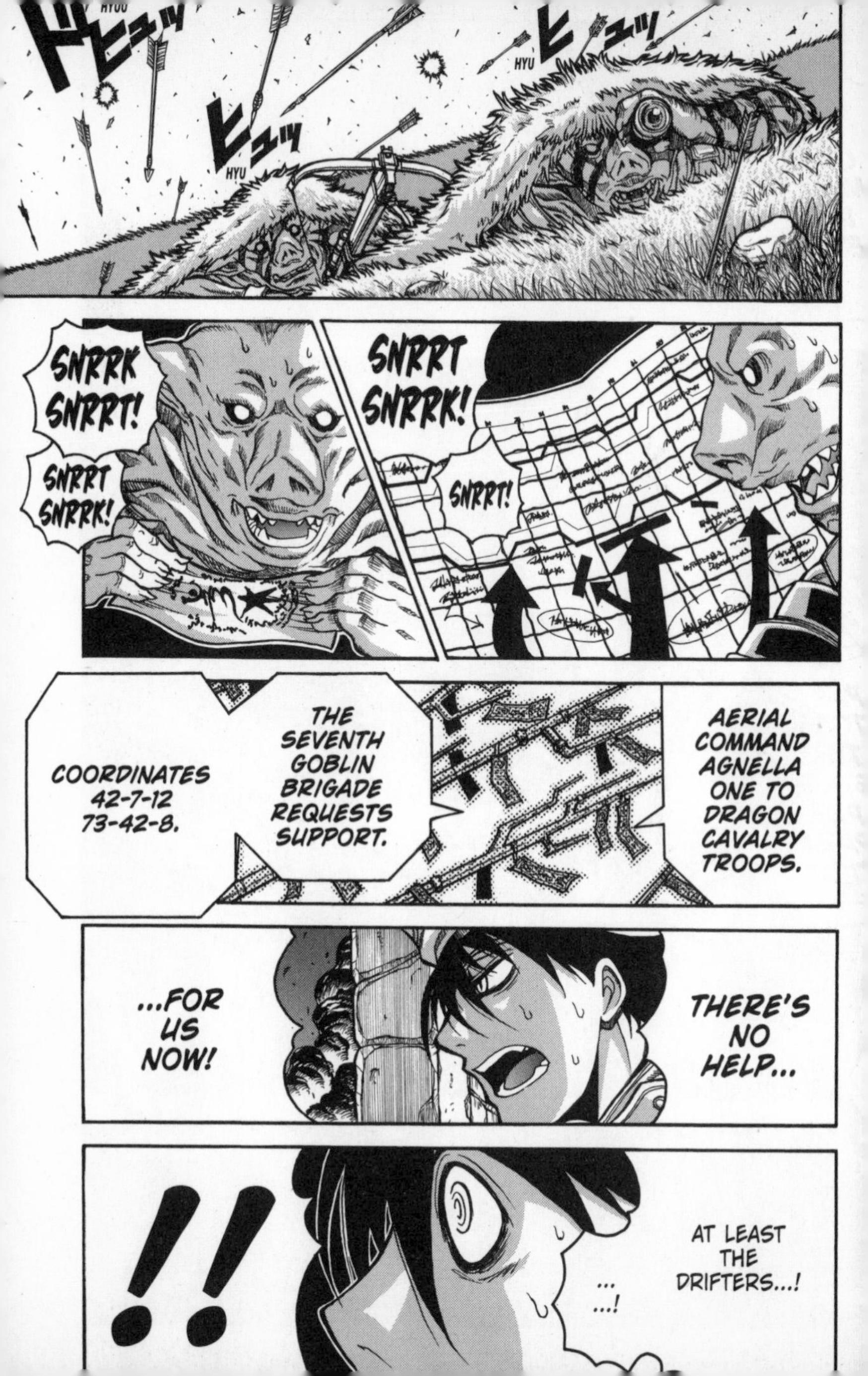
HYU
HYU
HYUU
SNRRT SNRRK!
SNRRT!
SNRRK SNRRT!
SNRRT SNRRK!
AERIAL COMMAND AGNELLA ONE TO DRAGON CAVALRY TROOPS.
THE SEVENTH GOBLIN BRIGADE REQUESTS SUPPORT.
COORDINATES 42-7-12 73-42-8.
THERE'S NO HELP...
...FOR US NOW!
AT LEAST THE DRIFTERS...!
... ...!
!!

KREEEE

KREEE

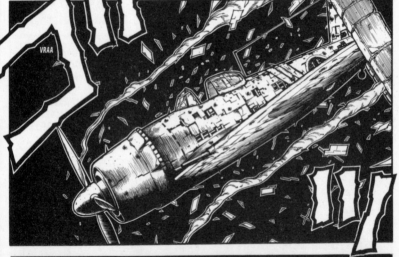

VRAA

ACT 9 / END

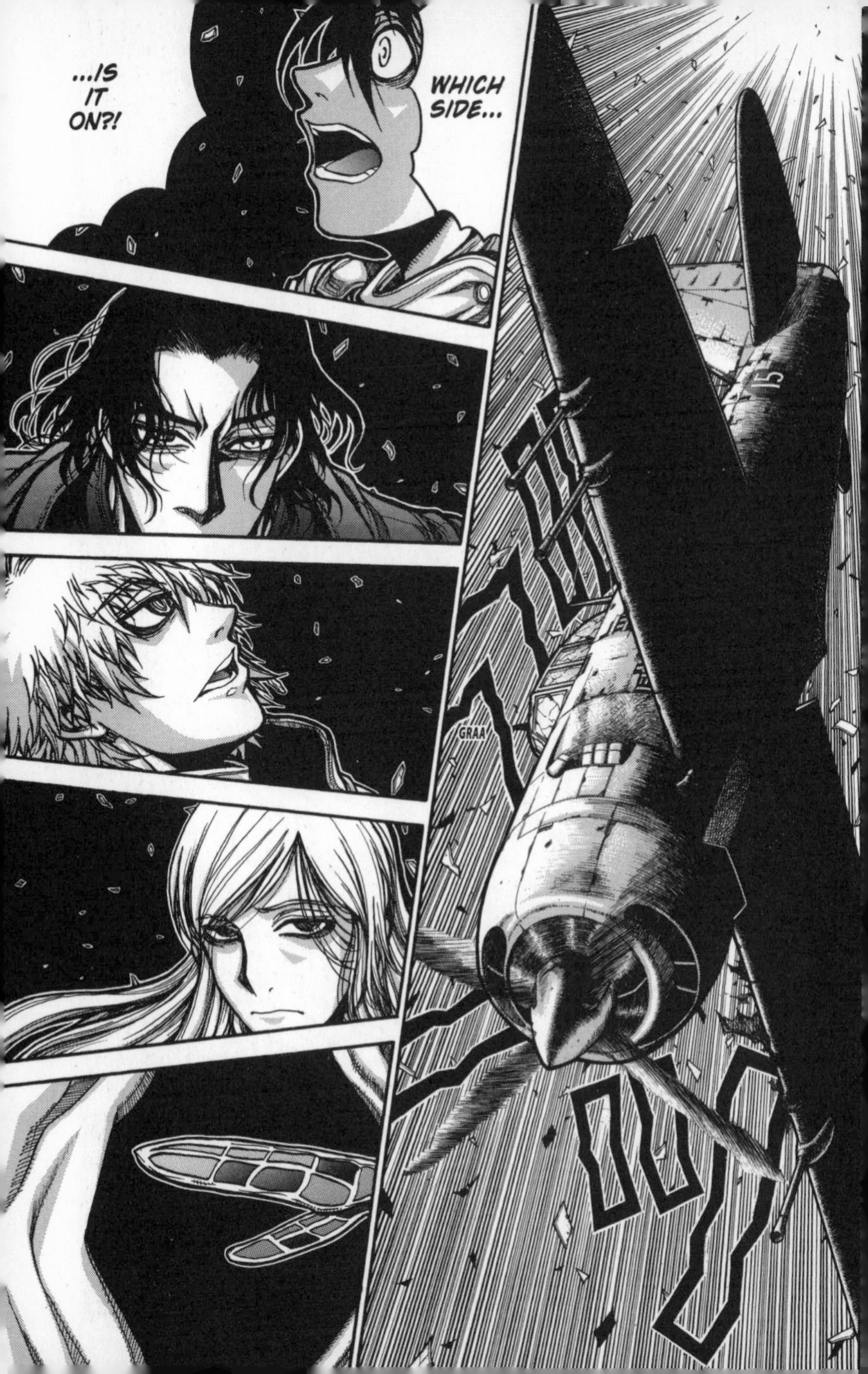
GRAA
WHICH SIDE...
...IS IT ON?!

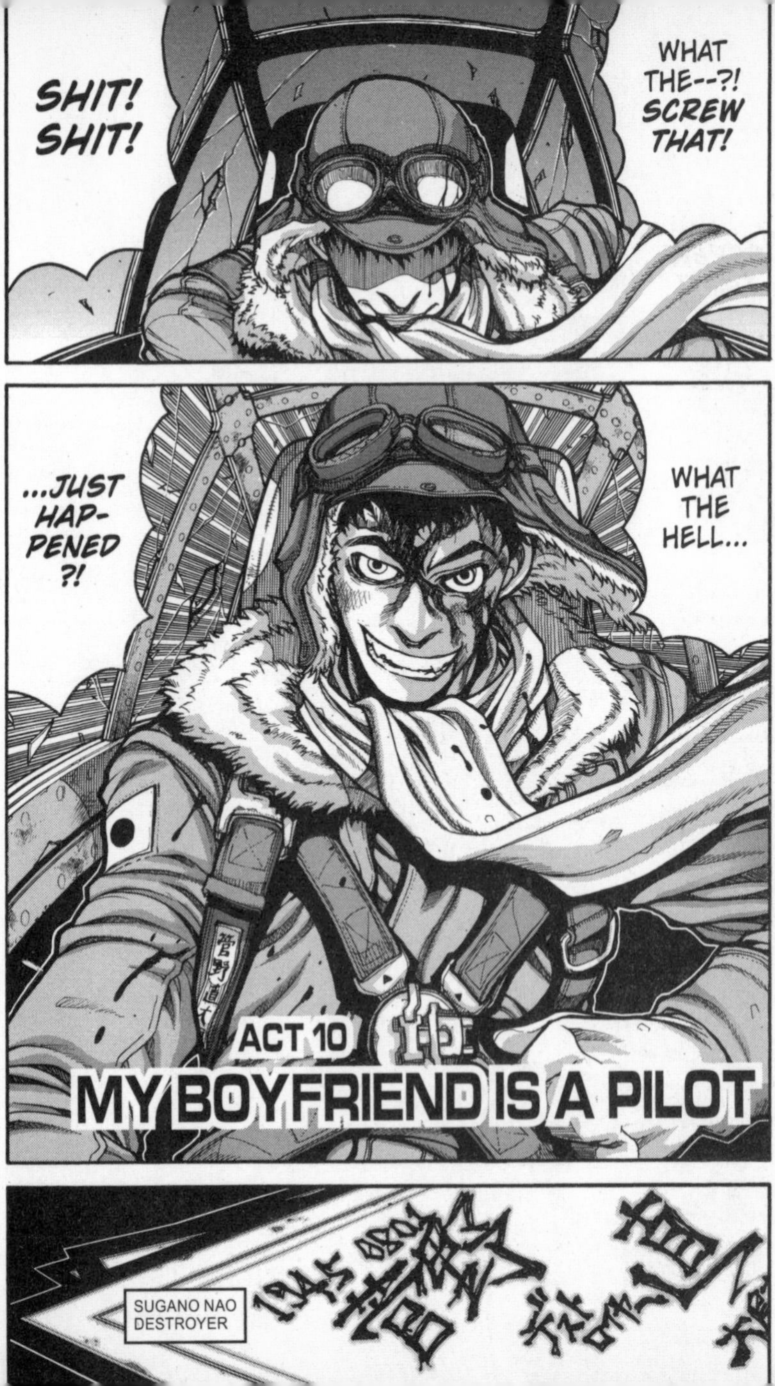
WHAT THE--?! SCREW THAT!
SHIT! SHIT!
WHAT THE HELL...
...JUST HAP-PENED ?!
ACT 10
MY BOYFRIEND IS A PILOT
SUGANO NAO DESTROYER

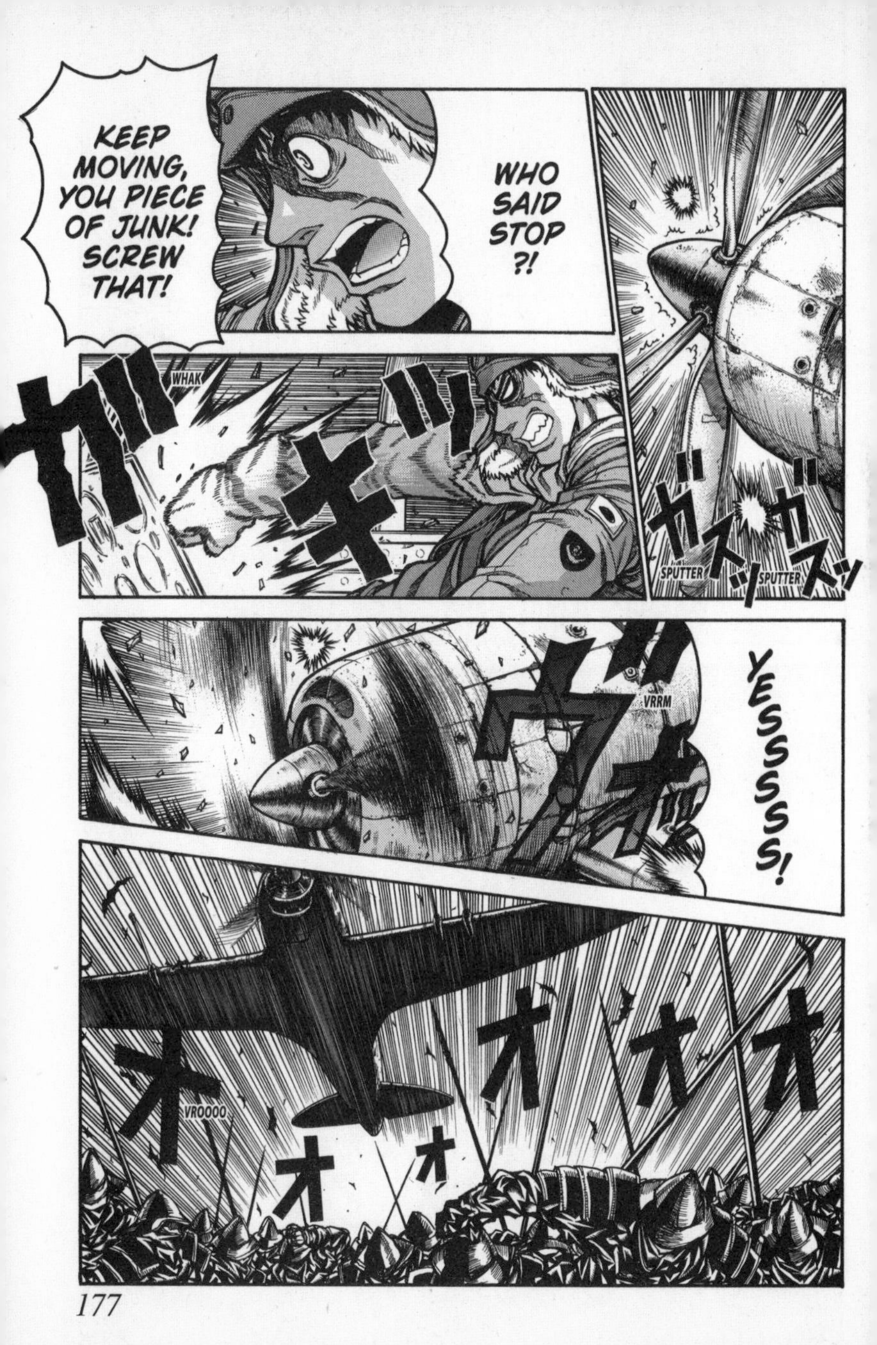
SPUTTER
SPUTTER
WHO SAID STOP?!
KEEP MOVING, YOU PIECE OF JUNK! SCREW THAT!
WHAK
YESSSSSS!
VRRM
VROOOO

SOME MOVIE STUDIO? **SCREW THAT!**

WHAT IS THAT?!

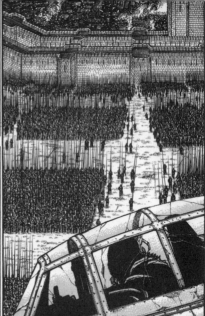

WHERE AM I? **SCREW THAT!**

WHAT THE --?!

FLAP

FLAP

...?

...!

...
...!

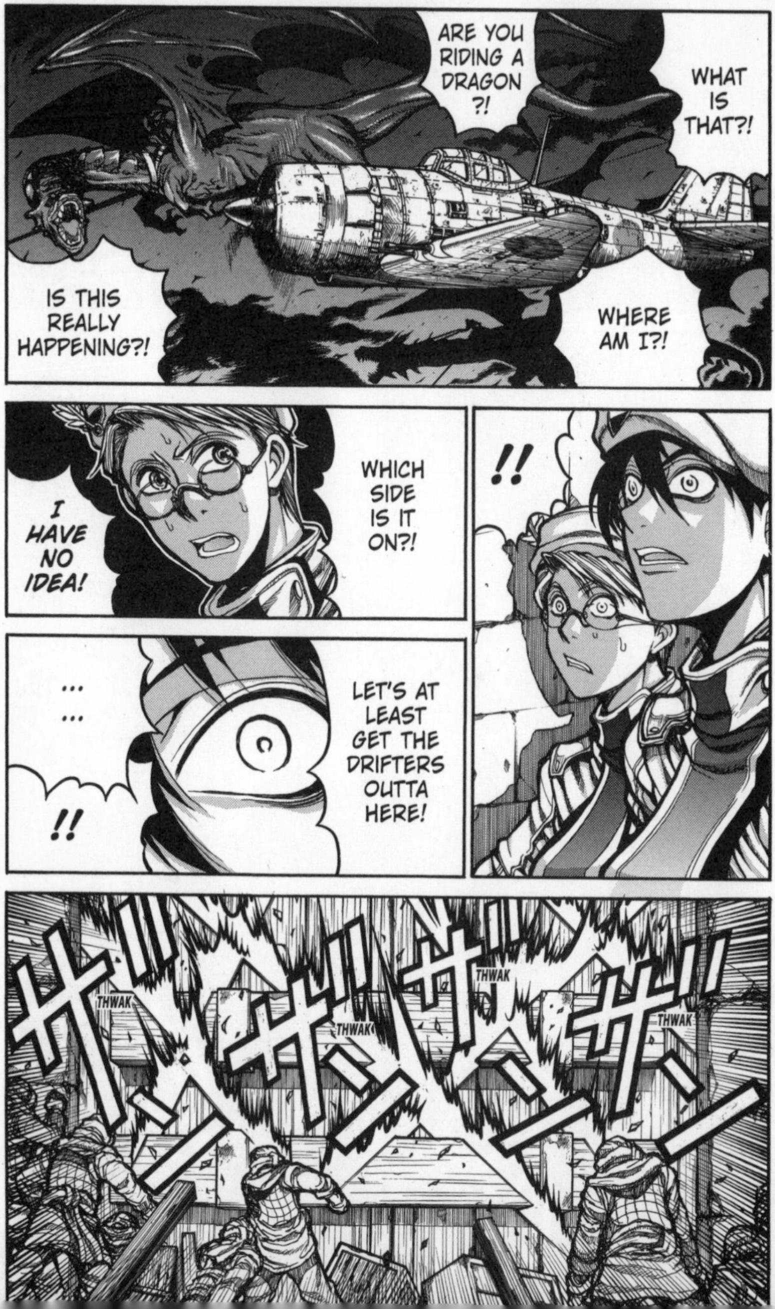
WHAT IS THAT?!
ARE YOU RIDING A DRAGON ?!
WHERE AM I?!
IS THIS REALLY HAPPENING?!
!!
WHICH SIDE IS IT ON?!
I HAVE NO IDEA!
LET'S AT LEAST GET THE DRIFTERS OUTTA HERE!
… …
!!
ザン
THWAK
ザン
THWAK
ザン
THWAK
ザン
THWAK

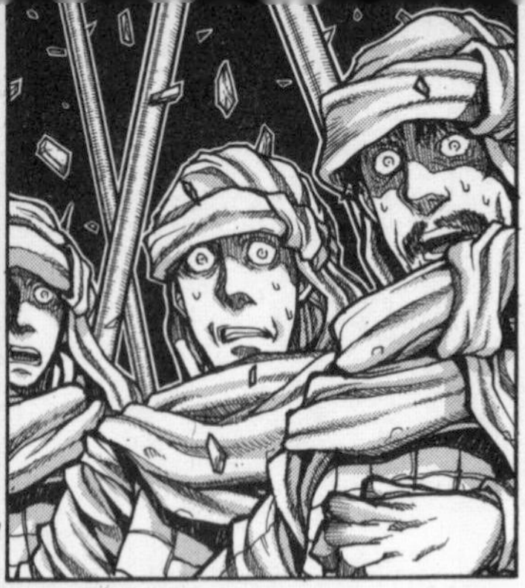

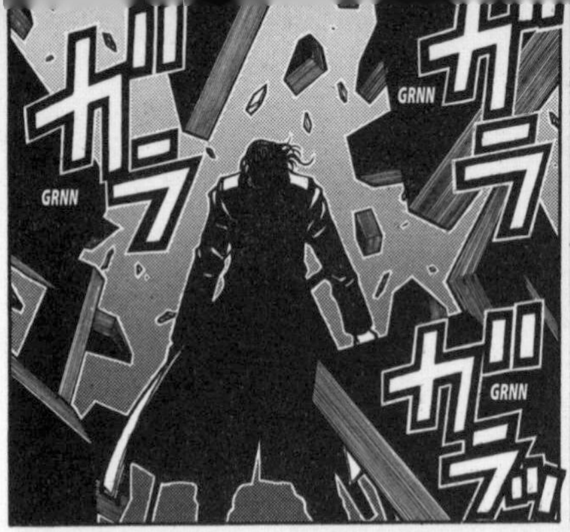
ガラ
GRNN
ガラ
GRNN
ガラッ
GRNN

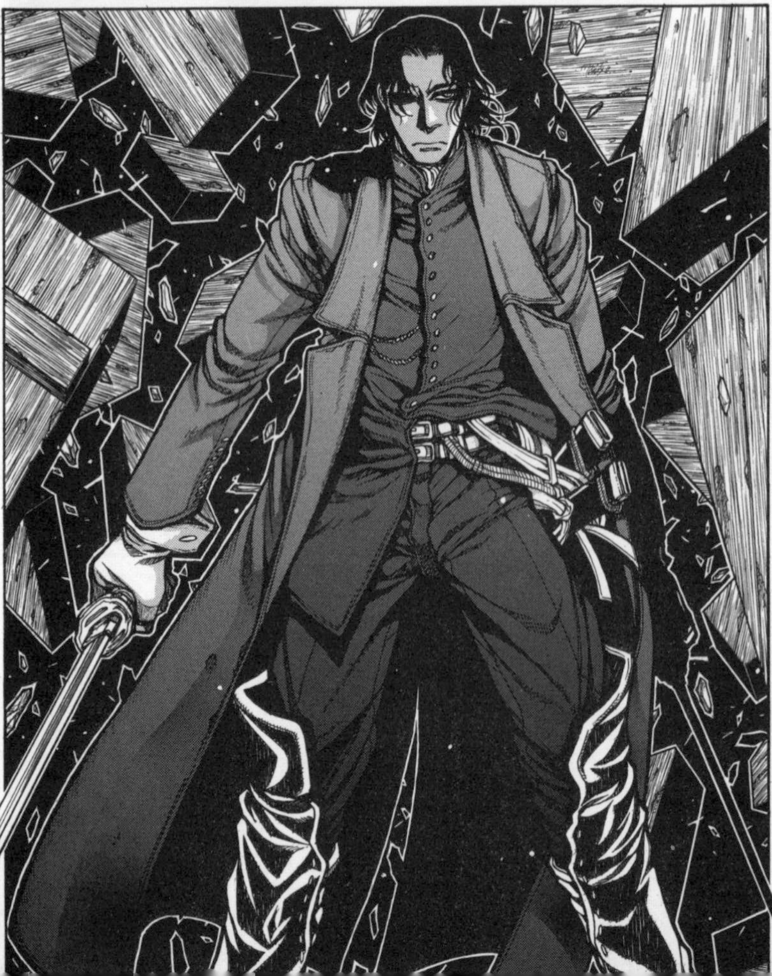

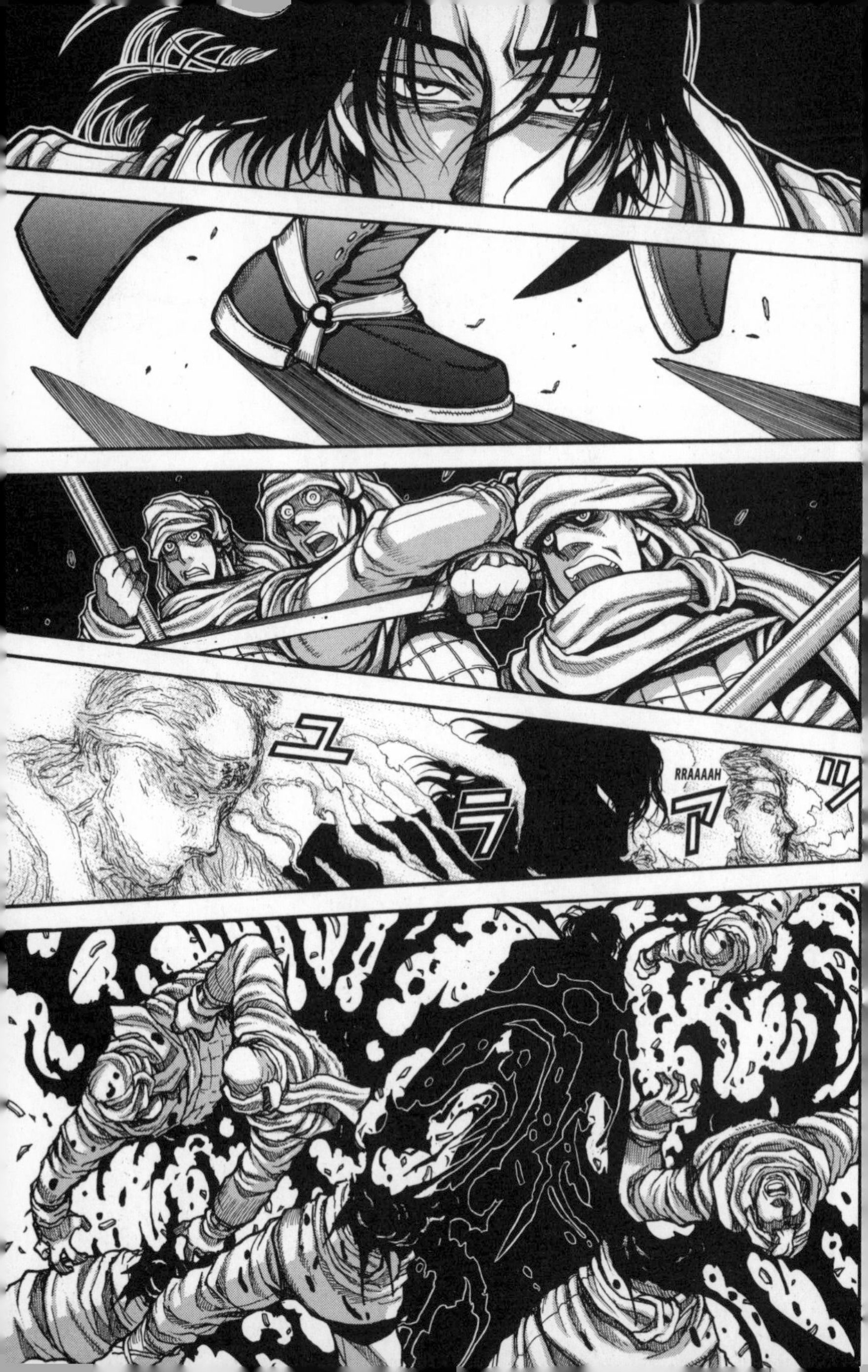
RRAAAAH

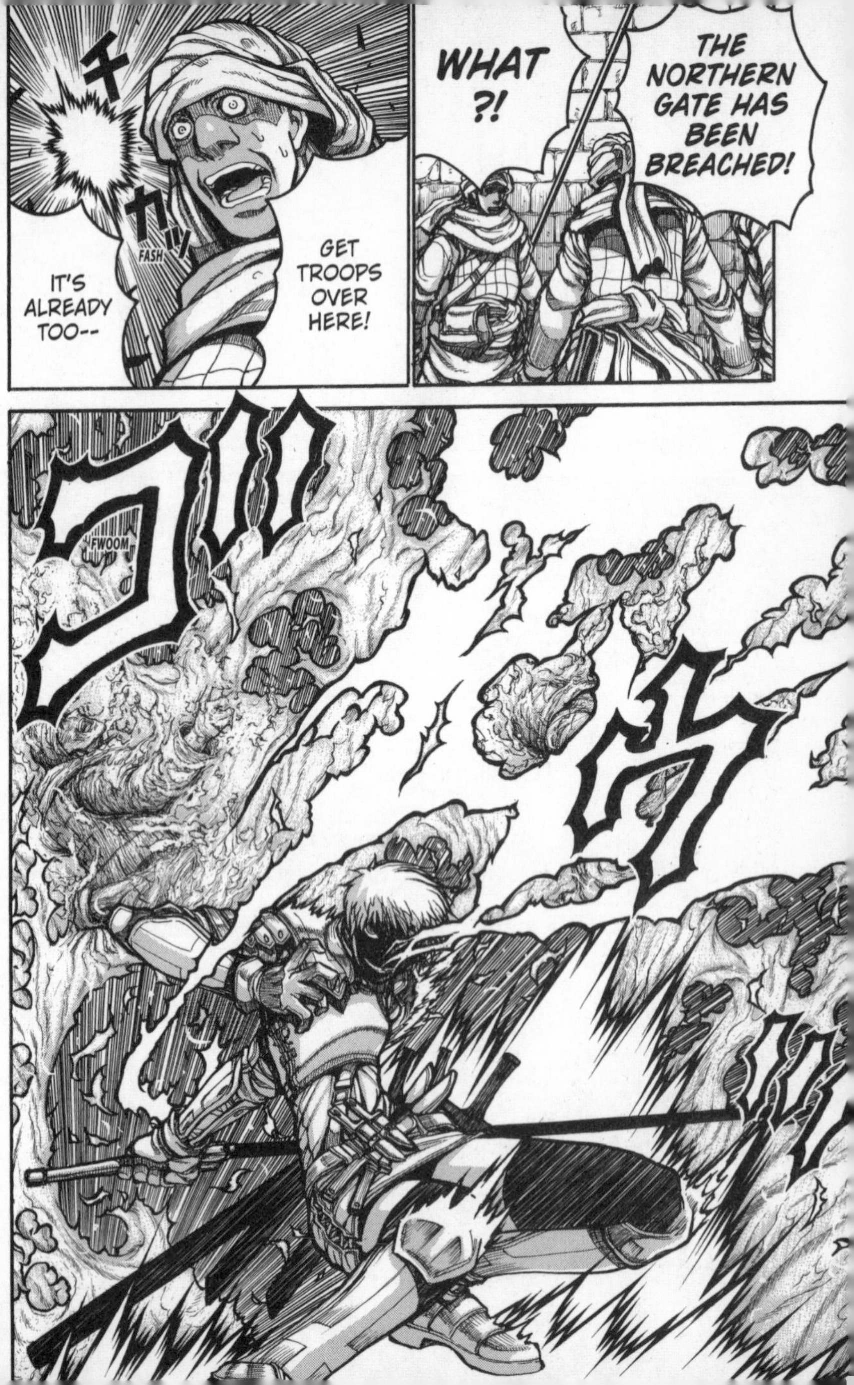
THE NORTHERN GATE HAS BEEN BREACHED!
WHAT ?!
GET TROOPS OVER HERE!
IT'S ALREADY TOO--
FASH
FWOOM

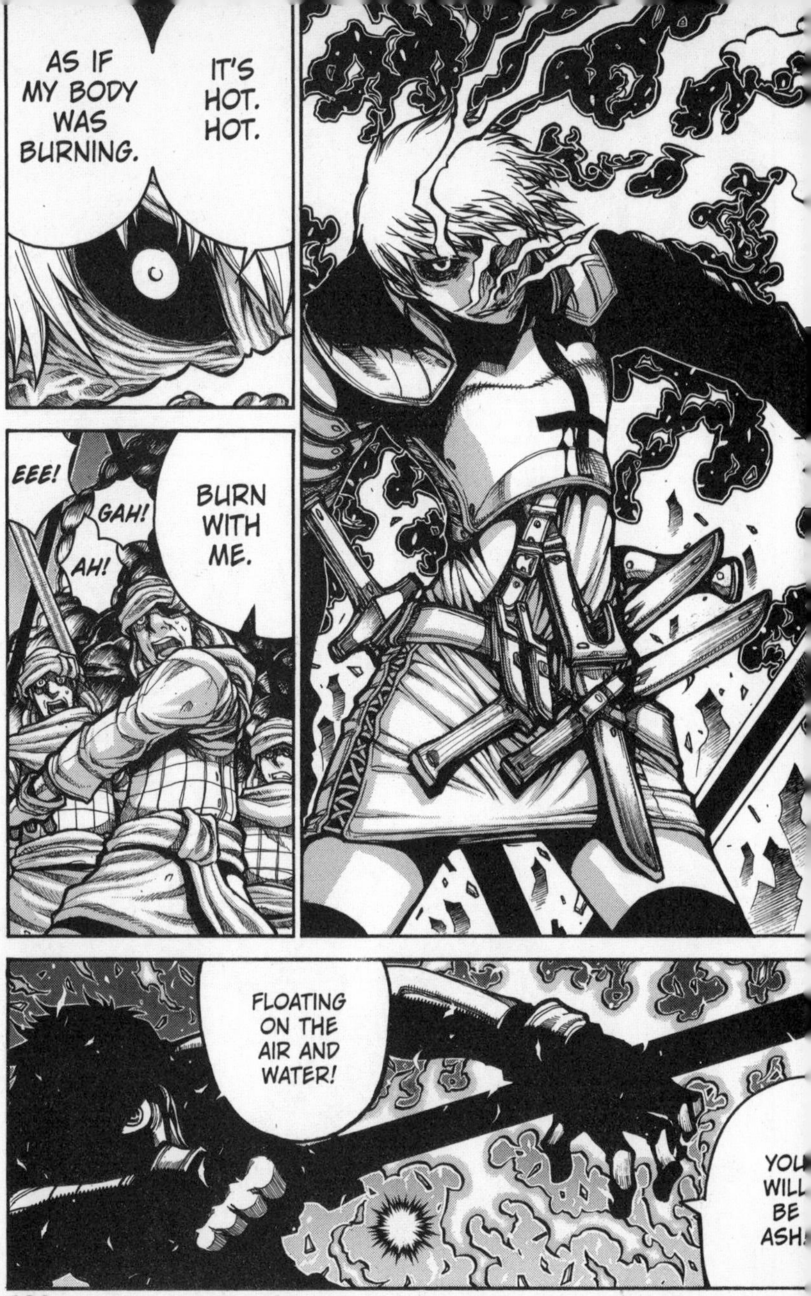
IT'S HOT. HOT.
AS IF MY BODY WAS BURNING.
BURN WITH ME.
EEE!
GAH!
AH!
YOU WILL BE ASH!
FLOATING ON THE AIR AND WATER!

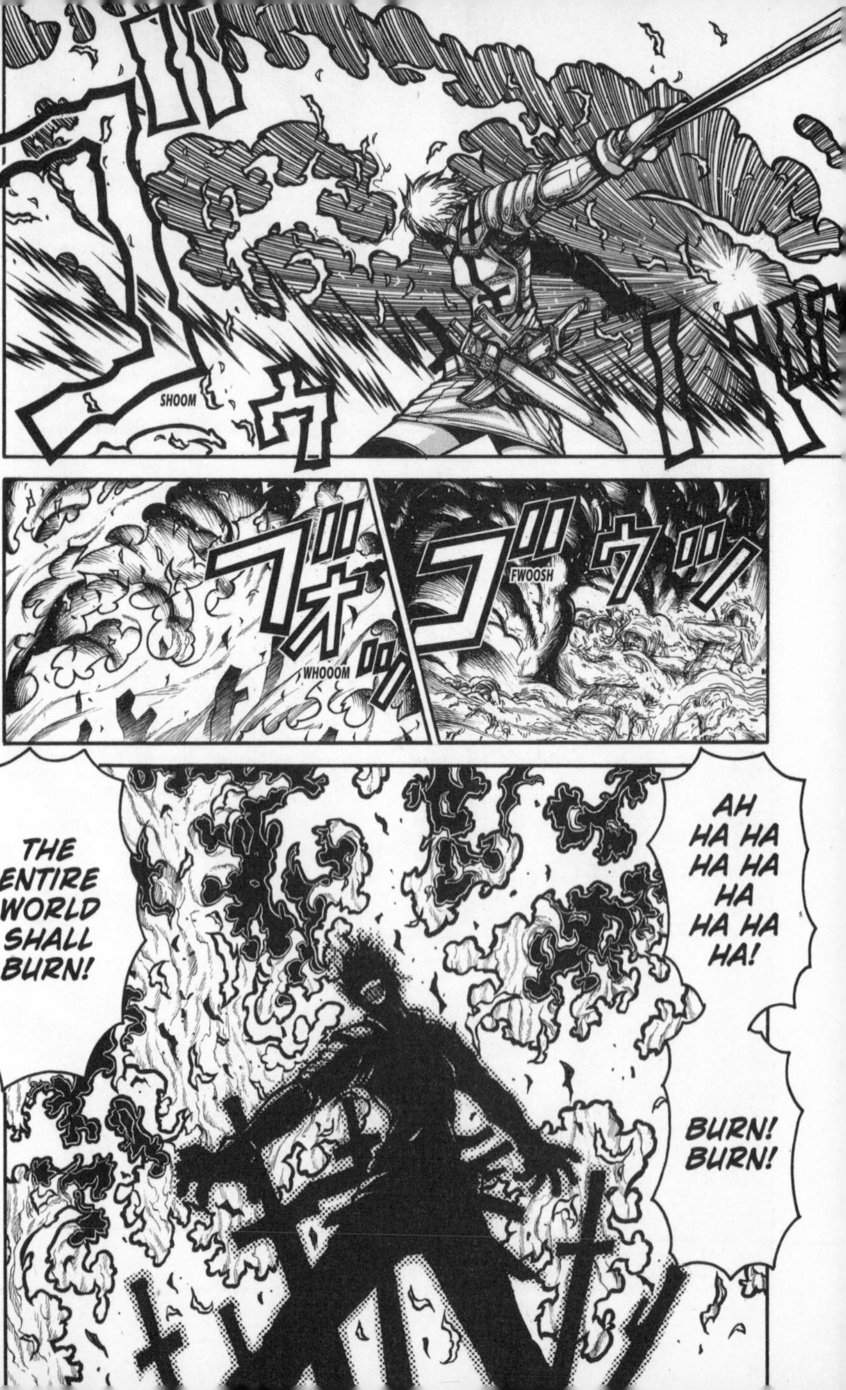
SHOOM
FWOOSH
WHOOOM
AH HA HA HA HA HA HA HA HA HA!
THE ENTIRE WORLD SHALL BURN!
BURN! BURN!

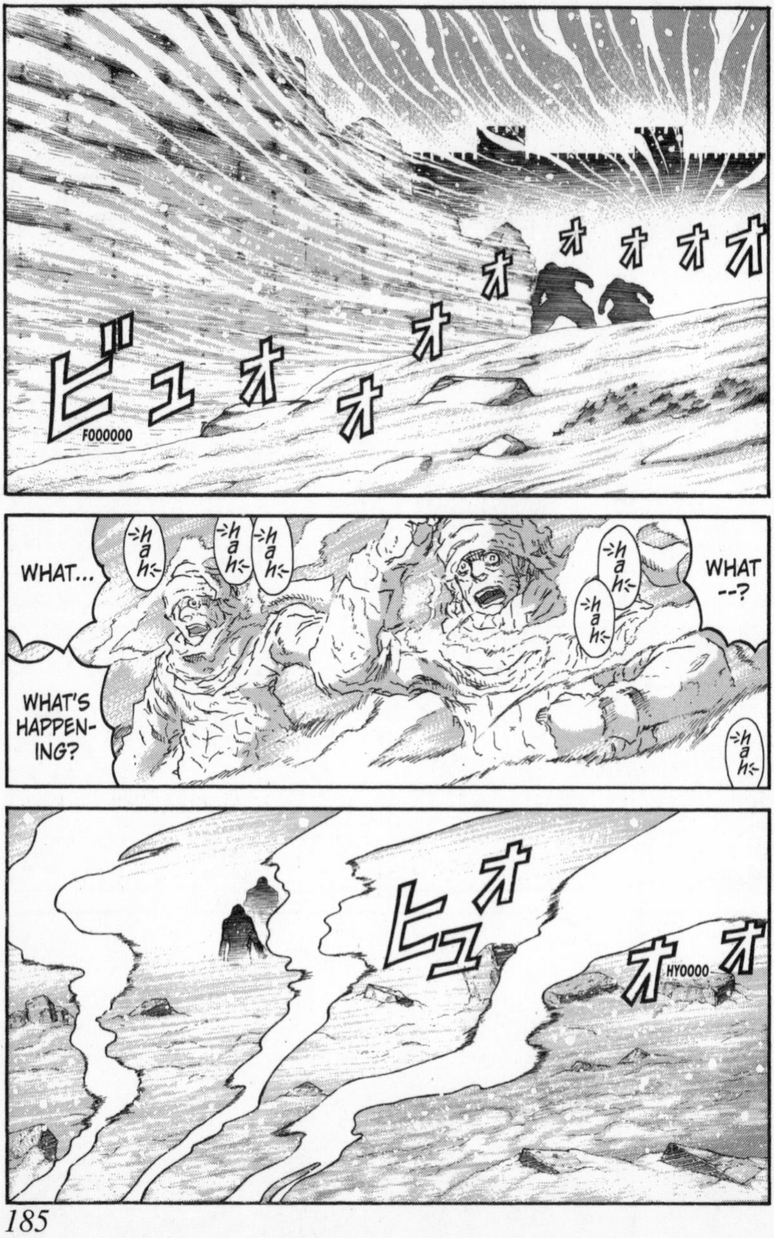
ビュオオオオオオオオ
FOOOOOO
WHAT --?
hah
hah
hah
hah
hah
WHAT...
WHAT'S HAPPENING?
ヒュオオオ
HYOOOO

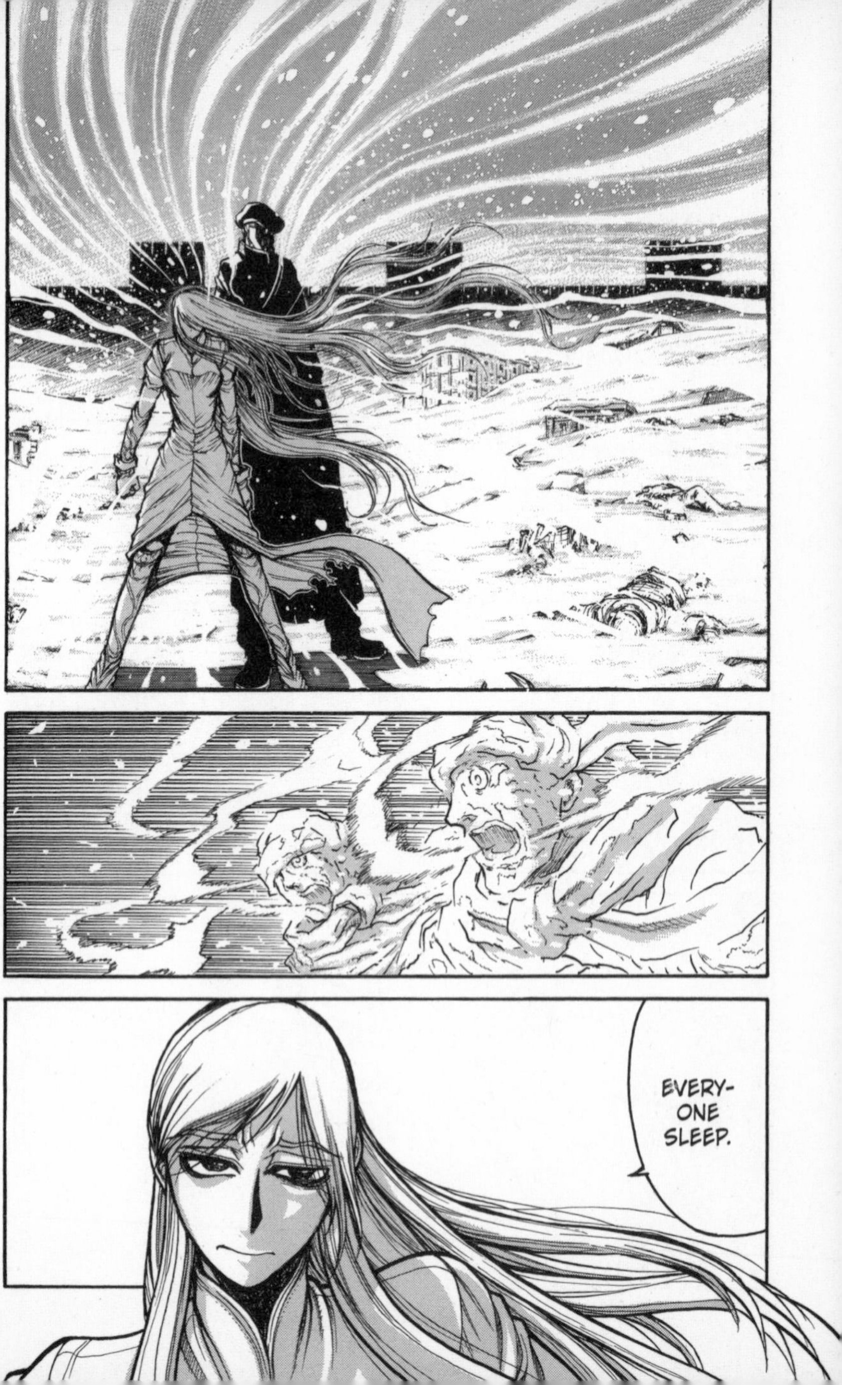
EVERY-
ONE
SLEEP.

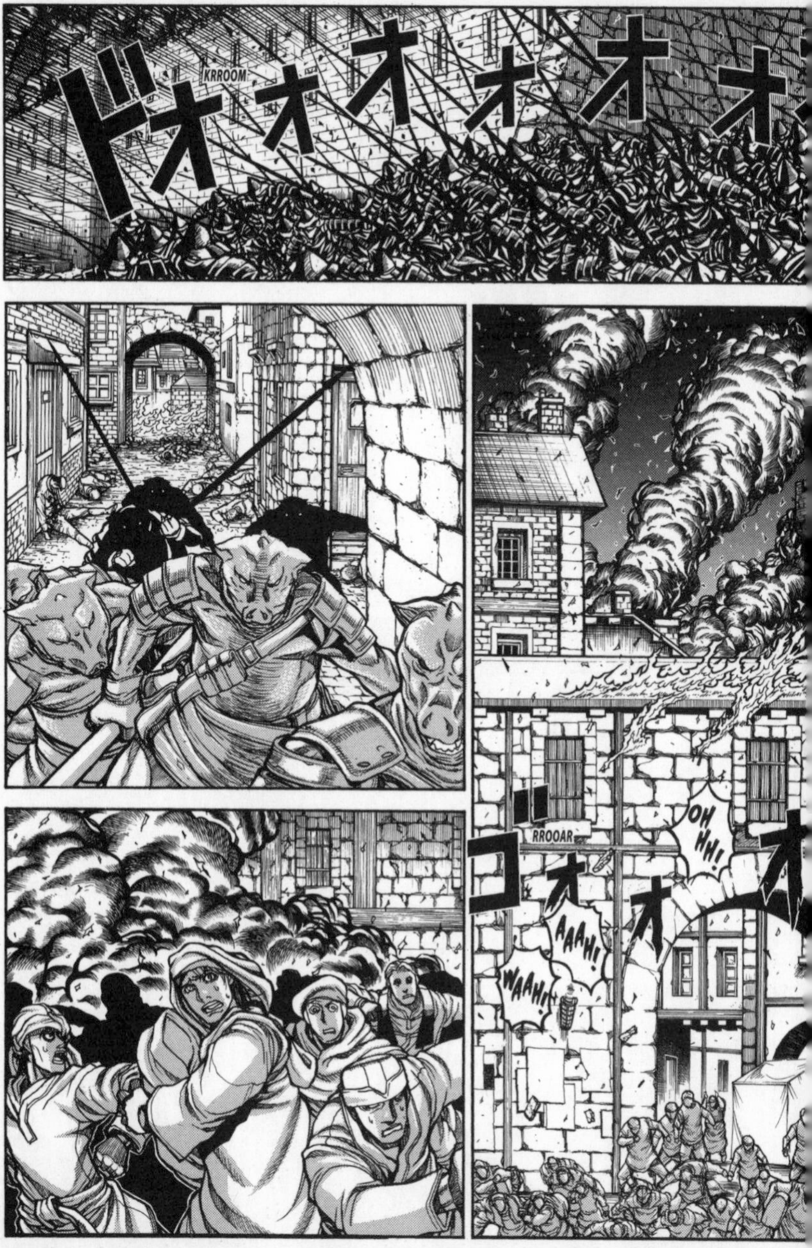
ドォオォオオ
KRROOM
RROOAR
ゴォオオ
OHHH!
AAAH!
WAAH!

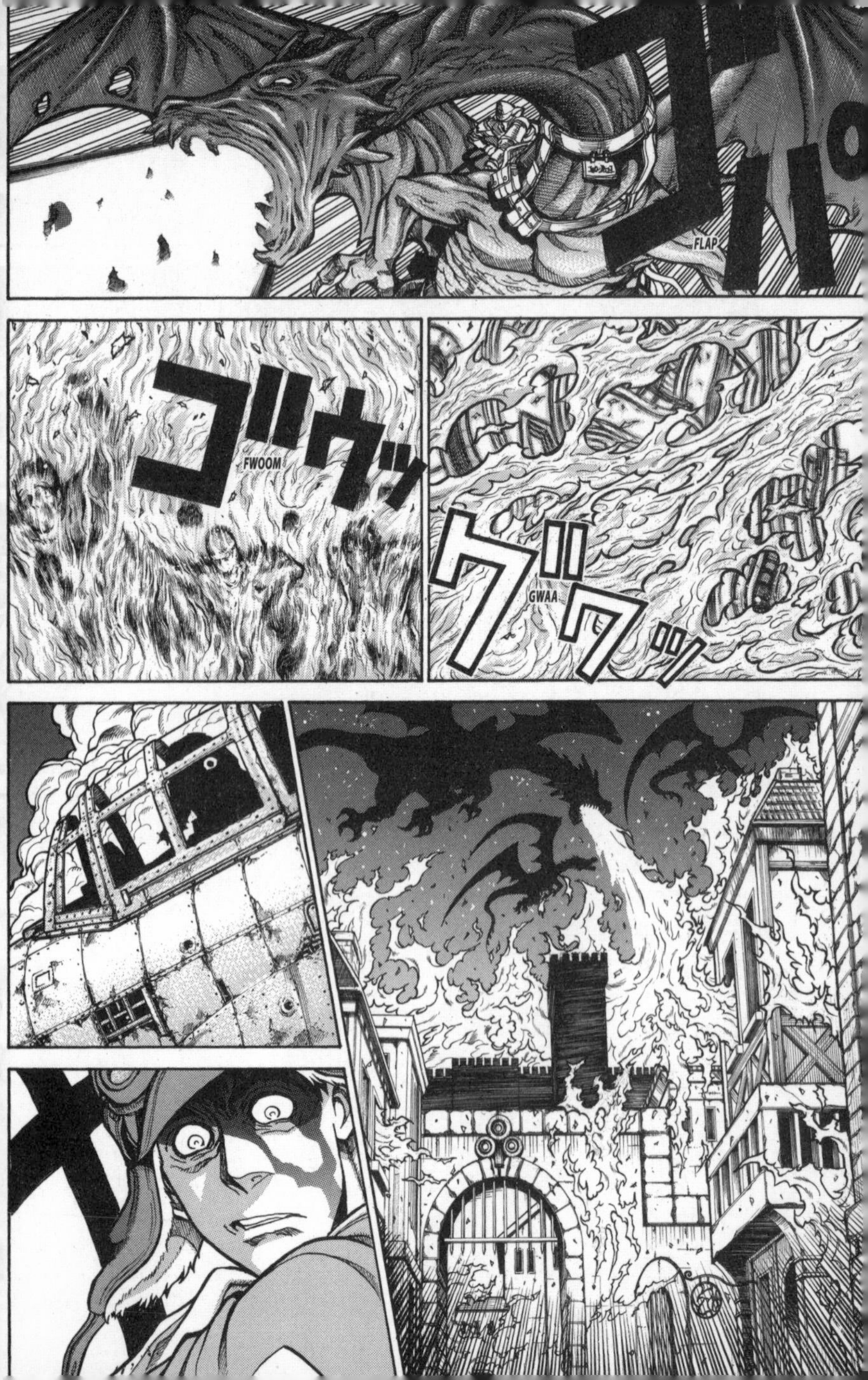
FLAP
GWAA
ゴウッ
FWOOM

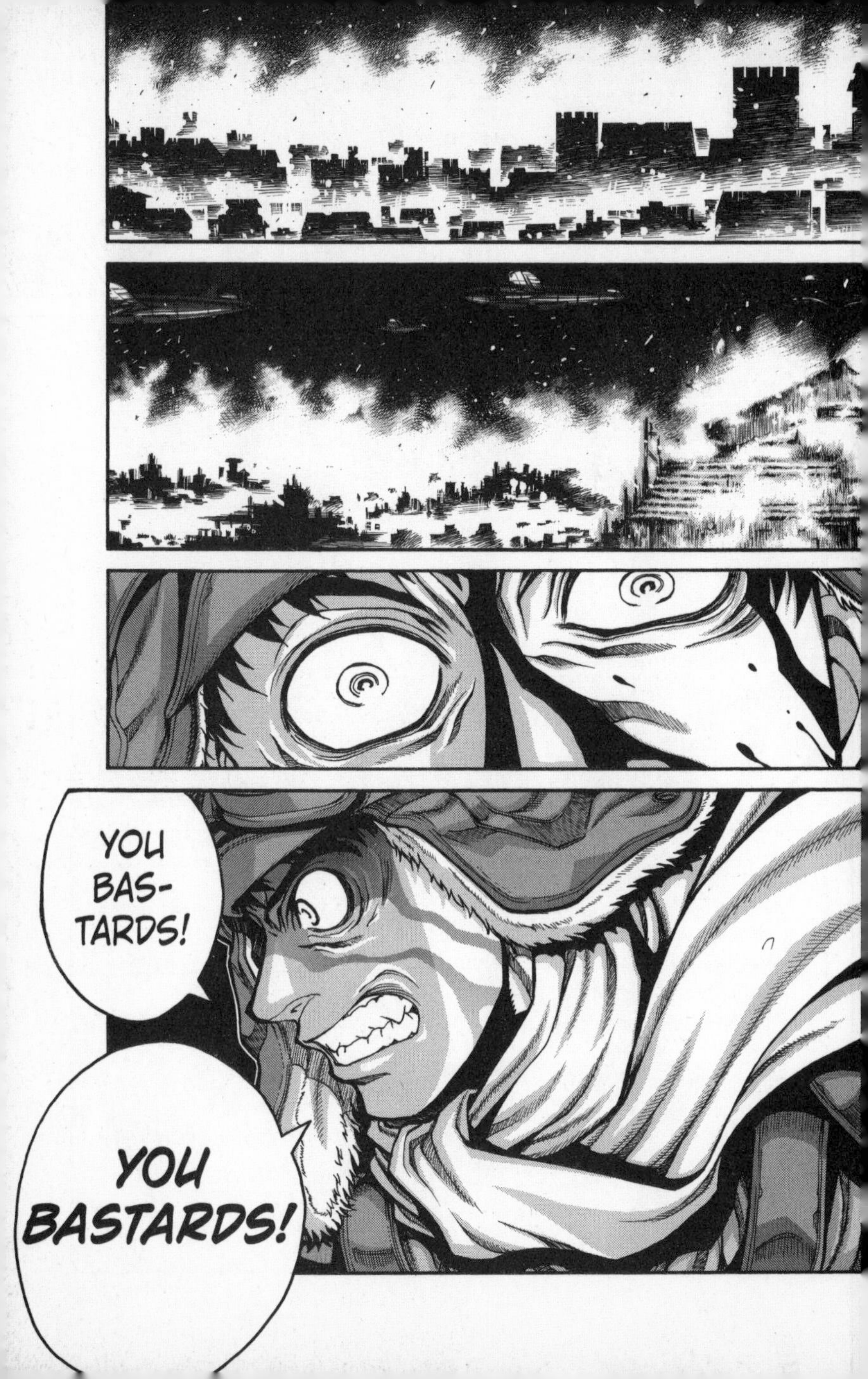
YOU BAS- TARDS!
YOU BASTARDS!

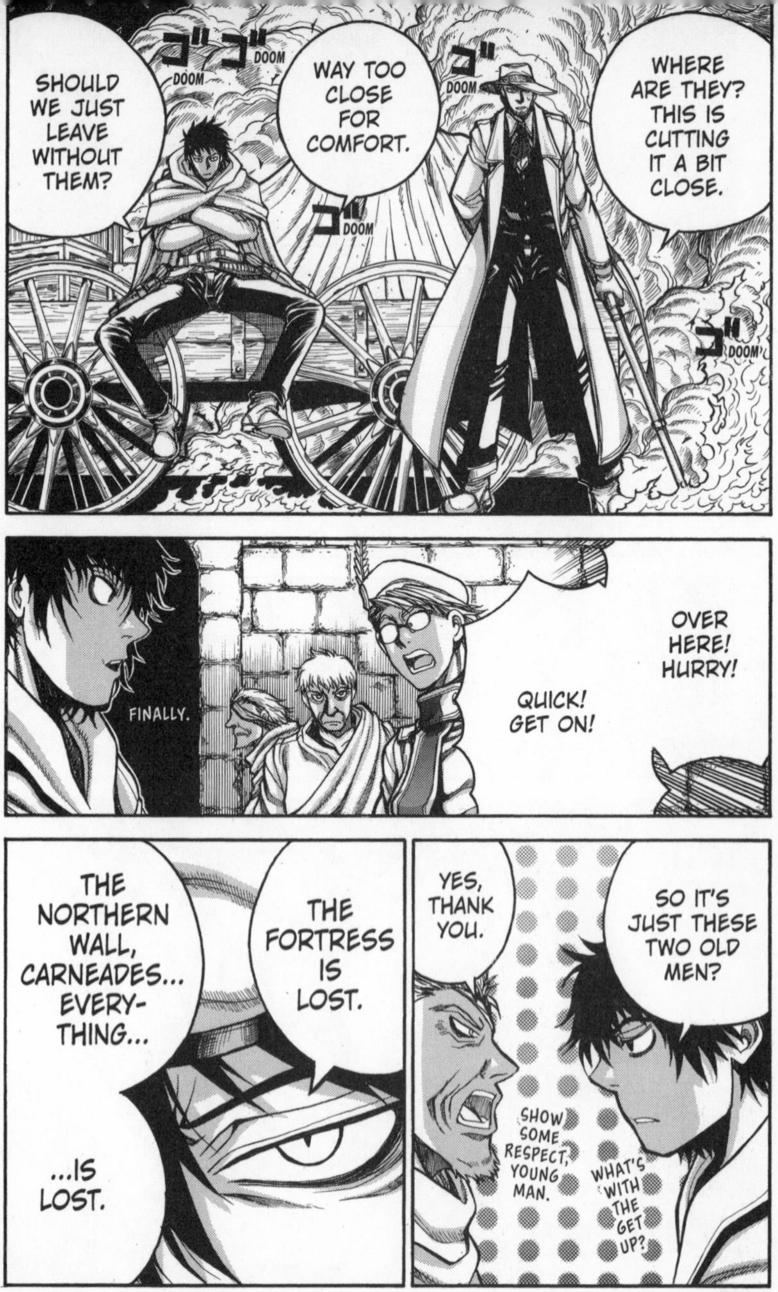
DOOM
WHERE ARE THEY? THIS IS CUTTING IT A BIT CLOSE.
DOOM
DOOM
WAY TOO CLOSE FOR COMFORT.
DOOM
DOOM
SHOULD WE JUST LEAVE WITHOUT THEM?
DOOM
OVER HERE! HURRY!
QUICK! GET ON!
FINALLY.
SO IT'S JUST THESE TWO OLD MEN?
YES, THANK YOU.
WHAT'S WITH THE GET UP?
SHOW SOME RESPECT, YOUNG MAN.
THE FORTRESS IS LOST.
THE NORTHERN WALL, CARNEADES... EVERY-THING...
...IS LOST.

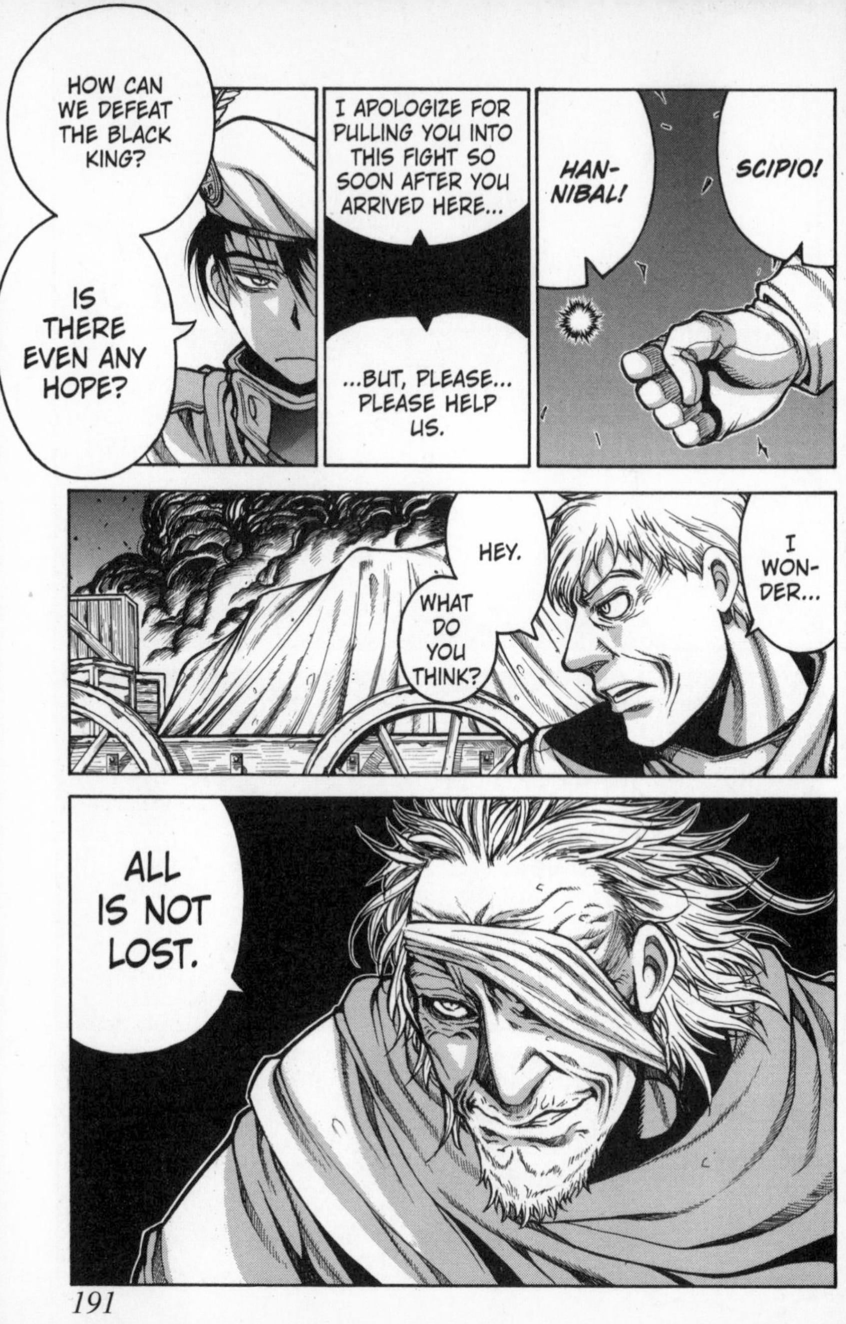
SCIPIO!
HAN-NIBAL!
I APOLOGIZE FOR PULLING YOU INTO THIS FIGHT SO SOON AFTER YOU ARRIVED HERE...
...BUT, PLEASE... PLEASE HELP US.
HOW CAN WE DEFEAT THE BLACK KING?
IS THERE EVEN ANY HOPE?
I WON-DER...
HEY.
WHAT DO YOU THINK?
ALL IS NOT LOST.

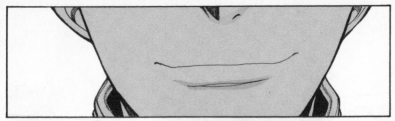

...THEY JOIN US...

ALL IS NOT LOST!

AND, IF *THEY*...

THERE IS STILL HOPE!

THE WARRIORS FROM THE CASTLE RUINS!

GO!

ACT 10 / END

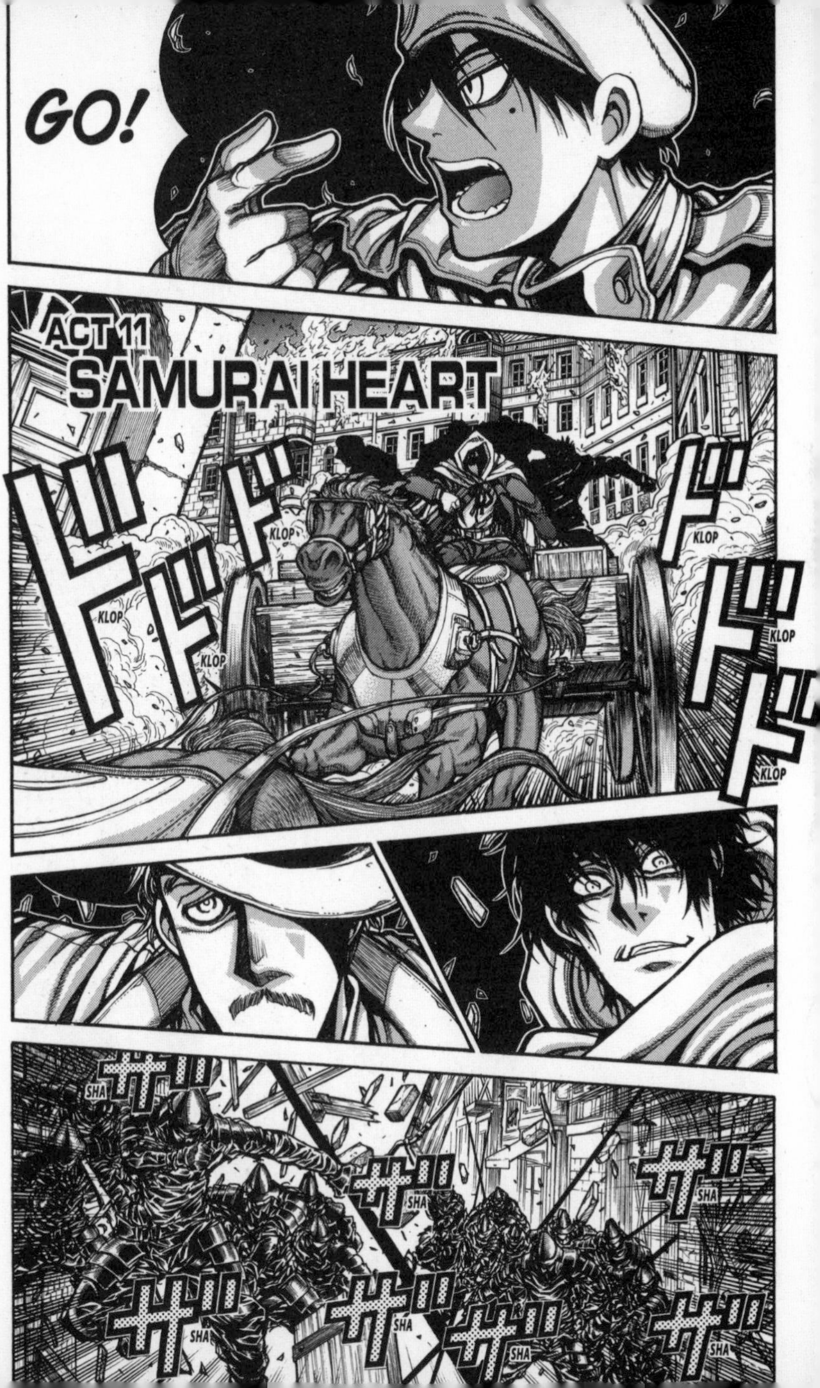
GO!
ACT 11
SAMURAI HEART
ドッ KLOP
ドッ KLOP
ドッ KLOP
ドッ KLOP
ドッ KLOP
ドッ KLOP
ドッ KLOP
ザッ SHA
ザッ SHA
ザッ SHA
ザッ SHA
ザッ SHA
ザッ SHA
ザッ SHA

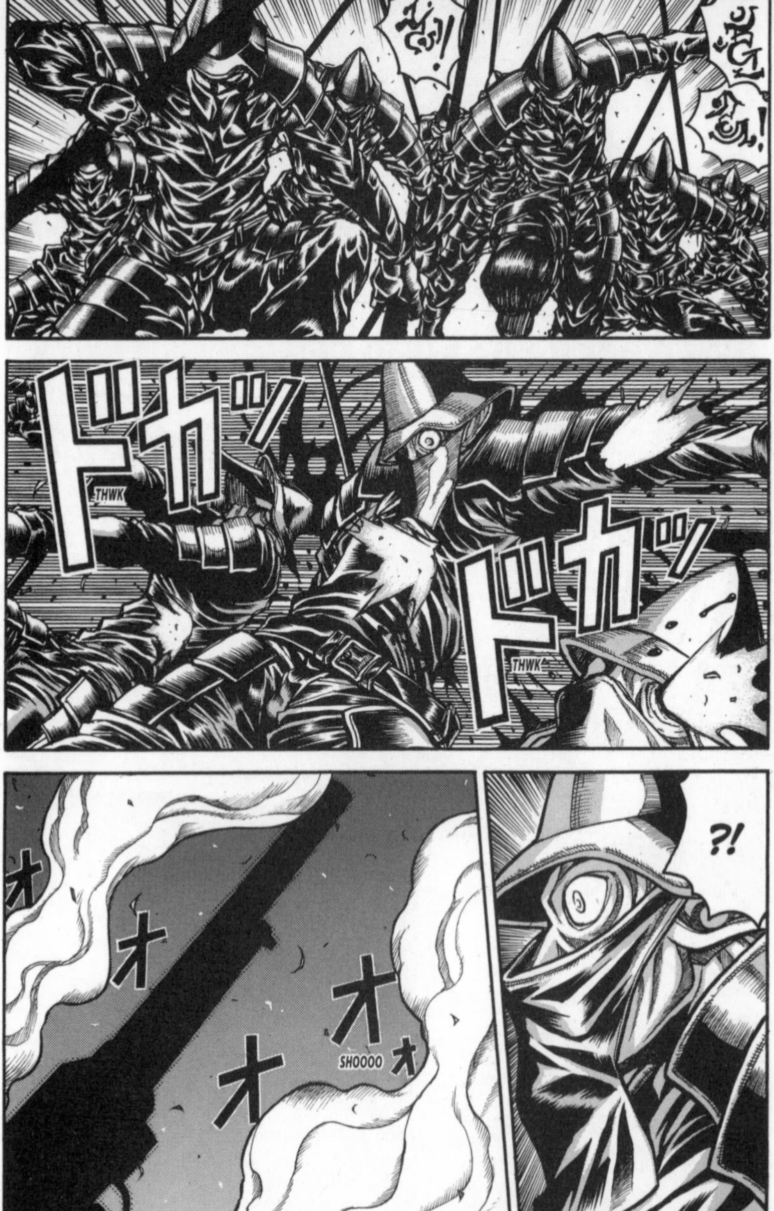
ドガッ
THWK
ドガッ
THWK
?!
オオオオオ
SHOOOO

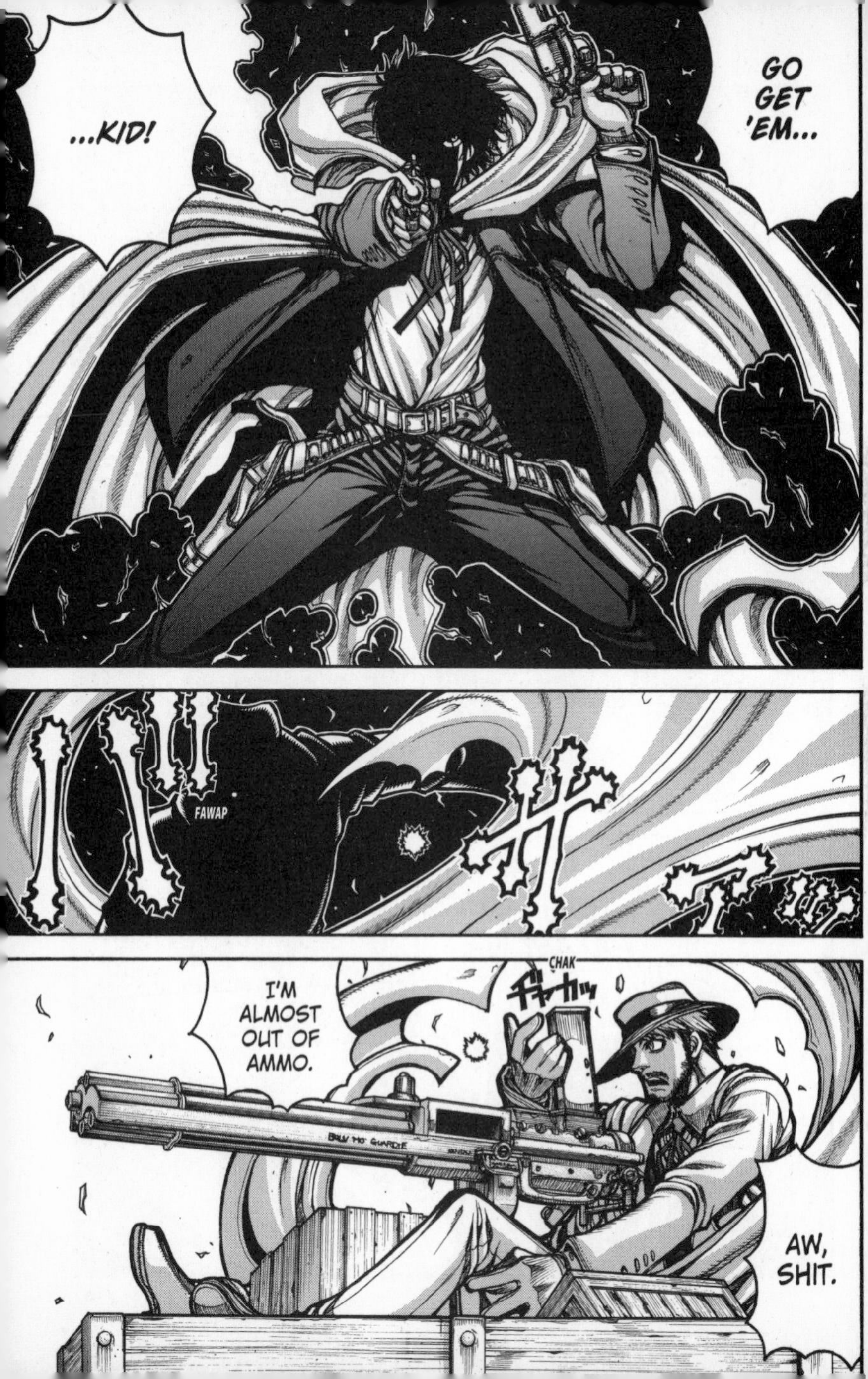
GO GET 'EM...
...KID!
FAWAP
CHAK
I'M ALMOST OUT OF AMMO.
AW, SHIT.

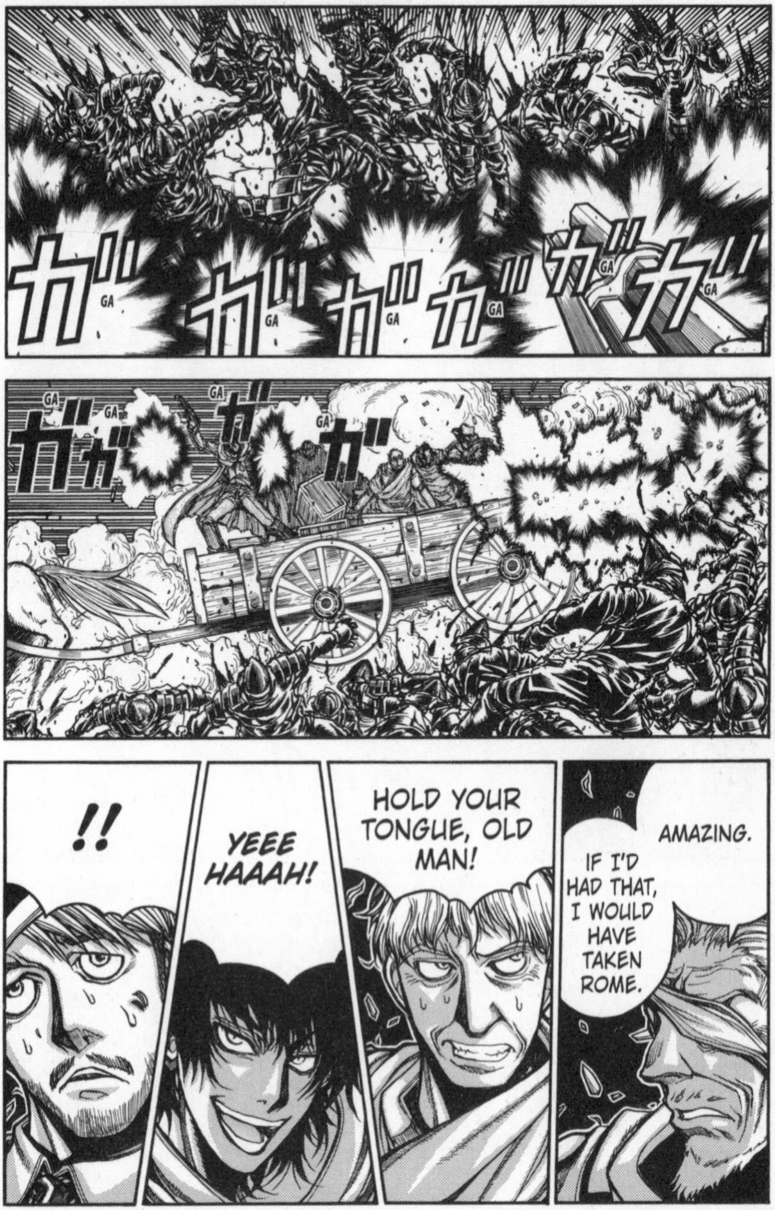
ガガガガガガ
GA GA GA GA GA GA
ガガガ
GA GA GA GA
AMAZING.
IF I'D HAD THAT, I WOULD HAVE TAKEN ROME.
HOLD YOUR TONGUE, OLD MAN!
YEEE HAAAH!
!!

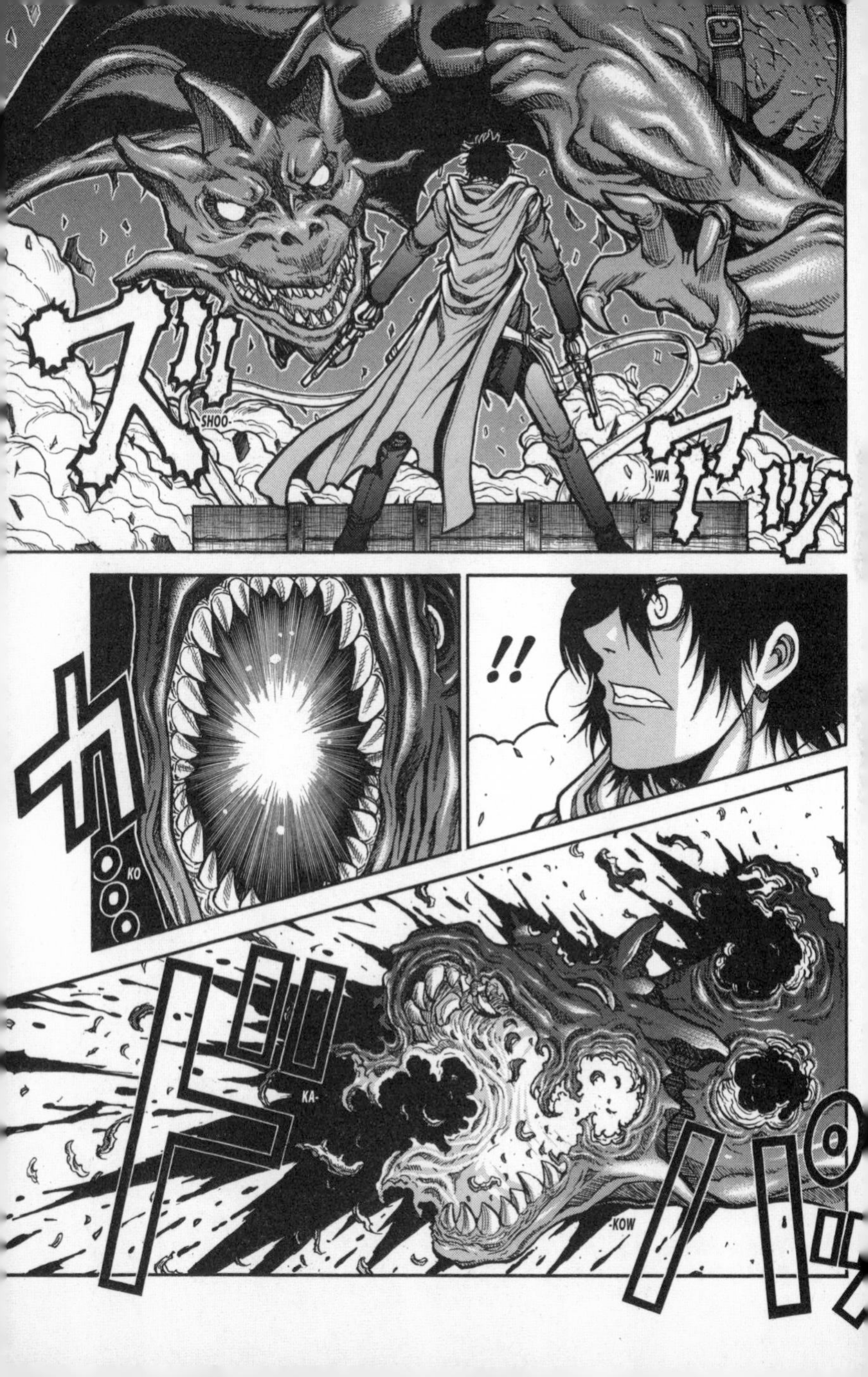
SHOO-
-WA
!!
KO
KA-
-KOW

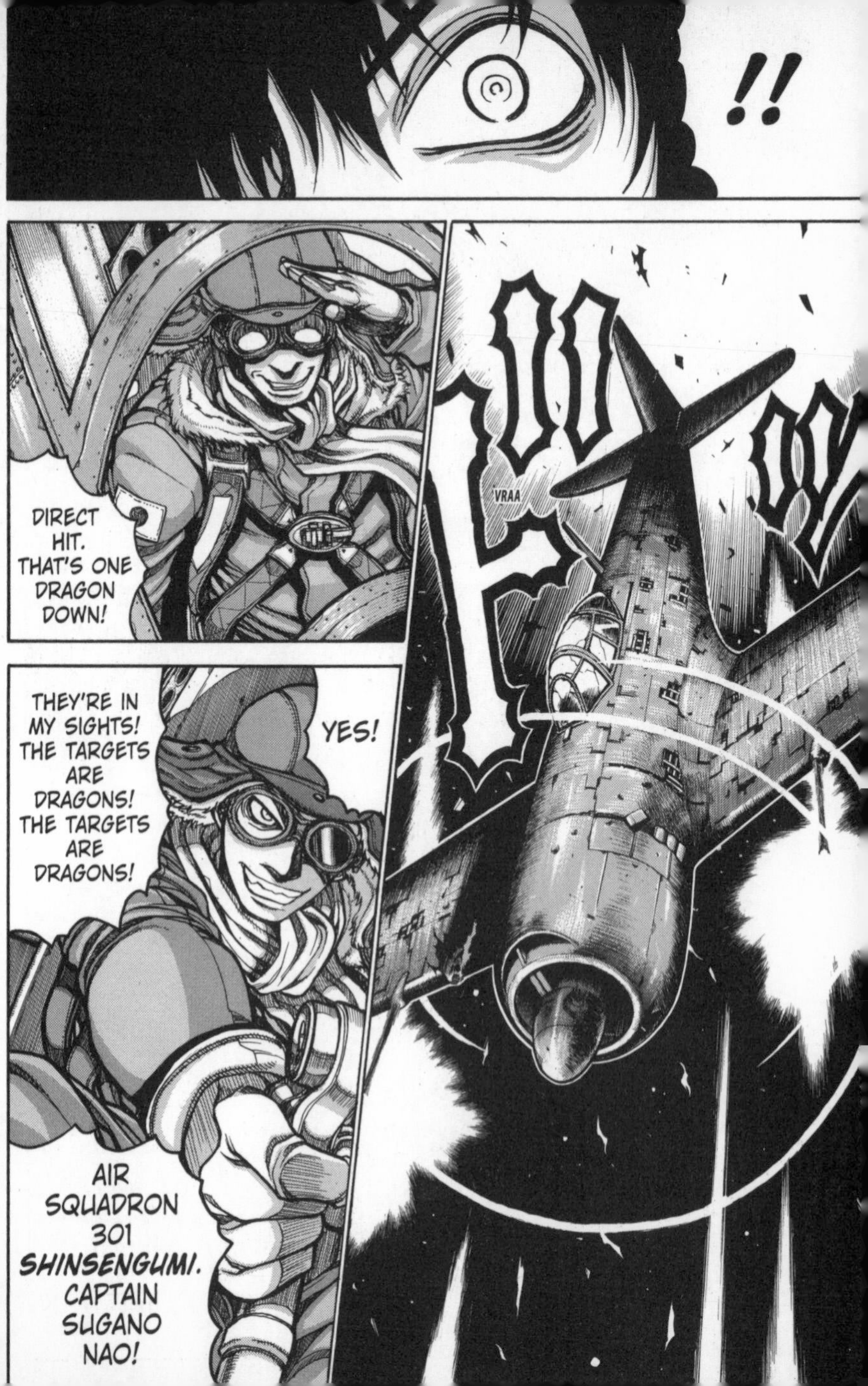
!!
VRAA
DIRECT HIT. THAT'S ONE DRAGON DOWN!
YES!
THEY'RE IN MY SIGHTS! THE TARGETS ARE DRAGONS! THE TARGETS ARE DRAGONS!
AIR SQUADRON 301 *SHINSENGUMI*. CAPTAIN SUGANO NAO!

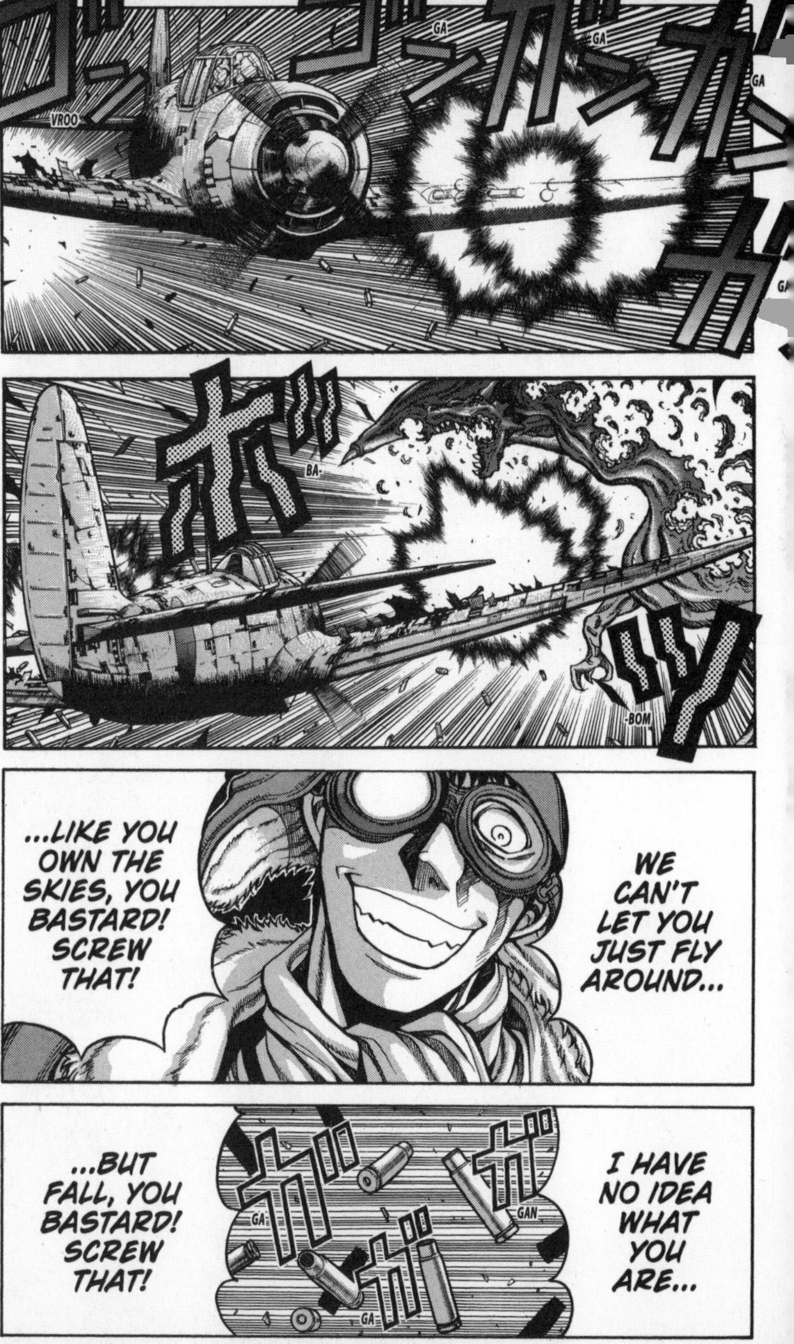
GA
GA
GA
VROO
BA-
-BOM
WE CAN'T LET YOU JUST FLY AROUND...
...LIKE YOU OWN THE SKIES, YOU BASTARD! SCREW THAT!
I HAVE NO IDEA WHAT YOU ARE...
GAN
GA
GA
...BUT FALL, YOU BASTARD! SCREW THAT!

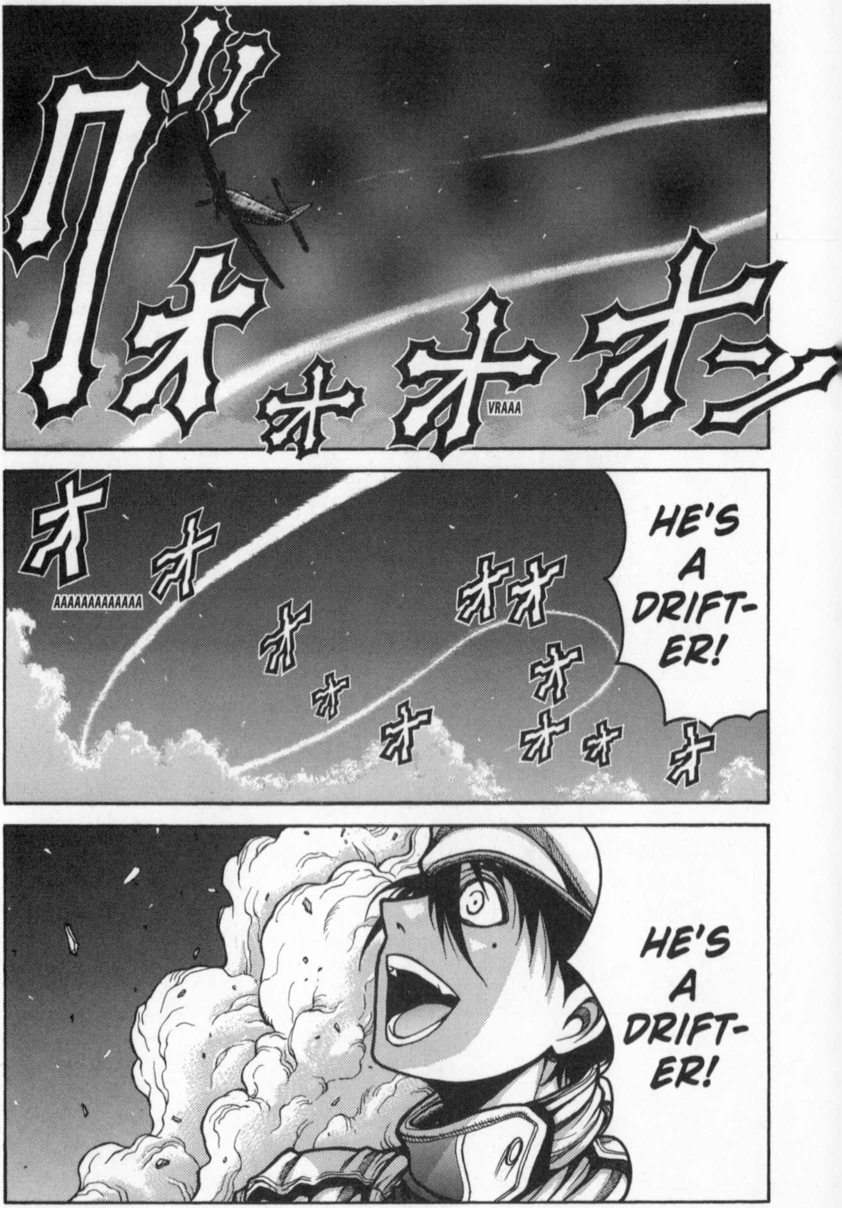
VRAAA
AAAAAAAAAAAAA
HE'S A DRIFTER!
HE'S A DRIFTER!

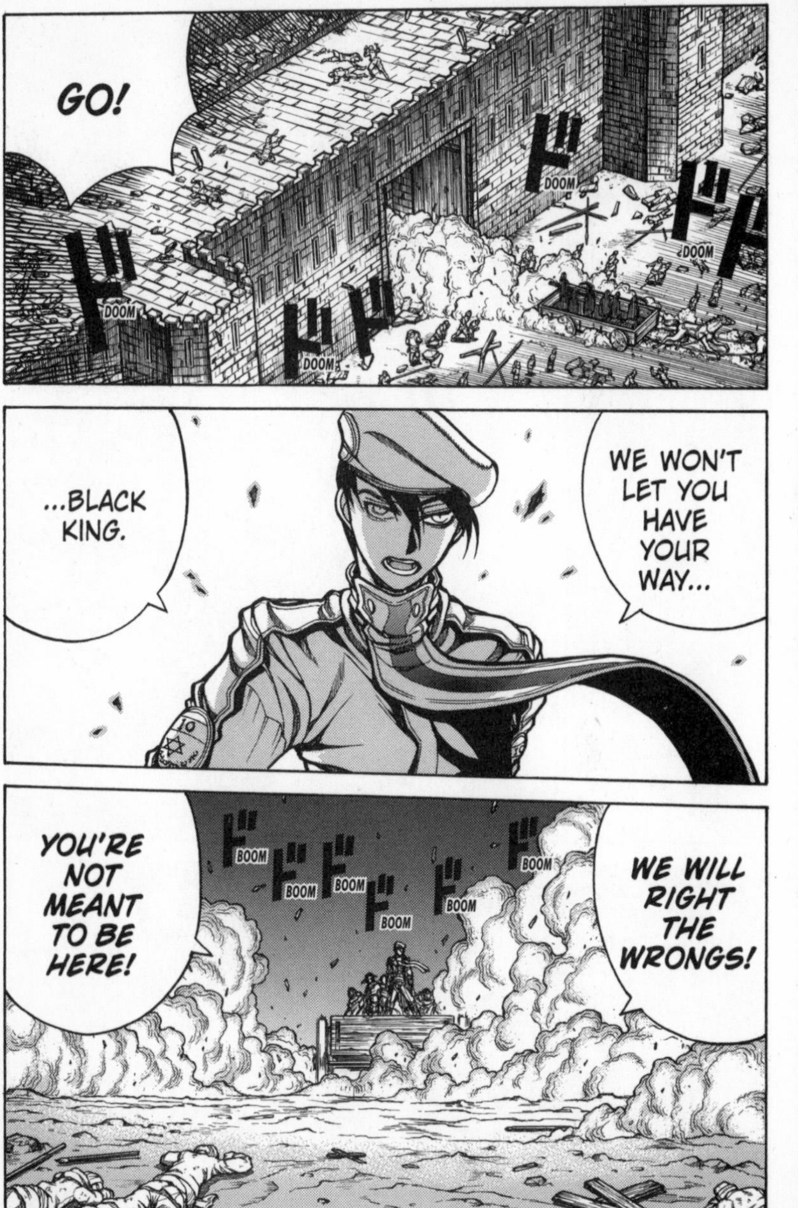
GO!
ドドドドドド
DOOM DOOM DOOM DOOM
WE WON'T LET YOU HAVE YOUR WAY...
...BLACK KING.
WE WILL RIGHT THE WRONGS!
ドドドドドド
BOOM BOOM BOOM BOOM BOOM BOOM
YOU'RE NOT MEANT TO BE HERE!

オオオオオオオ
FWOOOOOSH
SNRRT SNRRK.
SNRRT.
SNRRK SNRRT.
IT'S ALREADY TOO LATE.
IT'S FALLEN FRUIT.
SKOOSH
SKOOSH
SKISH

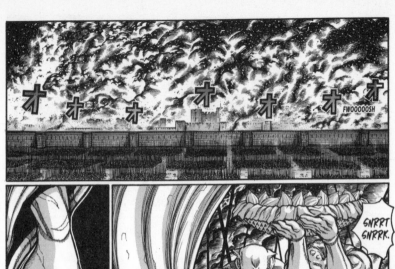

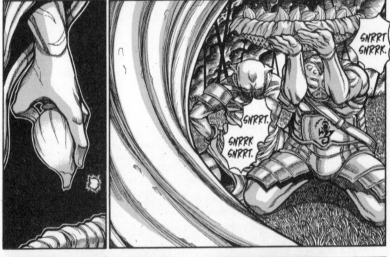

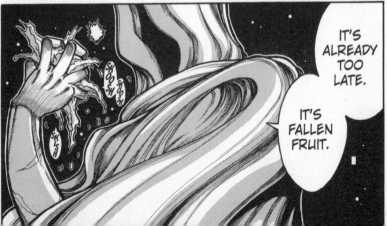

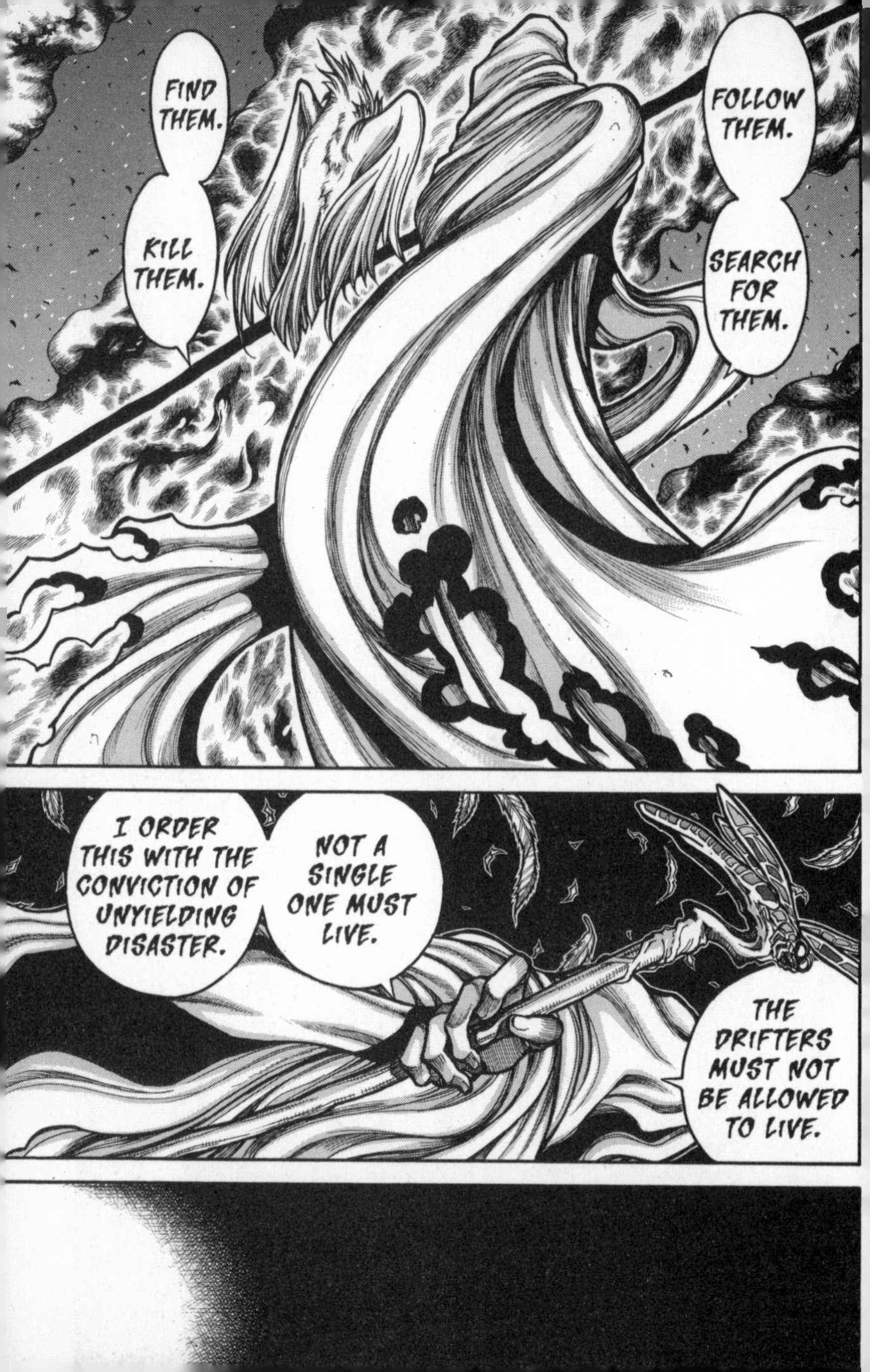
FOLLOW THEM.
SEARCH FOR THEM.
FIND THEM.
KILL THEM.
THE DRIFTERS MUST NOT BE ALLOWED TO LIVE.
NOT A SINGLE ONE MUST LIVE.
I ORDER THIS WITH THE CONVICTION OF UNYIELDING DISASTER.

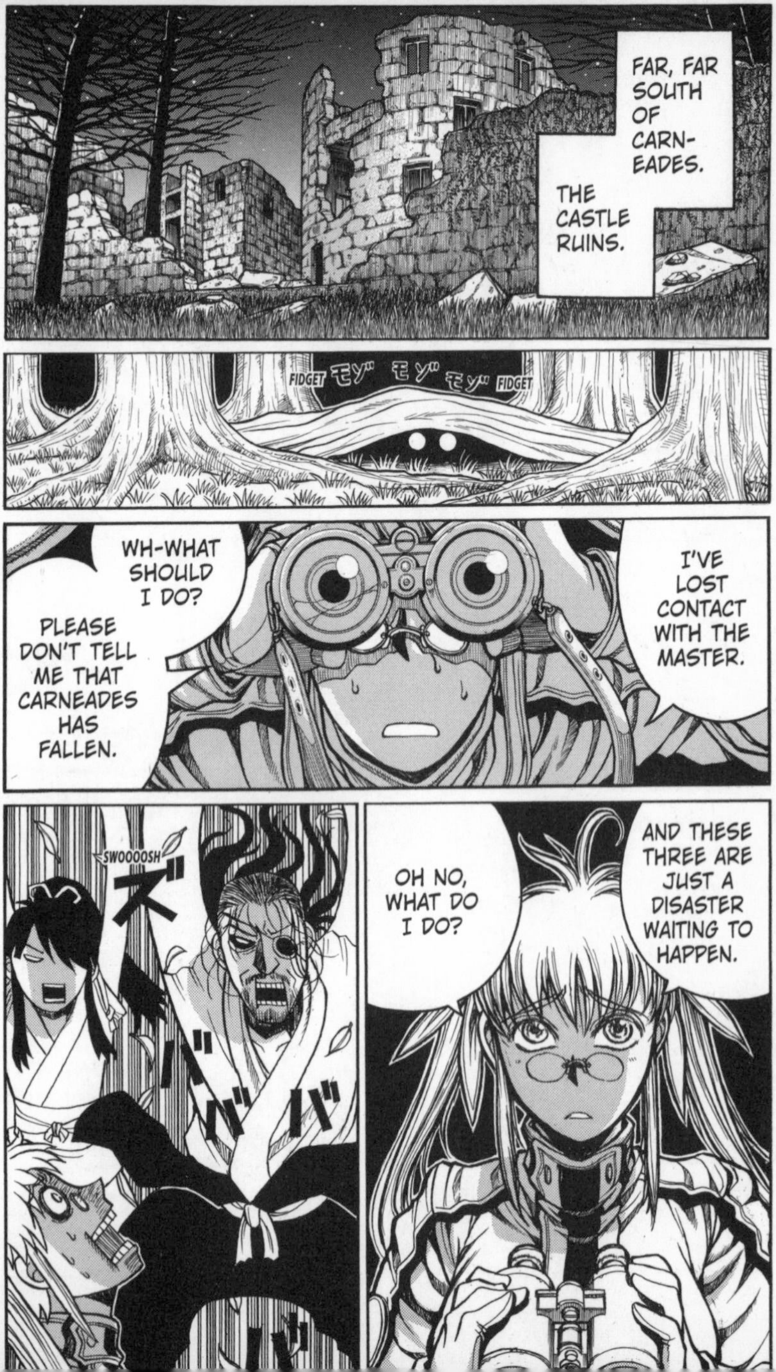
FAR, FAR SOUTH OF CARN- EADES.
THE CASTLE RUINS.
FIDGET モゾ モゾ モゾ FIDGET
I'VE LOST CONTACT WITH THE MASTER.
WH-WHAT SHOULD I DO?
PLEASE DON'T TELL ME THAT CARNEADES HAS FALLEN.
AND THESE THREE ARE JUST A DISASTER WAITING TO HAPPEN.
OH NO, WHAT DO I DO?
SWOOOOSH

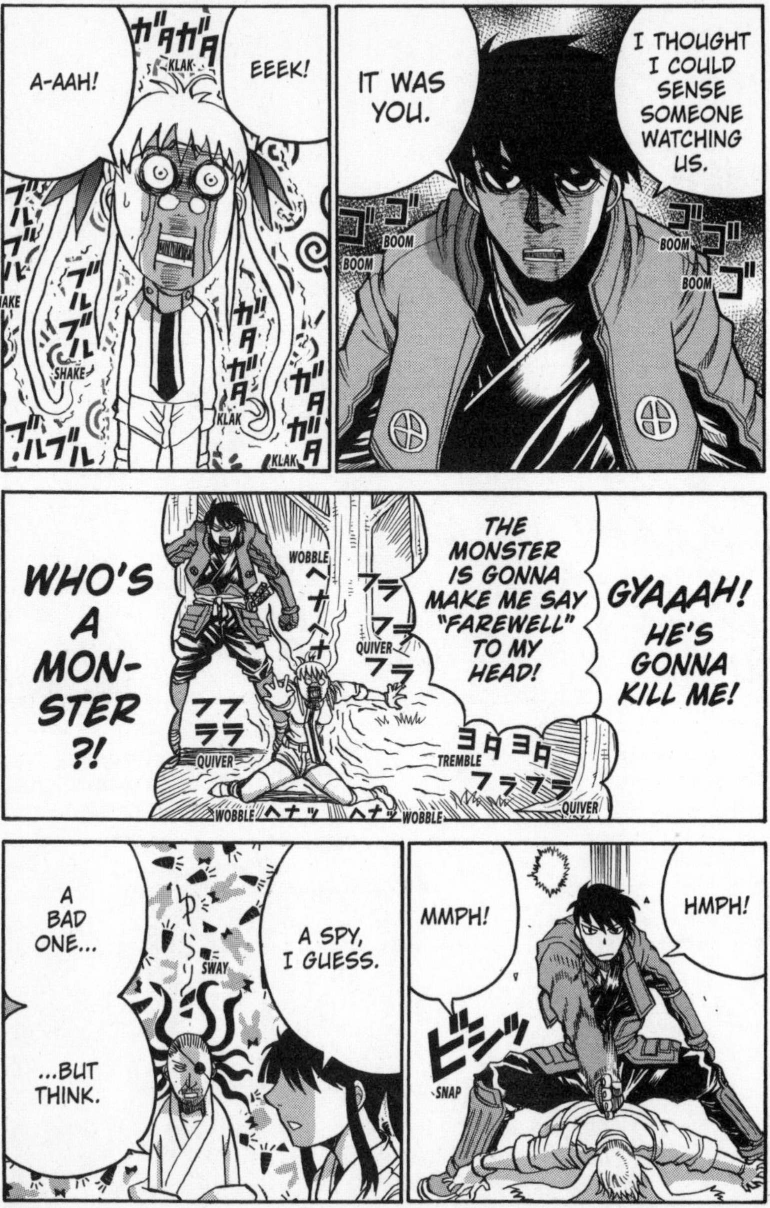
I THOUGHT I COULD SENSE SOMEONE WATCHING US.
IT WAS YOU.
BOOM
BOOM
BOOM
BOOM
EEEK!
KLAK
A-AAH!
SHAKE
SHAKE
KLAK
KLAK
GYAAAH! HE'S GONNA KILL ME!
THE MONSTER IS GONNA MAKE ME SAY "FAREWELL" TO MY HEAD!
WOBBLE
QUIVER
WHO'S A MON-STER?!
QUIVER
TREMBLE
QUIVER
WOBBLE
WOBBLE
HMPH!
MMPH!
SNAP
A SPY, I GUESS.
SWAY
A BAD ONE...
...BUT THINK.

TOYOHISA.
YES?
IF YOU HAVEN'T NOTICED, SHE SPEAKS JAPANESE.
AH!
C'MON, YOU!
CON-FESS! CONFESS EVERY-THING!
BOOM BOOM BOOM BOOM BOOM BOOM BOOM
HELP! I DON'T WANNA SAY FARE-WELL!
AAAH! EEE! AAAH!
CONFESS, OR I'LL TURN YOU OVER TO HIM.
YOU KNOW ME. THE ONE THEY CALL THE DEVIL.
MY HOB-BIES ARE BURNING EVERY-THING DOWN AND KILLING EVERYONE.
THEN SIPPING TOASTS FROM THE SKULLS OF THE VANQUISHED.
GREAT FAN OF POWER THROUGH THE SWORD.
LOVED TO DANCE "ATSU-MORI."
AAAAAH!

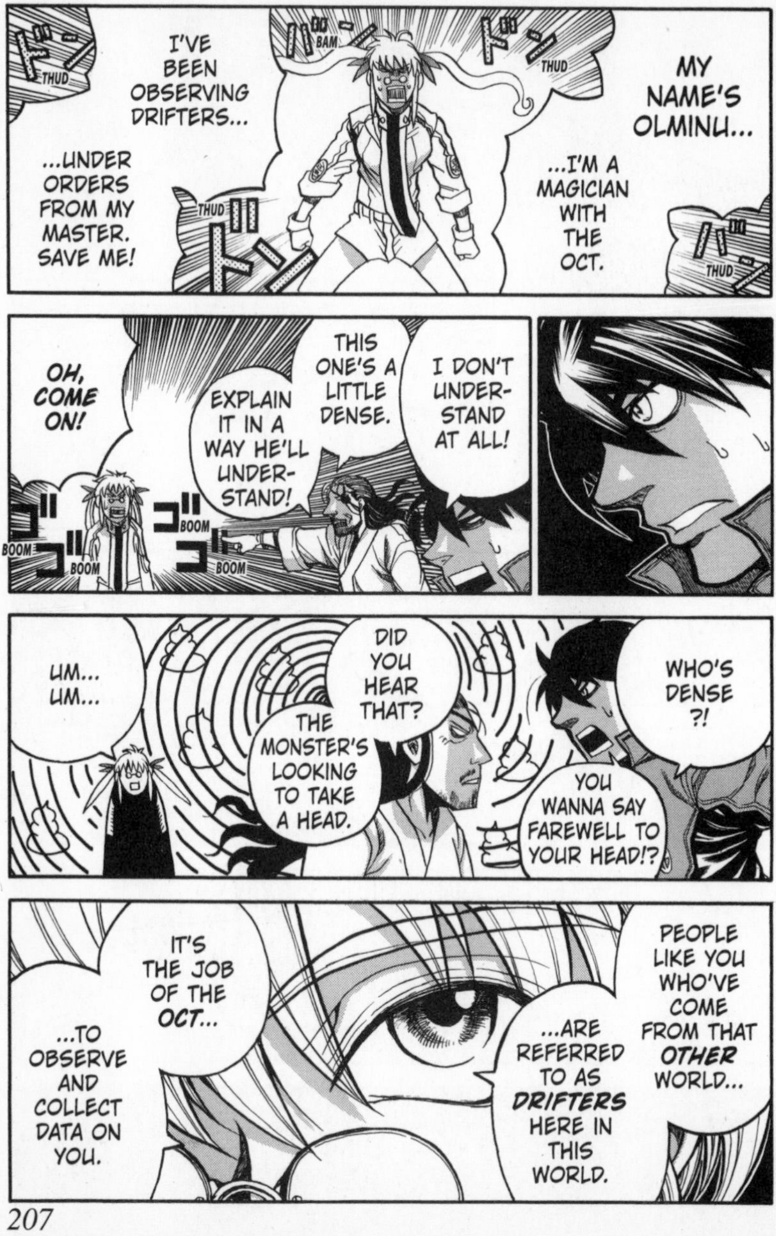
THUD
MY NAME'S OLMINU...
THUD
BAM
...I'M A MAGICIAN WITH THE OCT.
I'VE BEEN OBSERVING DRIFTERS...
THUD
...UNDER ORDERS FROM MY MASTER. SAVE ME!
THUD
THUD
I DON'T UNDERSTAND AT ALL!
THIS ONE'S A LITTLE DENSE.
EXPLAIN IT IN A WAY HE'LL UNDERSTAND!
BOOM
BOOM
OH, COME ON!
BOOM
BOOM
WHO'S DENSE?!
YOU WANNA SAY FAREWELL TO YOUR HEAD!?
DID YOU HEAR THAT?
THE MONSTER'S LOOKING TO TAKE A HEAD.
UM... UM...
PEOPLE LIKE YOU WHO'VE COME FROM THAT OTHER WORLD...
...ARE REFERRED TO AS DRIFTERS HERE IN THIS WORLD.
IT'S THE JOB OF THE OCT...
...TO OBSERVE AND COLLECT DATA ON YOU.

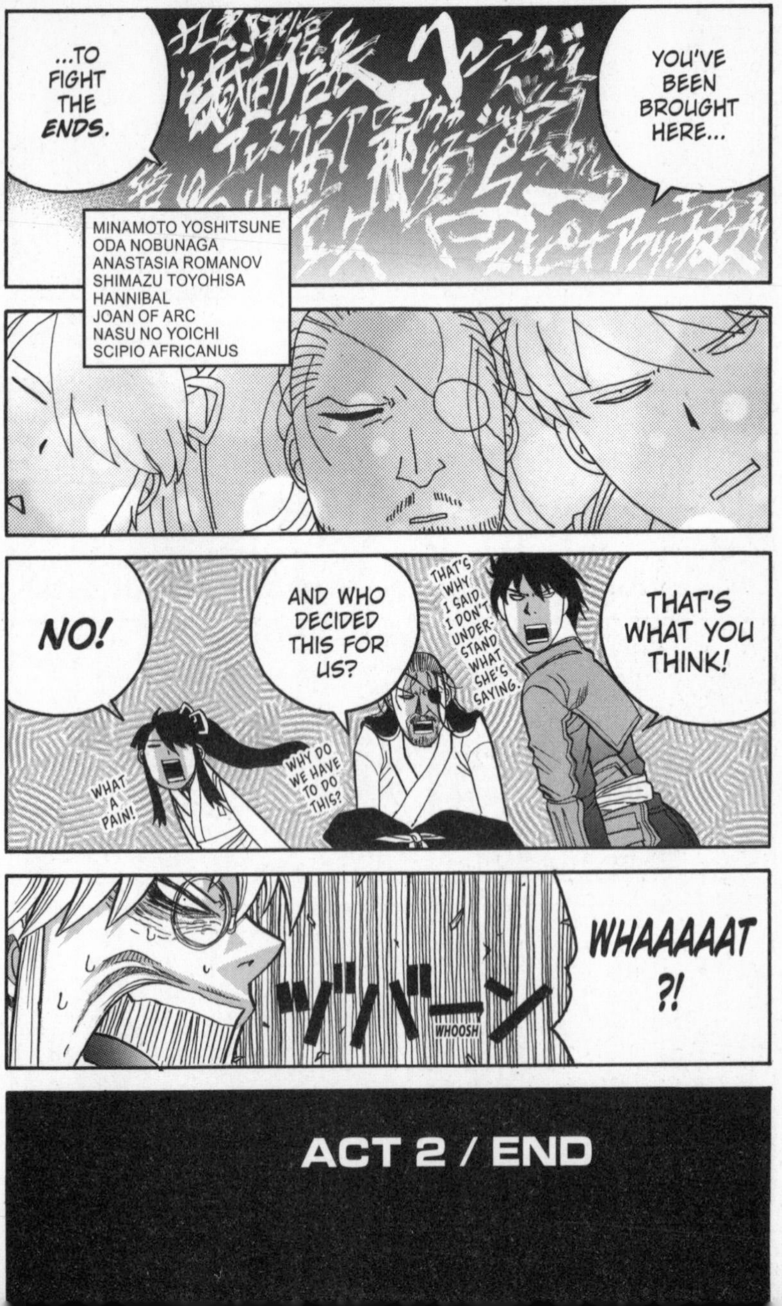
YOU'VE BEEN BROUGHT HERE...
...TO FIGHT THE ENDS.
MINAMOTO YOSHITSUNE
ODA NOBUNAGA
ANASTASIA ROMANOV
SHIMAZU TOYOHISA
HANNIBAL
JOAN OF ARC
NASU NO YOICHI
SCIPIO AFRICANUS
THAT'S WHAT YOU THINK!
THAT'S WHY I SAID I DON'T UNDERSTAND WHAT SHE'S SAYING.
AND WHO DECIDED THIS FOR US?
WHY DO WE HAVE TO DO THIS?
NO!
WHAT A PAIN!
WHAAAAAT ?!
WHOOSH

ACT 2 / END

CONTINUED IN THE NEXT VOLUME!

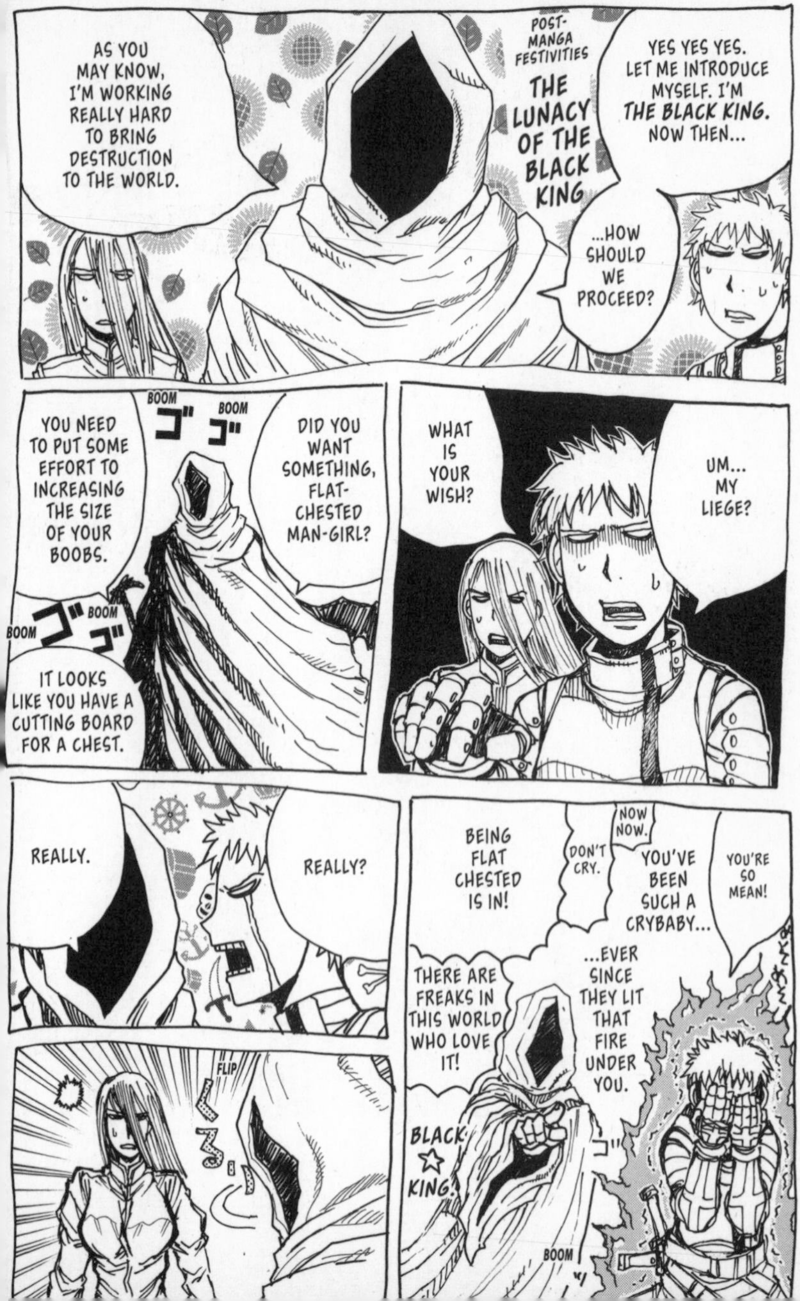
POST-MANGA FESTIVITIES
THE LUNACY OF THE BLACK KING
YES YES YES. LET ME INTRODUCE MYSELF. I'M THE BLACK KING. NOW THEN...
...HOW SHOULD WE PROCEED?
AS YOU MAY KNOW, I'M WORKING REALLY HARD TO BRING DESTRUCTION TO THE WORLD.
UM... MY LIEGE?
WHAT IS YOUR WISH?
DID YOU WANT SOMETHING, FLAT-CHESTED MAN-GIRL?
BOOM
BOOM
YOU NEED TO PUT SOME EFFORT TO INCREASING THE SIZE OF YOUR BOOBS.
BOOM
BOOM
IT LOOKS LIKE YOU HAVE A CUTTING BOARD FOR A CHEST.
YOU'RE SO MEAN!
NOW NOW.
DON'T CRY.
YOU'VE BEEN SUCH A CRYBABY...
BEING FLAT CHESTED IS IN!
...EVER SINCE THEY LIT THAT FIRE UNDER YOU.
THERE ARE FREAKS IN THIS WORLD WHO LOVE IT!
BLACK ☆ KING.
BOOM
REALLY?
REALLY.
FLIP

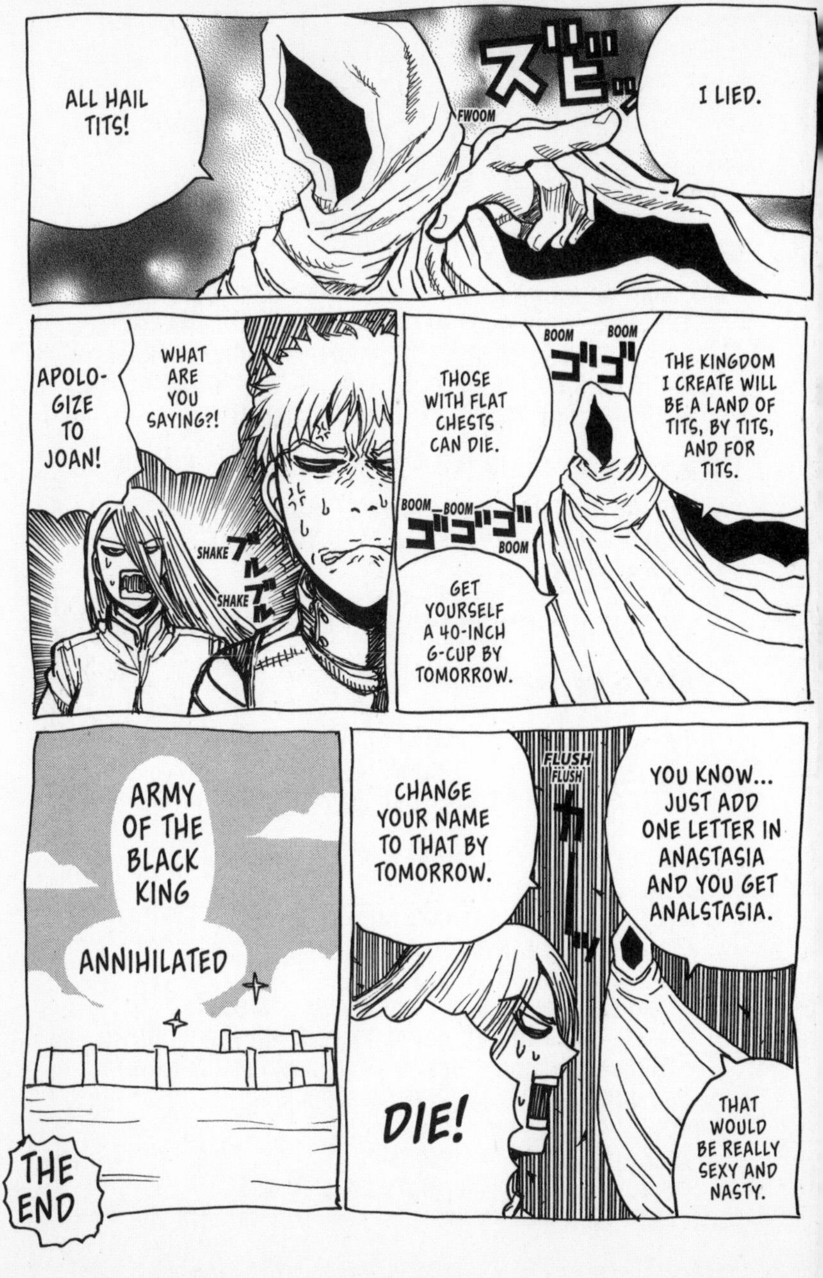
I LIED.
FWOOM
ALL HAIL TITS!
THE KINGDOM I CREATE WILL BE A LAND OF TITS, BY TITS, AND FOR TITS.
BOOM BOOM
THOSE WITH FLAT CHESTS CAN DIE.
BOOM BOOM BOOM
GET YOURSELF A 40-INCH G-CUP BY TOMORROW.
WHAT ARE YOU SAYING?!
APOLO-GIZE TO JOAN!
SHAKE SHAKE
YOU KNOW... JUST ADD ONE LETTER IN ANASTASIA AND YOU GET ANALSTASIA.
FLUSH FLUSH
CHANGE YOUR NAME TO THAT BY TOMORROW.
THAT WOULD BE REALLY SEXY AND NASTY.
DIE!
ARMY OF THE BLACK KING
ANNIHILATED
THE END

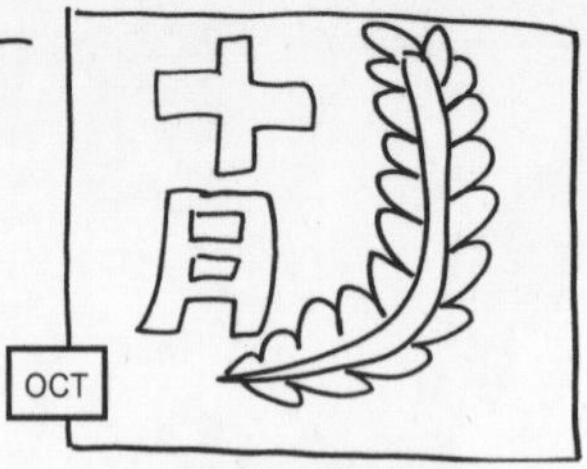
十月
OCT

POSTSCRIPT

- "BWA HA HA HA HA HA! FOOLS! THE MORE YOU STRUGGLE, THE MORE YOUR BODY BECOMES ENTRAPPED! THAT'S WHAT HAPPENS WITH A ROPE MADE EXCLUSIVELY FROM PUBIC HAIR COLLECTED FROM VIRGINS THIRTY AND OLDER! EVEN THE NINE-TAILED FOX COULDN'T CUT IT!"

("IT'S BEEN A WHILE" IN THE PARLANCE OF ADACHI-KU, TOKYO.)

- HA HA. THIS HAS BEEN THE FIRST VOLUME OF TANKOBON FOR *DRIFTERS*. WHAT'D YOU THINK? HOW WAS IT?

- UM...I REALLY DON'T HAVE ANYTHING ELSE TO SAY.

- CAKE IS SWEEEET.

- I STILL HAVE SOME ROOM LEFT, SO I'LL SING A SONG.

- ***BALLAD OF LOAN SHARK USHIJIMA***

NO NO, AIN'T GOT NO MONEY. TODAY IS ANOTHER
  SAD DAY FOR UTSUI.
HELP ME, USHIJIMA (SHAKE SHAKE)
WELCOME, MY SLAVE (DUM DUM DUM)
BEFORE YOU KNOW IT, DEBT IS UP
  ('CAUSE YOU KNOW, IT'S 50% EVERY TEN DAYS)
BEFORE YOU KNOW IT, HOUSEHOLD FINANCES ARE DOWN
  (I PROMISE, THIS STOCK IS GOING THROUGH THE ROOF)
OF COURSE, IT DIDN'T. REFI THE HOUSE.
NOW I'M LUCKY JUST TO BE ALIVE.
LUCKY, LUCKY, I'M A LUCKY MAN.
"IF YOU'RE GONNA DIE, MAKE SURE TO GET
  LIFE INSURANCE FIRST"

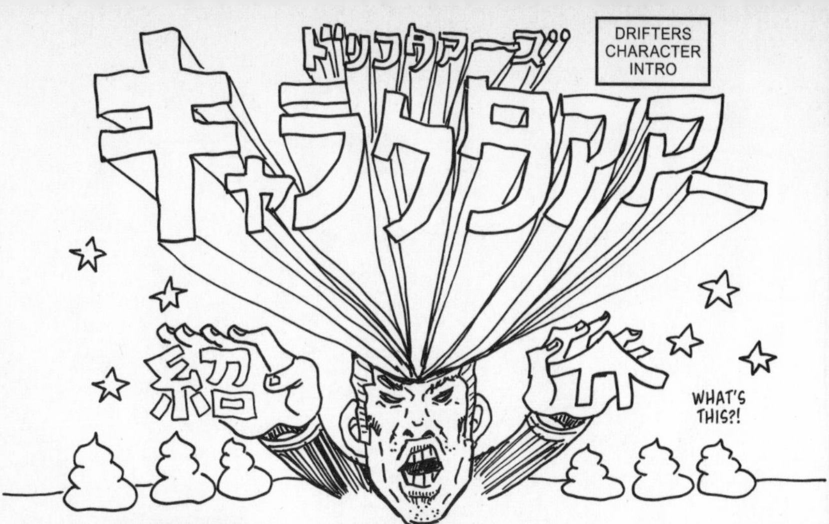
DRIFTERS CHARACTER INTRO
WHAT'S THIS?!

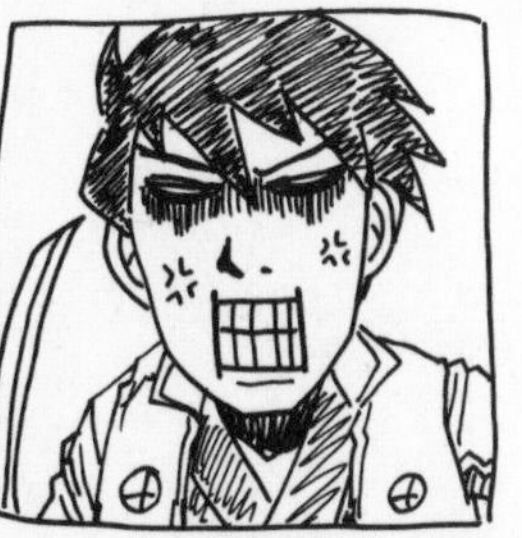

O-TOYOHISA

A VERITABLE KILLING MACHINE FROM THE SHIMAZU CLAN OF SATSUMA PROVINCE.
AS LONG AS HE GETS YOUR HEAD, HE'S HAPPY.
THOUGH SOMETIMES HE MIGHT PULL OUT YOUR LIVER IF HE HAS TIME.
TAKE YOUR EYES OFF OF HIM FOR A SECOND, AND HE'S PLANNING A SUICIDE SHIELD.
LUCKY JUST TO BE ALIVE.
FOLLOWS THE PHILOSOPHY THAT A MAN'S LIFE IS NO MORE THAN A SINGLE LEAF ON A TREE.

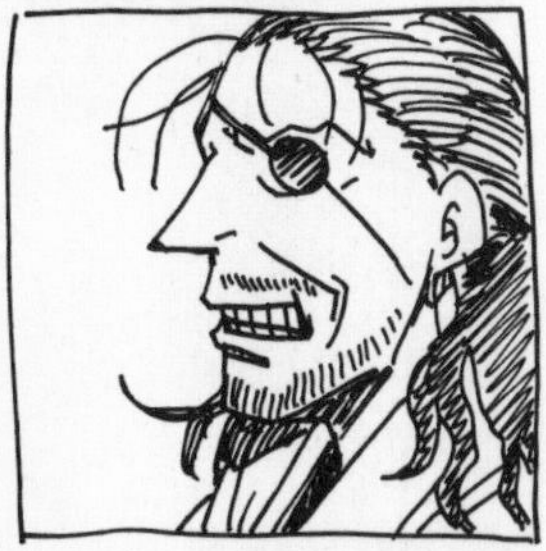

NOBUNAGA

FIRESTARTER FROM THE ODA CLAN.
A DANCE MANIAC WHO NEEDS LITTLE REASON TO BREAK OUT INTO A VERSION OF "ATSUMORI."
HIS DESCENDENTS ARE STILL DANCING ATOP ICE.*
AND EVEN MORE ARE SURELY DESTINED FOR "DANCING WITH THE STARS."
LA DEE DA. LA DEE DA.
ARSONIST.

*THIS REFERS TO FIGURE SKATER ODA NOBUNARI.

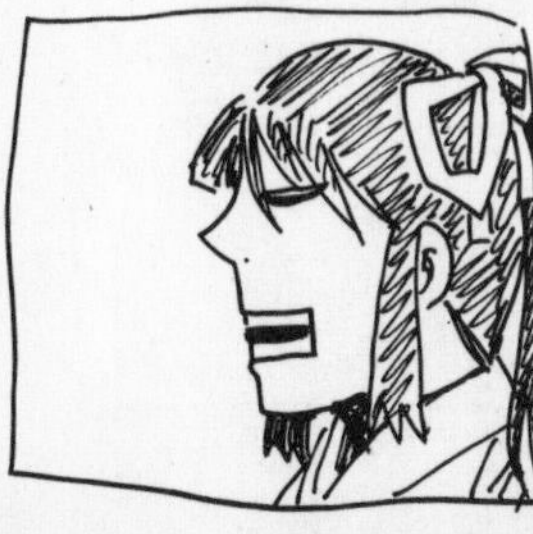

YOICHI

THE GOLGO 13 OF THE NASU CLAN.
STAND BEHIND HIM, HE'LL KILL YOU WITH A KARATE CHOP.
EVEN IF YOU'RE NOT STANDING BEHIND HIM, HE'LL KILL YOU WITH SOMETHING OTHER THAN A KARATE CHOP.
IF YOU FLY A FAN FROM A BOAT, HE'LL KILL THE FAN AND EVERYONE ELSE ON THE BOAT AS WELL.
KILL. SLAUGHTER.
PEW! PEW!

ALSO FROM KOHTA HIRANO

HELLSING